Praise for *Merciless*

"Lori Armstrong's writing is as smart, sexy, and ruthless as her characters. *Merciless* is her best novel yet."

—Allison Leotta, author of *Discretion* and *Law of Attraction*

"Armstrong's heroine blows away the stereotypes. Suspense lovers who haven't met Mercy Gunderson are missing out. *Merciless* has it all—a chilling mystery, smart dialogue, and memorable characters. Another riveting addition to the Mercy Gunderson series."

—Laura Griffin, bestselling author of *Twisted*

"Driven, damaged, and dangerous, FBI agent Mercy Gunderson is one of the best female leads to come down the pike since Eve Dallas. Lori Armstrong delivers the goods with *Merciless*."

—Cindy Gerard, bestselling author of The Bodyguards and The Black Ops series

Praise for *Mercy Kill*

"With a gutsy heroine, sharp humor, and a strong sense of place, Armstrong has created a winning series. The female veteran perspective is particularly fresh—not unlike a young V. I. Warshawski gone rural. Craig Johnson and C. J. Box fans should like it, too. Highly recommended."

—*Library Journal* (starred review)

"Sharp . . . An intriguing new character, FBI agent Shay Turnbull of the Indian County Special Crimes Unit, will leave readers eager to see how their relationship plays out in the next installment."

—*Publishers Weekly*

"[A] tough-mouth novel . . . [readers] will enjoy Mercy—tough, funny, and hardly a girl in a guy suit."

—*Booklist*

"Another surprisingly twisted tale leads readers into a thicket of relative good and evil."

—*Kirkus Reviews*

"This is a harsh tale filled with hard people but, like the South Dakota landscape, it's compelling and difficult to walk away from without being changed."

—*Romantic Times Book Reviews* (four-star review)

"Mercy is one of the best female characters around, and you can quote me on that."

—Lisa Gardner, author of *Love You More* and *Live to Tell*

Praise for *No Mercy*

"[A] smartly written, high-velocity tale."

—*The Wall Street Journal*

"Mercy Gunderson [is] a complicated and fascinating character whose presence in modern novels is way overdue."

—*USA Today*

"This is a new series to pay attention to."

—*San Jose Mercury News*

"Mercy is the kind of woman Lyle Lovett sings about with her scuffed boots, faded jeans, a hip flask instead of a purse, and enough attitude to rein in a steer."

—*Milwaukee Journal Sentinel*

"A voice laced with so much attitude and personality . . . Mercy is a take-no-prisoners toughie with (of course) a soft, vulnerable underbelly."

—*Boston Globe*

"Compelling . . . Mercy is as tough as an old army boot, with a vocabulary and weapons proficiency to prove it."

—*Publishers Weekly*

"[Armstrong] has created a grittier character in Mercy Gunderson. . . . Fans of the Collins mysteries should embrace this new novel with open arms, but the author could pick up some new readers, too, on the strength of this new heroine."

—*Booklist*

"Armstrong's writing is intense and passionate. With every turn of the page, she reveals more shocking revelations. This gripping story will undoubtedly become a must-read series. 4.5 out of 5 stars."

—*Romantic Times Book Reviews*, Top Pick review

"Within just a few pages of *No Mercy* I was gripped. . . . Lori Armstrong is the real deal and so is the setting and the characters in this novel which by turns is tough, sassy, sexy, and unique. As gritty, haunting, and authentic as South Dakota itself, *No Mercy* is a terrific series debut."

—C. J. Box, Edgar-winning author of *Below Zero*

"Mercy Gunderson shoots straight onto the list of my favorite heroines. A master of snappy dialogue and twisting plots, Lori Armstrong proves again why she is an award-winning author. *No Mercy* is a thrilling mystery, a hard-edged, fast-paced, no-holds-barred roller coaster ride."

—Allison Brennan, author of *Original Sin* and *Fatal Secrets*

"Mercy Gunderson, the protagonist in Lori Armstrong's wonderful new series, is everything readers hope for in a lead character: strong, capable, hot-headed, and soft in all the right places. Set in South Dakota ranch country that's so well evoked you'll smell things you wish you didn't, with a compelling cast of supporting characters and a dynamite mystery sure to keep you guessing until the very end, *No Mercy* is a no-holds-barred, flat-out winner of a series debut."

—William Kent Krueger, author of *Heaven's Keep* and *Red Knife*

"Step aside, cowboys, there's a new star on the horizon and her name's Lori Armstrong. With *No Mercy*, Armstrong introduces one of the most original heroes to come out of the west in years. Mercy Gunderson is a perfectly flawed woman; a tough-as-nails, take-no-prisoners kind of gal who'd just as soon outshoot or outdrink a man as bed him. Read this book or answer to Mercy."

"People always ask me what I read and I tell them Lori Armstrong. There comes a point when I need to read her like I need a shot of whiskey at the end of a hard day; Lori's writing is like that, unforgiving and deeply satisfying."

MERCILESS

A MYSTERY

LORI ARMSTRONG

A Touchstone Book
Published by Simon & Schuster
New York London Toronto Sydney New Delhi

Touchstone
A Division of Simon & Schuster, Inc.
1230 Avenue of the Americas
New York, NY 10020

First Touchstone trade paperback edition January 2013

TOUCHSTONE and colophon are registered trademarks of Simon & Schuster, Inc.

For information about special discounts for bulk purchases, please contact Simon & Schuster Special Sales at 1-866-506-1949 or business@simonandschuster.com.

The Simon & Schuster Speakers Bureau can bring authors to your live event. For more information or to book an event contact the Simon & Schuster Speakers Bureau at 1-866-248-3049 or visit our website at www.simonspeakers.com.

Manufactured in the United States of America

10 9 8 7 6 5 4 3 2 1

Library of Congress Cataloging-in-Publication Data
Armstrong, Lori
   Merciless: a mystery/Lori Armstrong.—1st Touchstone trade paperback ed.
      p.   cm.
   1. Women private investigators—fiction.   I. Title.
PS3601.R576M45   2013
813'.6—dc23   2012014752

ISBN 978-1-4516-2536-3
ISBN 978-1-4516-2541-7 (ebook)

May God have mercy upon my enemies, because I won't.
—*General George S. Patton*

1

I blamed my unrealistic expectations of becoming an FBI special agent on *The X-Files*.

Granted, Mulder and Scully were fictional characters, but working in the FBI was nothing like portrayed on any TV shows. Disappointment made me want to crawl inside the TV and kick some ass.

Figuratively speaking, of course.

So far my new FBI job hadn't entailed chasing down aliens—either illegal or the bug-eyed, misshapen-headed types.

I hadn't been assigned a trippy private office that I could decorate with funky, yet prophetic posters.

I hadn't met a weirdly wise, hip, confidential informant.

I hadn't participated in a raid where I got to yell, "Federal agents! Everyone on the ground!"

The brass hadn't issued me a shiny badge or one of those rocking black jackets with FBI emblazoned in big white letters on the back.

Heck, I hadn't even been saddled with an official partner.

I was damn lucky I'd gotten a gun.

Not that I'd gotten to shoot it yet.

Instead of chasing down bad guys and busting heads, I was trapped in an overheated office building in Rapid City with other agents, flipping though a stack of paperwork, listening to Director Shenker drone on.

And holy J. Edgar Hoover, did the man love the sound of his own monotone.

I sighed. A boot connected with my ankle, and I sucked in a quick breath at the sharp pain.

Of course, Director Shenker chose that moment to pause his lecture.

He peered at me over the top of his cheater bifocals—leopard print cheater bifocals, no less.

Peered was too bland a word. Glared was more fitting.

I fought the urge to squirm.

"Have something to add, Agent Gunderson?"

"No, sir." I pointed to my empty water glass. "Just a dry throat." I reached for the water pitcher—we'd been in meeting hell so long the ice had melted. When I thoughtfully refilled my tablemate's glass—oops, water splashed on his notebook, obliterating the elaborate doodle he'd been working on for the past two hours.

Served the bastard right for kicking me.

"Take ten, people," Shenker said, leaving up the PowerPoint presentation.

Didn't have to tell me twice. I was out of the room and down the hallway before my seatmate quit scratching himself.

Or so I thought.

A hand on my shoulder spun me around so I was nose to nose with Special Agent Shay Turnbull—my unofficial trainer, my doodling seatmate, the disher of a daily dose of snark that made me snicker like a teenage girl in spite of myself.

I shrugged him off.

"Follow me."

"Why?"

"Because I'm the senior agent, that's why. Do you have to make everything so damn difficult?" Turnbull headed for the door marked STAIRS, assuming I'd follow.

Another ass-chewing session. I grudgingly admitted I preferred Turnbull's private approach rather than our boss's public browbeating—not that I'd been on the receiving end so far.

We entered the small concrete landing to the stairwell. I rested my shoulders against the cement-block wall, half wishing I smoked. Would I look tough and cool if I flicked my Bic and squinted mysteriously at Turnbull through the smoky haze?

No. Turnbull would see right through me. He had that uncanny ability. Which sort of sucked ass for me.

"Would it kill you to look alive and at least partially interested in this training session, Gunderson?"

"Yes, it might kill me, because it's boring me to death. I don't see the importance of knowing riot procedure. There's not enough population base here to even *have* a riot. And historically, the guys in charge call the National Guard."

Turnbull lifted a brow. "Has it somehow escaped your notice, Sergeant Major, that more than half the South Dakota National Guard troops are currently deployed?"

I scowled at his pointed reminder of my army rank. "Doesn't matter. Training assignment is busywork. I wanna be out there doing something. Not sitting on my ass."

"The FBI's success rate is based on ninety percent office work and—"

"Ten percent fieldwork, yeah, yeah, I recently lived the manifesto." Standard training time for new FBI agents was five months at Quantico. I fell into the "special exclusion category" since at thirty-nine I was older than the federal government's mandated final hire age of thirty-eight for federal employees. With twenty years' service in Uncle Sam's army, and a pension in place, I'd been allowed to skip the firearms portion and specialized tactical maneuvers of the training program, allowing me to shave off four weeks in Virginia.

Agent Turnbull studied me in his usual fashion. Not looking me in the eye, because engaging in a stare down with me was an exercise in futility. And Special Agent Turnbull hated losing. So instead, he gifted me with the half-exasperated/half-amused look of superiority he'd perfected in his ten-plus years as a G-man.

"What? You can't fault me for hoping for something—anything—to happen."

"I'll say it again. Act like you give a damn about these training assignments. You're new. You should be enthusiastic. *Rah-rah! Go FBI!* and all that shit." His pocket buzzed, and he fished out his cell phone. He said, "Turnbull," and exited the stairwell.

I didn't move. Instead, I closed my eyes, still unsure if I'd made the right choice joining the FBI.

When I'd snapped out of the haze following the death of my former army buddy Anna, a death in which I'd pulled the trigger, I realized I needed more out of my life than being a retired soldier, part-time rancher, and full-time drinker. Since my skill set had been honed behind the scope of my sniper rifle, there wasn't much in the way of career opportunities in western South Dakota. I was zero for two on the attempted-career front; I'd made a lousy bartender and had lost when I ran for my dad's old job as Eagle River County sheriff. When the FBI had set their sights on me, it'd been a boost to my ego—although I'd never publicly admit that.

But again, I hadn't found out the job offer hadn't been about me personally until after I'd signed on the dotted line. The Rapid City FBI office was short on agents because no one in the vast resources of the FBI wanted to fill the agency opening in our state capital in Pierre, which meant the head of our division, Director Shenker, had to divide his time between that office and ours in Rapid City.

Since our district covered such a large area, and our staff was on the smallish side, we weren't a specialized unit like in more populated areas. We handled all the federal cases: everything from homicide to artifact theft. We weren't even partnered with other agents, although Turnbull was tasked with showing me the ropes as my unofficial partner.

Served him right, being saddled with a rookie, after flashing his specialized FBI badge at me, denoting him as part of the Indian Country Special Crimes Unit. What Turnbull hadn't told me? There was no such division within the Rapid City FBI unit.

After some kind of hush-hush dustup, he'd been transferred from the ICSCU in Minneapolis to "train" the agents of this smaller outlying FBI office in how to deal with Indian Country crimes. Which had pissed off the agents who'd been serving the Rapid City FBI office for years, dealing with Indian crimes without the official federal ICSCU moniker—or the funding—because for all of Turnbull's supposed training, he hadn't seen or done half the shit in his ten years as an agent that the Rapid City agents dealt with each year.

Guess he'd gotten quite an education for being such an *expert*.

Of course, I learned all this secondhand from Frances, the office manager, on my third day on the job at the FBI. She'd also shared the philosophy that when you work in Indian Country, *all* cases deal with crimes in Indian Country.

So far, I'd suffered with 95 percent office work, reading reports to familiarize myself with current events and cases. Nothing important had gone down since I'd punched the time clock as Special Agent Mercy Gunderson—not that I hoped for a horrific occurrence. But I hated sitting around talking about crap that'd never happen, wearing a gun I wasn't allowed to shoot.

The stairwell door opened, and Turnbull popped his head in. "Briefing room."

After a few moments I slipped into my chair, surrounded by a buzz of excitement. There was definitely something going on.

Director Shenker shuffled through a stack of papers as he entered the room. He glanced at the clock and stepped to the coffee center to fill his mug. "I've just been made aware of a situation on the Eagle River Reservation. The tribal police were brought in first, but given the sensitive nature, they've reached out to us for help."

The latest departmental catchphrase touted the "new spirit of cooperation" on the Eagle River Reservation between the recently elected new tribal president, the newly promoted chief of the tribal police, and the "local" fresh Indian blood in the FBI—aka me.

"What's the situation?" Agent Thomas asked. Technically, we weren't assigned to specific reservations, but Agents Thomas and Burke worked the northwestern part of the state. Turnbull and I concentrated on the southwestern section, and Agents Mested and Flack dealt with the central section on the west side of the Missouri River. As the lone female agent in this office it was hard not to feel like I was just there to fill a quota.

Shenker pressed his thumb between his eyebrows. "Three days ago, seventeen-year-old Arlette Shooting Star disappeared. The tribal police instituted a search of the reservation and found nothing. The highway patrol joined in searching the surrounding area and found nothing, either."

"No sign of her at all?"

"None. The last time her friends allegedly had contact with her was before lunch at the school on Friday. She did not report to her class after lunch. Her cell phone and her belongings were found in her locker."

"Does she have a habit of disappearing?" Turnbull asked.

"No. She's been living with her aunt and uncle on the Eagle River rez for the last year."

"Where'd she live before that?" Mested asked.

Shenker flipped through the pages. "Standing Rock, in North Dakota. They've checked to see if she's contacted anyone in that area, but no one is admitting they've seen or heard from her."

"She has family on Standing Rock?"

"Shirttail relatives. She had to move to Eagle River after her mother died and her aunt was named her legal guardian." Director Shenker put both hands on the conference table. "Here's why it's a sensitive situation. Arlette's aunt is Triscell Elk Thunder, married to tribal president Latimer Elk Thunder."

Silence. Then shifting in seats. No one spoke.

"And while the tribal president would like to avoid the appearance of impropriety, chances are, it's inevitable."

My thoughts rolled back to my nephew and how frantic I'd been after he'd been missing for only a few hours, not a few days. I'd tried to call out the cavalry, but no one had listened, so I understood Elk Thunder's intention to do whatever it took to find her. Still, it bugged me. Three days is a long time in a missing persons case.

"What's the plan?"

I glanced at Turnbull. The shrewd man defined *rah-rah!* FBI. The gleam in his eye indicated he was as antsy to get out of the office and into the field as I was.

"The plan is, you and Special Agent Gunderson will meet at the tribal police station at Eagle River first thing tomorrow morning. It's too late to do anything today. I'll pass along updates as needed. Any questions?"

"Will we be actively searching for the girl?" I felt Turnbull's eyes on me. Due to a cosmic debt I owed to the universe for being brought back from the dead, I'd become a sort of divining rod for the newly dead. Since Turnbull had pointed out this phenomenon to me before we'd become coworkers, I needed to know what role I'd be playing in the investigation.

Again, Shenker shrugged. "I can't honestly say what tack they'll take. Make no mistake—you two will be there in a secondary, not primary, capacity."

Agents Thomas and Burke stood, as did Agents Flack and Mested. At this point the case didn't affect them.

But Shenker wasn't finished. He gestured to the four men. "Not done with you guys. Turnbull and Gunderson, you're free to go."

Yippee.

Outside the conference room, Turnbull faced me. "You'll be all right in the field tomorrow?"

"Yes. Will you?"

He frowned. "Why wouldn't I be?"

I flashed my teeth at him. "Because you've been benched babysitting me since I finished Quantico. Just want to make sure *you* remember field-duty protocol, since this is my virgin voyage."

"Chances are high we'll be sorting through paperwork, so don't get excited you'll actually get to pull your gun, Gunderson."

"Dream crusher."

Turnbull jammed his hands in his pockets as we waited for the elevator. "I don't have to remind you not to talk about this case with Sheriff Dawson."

Not a question. Dawson and I were living together. He and I shared the same trepidation about my going to work for the FBI. A lot of secrets, mistrust, and half-truths had existed between Dawson and me from our first meeting. Getting over that hurdle, learning to trust each other, learning to separate our jobs from who we were when the uniforms came off had been a big step in our personal life together. I hated having to withhold information from him, but the fact that he was forced to withhold information from me put us on the same level. Our jobs hadn't created friction yet, but we were both aware it'd happen at some point.

"He's bound to've heard about this missing girl," Turnbull offered.

I shrugged. "Maybe. Maybe not. He's got today off."

"So he'll have supper waiting when you get home?"

I'd never get used to the rash of shit Turnbull gave me about Dawson, especially since when we'd first crossed paths, I'd denied anything was going on between the sheriff and me. "Why, Agent Turnbull. You sound . . . jealous."

He snorted. "Of your hour-long drive to reach home? I'll be fed, caught up on ESPN, and sweet-talking my most recent hookup into an encore before your truck turns up that bumpy goat path you call a driveway."

"Enjoy your Hungry Man TV dinner."

"I'm more of a Lean Cuisine guy."

I shuddered. Prepackaged dinners reminded me I'd had enough MREs to last a lifetime.

"If you don't hear from me, we're on to meet at the tribal police station at oh eight hundred tomorrow," he reminded me.

"Roger that." We parted ways in the parking lot.

The drive from Rapid City to the Gunderson Ranch might seem like a dull trek to him, but I loved it. I needed time alone, which had become a rarity in my life, and the hour drive was enough to change a bad mood into one of anticipation.

Dawson and I had gotten into the habit of eating supper one night a week with my sister, Hope, Jake—the ranch foreman who'd officially become Hope's husband four months ago—and their baby, Joy. My niece crawled as fast as a lightning bug and emitted babbling noises that sounded as if she was having a conversation with herself. I'd embraced being an aunt again, and I tried not to dwell on my morbid fears of how long it'd last this time.

The day had turned chilly, and it was full-on dark when I pulled up to the house. No sign of Dawson's patrol car. The lights were off in the kitchen, too.

So much for supper being on the table.

Neither Shoonga nor Dawson's dog, Butch, slunk out of the shadows to greet me with happy tail wags and excited yips.

I fumbled with my key to the back door. In all the years I lived here, we'd rarely locked our house, but that was one thing Dawson had changed after moving in. I put my foot down at springing for security lights. The strobelike effect was a pain in the ass when raccoons, turkeys, or other critters decided to explore the perimeter of the house.

Inside, I kicked off my boots and headed for the bedroom to store my gun. I had an attachment to firearms, but given that my sister had accidentally killed her best friend when she was a child, and that my niece loved exploring the house, Dawson and I had moved my gun vault into the bedroom.

I shed my unofficial uniform—any color of clean dress pants and a shirt I didn't have to iron—and hung it up, another habit of Dawson's I'd implemented. When the work clothes were off and the guns were locked away, we'd separated ourselves from our jobs. Since two of Dawson's three uniforms still hung in the closet, I knew he'd been called to duty.

After I slipped on my workout clothes, I scooped my hair into a ponytail and rolled out my yoga mat. Asanas would reset my mental and physical balance.

Half an hour later, I returned to the kitchen, my stomach growling. I checked my phone. No text message or missed calls. Strange. Dawson always kept me up to date on his whereabouts.

I checked the fridge and was happy to see that Sophie Red Leaf, the Gunderson family's longtime housekeeper/cook/counselor/meddler had left a foil-covered casserole on the top shelf with baking instructions.

These days, Sophie split her time between Hope's place and here, doing household things I could've done myself. Sophie was past retirement age, and I was past needing a surrogate mother, but I couldn't imagine my life without her so I'd keep her on the payroll.

I ate supper while I caught up on e-mail. I watched TV. Then I called it a night around eleven o'clock and crawled into bed.

Around two a.m. the bedroom door opened. I heard a thud as the gun vault closed and caught a whiff of shampoo and aftershave a couple seconds before the bed dipped. Then warm male skin pressed into my bare back as his arms came around me. He sighed.

"Hey, Sheriff."

"Sergeant Major."

"I thought you had tonight off."

"I did. Until Kiki started barfing in her patrol car with some stomach bug. Jazinski had already pulled a full shift, so I had to fill in."

"Lucky you." I repositioned the covers over us. "You really need to hire another deputy."

"I will."

"Soon."

"Mmm-hmm."

"Sophie made your favorite supper tonight. Corned-beef casserole."

"I'll have it for breakfast."

That's when I knew he was tired.

Dawson kissed the top of my head.

"Anything exciting happen on shift?" I asked.

"Nope." His breathing slowed.

"Wanna hear about a day in the life of an FBI agent?"

He made a noise in the back of his throat that I took as affirmative.

"I can give you very explicit information on the federal government's procedures and policy on riots."

Dawson made the noise again. A noise I now recognized as a snore.

Funny. That was the same reaction I'd had.

2

Since Dawson was still sleeping, I decided to stop at the Q-Mart for a cup of joe rather than waking him with the aroma of fresh-brewed coffee.

My cell buzzed right after I'd made the turn onto the main road leading to the rez. "Gunderson."

"Where are you?" Turnbull asked.

I glanced at the dashboard clock. I wasn't running late. "About ten miles outside of Eagle River. Why?"

"Because we just got word that Arlette Shooting Star has been found."

Found. Which equaled dead. "Where?"

"I'm not sure. Evidently, hunters found her at first light. The tribal police are on the scene."

"Where are you?"

"At the tribal police station. Officer Spotted Bear is catching a ride to the scene with me. Hang on a sec." The line went quiet. Then, "He said you're supposed to turn south on the Junction Eighteen cut across. Know where that is?"

"About four miles ahead of my current location."

"Entrance to the scene is marked at the first cattle guard. We'll meet you there."

Dammit. As much as I'd whined about wanting fieldwork, finding a young girl's body in a field wasn't what I'd had in mind.

At the turnoff, I slowed and hung a right over the cattle guard, where I saw the flashing beacon perched on the fence post. I wouldn't have needed the marker since I'd been to this make-out spot many times during my high school days.

Two older-model pickups were parked, the front ends pointed toward the tree line fifty yards ahead. Three guys wearing neon-orange hunting caps and camo clothes sat on the tailgates.

As soon as I exited my truck, I heard the muffled sounds of barking. I squinted and saw a flash of golden fur inside the cab of the closest truck. At least they'd had the sense to lock up the dog.

I didn't recognize the guys, so color me surprised when the oldest man spoke. "Hey. Aren't you Mercy Gunderson?"

"Yeah," I said to him. "Who are you?"

"Craig Barbour." He pointed to the younger version of himself; the guy sitting next to him was about fifteen. "My son. Craig Junior goes by Junior." Then he gestured to the smallish guy in the other pickup, who appeared to be the same age as Craig Junior. "That's Junior's friend. Erik Erickson."

"Wish we could've met under different circumstances. Thanks for sticking around."

"So what're you doin' here?" Craig Senior said suspiciously. "You lost the election for sheriff, right?"

"Right. Now I'm working for the FBI." It still felt ridiculous flashing the FBI badge, but I'd get used to it. "What were you guys hunting?"

"Geese. Got permission from Terry Vash to get rid of some of them. We were on our way to that pond." He jerked his chin to an area where cattails poked up.

"We'd hoped to get lucky right away, because we were supposed to go to school today," Junior added, "but Duke wouldn't stop his barking. So we locked him up, thinking maybe there was a mountain lion or a coyote close by. We moved closer to the trees, and that's when we saw her."

Silence.

When Craig Senior said, "Who'd do something like that to a girl?" I knew what had happened to Arlette Shooting Star was bad.

"That's what we intend to find out. Do any of you know her?"

Erik and Craig Junior looked at each other. Then Erik said, "I've seen her at school."

"Me, too, but I ain't never talked to her or nothin'."

"Thanks. We'll probably need you all to stick around for a little while longer."

I walked between the trucks toward the Eagle River tribal police patrol vehicle. The cop leaned against the driver's-side door so he could watch both the scene and the entrance to it. He pushed to his feet at my approach.

"Hi." I thrust out my hand. "Special Agent Mercy Gunderson. FBI."

"Officer Robert Orson."

Officer Orson had about as much Indian blood in his genetic makeup as I did—I was only a quarter Minneconjou Sioux, which was just enough to slightly darken my skin tone and lighten my hair color to light brown. I had at least a decade and a half on him, age-wise. But he had about a foot on me height-wise. Man. He was one tall guy.

"Wyatt Gunderson was your dad?"

I nodded.

"Didn't work with him much since he took ill right after I signed on with the tribal PD, but he seemed like a good guy."

"He was." A gust of wind blew, scattering dead leaves and bringing the wet scent of decay. I faced away from him, taking in the eerie scene. "I'm surprised there aren't more people here."

Orson shrugged. "It's early. And since she's the tribal president's niece, we've tried to keep it off the scanners. Brings out the gawkers, ya know?"

"What time did you get the call?"

"About an hour and a half ago. I was closest, so I drew the short straw."

"Me, too." I squinted at the tree line but couldn't see anything out of the ordinary from this angle. I let my backside rest against the hood.

"Aren't you gonna go poke around the crime scene?" he asked.

"Nope. My"—I bit back the word *partner*—"the other FBI agent en route has more experience. I'm new enough I'd probably muck it up."

"I hear ya there."

"Is this your first dead body?"

He gave me a strange look. "On the rez? Hell no. Not since I've been a cop and not before that."

"How long have you been a cop?"

"Four years. The first two I worked security for the jail. I got moved up after I finished the six-week training course."

I wasn't the type to make small talk, but something about this kid kept my gums flapping. "Is being a cop what you thought it'd be?"

"Honestly? No. I hate all the domestic calls. I spend most shifts busting up fights and arresting drunks. Seems nothing ever changes."

"You got family around here?"

"My wife does. Or else . . ." His gaze hooked mine. "Never mind. I'm tired and babbling like an idiot after working a twelve."

I leaned closer to him. "If you tell anyone I said this, I'll deny it. But the Eagle River Sheriff's Department is looking for deputies. It might be an option if you want to change it up and stay in the area."

Officer Orson nodded. "Thanks for the heads-up."

The suggestion was purely selfish on my part. I wanted to ease the sheriff's workload, and I suspected Dawson was in the interview process with applicants, although he never spoke of it to me. And this young kid would be a better fit in county law enforcement. Only so much room for advancement in the tribal PD if you were mostly white.

"When we got the BOLO on Arlette, I just hoped we'd find her alive."

Took me a minute to remember that BOLO was shorthand for "be on the lookout" and not a western string tie—worn by cowboys and Indians alike around here—instead of a real necktie. "Did you know her?"

"No. Pisses me off that someone did this to her. All violent deaths suck, but it's worse when it's a kid."

I shoved aside the images of the other dead teens I'd seen in the last year. "So when she went missing, and you were talking to her friends about why she might be missing, did anything strike you as odd?"

He cocked his head. "I didn't talk to her friends or family. I'm too low on the departmental totem pole for that job."

The sound of approaching vehicles brought us both to our feet. We watched as two SUVs and an ambulance bumped past the pickups, stopping behind Officer Orson's patrol car.

Special Agent Shay Turnbull was first out of the black SUV. Not only did he own an authoritative presence, I'd seen his charm work with nothing more than a smile. I'd watched him wrest control of a situation with a single word. I understood how lucky I was to be unofficially training with him, even while I also realized Mr. Perfect FBI Agent had done something serious to derail his promising career and end up in rural South Dakota. Not that he'd shared his deepest darkest secrets with me. Although mine were an open book, as he seemed to've memorized my military history.

The sun hadn't burned off the early-morning cloud cover, yet Turnbull wore dark shades in the dim gray light. He claimed his sunglasses provided anonymity. I think he believed the lenses gave off an air of mysterious badass. Must be a guy thing because Dawson wore his sunglasses all the damn time, too.

Three other tribal cops followed Turnbull. One carried a camera.

"Agent Gunderson," Shay said to me in lieu of a "good morning."

"Agent Turnbull, this is Officer Orson. He's been keeping an eye on the crime scene and the witnesses since the initial emergency call."

Turnbull nodded then addressed me again. "Have you been over there?"

"No, sir."

"Let's go." He tossed me a pair of latex gloves and signaled to the camera guy. "I want pictures of everything. And I mean *everything*."

I knew Turnbull preferred his own FBI team on crime scenes, but that wasn't always possible. This reservation was two hours out of Rapid City, so most agents were familiar with being their own Evidence Response Team, or ERT—in FBI speak.

I hadn't asked Officer Orson to describe the scene, so as not to skew my initial impression. When we reached the clearing where the body had been laid out, I wished I'd had more warning about the brutality of the situation.

Arlette Shooting Star was naked. A long piece of wood, driven directly through her heart, staked her to the ground. Dried blood spattered her chest. A dark stain spread across the dirt beneath her slim torso. Her arms and legs were precisely arranged in a T formation, not in the akimbo manner consistent with the randomness of a body falling to the earth. Her brown eyes, covered in a milky blue film of death, were wide open. Her top teeth covered her bottom lip, her face forever frozen in a grimace of pain.

The photographer began snapping pictures of the body from every possible angle. Turnbull said nothing. He just squatted as he moved in a crouch, scribbling in his notebook. The other two cops who'd arrived with him flanked Officer Orson. None of the men said anything. We all just watched, trying to reconcile the horror of what we were seeing.

I'd never been a fan of forensic shows. Since joining the FBI I'd had to learn forensic science, not just to look for the physical clues that often get left behind. The victim's body trauma leads profilers to a specific type of person capable of carrying out such a violent crime. I'd often wondered what these profilers would make of my sniper tactics.

You'll think of anything to take your mind off the reality of this young girl being abducted. Tortured. Probably raped before she was brutalized.

"Agent Gunderson?"

My focus snapped back to Turnbull. "Yes?"

Before he could give instructions, another vehicle screeched up. Doors flew open. The all-male tribal police were much slower to react than I was.

I heard the agonized shriek and managed to get ahold of the woman running toward the crime scene. Triscell Elk Thunder, I presumed. But she was determined, and she dragged me a few steps before I solidified my stance.

"Arlette?" she screamed, fighting me. "Arlette!"

"Ma'am. Stop. Calm down."

"Is that her?" She twisted and jerked.

I literally dug my heels in and held on.

She continued to flail. "Let me go!"

"No. You don't want to see her like this."

That angered her even more. "You have no idea—"

"Yes, I do." I shook her then. Hard. And got right in her face. "Listen to me. Trust me. You don't want to see her."

"Why not?"

"Because you can't erase it, once you see her like that. It'll never go away. It won't give you any closure. It'll haunt you. Is that what you want? To have that memory every time you think of her?"

She stopped thrashing.

I could feel everyone around us staring. Waiting. I wasn't certain I hadn't somehow overstepped my bounds.

Her resolve and resistance vanished. She crumpled to the ground with heart-wrenching sobs.

A tall, older Indian man—whom I saw only from the back and assumed to be her husband, Tribal President Latimer Elk Thunder— dropped to his knees in front of her, blocking her view of Arlette. He coaxed her back into their vehicle. He spoke briefly, angrily to a tribal cop, and then they left.

Numb from the cold, I waited by a fallen log. I remembered this area was lush and gorgeous in late spring. Sloping hills of green dotted with wildflowers. Cottonwood and elm trees budded out, sunlight glinting off waxy new leaves. The breeze blowing across the pond would be heavy with the scent of fresh vegetation and sun-warmed earth. Now this place was an ugly reminder of the encroaching harshness of winter.

Turnbull finished his instructions to the ambulance crew. I didn't know these EMTs, since they were from the tribal dispatch, although I'd been involved with the Eagle River County Emergency Services personnel so many times in the last year and a half I knew them all by name. Not exactly a badge of honor.

Agent Turnbull approached me. "I'm sending the body to Rapid City. Someone from the crime lab can pull the urine and blood tests. If not, we'll have the county coroner perform the exam."

"Exam? No autopsy?"

He shook his head. "Standard procedure in Indian Country. For most traditional Indian families, an autopsy is considered a desecration of the body and the spirit. Especially in children."

My gaze flicked to Arlette's bloodied, naked body being zipped in a black bag. "And what was done to her isn't?"

"I don't make the rules. But we've gotta follow them. See you at the tribal police station."

My first official murder case as an FBI agent.

The prospect of an interview with Triscell Elk Thunder tied my stomach in knots. I understood the necessity of questioning the victim's family ASAP, so I was grateful that Carsten McGillis, a victim specialist—VS—with the FBI, had driven from Rapid City.

Given how Triscell had acted at the crime scene, I half expected that she'd burst in and act hysterical, spouting threats. But her stoic demeanor, her weariness, dug into me like a hidden thorn.

Witnessing her grief sent me spiraling back to the day of Levi's murder. Sadness and horror warred with my need for vengeance, not justice. I participated minimally in the interview, taking my own notes of what I believed would be pertinent information. A couple of things stood out to me:

(1) Arlette didn't have her cell phone on her person when she disappeared. What I knew of teens? They *always* had their cell within reach. The fact that Arlette's phone was in her locker made me wonder if the killer had put it back after the fact.

(2) Arlette's status as the niece of the new tribal president made her a higher-profile victim. Arlette's murder could've been a calculated move aimed at Latimer Elk Thunder in an attempt to distract him from tribal business. I put a question mark after that.

(3) But if the distraction angle was the intent, why wasn't the tribal president here holding his wife's hand? According to the tribal cops, he'd

gone back to work at tribal headquarters immediately after leaving the crime scene. Arlette's murder hadn't seemed to cause more than a hiccup in his normal schedule.

(4) Why weren't any of Triscell's friends or other family members with her, lending support in her husband's absence? In a community this small, even a fair-weather friend would offer to stand by her, if only for the opportunity to get the inside scoop for gossip.

Turnbull's interview technique resembled a disorganized fishing expedition. I'd had my fill of his borderline bullying tactics when I saw fresh tears rolling down Triscell's cheeks.

Carsten jumped in before I did. "Enough, Agent Turnbull. Mrs. Elk Thunder needs a break. Let her go home. She's been extremely helpful."

Turnbull offered an imperious "A word, Miz McGillis?" and stood. He probably intended to blister her ear about undermining his leadership role. He thanked Triscell Elk Thunder for her cooperation. Then he ushered Carsten and the others from the room, leaving me alone with her.

A sigh echoed to me. I figured she wouldn't stick around, but I felt her stare as I feigned concentration on shuffling and reshuffling the papers in front of me like a Deadwood poker dealer.

"You've been through this before." She paused and clarified, "On the civilian side, not as an FBI agent."

Astute. I nodded.

"With who?"

"My nephew. Levi Arpel."

"I remember that. Happened about a year and a half ago?"

"Sixteen months." Hard not to keep track. Sometimes it felt as if that brutal day had been yesterday; other times it seemed years had passed since I'd found him.

"That's right. You shot the guy who did it. Leo . . . what's his face. The hippie teacher."

I almost corrected her—it was Theo—but refrained because I refused to speak the man's name. Still, I tensed. I suspected her next question would be to ask if killing him had offered me any closure.

Goddammit. I did not want to justify my act of self-defense, which had ended Theo's life, or to wait for her to ask about some magical coping mechanisms for grief after a violent death. That fit into Carsten's job description as VS, not mine.

I pushed back from the conference table, focused on sliding all my papers into a manila folder. "You're free to go, Mrs. Elk Thunder."

"Wait, I'm sorry. I don't mean to pry. I just . . ." She sighed. "I feel guilty. Arlette had changed in the last month, and I just went about my own life, assuming she was just being a teenage girl. I should've tried harder, and I have to live with that."

Big mistake looking at her. Her dark brown eyes brimmed. I softened my tone. "We will do everything we can to find out who did this to Arlette."

"FBI party line." She sniffed.

I rather pointedly held the door open for her. After she sailed through it, I pressed my back against the wall, waiting three full minutes before I ventured out of the room.

The building, constructed in the 1950s, had weathered tornados, an attempted burning, and vandalism—the aftereffects still lingered inside, years later. The place was a disaster. Shit was piled everywhere: broken office equipment, empty coffee cans, old uniforms, boxes overflowing with papers. I hoped they weren't important papers, but since they were stacked next to filing cabinets marked ARREST RECORDS, I had to assume they were.

I wondered why no one cared to clean up or at least attempt to organize the mess. Taxpayers who complained about red tape and lost paperwork would have a field day in here. But the tribal police didn't have to play by the same rules as county or federal cops. All areas, with the exception of the conference room, were dirty and jam-packed with junk. No wonder my dad had hated coming here. Now I understood Dawson's frustration, too.

By the time I'd navigated my way into the break room, I'd decided against a cup of coffee.

No sign of Carsten.

Agent Turnbull's shoulders rested against the door frame as he spoke to Officer Spotted Bear. My anxiety kicked in. In the military I'd stand off to the side, at rest, waiting to approach a superior officer until I received acknowledgment. Protocol wasn't defined within the FBI. So I hung back awkwardly, pretending to study the topographical map on the wall, splattered with dark splotches that looked like blood.

"Something you need, Gunderson?" Turnbull finally asked.

I faced him. "Just wondering what's next on the agenda today?"

"Nothin'. But two of the victim's friends scheduled interviews tomorrow."

"Really? They volunteered?"

Turnbull gave me the assessing stare that signaled he was in senior agent mode. "Apparently. Why?"

"Didn't you get the impression from Mrs. Elk Thunder that Arlette didn't have any friends?"

"Adults know way less about what their kids are up to than they wanna admit."

I couldn't argue with that. "So are we done for the day?"

He sipped his coffee. "Yep. Looks like I'm the one with the long commute today, hey?"

Reverting to Indian speak. How . . . calculating of Special Agent Turnbull. Did he think the change in speech pattern gave the tribal cops the impression he was just another rez kid who'd made good? Please. He'd been raised in Flandreau. The Santee tribe had piles more money than the Minneconjou Sioux. "Can't say I'm unhappy about being so close to home. I just needed to clarify if we're meeting here tomorrow, and not at the VS offices."

"Far as I know. Carsten is scheduled in court and won't be assisting us with the interviews."

"Thanks. Have a good evening, sir."

He nodded and gave me his back, returning to his conversation with Officer Spotted Bear.

The wind sliced into me as I crossed the parking lot. The temperature must've dropped twenty degrees in the last few hours. Pewter clouds hung low, heavy with the threat of snow.

I climbed into my new—albeit used—Ford F-150. My dad's old truck had finally crapped out and had been relegated to feed-truck status on the ranch. As I zipped down the black ribbon of empty highway, darkness already obliterating the foggy tinge of daylight, I sang along with Little Big Town about living in the boondocks, realizing I didn't want to go home. Dawson wouldn't be there, which was a total fucking girly excuse for avoiding the place.

I hadn't been in Clementine's for a month, which might have actually been a new record for me, not counting the months I was out of town. But I wasn't in the mood to chitchat with John-John or any of the regulars I had slung drinks for during my stint as a bartender. Lunch had been the last thing on my mind after I'd spent the morning at the crime scene. Now it was close to suppertime, and I was starved.

Once I hit the outskirts of the Eagle Ridge Township, I parked in front of the Blackbird Diner. If Dawson just happened to see my vehicle, maybe he'd amble in from the sheriff's office. Be nice to see his face across the table from mine for a change.

The homey aroma of warm bread and strong coffee enveloped me as I headed toward my favorite booth in the back. I hung my wool coat on the peg and slid in, reaching for the menu strategically placed along the wall.

A glass of water plopped down in front of me. I looked up at Mitzi and smiled. "Thanks."

But Mitzi wasn't returning my smile. "You ain't supposed to be carryin' in here, Mercy."

Having a gun on my person was second nature. I opened my mouth to argue, but Mitzi beat me to the punch.

"Only people I let carry in here are Dawson and his deputies. You know that."

We'd had this argument before. I usually acquiesced and trotted out to my truck, dutifully locking my gun away. I wasn't feeling so cooperative today. "I'm a federal officer on a case. Dawson enforces county regulations. Go ahead and call him. Tell him I'm in your booth with a loaded weapon. Let's see what he does."

Mitzi harrumphed. "Beings you're livin' with him, I doubt he's gonna make you take it off. I really doubt he's gonna write you a ticket. Or put you in jail again." The ruby slash of her mouth was a clownishly grotesque smirk. "Then he'd probably have to wash his own socks and boxers, huh?"

I don't know which annoyed me more—that Mitzi assumed because I'm a woman I did all the laundry in our household, or that she'd somehow known that Dawson wore boxers. I managed to hold my tongue. "What are the specials tonight?"

"Mushroom meat loaf with country gravy, mashed potatoes, and steamed veggies."

Steamed veggies as a side dish nixed that choice. "What's the soup?"

"Borscht or chicken noodle."

Beets. Yuck. "I'll have a bowl of chicken noodle, a side of hash browns with country gravy, and a basket of wheat rolls."

"I'll have to charge you for the bread," she warned.

"I know. Water's fine to drink."

As she spun away from the table, her support hose eked out a *scritch-scratch* sound with every step.

I propped my feet up on the opposite bench seat and let my head fall back. Keeping my eyes closed, I focused on *uji* breathing to center myself.

But no matter how hard I tried to clear my mind, the image of Arlette Shooting Star's body impaled by a wooden stake kept popping up. In a moment of clarity, I realized what had bugged me: the positioning of the body. Like a ritual killing. Like I'd seen in the forensics classes I'd taken at Quantico.

Had Turnbull gotten the same impression? If so, why hadn't he said anything to me? As a test? To see if I'd ask about bringing it to the attention of an FBI profiler?

I couldn't fathom being an FBI profiler. Sitting in an office, running probability and statistics on potential violent behavior. Knowing someone was out there waiting to strike again and being unable to stop it would be worse than dealing with the victim, the family, and the crime scene.

Dishes rattled, and I opened my eyes as Mitzi slid my soup in front of me, hash browns to the left, bread to the right. "Anything else?"

"Nah. I'm good for now."

The soup was hearty, the hash browns crispy and greasy. I was mopping up the last of the gravy with my dinner roll when the bench seat across from me creaked. I glanced up into Rollie Rondeaux's placid face.

That was a surprise. Rollie had all but vanished from my life. I'd called him after I returned from Quantico, but he had never called me back, or stopped by the ranch just to shoot the breeze, or take me for a joyride in his crappy truck. It'd been months since we'd laid eyes on each other. And to be honest, I was a little pissy about the situation, even when I knew what'd changed things between us: my status as a federal employee.

Mitzi clomped over with a cup of coffee for Rollie and rattled off the pie selection.

After he ordered pie, I wiped my mouth and casually asked, "What brings you into town?"

"Outta diapers, and Besler's is the only place that carries the tiny ones Verline wants."

"How is Verline?" Rollie's live-in, Verline, had given birth to their second child prematurely, right after I'd returned from Virginia. I'd made a care package. Okay, Hope had done all the work, but I'd delivered it to their trailer.

A package neither Verline nor Rollie had acknowledged.

Rollie rubbed his fingers over his jaw. "Verline is . . ." He sighed. "Ain't no way to describe how she's been actin' lately. I volunteered to go on a diaper run. Now that I'm out of the house I don't wanna go back."

"That doesn't sound good. Trouble in paradise?"

"Paradise." He snorted. "Like hell most days. I'm too old for this cryin'-baby stuff, Mercy. I'm definitely too damn old to deal with a temperamental woman. Half the time I wanna throttle her."

I frowned.

"She's drivin' me crazy, hey. Drivin' me to drink."

"Like you've ever needed an excuse to drink. Besides, you've always said Verline makes you crazy. It'll blow over."

His braids swayed when he shook his head. "Not this time." He sipped his coffee. "What's goin' on with you and Dawson?"

"You'd know the answer to that if you ever called me, *kola*."

He shrugged. "Been too busy dealing with my own stuff to worry about someone else's." His gaze dropped to my left hand. "You ain't wearing his ring."

"I doubt you've dropped to one knee and proposed to Verline, and you've been with her longer than I've been with Dawson."

"Ain't the same thing. I know he's asked you."

No reason to lie. Dawson asked me to marry him every week. He just brought it up when the mood struck him. But I kept hedging. Not saying no, but more along the lines of, *Can we talk about this later?*

"Mebbe the fact you ain't said yes means he ain't the man for you."

"As if I'll take relationship advice from the old-timer who's been divorced multiple times and is shacked up with a girl who can't legally buy a six-pack."

"You got a mean streak, Mercy."

"Like that's news. Besides, you've had issues with every man who's ever been in my life, starting with my father."

That shut him down.

Mitzi swung by with Rollie's pie.

"What's goin' on at the FBI?" he asked after a bite of lemon meringue.

"Mostly procedural courses behind a conference table."

He lifted a dark brow so high it moved his PI hat up an inch. "That's it? I heard Hoover's henchmen are involved in the Shooting Star case."

Nothing stayed secret for long on the Eagle River Reservation. "Yeah.

Didn't take long for her to go from missing to dead." I paused to sip water. "What do you know about it?"

"Nothin'."

Bullshit. Rumor was Rollie was more aware of rez happenings than the tribal cops. I'd have to ply him with flattery to unlock his lips. "Come on. You've got your ear to the ground. What's your take on this?"

"I ain't ever gonna snitch for the feds."

"If you don't want to give information to the feds, then why are you talking to me?"

Rollie's gaze searched my face. "Mercy, we both know being a fed ain't really you. How long you think you'll last in the FBI?"

I bristled. Why would he imply I'd fail after having the badge for only a few weeks? "So I'd be better off pulling taps at Clementine's?"

"Mebbe. At least when you were working for the *winkte,* you weren't drinkin' as much. And I guarantee what you see in this job will send you straight back to the bottle."

"How can it be worse than what I dealt with in the army?"

He curled his hands around his coffee cup. "The feds in Indian Country deal with the bad stuff. The really bad stuff. Not just murders, but rapes. Child abuse. Sex crimes. All the sick stuff most people, even the cops, on the rez turn a blind eye to."

"Why is that kind of shit allowed to slide?"

"Because it's easier to ignore it than admitting one of your relatives is capable of raping a two-year-old. Or that burning a six-year-old with a cigarette is an acceptable form of discipline. Or sexually assaulting an eight-year-old with beer bottles and kitchen utensils is a form of entertainment. And those I mentioned? They're not the worst cases."

Bile rose, and I swallowed it down with a gulp of water. "How do you know that?"

"I've lived here my whole life. I've watched how no jobs, no purpose, and too much alcohol affect the tribe."

"What if I can make a difference?"

Rollie raised his eyes to mine. "Because you've got a dab of Indian blood?"

I blinked at him. That was more than a little snarky coming from the man who'd encouraged me to enroll in the tribe about eight months ago.

"Besides, you can't make a difference. No one can. Watch yourself, Mercy, when you go digging into this bad stuff. There's always someone wantin' to keep their sick little secrets. There's always someone wantin' to prove they're smarter than you."

"Can you stop talking in riddles for one damn minute?"

He picked at the toasted meringue. As I formulated my next question, Rollie demanded, "Did Latimer bring in the feds right away when she went missin'?"

"Why?"

"'Cause he'll milk this tragedy for all it's worth, even though he really don't give a damn about that girl."

"No love lost between you and the tribal president?"

"He's a self-serving prick who reeks of false piety."

Harsh. "That doesn't seem to be the general attitude on the rez. People have great hopes he'll implement changes."

"Two words that mean nothin' in politics: hope and change. Especially not when it comes to his ideas."

That didn't sound like differing philosophies; it sounded personal. "How long have you known Latimer Elk Thunder?"

"Since before he became a white man in Indian skin."

For Rollie that was an unforgivable offense—in men, anyway. "Are you guys business rivals or something?"

"Since he owns the only gas station on the rez, he ain't got no rivals."

"So were you rivals over a woman? You said some nasty stuff about my dad because you believe he stole my mother from you."

He harrumphed and ate another bite of his pie.

"So you weren't in love with his wife and she threw you over for Latimer?" I joked.

"Not hardly. I ain't ever been impressed with her, either. Though she's awful damn impressed with herself." His black eyes met mine. "How was the niece killed?"

That was an abrupt subject change. "I'm not at liberty to disclose that information."

"Was she brutalized before her body was discarded like an unwanted animal? Or after, at the dump site? I'm betting after."

"Who told you this?"

He clammed up when Mitzi refilled his coffee.

"How did you know?" Dammit. I shouldn't have let that slip. "Are you having some kind of visions like John-John?" I demanded.

Rollie snorted. "If I did, I sure wouldn't tell nobody."

"Then why are you telling me this?"

He shoveled in a bite of white fluff. Then pointed his fork at me. "I didn't tell you nothin'. I hazarded a *guess*."

Outwardly, I managed a bored look. Inwardly, I imagined snatching away his pie.

"Ain't ya gonna pull that high-handed fed crap and threaten to haul me in if I don't cooperate?"

I offered a half shrug. "You haven't actually given me any useful information, Rollie. You're just guessing, right?"

"Guess you don't know that Arlette Shooting Star ain't the first dead girl to show up around here, and I doubt she'll be the last."

My jaw nearly hit the table.

Before I could formulate a response, he was gone.

3

On the drive home I couldn't help but wonder what Rollie's angle was. How could the FBI not be aware of other female deaths on the reservation that might relate to the Shooting Star case?

The crotchety old man had a bug up his butt about all law enforcement agencies—especially federal—since the American Indian Movement, known as AIM, uprisings in the 1970s. He refused to admit whether he'd been involved in the AIM violence. But given his issues with the government after his military discharge during the Vietnam War, I wouldn't be surprised if he'd masterminded some of the shit that'd gone down.

My dad hadn't been sheriff during those rocky years, so I hadn't known details about the outbreaks of fatal violence until I'd studied the case histories and investigations during my training at Quantico.

Since I'd already been assigned to an FBI office with multiple Indian reservations in the jurisdiction, I'd had to take extra classes on racial sensitivity and honoring traditional Indian customs within the confines of federal laws. Not even being a registered member of the Eagle River tribe had let me klepp out of the courses.

Although I'd been armed with information after the lectures, nothing I'd learned about that turbulent time was cut and dried. Emotions ran high, untruths abounded, subterfuge on both sides culminated in tribal members and FBI agents dying. Not a particularly proud moment for either AIM or the FBI. But I had a better understanding of Indian resentment . . . as well as the feds' frustration.

So I had to question Rollie's motive in telling me to look deeper. Was he trying to lead me off course? And if so, why?

At home I flipped on the TV and my laptop, nestling into the living room couch with a beer. I started my Internet search wide, going back twelve months, using the keywords: Indian reservations, women's deaths, accidents, violence.

1,379 results popped up.

Well, wasn't that a kick in the ass. I narrowed the search to the local papers in western South Dakota and retrieved more manageable data. I started clicking on links, copying pertinent ones into a separate document.

Three obituaries from last year caught my notice. Each a month apart. The first one was for Tunisia Broken Arrow, age twenty-two. Nothing in the obit about cause of death. The second one for Minneola "Mimi" Diggeman, age thirty. Again, nothing in the obit about cause of death. The third obituary was for Delia Moss, age twenty-seven. No listed cause of death.

How could all of these young women have died of natural causes? I cross-referenced the time frame, and none of the names were listed as car accident victims. Illness possibly? Or suicide?

I changed the parameters, going back twenty-four months, and found three more obituaries. All young women, all dead within a month of one another. None of the obits listed cause of death.

What the hell was going on? The only way to make any sense of this was to see the tribal PD's report logs. There'd be a written report for a suicide. As well as a written report on a death due to exposure—I noticed these obits were mostly from the late fall/early winter months.

I knew I'd have to bring this up with Turnbull.

My cell phone buzzed with a text message from Dawson: *Crushed under the weight of unfinished paperwork. Trying to catch up. Late night and early-morning shift means I'm crashing in my office tonight. Sorry. Miss you.*

I miss you, too.

I hated that our schedules didn't mesh, but that would probably always be a wrinkle in our private life together. No wonder cops had such high divorce rates. I sucked it up, swallowing the missing-my-man girly whine, then shut everything off and went to bed.

My sleep was fairly restful, considering the previous day's disturbing events.

But as I drank coffee and looked at what the computer search engine had dredged up the night before, I knew I needed to talk to Rollie again—before I brought up my suspicions with Shay. Since we had interviews scheduled for first thing this morning, I'd drop by his place at the Diamond T after work tonight.

Jake must've come by early because the dogs weren't around when I stepped onto the porch. I squinted at the sky. Another dreary day. The moist air seeped into my bones, and I shivered. Wet cold is worse than dry cold. I'd take winter in the high plains desert over winter in the supposed warmer clime of North Carolina. At least if it snowed, the dulled, gray, lifeless tones of late fall would be hidden beneath a blanket of white.

The parking lot at the tribal police station was nearly full—an odd occurrence this early in the morning on the rez. I remembered to put my FBI parking tag on the dash. Hopefully, that wouldn't earn me a tire iron to the windows or headlights.

Inside, a dozen or so people crowded around the receptionist's desk, arguing about wrongful incarceration of a family member. I dodged fighting kids and skirted a hefty woman in a wheelchair who was blocking the door. After winding my way through teetering boxes in the hallways, any calmness evaporated once I reached the conference room. I hated that I wanted Agent Turnbull here. I hadn't dealt with the tribal cops much, and I was still finding my footing as to who was in charge in what circumstance.

Officer Ferguson was kicked back, with her boots on the table and a file folder obscuring most of her face. Those boots dropped with a thump when she saw me. "Sorry, Agent."

"No problem." I spied a coffeepot and poured myself a cup.

"Is your partner coming today?" she asked.

No surprise she'd be asking about Shay. The man's amazing looks could've landed him on the cover of a historical western romance, where the scantily dressed, brave Brave held the virginal white girl in his big strong arms. "Special Agent Turnbull is not my partner. He's my supervisor. So I assume he'll show."

"Oh, I didn't know." She gave me a curious look. "Do you think the reason we're interviewing Arlette's friends is because we're women?"

Oddly enough, that comment relaxed me, because I'd had the same thought. "Probably. But I'll take a dozen teenage girls in interview any day over one strung-out male meth head." I sat across from her and sipped my coffee. "Do you know these friends of Arlette's?"

She shook her head and slid me a file folder.

I skimmed the lone document. "Where's the other girl's statement?"

"That's all we've got."

I bit back a comment about the seemingly haphazard treatment of documents at the tribal PD. When I glanced up, I noticed the curtain to what I'd assumed was a window was now open. It wasn't a window but a two-way glass to a viewing room. That's where Turnbull would be.

Three raps sounded on the door, and the receptionist stuck her head in. "Fergie? Are you ready for Naomi Malloy? The Kicking Bird family has taken over the front office, and she's getting spooked."

Officer Ferguson looked at me and I nodded. "Bring her in."

After the door closed, I said, "So . . . Fergie, huh?"

She rolled her eyes. "I got that nickname after Fergie, the former Duchess of York, became a household name, but before Fergie, from the Black Eyed Peas, became popular." She smirked. "But I'm sure you can see my resemblance to the latter."

Redheaded Officer Ferguson was about five feet three and as curvy as a tipi pole.

"One of my nicknames in the army was Gunny, which pissed off the marines we were stationed with, because that name is used exclusively for a male gunnery sergeant. They still gave me the stink eye after I pointed to my name patch and explained Gunny was short for Gunderson."

"Fucking jarheads," she muttered. "I was in the air force for a decade, so I know how they are."

"You were military police?"

Fergie nodded. "Ended up stationed at Ellsworth for the last of my enlistment. Met a native guy, moved to the rez, got a cop job . . . and here I am."

"He fell in love with your lovely lady lumps?"

She grinned and started to retort, but the door swung inward, sucking the humor from the room. The ashen face of a young Indian girl reminded us of our unpleasant task.

I stood and offered my hand. "Naomi? I'm Special Agent Gunderson of the FBI. Thank you so much for coming in to speak with us."

"Why don't you sit here." Officer Ferguson offered her a seat between us. "That way we won't have to shout at each other to be heard. You want coffee or water?"

Naomi shook her head and slid into the chair.

I studied her openly. Long, straight hair scraped back into a ponytail. Eyes heavily lined with black eye shadow. She peeled back the oversized, black ski jacket. The puffiness of her down-filled coat made her look much huskier than her actual slight stature. Rings adorned all ten of her fingers. Her fingernails were painted black, but the polish was mostly chipped off.

She tugged down a black T-shirt emblazoned with the words TEAM JACOB, and I bit back a groan. A *Twi*-hard. My sister had convinced me to watch the first *Twilight* movie, and I had done so with extreme cynicism, leaving on my running shoes to make a fast getaway. But the flick was entertaining, despite the bucket loads of teen angst.

"Since you're a minor, we can wait to begin until there's a parent or guardian present."

"My mom's dead; my dad's in jail. I live with my grandma, and she don't get around too good. I don't need anyone's permission to talk."

I glanced at Fergie, and she shrugged, as if to indicate that this happened regularly. "If it's all right with you, we'll start with the basics. How well did you know Arlette?"

Naomi twisted her rings. "We hung out. We liked the same books."

"What kind of books?"

"Vampire ones, mostly." Her chin came up, daring me to make fun of her.

I played dumb. "Vampire books like *Dracula* or the ones Anne Rice writes?"

"No. Like the *Twilight* series." She pointed to her T-shirt. "Like the *Vampire Academy* series. *The Vampire Diaries*."

"Ah. Did you and Arlette see each other outside of school hours to talk about your shared interest of vampire books?"

"Yes, as often as we could."

"Would you meet at her house?"

She paused. "Sometimes. But her uncle hated when she had people over. He complained he wanted to watch his TV in peace and quiet without loud teenagers around."

"How was her relationship with her uncle?"

"In front of other people, like tribal members, he acted as if he liked having her around. But when it was just them two and her aunt? He wasn't nice to her, and she heard him say he couldn't wait until she was gone."

My gaze narrowed. "Did you hear him say that?"

"Once. On one of the rare times I stayed over at her house. I needed a drink of water, and I overheard him and Arlette's aunt arguing in the living room. He said he'd never wanted kids—his own or anyone else's—and maybe if they were lucky, Arlette would screw up just like her mother had, and then they'd be rid of her."

"Did you tell Arlette what you overheard?"

She shook her head. "It would've made her feel worse because she knew her uncle didn't want her around."

Rotten luck to overhear such a cruel remark in light of what

happened to her friend. "Did Arlette ever tell you that her uncle physically hurt her? Or threatened to hurt her?"

"I don't think so. He just said mean shit to her all the time. Especially
after he'd been drinking." Naomi's eyes widened with fear. "You won't
tell him I said any of that?"

"No. Everything you tell us is confidential." I glanced up from the
scant notes I'd jotted in my notebook. "Who else did Arlette hang
around with?"

"We were both kinda loners. People made fun of our interest in vampire books." Naomi scowled. "She sometimes hung out with Mackenzie
Red Shirt. But only when Mackenzie wanted something."

"Like what?"

"Like a ride to one of the parties out at Dickie's slough. Or if she
wanted Arlette to do a report for her."

"What would Arlette get in return?"

Naomi became interested in the frayed end of her scarf.

After a silent minute or two, Officer Ferguson prompted, "Naomi?"

She looked up at me. "Mackenzie kept promising to introduce Arlette
to this older guy she'd been crushing on."

"Did Mackenzie ever follow through?"

"Yeah." Tears swam in her eyes. "That's when everything changed.
When Arlette changed. She started lying to her aunt about where she
was going. She stopped caring about her schoolwork."

Now, maybe this was making sense. "Who was the guy?"

"I don't know. She wouldn't tell me. She just called him J."

Naomi must've sensed my skepticism because she blurted out, "I
swear it's the truth! Arlette said she found her Jacob but he wanted to
keep their relationship secret. When I told her that was a bad thing, she
accused me of being jealous. I should've made her tell me! I should've . . .
done something, because now she's dead!" Naomi set her head on the
conference table and sobbed.

I wished Carsten was here. I stared at the bawling girl, unable to comfort her because petting and soothing weren't my way. I waited, quietly

tapping my pen on my notepad to the same cadence of my boot tapping on the floor. Fergie poured a glass of water and passed it to Naomi, offering the gentle, encouraging pat on the back I couldn't.

The girl lifted her head and wiped the moisture from her face. "Is it true?"

"Is what true?" I asked.

"That Arlette was staked through the heart. With a wooden stake? Just like . . ."

A vampire.

Another chill zigzagged up my spine. Why hadn't Triscell Elk Thunder mentioned Arlette's obsession with the *Twilight* series and anything vampire-related?

She had to've known.

Did you know everything about Levi's interests?

No. But I hadn't lived with Levi, either.

"Yes, Naomi, I'm afraid it is true," Fergie said gently.

"Oh God. That's so sick—" Her voice caught on a sob, but somehow she didn't break down.

"When was the last time you saw her or talked to her?"

She sniffled. "The day we had the fight."

Poor girl. Talk about guilt. A fight with her friend, and then she winds up dead. I handed her a tissue. "How long was that before Arlette disappeared?"

"Three days."

"Had Arlette ever mentioned wanting to run away?"

"No. She didn't like it here, but she knew she'd have to graduate to get outta here for good." More tears welled up. "We talked about leaving together. Until she started spending all of her time with J."

Jealousy was a powerful emotion. Still, I had a hard time believing Naomi would murder Arlette because she'd ditched her for a guy. Even if the guy Arlette bragged about was her "Jacob."

God. Teens really took the fictional world that seriously?

My freakin' head was about to explode.

Officer Ferguson jumped in. "Did everyone know you and Arlette had a falling-out?"

Naomi shook her head. "And no one would've cared anyway."

"Anything else you care to add?"

Another head shake.

"Okay. Thanks for your help. If we think of anything else, can we call you?" I glanced down at the paperwork and rattled off the numbers. "That's your cell phone number?"

"Yeah."

"I imagine it goes everywhere with you."

"I guess."

"Did Arlette always have her phone with her?"

"Not during school hours. She kept it in her locker because she got it taken away by the principal once and her uncle freaked out. Why?"

"Because Arlette's phone was found in her locker. You think she just went someplace and forgot it?"

Naomi slid her arms into her coat sleeves. "Nope. That means she left school before lunch and planned to come back."

Mackenzie Red Shirt, our next interviewee, didn't show.

I returned to the empty conference room after a brief bathroom break, trying to sort through my notes. What would be the best way to track down Miss Red Shirt and convince her to tell us Arlette's mystery guy's name? I also wanted to talk to Triscell. I'd taken her vague, flustered state as a result of grief. So it surprised me to see a "No contact without permission from the tribal president" note on the file. That made zero sense.

I was lost in thought and didn't notice that Turnbull had entered the conference room until he parked his butt on the table next to my papers.

He actually gave me a warm smile. "Great job with the friend."

I leaned back in my seat. I hated how he invaded my personal space—and he was aware of it, so naturally he did it as often as possible. "Had you made the connection between the stake in the victim's heart and vampires?"

"The thought had crossed my mind, but I dismissed it. I'm still not convinced there is any correlation. But I ain't gonna write it off as coincidence." Shay spun my notebook around to read my notes. Then his gaze hooked mine.

Damn man had the most compelling eyes. I could say that objectively, when he wasn't annoying the piss out of me. He'd hit the lottery as far as good looks. Sporting the best of his Native American ancestry, he had chiseled cheekbones, smooth skin, and hair as black as tar worn long enough to brush the edges of his prominent jaw. His body appeared long and lean, but I'd trained with him at the gym and knew firsthand that well-honed muscles lurked beneath his casual work clothes. Add in his dazzling smile, an abundance of charm, and Shay Turnbull was a force to be reckoned with.

When he wanted to be.

So I wondered what he wanted now. "What?"

"Have you had lunch?"

"No. Why?"

"I'm following up on another case and wondered if you wanted me to bring you something back from Taco John's?"

Thoughtful. And so very un-Shay-like. "Sure. Whatever you're having is fine."

"Cool. Oh, and while I'm gone, could you make copies of the files I gave the receptionist?" He leveled that charming smile on me.

And . . . that was *very* Shay-like. But I'd get lunch out of the deal, so I wouldn't complain.

After lunch, I headed to my pickup to grab a sweater because the conference room we were working in was like a meat locker.

It'd been a while since I'd been waylaid in a parking lot during the day. To my credit, I didn't pull my gun on the young Indian woman leaning against my truck, angrily puffing on a cigarette.

"Are you Gunderson?" she demanded.

"Yeah. How'd you know this was my vehicle?"

"FBI tag in the window. Good way to get your tires slashed."

"I'll take that under advisement. Who are you?"

"Mackenzie Red Shirt."

Ah. The no-show teenage interviewee. "Well, Mackenzie, you're late. I can spare a half hour if you wanna go back inside—"

"No fuckin' way am I goin' into the cop shop."

"Why'd you volunteer to come in?"

"I *didn't* volunteer." She inhaled quickly and blew out a violent stream of smoke. "That little bitch Naomi called and told me she signed me up. She set me up."

My gaze flicked to the main road. We weren't exactly inconspicuous. "So why are you here?"

Mackenzie glared at me. "To find out what Naomi said."

"Why not just ask her?"

"I tried, but she wouldn't tell me nothin'."

I crossed my arms over my chest. "So you what . . . jumped Naomi after she left?" I tsk-tsked. "Not the brightest crayon in the box, are you, Mackenzie? Threatening another minor in full view of the *cop shop*."

"I didn't leave a mark on her."

A bully. Lovely. One who used words was no different than one who used fists. The only thing a bully understands is another bully. "Am I supposed to be impressed? Here's the truth: leaving bruises is a more effective threat than reducing a girl to tears." I leaned closer. "Need a personal demonstration on how that one works?"

Her eyes showed a hint of fear. "No."

"First smart thing you've said. Now move it so I can get to my truck."

That caught her off guard. "But . . . I thought you wanted to talk to me."

"I did. But now after meeting you? I doubt anything you'll tell me will help our case."

"Oh yeah?" An indignant Mackenzie aimed a cool look at me. "What's it worth to tell you the name of the guy I hooked Arlette up with?"

"You're expecting I'll pay you for that information?" I laughed. "Wrong. Besides, Naomi already told us." I tossed the baited hook out, waiting for her to jerk on the line.

"Bullshit. How could she've told you when she don't know his name?"

"What makes you think Naomi doesn't know?" I paused a beat and feigned surprise. "Oh. Right. I'll bet when you threatened her, she swore she didn't know anything and didn't tell us anything. And you believed her." I shrugged. "I would've lied, too."

"What did that bitch tell you?" she snapped.

"Sorry. Confidential information."

Mackenzie whipped her cigarette down, not bothering to tamp it out before she stormed off.

I braced myself for more accusations when she stomped back.

"Since this is all so freakin' *confidential*, you'll keep my name out of it when you talk to Junior?"

I knew a Junior. Problem was, I knew several of them, including the teenage Junior who'd been part of the trio to discover Arlette's body. "Of course. But Naomi didn't tell me how *you* knew Junior."

She slumped beside me. "We lived in the same trailer court for a while, until my stupid mom got us kicked out."

"Which trailer court?"

"The Diamond T, outside of the rez."

Goddammit. The Junior I was thinking of *was* Junior Rondeaux— who lived in that same trailer court with his dad and Verline. Now I was more than a little pissed that Rollie hadn't mentioned his son Junior's connection to Arlette Shooting Star.

A chill raised gooseflesh on my arms. Was that why Rollie had sought me out? To share his suspicion that his son was somehow involved in Arlette's death?

No. He'd never tip off the feds, especially not when it came to family. My silence must've been the signal for Mackenzie to talk.

"Look, I was just playin' with Arlette, introducing her to Junior. She and Naomi were so freakin' . . . ridiculous about that *Twilight* shit. Talking about it all the time. Acting like it was real. I overheard them talking about wanting to meet someone like Jacob—a mystical Indian with family ties to the old ways. People around here whisper about Junior's old man bein' all-powerful, so I teased Arlette about knowing a guy like that. I didn't expect she'd become obsessed with him. I strung her along for a while before I introduced them. But I didn't know there was such bad blood between Junior's old man and Arlette's uncle."

"Did Arlette's uncle know she was seeing Junior Rondeaux?"

Mackenzie shook her head. "But Junior's dad knew about Arlette and told Junior to break it off with her."

"Did he?"

"I don't know. They both stopped talking to me."

"How long ago was this?" At her blank look, I clarified, "When did you introduce them?"

"Over a month ago."

That fit with Naomi's time frame of when Arlette started acting strangely. But something else didn't fit. No one in the entire Eagle River community knew about Junior and Arlette sneaking around? Bull. The rez was a hotbed of gossip. Why hadn't anyone come forward with this information?

You're surprised no one is spilling their guts to the tribal police? Or the feds?

I glanced at Mackenzie and was shocked to see her hands covering her face. "What's wrong?"

She raised her head and stared at me through teary eyes. "Arlette was a dork, but I didn't want her to die."

"Do you think Junior could've killed her?"

No answer.

I looked away when a car door slammed, and when I refocused on

Mackenzie, she'd ducked down, vanishing into the sea of cars. The abrupt end to our conversation left me unsettled.

Officer Ferguson frowned as she approached me. "I figured you'd be back from lunch before now."

I pulled my cell phone out of my pocket and waggled it. "Got waylaid by a phone call. What's up?"

"Nothing. I thought I saw you talking to someone, but you must've been talking to yourself."

"Hazard of the job." I shoved my cell in my pocket. "I came out here to get a sweater. Can't you guys crank the heat up in that conference room? I think I have frostbite."

She laughed. "I'll see what I can do for you, Gunny."

A few hours later I drove to the Diamond T.

The trailer court looked as crappy and run-down as it always had. Busted windows in the trailers, broken-down cars parked everywhere, trash blowing back and forth between falling-down fences. Talk about a rural slum.

It was early enough in the day that kids weren't home from school yet. Their suspicious stares on my last visit reminded me of the ragged children in war-torn Iraq; their smiles had never quite masked the hatred in their eyes.

I parked behind a blue Dodge Caravan with a broken rear window that had been repaired with plastic dry-cleaning bags and lime-green duct tape. The back end of Rollie's truck jutted out from the gravel driveway between the doublewide and the garage.

A dog barked, starting a chain reaction of howls, from one littered yard to the next, as I got out of my pickup.

I climbed the rickety steps and knocked on the screen, expecting to wait. But the inner door swung open immediately. Verline stood inside the jamb, a diaper-clad toddler cocked on her hip. "Rollie ain't here."

"Thanks for the update, but I'm looking for Junior."

She shifted the fussy boy. "Why?"

"I need to ask him a few questions."

"It'd be a waste of time. Unlike his father, he ain't gonna talk to you."

"So does Junior still live here?"

"Not since Rollie kicked him out."

I resisted asking if that'd happened after Rollie found out about Junior's alleged involvement with Arlette Shooting Star. "Have you seen him recently?"

An anxious look flitted across her weary face. "He shows up when he knows his old man ain't around."

"Do you know why Rollie sent him packing?"

Verline shook her head.

"Did Junior mention where he was staying the last time you saw him?"

She averted her eyes, and then tugged on the boy's diaper before she looked at me again. "I didn't ask."

I let it slide, even though I was sure she was lying.

An excruciatingly loud wail came from inside the house. Holy crap. Did that new little baby have a monster set of lungs. Then the toddler started shrieking and hitting Verline on the shoulder with his tiny fists.

"I gotta go." And she slammed the door in my face.

4

And once again, Dawson wasn't home.

The dogs were happy to see me. I rewarded their enthusiasm by playing fetch, whipping the tennis ball across the yard.

Over the past few months Shoonga and Butch had become best buds. Shoonga was clearly the alpha dog, since the ranch was his turf. Butch followed Shoonga around, content to follow his lead—except when it came to fetch. Butch turned fiercely competitive whenever a bouncing ball appeared. He'd knock Shoonga's doggie mug into the dirt every chance he could. It amused the heck outta me seeing the two dogs yipping and nipping at each other, hackles raised, teeth bared and fur flying whenever that yellow fuzz-covered ball bounced.

Kind of reminded me . . . of Shay and me.

I petted and praised the pups, poured extra food for them on the porch, and entered my empty house.

The kitchen sparkled thanks to Sophie's efforts. She'd left a note on the table about laundry.

Although Sophie had been doing domestic chores for our family since my mother had died, she was more than a housekeeper. She'd helped raise Hope and me. She'd taken care of the household and my father. This house seemed as much her home as mine.

Dawson understood my reason for keeping Sophie on the payroll, but he refused to let her do his laundry. I understood where he was coming from. It'd taken me a couple of months after I'd returned from Iraq to hand over my dirty clothes to her.

I figured he'd cave in. He hadn't. So it made no sense to me why

Dawson was perfectly content to let Sophie cook for us. Probably because she kept him well supplied with his favorite cookies.

But according to the note, she had to leave early to take her daughter Penny to the doctor, so no tasty supper awaited me. If Dawson didn't show up, I'd probably just eat yogurt.

I changed, rolled out my mat, and practiced yoga until sweat stuck my clothes to my skin.

As I stood under the tepid shower spray, I wondered how my life had become so mundane. I went to work. Came home and played with the dogs. Worked out. Showered. Ate supper. Watched TV, looking at the clock every ten minutes and wondering when Dawson would show up. Then I'd hit the hay.

I'd always been fairly solitary, but tonight it almost seemed . . . forced. By the time I'd dried off, combed out my wet hair, and slipped on a robe, I'd decided to partake of a little nightlife at Clementine's. I wandered into the kitchen for a pregame beer when the dogs started barking. Dawson's deep voice soothed them, and I could practically hear their tails thumping against the boards on the porch.

God, I knew the feeling. I was tempted to give a little yip of excitement myself.

The door opened. Dawson didn't notice me at first, as he was too busy taking off his butt-ugly hat, hanging up his coat, and toeing off his boots. When he lifted his head and looked at me, my belly jumped like I was a teenage girl with a crush.

Dawson smiled. "Hey."

"Hey, yourself." I took a sip of beer. "You done for the night? Or just stopping to get something to eat before you head back out?"

"I'm done." His gaze started at my forehead and leisurely traveled the length of my body, down to my bare toes, and then back up.

By the time his eyes met mine, they held that look. The look I'd been missing for the last week.

Then he stalked me until my spine hit the counter. "Whatcha got on under that robe, Sergeant Major?"

"Just my skin, Sheriff."

Dawson made a noise that resembled a growl before his mouth covered mine. I fell into him, fell into the kiss, blanking my mind to everything except the happy fact that he was here.

His hands cradled my face then slid down my neck to the gap in my robe. Then his hands were on my bare skin, cruising down my chest over my rib cage to circle my waist. The way the ragged pads of his fingertips stroked my breasts made me arch into him harder. Kiss him harder.

Then he dropped to his knees.

He chuckled against my lower belly at my moan of delight. Then his hard-skinned hands were on the inside of my thighs, pushing them apart so he could settle his mouth on the damp flesh within.

I held on to his head with one hand, the edge of the counter with the other, and gave myself over to his intimate kiss. He had me panting, begging, and quivering in record time—a feat that might've been embarrassing for me if I hadn't already known this man took tremendous pride in turning me inside out as fast as possible.

As I regained my sanity, Mason treated me to sweet, lingering kisses everywhere on my body, letting his mouth roam. Once he was back on his feet, he murmured, "Jump up," in my ear, as his hands clamped onto my butt.

Then I was on the counter, my robe was on the floor, and Dawson was unbuckling his belt. The moment his body powered into mine, my world became him: his taste, his scent, his heat.

After he rocked me so hard I swear he rocked the cabinet off the floor, he yanked up his pants and carried me to bed.

Looked like we were making up for lost time.

Not a single complaint from me.

I'd never sexually clicked with any man the way I did with Dawson. Living together hadn't cooled our passion one iota. In fact, being in close quarters and able to act on impulse whenever we wanted had ramped it up a notch or twenty.

Later, as I was spent and sprawled on my stomach, he'd propped himself on his side, letting his fingers follow the curve of my spine.

"Guess what I got today?"

"A qualified applicant for the deputy's position?"

"Funny. Try again."

I lifted my head and looked at him. "You really want to play twenty questions?"

Dawson sighed. "Sometimes your cut-to-the-chase attitude is annoying. Indulge me. One more guess."

"Fine. You got a commendation from the governor."

"Nope. I got our hunting licenses." He toyed with my hair. "I applied for both of us when you were busy at Quantico."

"What we get?"

"Antelope. Bucks. I thought we could go hunting on Saturday."

I grinned. "Really? You did that for me?"

"Yep. I reckoned a box of bullets would mean more to you than a box of chocolates."

The man knew me so well. But that was a two-way street. He had an ulterior motive. "First, you ply me with smokin' hot sex, and then, you dangle the prospect of killin' something . . . What do you really want?" My eyes narrowed. "No way, copper. You aren't shooting my new AR-15."

He chuckled. "So suspicious and so freakin' protective of your firepower. But you are half right." Teasing aside, he wore a serious face. "There is something I want to talk to you about." He continued to stroke my arm, almost absentmindedly. "Mona called me yesterday."

Who was Mona? Took a second for the name to register. Ah, right. The cocktail waitress he'd knocked up; the mother of his son, Lex. "What did she want?"

"Mostly to complain about how hard it is to be a single mother. But the point is, seems Lex has been in trouble, and he's been suspended from school. Mona is at her wit's end. She asked if Lex could live with me for a while."

Silence lingered for what seemed like an eternity before I asked, "What did you say?"

"I said I had to talk it over with you first, since I am living in your house."

"What did he do to get suspended?"

Dawson started that soothing stroking motion on my back again. "He brought a switchblade to school. For protection, he claims, because some older kids had been threatening him. Unfortunately, this school has a zero-tolerance policy for weapon violation. First strike and you're out."

"When did this happen?"

"Two weeks ago. But Mona was too deeply involved with her own shit to let me know, which is about par for the course with her. Apparently, Lex has been parked on the couch playing video games for the last two weeks, since he hasn't been in school."

"So you've talked to Lex about moving here?"

He nodded. "Today. Lex actually seems excited about it. I don't know if he's playing me or what, since it's only in the last six months he's been interested in spending time with me. Anyway, this is something you and I haven't talked about, besides me asking if you'd mind him being here over Thanksgiving or Christmas break. But it's a big difference—"

I rolled to face him and placed my hand on his chest. His heart pounded beneath my palm. "Mason. It's all right. I know how much you've wanted—how hard you've tried—to have a relationship with your son. I'd never stand in the way of that. Lex is welcome here."

He pressed his forehead to mine. "Thank you. You have no idea what this means to me. To be honest, as much as I've always said I wanted Lex around, this whole thing scares the living shit outta me, Mercy."

"I know."

"I mean, we'll get the logistics of how he's getting to and from school figured out, but I don't know if I have . . . hell, I've never been around kids that much. Sometimes—most times—Lex doesn't feel like mine. He just seems like a kid I know that I see once in a while. What if I'm a shitty father?"

That confession made me ache. "I think the fact you're worried about being a good father indicates you've already won half the battle. Once he is around you, day in and day out, he'll see what an awesome guy you are."

"I like this flattering side of you, Sergeant Major." He brushed his lips across mine. "So since you admitted that I'm an awesome guy, does that mean you're ready to marry me?"

I tried to keep it light. "I'm still weighing my options."

"What options?"

"I hear that Dick and Alice Anderson might be headed for divorce court. And you know I have a thing for former rodeo cowboys. So I might wait to see what happens there."

"Dick Anderson is seventy. Been a long time since he's been on the back of a bull. Plus, rumor is . . . the reason Alice wants to call it quits after forty-five years? Dick ain't performing his husbandly duties any-more."

"Who'd you hear that from?"

"Lila, at the diner. And apparently, Dick ain't the type who believes in Viagra." He pinned me to the mattress, rubbing his third erection of the night against my belly. "So maybe you oughta put *this* on the plus side of staying with me for the long haul."

"Cocky man."

"And I'll prove it."

Sophie lured us out of bed early the next morning with the scent of bacon, eggs, and fried potatoes.

I noticed she'd folded up my robe and set it on the kitchen table, but she didn't tease—a rarity for her.

"You're here early," I said.

"Couldn't sleep. Pain in my hip kept me awake."

Wasn't like Sophie to complain. "Maybe you should have the doctor check you out the next time you take Penny in."

She gave me a considering look. "You worried, hey?"

"Yes, because you haven't been your bossy self lately. I wondered if it's too much, splitting time between here and Hope's place."

"You askin' if I'm getting a little long in the tooth to be doin' my job?" she asked sharply.

"No. And you don't need to snap at me for caring about you, Sophie."

She made that sound between a sigh and a harrumph. "Sorry, *takoja*. I've got a lot on my mind, with Penny's cancer and all."

Penny was Sophie's last living daughter. All of her Red Leaf kids had passed on, and her son Devlin Pretty Horses was the only remaining male child. "Anything I can do?"

"Nothin' no one can do." She offered a tremulous smile through the sheen of tears. "Workin' takes my mind off it."

"We'll be able to oblige you on that, because Mason's son Lex is coming to stay with us for a while."

"Really? When?"

"Soon, I think."

"Oh, the sheriff's gotta be happy about that." Her sharp brown gaze locked onto mine. "But are you happy?"

I don't know. "Yeah, I am."

"That don't sound convincing, Mercy."

"I just . . . don't want him to get hurt. He has wanted a chance to really be Lex's father for longer than he's willing to admit. I hope this kid isn't the type to take advantage of him."

Sophie patted my arm. "Me, too. Now how about if we get you fed, eh?"

Dawson's arms came around my waist, and he squeezed me. When he left a sweet, lingering kiss on my temple, I knew he'd heard the entire exchange.

"Mornin', Miz Red Leaf," he said. "That smells awesome."

"It is. Sit down, both of you, and I'll dish up."

"Why don't you sit down, Sophie. Get some of your questions about Lex living here out of the way while I dish up."

Sophie grinned. "Seems someone's in a *very* good mood this morning. I wonder why? Any theories, Sheriff?"

Dawson smirked. "I ain't touching that one." He poured three mugs of coffee and sat across from Sophie.

"When will your son be here?"

"Sunday night. Mercy 'n' me are goin' huntin' Saturday. After I bag a bigger buck than her, I'm driving to Denver. We'll be back Sunday so I can get him enrolled in school Monday."

I snorted. "In your dreams about bagging the bigger buck, marine." I slid the plates on the table and took my seat next to Dawson.

"I love a challenge." He snatched a slice of bacon off my plate and shoved it in his mouth.

I whapped his knuckle with my fork.

"You two behave," Sophie warned. "What room were you thinkin' of putting Lex in upstairs?"

"Not my old room, since Joy's crib is in there. Probably Hope's old room. It's empty, right?"

"Yeah, but it's got a floral bedspread and curtains," Sophie pointed out.

"That'll be fine," Dawson said. "I don't think Lex will care."

Sophie and I exchanged a look. "Uh, yeah, he's gonna care. I'll stop at Walmart on my way home tonight and pick out bedding that's plain and . . . manly."

"Fine, but I don't see the big deal. You've got girly sheets on our bed, and I haven't complained."

Not the same. He'd sleep on burlap if he was getting laid regularly, but I didn't want to argue with him. We tucked into the food, and no one spoke until our plates were empty.

As we finished our coffee, Sophie said, "Such a pity about that Shooting Star girl. So young. I know not everyone likes that family, but it's hard not to feel sorry for them, hey."

Leave it to snoopy Sophie to bring up a case I'd hoped to avoid discussing with the sheriff.

"I assume the FBI was brought in?" Dawson asked me.

"It's under investigation."

"Well, good luck with that. I'm just damn happy it didn't happen in my jurisdiction." He pushed back from the table and took his plate to the sink to rinse it. "Miz Red Leaf, outstanding breakfast. Thank you."

She waved him off with a smile.

"Mercy? Got a minute to talk to me before I head out?"

"Sure." I followed him to the bedroom and watched as he strapped on his gun. "What's up?" I formulated a half-dozen responses to his inquiries about the Shooting Star case, hoping I could hit the balance between evasive and professional.

"Don't spend a lot on the bedding stuff for Lex's room, okay?" He opened his wallet and passed me three twenties.

I nodded, happy that Lex was the buffer between our jobs. For now, anyway.

"I'll be late tonight." Dawson kissed me thoroughly. Then he held my face in his hands and locked his steely gaze to mine. "You know I love you, right?"

"Right."

He waited for a better response.

Might be perverse, but I let him wait.

"And?" he prompted.

"And I love you, too."

His smile had me smiling back at him as I watched him walk out. This frequent admission of how I felt about him was a whole new experience for me. During my stint in the army, I'd had to hide my true occupation from my fellow soldiers. So because I really couldn't be myself, I'd formed no long-term emotional attachment to any man during those twenty years. Which left me the emotional equivalent of a robot.

Dawson saw beyond the facade—almost from the moment we'd met—which was part of the reason he'd had me running scared. It took a tragedy—a near mental meltdown—for me to stop finding excuses for why he and I would never work, to see him as the man who wanted me, the real me, no matter what I'd done in the past.

I relied on him—emotionally, physically. Me, Mercy Gunderson, badass former sniper who never needed anyone, needed him. Once I admitted that need to myself—and to him—I honestly felt more in control of my life than I ever had.

I must've been smiling when I wandered into the conference room, because Shay muttered about someone getting lucky. I ignored him and studied my notes. As the newbie agent in the office, I listened a lot because I had a lot to learn. But today I was determined to bring up my preliminary discovery on the unexplained deaths on the reservation over the last two years.

Director Shenker ended his phone call as he sailed into the room. "Morning, all. Agent Turnbull? If you want to get started?"

"Sure. I just got off the phone with the crime lab regarding the samples taken from the victim in the Shooting Star case. No tissue from her attacker was found under her fingernails. No evidence of rape."

"What about defensive wounds?" Director Shenker asked.

"None. The tox results came back with high levels of digitalis, which is unusual. I did some research. Evidently, its intended use is for heart arrythymia. Given to patients with congestive heart failure."

"But if you aren't suffering from congestive heart failure? What does the drug do?"

"Causes irregular heartbeat. And all sorts of other nasty side effects, like vomiting, diarrhea, hallucinations, listlessness . . . almost always resulting in death. I also learned the foxglove plant is the most widely known source for digitalis. The leaves, the roots, the flowers are all poisonous."

"Is it a controlled substance?"

"Yes and no. In prescription form it's controlled. But the plant itself is for sale in greenhouses across the country."

Something occurred to me. I looked at Shay. "Could Arlette have taken it as a suicide drug? Along the lines of *Romeo and Juliet*? She drinks the poison because she can't be with her true love?"

He leaned back in his chair. "It might be plausible . . . except for the fact that somebody drove a stake through her heart."

Male chuckles sounded around the table.

Ooh. Smackdown. But I wasn't about to be deterred. "Or maybe she tried to kill herself and was wandering around aimlessly, confused, with the toxin in her system, and—"

"Some random guy saw her, picked her up, stripped her, and staked her? I don't think so," Turnbull retorted.

"Fine. But don't you agree that the murderer seems to have a sense of irony with that stake, given Arlette's love of vampire tales? Wouldn't feeding her poison before he killed her play a part? The guy didn't rape her," I reminded him. "And he had her for a couple of days before she turned up dead. So maybe this sicko played with her. She'd be easy to lug around if she was drugged up. But he'd still get to kill her, she just wouldn't fight him."

"Good point, Agent Gunderson," Shenker said. "Do we know what form she took the drug in?"

"Nope. But the best guess at this point was she consumed it in liquid form." Turnbull sighed. "And here's another bizarre twist. The comfrey plant is used in teas and herbal remedies, and the leaves are so close in appearance to the leaves of the foxglove plant that sometimes foxglove is mistaken for comfrey. There've been several cases of accidental poisoning."

"So the poisoning could have been accidental and unrelated to her murder," I said.

"We cannot rule out that theory entirely."

Somewhat vindicated, I pushed my next point. "With the absence of defensive wounds, it would appear Arlette knew her attacker."

"Yes, but remember, we're dealing with a small pool of people on the rez, so chances are just as likely it wasn't a male she knew intimately, but a male she knew in passing."

"We're assuming it's a male?" Agent Mested asked.

"Isn't it always?" Agent Flack shot back.

Strained laughter.

"Director Shenker?"

His gaze bored into me. "Yes?"

"It's come to my attention that there have been quite a few young women found dead on the reservation in the last couple of years."

Agent Flack snapped his gum and whipped around to face me. "You talking about that Good Shield woman? Victim found gut shot out in the middle of nowhere?"

I hadn't seen that obituary, and it bothered me there was one or more I'd missed in my small bit of research. "Was the FBI called in on that one?"

"Called, yes. We didn't get involved because I agreed with the tribal cop who suspected a domestic dispute. Evidently, nine-one-one dispatch had several emergency calls involving the vic and her partner, going back a couple of years. The last time cops were called to the scene, guns were involved."

"So the partner is in jail?"

Special Agent Flack blew a big pink bubble, then popped it loudly. "No. The dude was alibied. Happens all the time down there, cousin vouching for cousin, hey." Laughter. "Nothin' the tribal cops or nobody else could do."

Seemed too cut and dried. Too . . . easily dismissed.

"Is there a reason to get this backstory on previous and unrelated cases, Agent Gunderson?"

"Yes. I have a gut feeling some of those old cases are somehow related to this new one."

Silence. Except for Shay's disgruntled sigh.

"Here in the bureau, we're less about gut feelings and hunches than we are about solid evidence," Shenker said.

I let his doubt bounce off me, but I couldn't keep the blood from rushing to my face. "Even if solid evidence is ignored? Or dismissed?"

Shenker stared at me thoughtfully. "No offense, Agent Gunderson, but you are new to the bureau. Why haven't the tribal police picked up on it? If it's so obvious to you?"

Since I'd started working here five weeks ago, I had mostly observed. I asked questions only when I hadn't been able to find the answers myself. I wasn't the timid mouse in the corner, but neither was I the roaring lion. I'd backed down on a couple of occasions. But I would not back down on this. "Maybe due to budgetary and manpower constraints, the tribal cops are conditioned to look for the easiest answer first, in order to get the case resolved and move on to the next one. Those officers see a lot of bad shit. It'd be easy to get jaded. My dad dealt with them when he was Eagle River County sheriff. And yes, he complained about the tribal police not wanting to cooperate with any other law enforcement agencies. Not on any level. Something as simple as the tribal police refusing to fax paperwork meant he had to drive from Eagle Ridge to Eagle River. Half the time they'd have no record of the paperwork he'd requested.

"And now after I've been in the tribal police headquarters? I see the same problem. To be perfectly blunt, the place is a disorganized pigsty, with who knows what files spread everywhere. So if there is a connection or pattern to these deaths, I wouldn't be the least bit surprised if the tribal cops didn't catch the similarities because they wouldn't know where the hell to find the information."

No one looked at me.

Maybe I had gotten a little vehement, maybe it was a shot to my ego they wouldn't listen. As the highest enlisted rank in my squad, my opinions always commanded attention. I didn't expect special treatment as an agent, but I sure as hell hadn't expected my observation to be discounted immediately.

Director Shenker steepled his fingers, just like the FBI honchos on TV. "Tell you what, Special Agent Gunderson. I'll let you put your money where your mouth is. I don't know what important case files you think you saw carelessly strewn around the tribal police department, but

I have it on good authority the arrest records, case reports, and official police logs are locked up tight in the tribal HQ archives department. Alongside other sensitive matters to members of the tribe, like family lineage, land succession, recorded oral histories, births, deaths, marriages. You know where that department is, right? Since you registered as a member of the tribe, what . . . eight months ago?"

"Yes, sir."

He tapped his fingers on his lips a couple of times. "Since we have meetings scheduled Monday, starting Tuesday, you'll backtrack through all the police files—cases, arrest records, police logs, plus the obituaries, the official death records, media articles, and whatever else you can find to document your theory. Get me proof. Then I'll listen to your gut."

I'd just been demoted to flunky.

I'd suck it up, like a soldier, and do my job, because I'd done a lot worse things under orders than paw through musty file folders. I managed a tight smile. "Thank you, sir, for the opportunity to test my theories."

Director Shenker frowned, unsure if I was being sincere or sarcastic.

I wasn't quite sure myself. As much as I loathed the idea of being stuck underground like a mole, I'd prefer doing something that might make forward progress on this case, or reopening cold cases, rather than sitting through more courses on FBI procedures.

Turnbull could handle the particulars of the current investigation. He'd be thrilled I wasn't impeding his lone-wolf investigative prowess anyway. I sent him a sidelong glance, expecting to see his superior smirk.

But he was pissed, as evidenced by the telltale clenching and flexing of his jaw.

Screw him. Nothing I ever did made him happy.

"Now, on to the next order of business," the director said.

I listened, ignoring Shay's stealthy interest in the notes I jotted down.

As soon as Shenker announced the break, I booked it to the one place Shay couldn't follow me: the ladies' room.

Might make me a chickenshit, especially when I'm normally ready to fire—either a gun or my mouth—but I didn't slide back into my chair until after the meeting reconvened.

Director Shenker liked to hear himself talk. And he didn't seem to notice I didn't participate. He dismissed us—not for lunch, like I'd expected, but for the rest of the day. He stopped my rapid exit with a curt "Gunderson."

"Sir?"

"I'll clear you to be at tribal headquarters archive department. You'll be assigned on this task until further notice. Understood?"

"Yes, sir."

"Turnbull, I'll need you to stick around for a bit," Shenker added, allowing me to make a clean getaway.

5

It was an indication of how crappy my morning had been that I was actually looking forward to my trip to the dreaded Hellmart—aka Walmart. As usual, the parking lot was jam-packed, and I practically had to park on the moon. But I gave myself props for remembering to remove my gun, since I was always way too temped to use it in the store.

Once inside the building, I cut through the health and beauty aisles to reach the dog food. Might as well stock up. I zipped past the gun department, briefly stopping to price bullets.

I spent so little time in the household-goods section of the store it took me a couple of rows to find it. And holy hell, the color choices for comforters fanned out before me like a rainbow. Couldn't go wrong with navy blue. I piled a blanket, a comforter, a sheet set, and matching plaid curtains on top of all the other junk.

Seemed Hope was always running out of diapers, so I detoured to the baby section and threw two packs into the cart. I couldn't resist a new outfit for Poopy, a darling pair of denim overalls with glittery butterflies appliquéd on the butt.

I skipped the food section and wished for the hundredth time Sophie knew how to text so she could send me the weekly grocery list since I was already here.

My cell buzzed while I waited in line. I debated ignoring it, except I wouldn't want to miss sexting with Dawson because I was avoiding Turnbull. The text wasn't from either man, but from Hope, asking me to pick up diapers. *One step ahead of ya, sis.*

Since I had no place to be, I stopped at Wendy's for lunch. Afterward, on a whim, I pulled into Runnings, a ranch supply store. Seeing the display of hunting gear, I realized I didn't have the mandatory neon orange article of clothing required for all hunters. It went against everything ingrained in me to wear something so blatantly obvious. I picked the least offensive item I could find: a knit hat. I tossed one in the cart for Dawson, too. Checking the prices of various calibers of bullets, I was surprised they were a buck less a box than at Walmart, so I scooped up a box of .308 for my rifle, a box of .270 for Dawson's Remington bolt action, a box of .223 for my AR, and a box of .22 for target practice.

Since I'm a sucker for western clothes, I detoured through the women's clothing department and found two rhinestone shirts a little on the tacky side that I couldn't live without.

My last stop was the candy aisle. I don't have much of a sweet tooth, but I'm the only one in my family. Sophie loved old-fashioned horehound candy. Jake had a thing for lemon drops. Dawson could eat black licorice by the truckload, and Hope preferred maple nut goodies. I bought two packages of each and wondered what kind of candy Lex liked.

I flashed back to Levi as a kid and how crazy he'd been for circus peanuts—those disgusting molded blobs of orange fluff. But I hesitated to throw in a package. Sometimes the simplest thing would start Hope on a crying jag. She'd gotten better in the last few months. At least now she and I could talk about Levi without either of us breaking down every time.

I loaded everything into the truck and finally started for home. I'd managed to shove aside the morning's events during my shopping foray, but as soon as Rapid City reflected in my taillights, those suppressed thoughts surfaced unbidden and unwanted. Dammit. I'd been in such a happy—albeit girly—place with the lunch and the shopping. Needing to stay out of my head, I cranked the country music and belted out tunes about cheating, drinking, and more drinking.

Hope's car was parked next to Sophie's. I unloaded everything myself. After I dragged the last bag into the kitchen, I heard Sophie and Hope talking in the office. Or were they arguing?

"She says she's fine, but I know she ain't telling me all of what the doctor said."

Another conversation about the perils of Penny Pretty Horses.

"Well, it's stupid that she doesn't let you go to the doctor's office with her," Hope retorted. "You never should've let her get away with it the first time. Demand to go with her."

Sophie shook her finger. "Don't be pretending you know what it's like to have this kind of confrontation. You always back down from conflict. Always. And you're tellin' me to make demands of my daughter . . . who is dying?" She snorted. "You have no idea—"

"I've lost a child, too," Hope snapped.

This discussion was headed into dangerous territory, so I cut in. "Hey, ladies, what's going on?"

Hope's angry gaze flicked to me from behind our father's desk. "Hey, Mercy. Sophie is leaving early to spend time with Penny."

Sophie gave Hope her back. Her eyes were hard, and her jaw was tight.

"I know this is hard on you. Is there anything I can do, Sophie?"

A beat passed. She shook her head, but a sly smile appeared. "Just don't leave no more of your clothes in the kitchen, hey."

I would not blush.

Sophie patted my arm as she walked past me, and I wanted to hug her. Normally, I squashed such impulses, but today, I gave in to it. Her familiar scent, a scent that hadn't changed in thirty years—Jovan musk perfume, a faint whiff of cooking grease, laundry soap, and Lemon Pledge—enveloped me, and I sighed. Maybe I'd needed the hug more than she had. "Tell Penny hi from me."

"Will do." She stepped back and straightened her coat. "I stripped the bedding in Hope's old room, so it's ready for the boy." Her dark eyes pinned me. "You'd better be washing them sheets before you put 'em on the bed, 'cause who knows what kinda chemicals and junk they got on 'em in China."

I was happy to see the flash of the old bossy Sophie. "Yes, ma'am."

After Sophie left, without saying good-bye to Hope, my sister said, "Since Sophie feels entitled to interrupt me whenever the hell she wants because I have nothing important to do"—she sneered the last part—"I have about an hour and a half left of bookwork. Are you gonna be around to listen for Joy?"

And despite the tension in the room, my day just got a whole lot brighter. "Sure. Do your thing."

I shoved the bedding in the washer. Then I snuck upstairs to peek at my niece, indisputably the cutest baby on the planet. Tempting, to pick her up and snuzzle her chubby cheeks just to hear that darling giggle. But Mama would whup my ass if I woke her. Plus, the kid was so sound asleep, she snored.

I ditched my FBI duds for my favorite pair of Aura jeans and slipped on my new red-and-black thermal "burnout" western shirt dotted with what looked like bloody roses. In the living room, I opened my laptop and logged on.

Feet propped on the coffee table, pen jammed in my mouth, I didn't move beyond getting up to toss the bedding in the dryer when the cycle beeped. I hadn't found much information, and I suspected that was because the two local Indian papers had only recently started uploading content to the Internet.

Hope passed by the living room with a blithe, "Joy's up."

"What? I've been listening, and I haven't heard her."

"She turned over in her crib, which is a signal naptime is over."

Whoa. Hope had heard that all the way in Dad's office? Talk about batlike senses. I shut down my computer and grabbed the clean bedding. I met Hope halfway up the staircase.

"False alarm. Joy is still sacked out." She pointed to the bundle in my arms. "Need help?"

"Sure."

In the bedroom, I stretched the fitted sheet across the top corner of the mattress.

Hope tucked her end of the sheet around the opposite corner on the bottom of the bed. "So . . . Dawson's son is coming to stay for a while."

We each automatically moved to the other end of the bed, the motions familiar from doing this a hundred times. "I guess."

"Have you ever talked to Lex?"

I shook my head. "Dawson talks to him in the afternoon when Lex gets home from school. It worries him that Lex is a latchkey kid."

Hope snapped out and smoothed the top sheet. "Will that be different when he's living here?"

"A lot of that is up in the air until Lex is enrolled in school."

"Middle school. God, Levi hated middle school. Kids were so mean. It was probably the only time I thought about pulling him out and homeschooling him, but Daddy wouldn't let me. Said I wasn't gonna coddle the boy and Levi had to learn to deal with adversity."

"That sounds like something Dad would say."

"He also told me that since I'd barely graduated high school, I had no business teaching."

I hugged the pillow to my chest instead of punching it. "Hope, did Dad say mean shit like that to you all the time?"

She shrugged. "When I look back on it, usually he only said that stuff when I was being a brat about something. It made him crazy because he always wished I'd be more like you. He'd hoped for that up until the day he died."

My sister knew so many more facets of my father than I did. In the time I'd been home, I'd discovered not all of those facets put Dad in a good light.

We adjusted the comforter and piled on the pillows. I stood on the step stool to take down the sheer baby-blue curtains with layers of ruffles and hung the navy-blue and hunter-green plaid panels.

"It looks great, Mercy. No remnant of me in this room at all." She smiled wistfully and balled up the curtains. "Levi would've loved to have another boy around."

I experienced that crushing sensation around my heart again. "Think Lex will push boundaries with me because I'm not his mother?"

"Yes. But you've got the tough love down pat, sis. Levi called you a ball buster, but he knew you'd give it to him straight. You expected more out of him than I did."

Joy screeched and added a ma-ma-ma-ma-ma that sent Hope scurrying. When I heard my niece bouncing up and down with happiness at seeing her mama, I smiled. The baby girl's name was apt; she'd brought such joy into all our lives.

Dawson and I were up well before the crack of dawn on Saturday, eager as two kids on Christmas morning for our first hunt together.

He hadn't had a chance to scout the ranch for the best place to find antelope. Although it'd been several years since I'd done any hunting, I figured animal behavior patterns probably hadn't changed. I'd find antelope in the same place I had two decades ago.

We opted to use the ATVs rather than drive a pickup. Antelope were smaller than deer, and we could each easily strap a carcass onto the back of an ATV and haul it home before the meat spoiled.

By first light, we'd arrived at my suggested starting point and left the machines parked at the bottom of a small hill. At a balmy forty-five degrees, it didn't feel like November. The wind blew like a bitch, which was actually good—antelope have a finely tuned sense of smell. With the fastest animal land speed in North America, once antelope catch a whiff of human, all you see are those white butts bouncing away.

Antelope prefer wide-open spaces, so I'd chosen a two-mile-long bowl-shaped draw with water at the bottom and great vantage points above. The grass was tall in some places, providing excellent cover and hidden resting points as we zigzagged over the terrain.

I'd slung my H-S Precision .308 takedown rifle over my shoulder. As a kid I'd hated using a shoulder strap. I preferred to carry my gun as I belly crawled. As an adult I wanted both hands free.

Dawson wasn't one of those never-shut-up types of hunters. The ones who really don't give a damn if they shoot anything. For them, securing a hunting license, slipping on camo clothes, and toting around a fancy gun were really just excuses to hang out with the guys and drink beer.

I kept my binoculars trained on the area around the water, while he kept scanning the ridges and hidden dips in the vast landscape. There wasn't a speck of snow on the ground, allowing the antelope to hide in plain sight. The dead grasses with hues ranging from the faded gold of dried corn stalks to the darkness of coffee grounds provided perfect camouflage. The one advantage we had? This time of year the males were slaves to their baser instincts and deep in rut. The bucks were constantly sniffing for females, which meant they were always on the move, looking for more action. And if they couldn't fuck, then they'd lock horns with other horny males of their species, trying to keep them from fucking.

Dawson tapped my arm and pointed.

I refocused, making minute adjustments for the change in distance and my eyes. About twenty antelope were hunkered down, on the edge of a ridge. But they were a good fifteen hundred yards away.

Over the next ten minutes, we watched the group, comprised of does, probably hiding from the amorous attentions of the bucks. But rest assured, our targets were very close by.

Target. How quickly I slipped back into sniper lingo when I wore camo and held a gun in my hand.

We moved our position closer to the watering hole. Ducking low. Moving slowly. Creeping quietly. My guess was the bucks would wander from their hidey-holes to the water and quench their thirst before seeking out the herd of females. The harem was farther downwind than we were, so chances were good we'd have first crack.

After we settled into our new position, I nudged Mason and whispered, "We didn't talk about who gets first shot."

"I'm sure you think you do, Sergeant Major, since you outrank me."

"Yep."

"Not a fuckin' chance," he hissed. "I should get the first kill since I applied for the hunting licenses."

"Yeah? You wouldn't *be* hunting if not for the fact I own this chunk of land, Sheriff."

"How do you suggest we decide this problem, now that you're a crime-solving specialist in the FBI?"

A pause.

We said, "Rock, paper, scissors," at the same time.

Dawson grinned at me, and I grinned back.

Hands out, fists on palms, we locked gazes, whispered, "One, two, three," and looked at our hands.

He'd chosen rock.

I'd picked paper.

I won.

I leaned over and pecked his puckish mouth. "Don't pout. Maybe you'll get lucky, and I'll miss."

He snorted. "Not likely. And that's the first time I've ever had a huntin' buddy kiss me. It's kinda weird."

We returned to our watchful stance.

As much as I loved the pulling-the-trigger part of hunting, I also loved this quiet time. I might've felt differently if I was stretched out on frigid snow-covered ground, trying to hide my white puffs of breath as the cold seeped into my bones. But I was content, lying on my belly in the tall grass, scanning the area with my binoculars, grateful my hood blocked the wind from my face.

I never thought I'd miss spending my days and nights in the great outdoors. While lying in the sand or on a rooftop, or standing in the back of an assault vehicle, I had dreamed of a soft mattress. Of crisp sheets that carried a freshly laundered clean scent. Of cool, puffy pillows beneath my weary head. Of one night of uninterrupted slumber. Of early-morning tendrils of light teasing through the window blinds as a gentle wake-up call. Not mortar rounds. Not machine-gun fire.

After all the years I'd spent in the army, my days and nights fighting heat, cold, bugs—intestinal and the creepy-crawly types—insurgents, insomnia, cramped quarters, and no quarters, and the weeks without a shower, I swore I'd never willingly subject myself to such primitive situations ever again. No camping, no hiking, no wilderness treks for me.

My new idea of roughing it would be no complimentary breakfast at my vacation hotel.

So why was I stretched out in the dirt, weeds poking me in the face, surrounded by the warning scent of male animal urine?

Because my man had done something special for me, reminding me that I'd missed this. Reminding me this reconnection with nature and where I was raised also defined me.

I hadn't been to this part of the ranch for years. I suspected the watering hole had dried up during the almost decade-long drought. For a few decades, the Gunderson family had hayed a small section at the bottom, leaving the bales as emergency feed if any of the cattle got stranded during a blizzard. This area didn't produce enough feed in comparison to other areas with easier access, so it'd been allowed to go fallow.

Fallow was good for wildlife. With access to water, and a stand of scrub oak and pine trees to run and hide in, this was an ideal place for them to gather.

Time passed in a pleasant void. I wasn't getting antsy as much as worried our entry into the animals' domain hadn't been stealthy enough. Were the bucks hunkered down watching us?

I considered asking Mason how long he wanted to wait these animals out, because he had to leave for Denver today, when three big bucks picked their way to the edge of the water.

Hello, boys.

They didn't seem to be in a hurry. When they were spread out, I whispered, "Mine is the far right."

"I'll take the left side."

Chances were high this would be our only shot today, so we had to make it count. "You sighted in?" I asked Dawson, keeping the antelope in my crosshairs.

"Yep."

"Count of three."

"One," he said.

"Two," I said.

"Three," we said together.

Ba-bam. Ba-bam.

Near perfect symmetry.

My buck dropped.

Dawson's animal struggled and acted confused. By the time it staggered a few steps then lay down, the third buck was long gone.

As soon as Dawson's buck quit twitching, we grabbed our stuff and hightailed it down the hill.

We stopped first and looked at his buck. Nice clean kill, a few inches behind the front leg, which was a perfect heart/lungs shot. The buck had a decent set of horns. Then we walked to my kill.

Dawson said, "Jesus, Mercy. That's fuckin' nasty."

My shot had been a head shot. The buck's brain had exploded, horns hanging off what was left of the skull. I found Dawson staring at me strangely. "What?" I asked.

"Why would you shoot . . . ?"

Because I was used to taking head shots.

Other snipers might talk about hitting center mass. But at ranges below two hundred yards, I always aimed for the head.

A habit that was hard to break, apparently. I also had no intention of having a mount made. Another habit I shunned—showing off a kill. Just knowing I'd hit my target satisfied me.

But maybe . . . I should've done it differently. Should I pretend I'd missed the spot I'd aimed for?

"If I'da known you weren't interested in mounting it, I'd have gotten you a doe tag."

"Ha-ha."

"Good thing I brought a hacksaw. No need to drag the head back now," Dawson said dryly.

"Yeah. Good thing. 'Cause all I brought was a knife."

Mason stood and smirked at me.

"What?"

"Is that your way of asking me to gut your antelope, little lady?"

"Fuck off." I unsheathed my knife. "And just for that smart-ass remark, I'll race you. Let's see who gets their kill cleaned up fastest."

"God, I love you."

I blew him a kiss before my hands were covered with blood.

As soon as he stood above his buck, I said, "Ready?"

"Yep."

"Go." I dropped to my knees. I rolled the buck on his back and carefully sliced through the hide and muscle, starting at the sternum and ending at the tail. Then on the second pass, I separated the tough membrane covering the body cavity. Using the tip of the knife, I cut around the anus and the genitals, mindful not to cut into the urinary tract or the poop chute. Then I sliced into the body cavity itself, turning the blade side up as I cut, so the knife didn't go in too deep and nick the stomach. I scored the breastbone with the blade three times and pushed down, cracking it.

I took a break and glanced over at Dawson, who already had his hand in the cavity and was pulling out the guts.

Son of a bitch.

He flipped his buck over to drain the last of the blood, resting on his haunches.

I half expected him to throw up his hands like a tie-down roper.

Mason ambled over, and I still hadn't gotten to the gut-removal portion yet.

"Lagging behind, Sergeant Major."

I grunted, then made the cut across the esophagus that allowed my hand to get inside that still-warm cavity and start yanking out innards.

Point for Dawson that he didn't offer to help.

Minus two hundred points that he started whistling "No Guts, No Glory" while I was shoulder deep inside my kill.

"It's too damn warm out to let these hang once we get them back to the ranch," he said. "We'll have to get the meat cleaned up and frozen as soon as possible."

"I'll bow to your expertise. To be honest, I've never butchered my game."

"Never? Why not?"

I rubbed the end of my nose. "My dad usually struck a deal with someone at Baylor Brothers Meat Processing." That wasn't the whole truth. For some reason, it hadn't bothered my father to watch me kill something, but it'd bothered the heck out of him to watch me butcher it. In fact, counting this antelope, I'd only gutted a kill three times. My father had taken over, gutting the animal himself. Which seemed strange, because Dad never treated me like a girl who might be squeamish. I hadn't been, but that hadn't mattered. Every time we'd gone hunting, I made the kill shot; someone else cleaned up the mess.

It struck me, then, how I'd carried that mind-set with me during my sniper years.

Dawson made a disgruntled noise and pulled me back to the present. "It ain't that hard to butcher. There's not that much meat on antelope anyway."

I finally scooped the last of the innards out and rolled my buck to let the blood drain out.

He crouched down and scrutinized my kill. "This is one plump little sucker. He'll have more meat on him." Then he said, "Hold still," and took out a handkerchief. "You've got blood on your face." He dabbed at it. "It's gone."

"Thanks."

"You want that hacksaw now?"

"Yeah."

Really didn't take much effort to lob off the head.

We both pushed to our feet, and he handed me another hankie to use on my hands and arms. "Seems crazy that we both got our bucks on the very first shot."

I shrugged and wiped at the blood. Didn't seem that odd to me. The *one shot, one kill* mantra had been drilled into my brain during sniper training.

"Did you bring another gun?" Then he laughed. "Of course you did."

"You wanna have a little shooting contest? I gotta redeem myself somehow since you whipped my butt in quick field dressing."

"What'd you bring?"

"H&K P7. Nine mil."

Dawson shook his head. "I'm not easily intimidated, but Christ, woman, you have a lot of guns."

"Think of it as the equivalent of other women's obsession with shoes."

He laughed again. "Show me."

I let him go first.

I still won.

By a lot.

Even with my bad eye.

Luckily, my man was a good sport—even if I was a much better shot.

We wrapped and strapped up the kills, then started toward the ATVs. Packing out the animal was probably the worst part of hunting. I was surprised birds weren't already circling above the two piles of guts, waiting for us to leave so they could fight over a quick-and-easy meal. The birds would get the first go, and then the bigger predators would come in and chase them out.

Circle of life and all that shit.

Dawson shouted, "Double time, Sergeant Major, you're lagging behind."

At the ranch, we had to lock up the dogs.

I watched Dawson part out the carcass. He'd rinse and cut and rinse some more. Antelope were hairy creatures, and nothing ruined a piece of meat like a bunch of hair frozen to it. But luckily, antelope hair was very fine, and once it floated to the top of the water, it could easily be skimmed or poured off.

His expertise didn't surprise me, but his efficiency did. He had both bucks skinned, butchered, cleaned, and parted out in two hours. I helped as much as I could—or as much as he'd let me. I was secretly happy I wouldn't have to walk past an animal kill for several days waiting for the meat processors.

As soon as he finished, he hit the shower. By the time I cleaned myself up, Mason was packed and anxious to go. It'd take at least seven hours to reach Denver.

"Are you sure you don't want to come?" he asked.

"It's best if you and Lex have time to talk, without his mother or me around." I kissed his cheek. "Besides, you'll be back in twenty-four hours. I can find something to occupy myself."

He kissed me. Hard. "I'll text you when I get there."

"Drive safe."

"What are your plans tonight now that the sheriff is gone?"

I tore my attention away from a riveting episode of *Ice Road Truckers* and looked at my sister. "Been a while since I've been to Clementine's. Thought I'd catch up with the crew and the regulars."

Hope swayed with Joy on her hip, softly biting her lip. I braced my-self for the don't-start-drinking-again plea. But she blurted, "Can I go with you?"

I think my jaw hit the floor. "What?"

"I never get to go out. I'd like to have a conversation with an adult that's not Jake, Sophie, or you. No offense."

Had Hope ever been to Clementine's? The place had a bad reputa-tion—deservedly so. Plus, I considered it my bar. Might be stupid, but I had the urge to protect it even from my sister.

"Of course, me goin' would boil down to Jake watching Joy for a few hours." She bit her lip again.

The fact Hope was willing to leave her baby, a baby she rarely let out of her sight, proved to me she needed a break. I smiled at her. "Sure, if you wanna come along, that'd be great. You can keep me from drinking until the wee hours so I'm not hungover when Lex gets here tomorrow."

"Great. Umm . . . what should I wear?"

I checked out her outfit, a brightly patterned blue-and-black poet's shirt paired with black leggings. "You look awesome. I'm not changing. I'm wearing this."

"Can I borrow some makeup?"

"Knock yourself out. It's in the top drawer on the right side."

"Okay. Be right back." Hope passed me Joy.

"Hey, Poopy." When I smooched her crown, her little bitty pigtails tickled my nose. She smelled like graham crackers, apple juice, baby powder, and sweet innocence. I'd dealt with my fears—a butt load more than I'd first suspected—and let her become part of my life, which might seem like a no-brainer to most people, but I was at a dark place after I killed Anna. I thought by staying away from Joy, I was actually doing her a favor.

But Hope hadn't allowed my distance from her child. It amazed me when I uncovered my sister's pockets of strength.

The barking dogs alerted me to Jake's presence right before he walked in. Joy squirmed and tried to jump from my arms to get to her father.

Jake only had eyes for her. He plucked her away and blew a raspberry on her neck until she squealed. Only then did he acknowledge me. "Hey, Mercy."

"Jake. How did things go today?" He'd been dreading moving cattle. I didn't know enough about what that entailed, except he did it multiple times a year.

"Better than I expected, to be honest. I had good helpers with Luke and TJ and their boys. Where's Hope?"

"I'm right here."

We both turned to see Hope leaning against the doorjamb.

"Wow, babe, you look great. Do we got a hot date or something I forgot about?"

She laughed self-consciously. "Mercy's going to Clementine's to have a drink, and I asked if I could tag along." Her eyes anxiously searched his face. "That's all right, isn't it?"

"Of course it is. You deserve a night out." He paused and looked from me to Hope and back to me. "Who's your DD?"

"I plan to have only one drink, Jake. So we should be fine. Besides"— Hope smirked at me—"Mercy don't want the sheriff to get wind of her arrest while he's out of town."

"You're hilarious, sis."

"Well, you two have fun. I'll take lil' punkin home." He mock-whispered, "Now that your mama's outta the picture for the night, I can teach you how to wrassle gators." Jake shot me a smile before he took off.

Hope insisted on driving. Which meant it took us fifteen minutes longer to get there than if I'd been behind the wheel.

Clementine's was hopping. Something had put this out-of-the-way, hole-in-the-wall bar on the map in the last year. John-John halfheartedly complained about Clementine's becoming mainstream, but the steady stream of income softened the blow.

Muskrat was the bouncer. He didn't give me one of his signature bear hugs, where I felt my spine brush the skin behind my belly button as he squeezed me tight. Maybe his lackluster response was a result of seeing Hope, since, like John-John, he wasn't fond of Jake. "So what brings the Gunderson girls by tonight?"

Hope tittered. God. I hoped she remembered she was a married woman and didn't flirt with every guy who paid attention to her, as the old, needy Hope would have. "Just looking to get out of the house for some social time."

Some of the same regulars filled the bar. Vinnie, the biker, and his posse holding court beneath the TV. Construction workers and cowboys in the back shootin' pool and shootin' the shit. Lots of folks in here I didn't recognize. I weaved through the crowd until Hope and I reached the main bar.

John-John saw us, but he was too busy mixing drinks to do more than nod.

I could tell Hope was trying to play it cool and not gawk at the customers who were blatantly checking her out.

Winona gave me a one-armed hug from behind. "Mercy! Damn, girl, I miss working with you. Why you hauling yourself in this mangy hole? You and the sheriff have words?"

"No, smart-ass. I'm here with my sister and we're thirsty."

"I'll get you two beers since John-John's glaring at me." She slid two bottles of Bud Light in front of us.

Hope was stuck sitting next to Lefty. I intended to warn her about the crotchety old rancher. But Lefty, who hated everyone, seemed taken with my little sister.

I sipped my beer and kept playing Name That Regular to amuse my-self. I was more happy about who I didn't see—no Cowboy Trey, no Kit McIntyre, no Tiny, no Laronda. Didn't appear Saro's group was around, but that didn't shock me.

I'd learned through the FBI that Saro was restructuring his organization after his brother Victor's murder. Shay had hoped the resident rez drug runner would be crippled by the loss, but Saro rallied, although he and his group were staying pretty far off the radar.

John-John stopped in front of me and wiped his brow.

"Looks like business is booming."

"I'd hate to see what crazies it'd bring out if we actually ran happy-hour specials." He tossed a handful of nuts into his mouth. His eyes locked onto mine. "Why are you palling around with Hope?"

"Last-minute thing," I said, and didn't explain further. "When it dies down, I'd like to pick your brain about a couple of things."

"Did *Unci* put you up to grilling me about my mom?"

"No." Was he touchy and snappish tonight, or was it just me? "She's worried about Penny."

"Join the club." He pulled taps and opened the cooler.

I should've waited to get a better bead on his mood, but the question had just popped out. "Has Saro been in lately?"

John-John lifted his head abruptly. The war braid with the red feather tip swung into his face, and he impatiently batted it aside. "Why are you asking me for this information?"

"I'm asking because I've had Saro's blade at my throat, and I'm not eager to repeat the experience."

He shot me a look that I interpreted as distrustful. Before I could cajole him or try charm, he said, "Why don't you ask your partner? He's been in here several times."

Partner? At first I thought he meant Dawson, but I figured out he meant Shay. "Why has Turnbull been in here?"

"I asked him the same thing. He said he can drink anywhere he wants. Which sucks for me. If I blackball him, he'll show up with a federal raiding party to see what I'm hiding, even though I ain't hiding a damn thing."

Christ. Talk about paranoid. But my defense of my employer and Shay would only piss him off, so I bit my tongue.

"So I serve him. He's been in here once when Saro showed up. They ignored each other, although the brooding G-man was awful damn interested in Saro's new recruits."

"And here I hoped Saro had given up his evil ways after his brother was murdered." I sipped my beer. "Is Saro recruiting in here?"

"Doubtful. He's only been in a half-dozen times in the last five months. But he don't have to do much to recruit anyway. People line up to get in with him, even after all the shit that went down. People you'd never expect."

That comment caught my notice. "Like who?"

"Like punks with no other job choice. Like idiots who have a falling-out with their family."

I frowned. He wouldn't give me names; he expected me to guess. Or he expected me to know. Except I didn't have insight on the inner workings on the Eagle River rez. I never had. The one person who had that knowledge, Rollie, was currently pissed off at me. Rollie was pissed off at everybody, it seemed. Me. Verline. His son.

Wait a second. My eyes met John-John's. "Junior Rondeaux?"

He nodded.

"Holy shit." Jesus, I was an idiot.

It hit me, then, the seriousness of my rookie mistake, keeping the information Mackenzie Red Shirt had given me about Junior Rondeaux to myself. It could have tremendous impact on this case, since Junior had ties to that murderous bastard Saro, and to Arlette. Turnbull would have every right to dress me down when I finally came clean with him.

John-John leaned closer. "Why's this so surprising to you?"

"Because I tried to track Junior down yesterday."

"Why?"

"Some of that pesky fed stuff you don't wanna know about and I can't tell you about anyway."

He shrugged. "Well, you ain't gonna find him in here because he's banned."

"For how long?"

"Forever."

"What did he do to get blackballed?"

"He's a Rondeaux."

"That's it?"

John-John glanced away and then refocused on me with eyes as hard as concrete. "I know you're friends with Rollie. But he ain't no friend of mine or my family. I'd lose customers if him or any of his spawn stepped foot in here. So they ain't welcome. Ever."

"Rollie knows this?"

"Yep."

"But . . . you let him in when Geneva's group talked me into running for sheriff."

"They didn't give me a choice."

"Why didn't you tell me about this Rondeaux clan ban when I worked for you?"

John-John ignored me and walked to the end of the bar.

Goddammit. I hated not knowing shit like this, even when I told everyone to leave me out of their family dramas. For years Rollie had made barbs about John-John's psychic abilities. And about Sophie being uppity. I don't know why I hadn't drawn the parallels that there was bad blood between him and the whole Red Leaf family. I'd always chalked it up to Rollie being an ass.

I spun my bar stool toward Hope.

"What's wrong?"

"Do you know why the Red Leaf family and the Rondeaux family are enemies?"

She picked at her thumbnail before she met my gaze. "No. And that's not me protecting Jake. He won't talk about it, Sophie won't talk about it. But it seems to be more a problem between the Pretty Horses and the Rondeaux. The Red Leaf kids and grandkids got caught in the middle."

Sophie had two kids—Penny and Devlin—with her first husband, Von Pretty Horses. After he died, she remarried Barclay Red Leaf, and they had three sons: Del, Jake's dad; Terry, Luke and TJ's dad; and Ray, who'd fathered a half-dozen kids before he'd passed on, leaving the small Red Leaf Ranch, adjacent to our ranch, to Terry. I'd never met Del or Ray. They'd both died by the time Sophie came to work for us.

"Even now that I'm married to a Red Leaf, they won't discuss family matters if I'm around," Hope said.

"But you're family to them. Hell, I'm practically family to them."

Hope shook her head. "Not in their minds."

Maybe it was beer causing the sudden ache in my belly. "Is that because so many of them have worked for us for so long?"

"That's part of it. Sophie is different to me when we go over to her house. She . . . snaps a lot. Not at me. Then she and her grandkids start speaking Lakota, and I can't understand. It makes me uncomfortable."

That piqued my anger, but I also realized Hope might be a wee bit paranoid. "Do they treat Joy like an outsider, too?"

"No." Hope reached for her beer and sipped. "Still, because of . . . that and some other stuff, Jake's even suggested to Sophie that she retire from workin' for us."

"Yeah, I've heard Sophie's response to that. Do you think—"

Out of the blue we heard, "Hope Gunderson? Is that you?"

Hope faced the woman bellied up to the bar next to her where Lefty had been sitting. "Betsy? Omigod! What are you doing here?"

A lot of squealing and hugging, and then my sister disappeared into the back room with her old high school friend.

And once again, I was drinking alone.

After five minutes, the rush of people up to the bar sent me outside for fresh air. In hindsight I should've snuck out the back door. My one complaint about Clementine's has always been the lack of lighting in the parking area. It's a bitch even for people who don't have my night vision problems.

I jammed my hands in my pockets and glanced up at the sky. No stars. No moonlight peeked through the thick cloud cover. I half expected to feel snowflakes hitting my face, the temperature had dropped so drastically since this morning.

I paced, mind racing, and I'll admit none of my thoughts were very flattering to the Red Leaf, Pretty Horses, or Rondeaux families. But I wasn't so deep in thought that I wasn't aware someone moved between the parked vehicles off to my left.

Of all the times not to be carrying. I called out, "I know you're there."

No response.

"I'm not in the mood to play hide-and-seek."

No response.

Screw this. I started to back up, slowly, facing forward, hoping like hell I didn't stumble into a hole and fall on my ass before I reached the bar door.

A shadow solidified into a man. He moved toward me, both his hands up in the air, his head covered by a hood so I couldn't see his face.

"Stop right there. Keep your hands where they are and identify yourself."

He stopped. "It's Junior."

"Junior . . . as in Junior Rondeaux?"

"Uh-huh. I heard you was lookin' for me yesterday."

"How'd you know I was here?"

"I got my ways."

Somebody was spying for Saro at Clementine's. "So Junior, you were just waiting out here in the cold hoping I'd come out alone so you could jump me."

"I wasn't gonna jump you. Doncha think I learned that shit don't fly with you last time? When you held a fuckin' gun to my head."

"You armed?"

"Nope. Left it in the car."

"You alone?"

"Yeah."

"Good. Drop the hood. I feel like I'm talking to Kenny from *South Park*."

He used one hand to slide the hood back.

I took two steps closer. I'd seen Junior Rondeaux one time. During our lone meeting I'd used my gun barrel to shove his face into the dirt so I really didn't remember what he looked like. Junior didn't strike me as handsome. He looked nothing like Rollie. He resembled any number of the young Indian men on the reservation; pockmarked skin, prominent nose and cheekbones. His unkempt black hair hung past his shoulders. He topped my height by four inches, but with his baggy clothes I couldn't tell if his build was lanky, muscular, or flabby.

"Who told you I was looking for you? Mackenzie? Or Verline?"

"Verline. But I'm sure Mac was talkin' smack about me."

"Why would you say that?"

Junior scowled. "She's a drama queen. She lives for that shit."

"Is that why she introduced you to Arlette Shooting Star?"

"Yeah. Mac's the type of girl who racks up and trades favors. I owed her one. So when she asked me to meet this high school girl, I said no. At first."

"What changed your mind?"

"Mac told me Arlette was the tribal president's niece. I knew it'd piss my old man off when he got wind of it, because he hates Latimer Elk Thunder. And I thought, What the hell, right? It was only one time."

"Did you meet with Arlette more than once?"

He nodded. "I was supposed to flirt with her, get her to like me, then Mac was gonna tell her a bunch of that catty, mean-girl bullshit to make her cry. I didn't want no part of that."

"So what happened?"

Junior blew out a short burst of air. "I realized that Mac is a bitch. She zeroes in on another girl's weakness and goes for the throat. After I met Arlette, I told Mac to back off and leave 'n' Arlette alone, which is probably why Arlette thought we had a thing goin' on. We didn't. I hung out with her. We were friends."

"Why? I mean, it started out as a prank. And you're what? At least five years older than her? What was Arlette's appeal?"

"Gimme a break. I wasn't banging her or nothin'. Arlette knew a lot of history and Indian legends. The cool stuff that we didn't learn in school. I didn't tell no one about it, 'cause none of my friends would believe I cared about that kinda junk. Our meetings were on the down low, know what I mean? Her uncle woulda freaked if he heard we were hanging out."

"Like your dad freaked when he found out?"

"Yeah. Like, I thought the old man was gonna have a stroke."

Rollie. That lyin' SOB. I don't know what the hell kind of game he was playing with me. It was almost as if he wanted me to consider his son a suspect. "When was the last time you saw Arlette?"

"A little over a week ago. She told me she thought we were soul mates or some stupid thing like that. But we were *friends*," he reiterated. "That's it."

"Did your friendship with Arlette contribute to your dad booting you out of his house?"

Junior muttered about Verline having a big mouth. "That had nothin' to do with it."

Since this wasn't an official FBI interview, I could be more blunt in directing the conversation. "Why did Rollie kick you out, Junior?"

His attempt at a withering stare was almost laughable. But after a minute of silence, I knew I had to play my card first.

"Lemme guess when this all went down. When Rollie found out you were working for Saro?"

"Who says I am working for him?"

"Are you?"

Junior shifted his stance, making his answer obvious.

"Come on, Junior. Don't try to bullshit me now. How long have you been Saro's"—*lackey*—"associate?"

"Two months. And my old man can't blame me for doin' exactly what he told me to do: get a job. He'd been a real dickhead about it, too, but he wouldn't hire me to work for him, even when I'm his kid."

Unemployment on the Eagle River Reservation was around 70 percent, so jobs were damn scarce. I realized the appeal for young guys like Junior, working for Saro. It gave them something to do, money in their pocket, and a place to belong.

Too bad Saro was a crazy murderous bastard who used and discarded these young men just because he could.

"Do you wanna know what he did? He pointed a gun in my face and told me to get out of his house and his life and never come around again. Verline tried . . . to stand up for me. But Rollie told her if she sided with me, he'd kick her ass out, too. She don't have anyplace else to go." He clenched his hands into fists at his sides. "Sometimes I fucking hate him."

I waited until he'd calmed himself. "I appreciate you tracking me down and explaining your side of the situation. But you will need to come in and repeat this on record."

He took a step back. "No way. You think I did it. That I killed Arlette. You get me there as a trick, and then you'll throw my red ass in jail."

"Which is why you need to tell my colleagues exactly what you told me. It'd be best if you came in on your own instead of us trying to track you down."

"I can't. Don't you understand? If Saro catches me showing up to talk to the FBI, he'll never trust me again."

"Hate to break it to you, but Saro doesn't trust you *now*."

"So you say," he spat. "Typical bullshit FBI move. Man. I thought I could trust you."

"Why? Because I'm friends with your dad? Wrong. My priority is to figure out who killed Arlette. And right now you're pretty high on the suspect list." I got right in his face. "Prove me wrong, Junior Rondeaux. Show up to talk to us."

"I can't." Then he ducked and disappeared into the darkness before I could grab him.

Shit.

My first lead, and I'd let it slip through my fingers.

I returned inside, my foul mood palpable.

Some bimbo—around my age, wearing an extra hundred pounds and a polyester shirt straight out of the '70s—had parked her fat ass on my bar stool. Looked like she'd even helped herself to my beer. She yakked at a guy who had the expression of a trapped rabbit.

I tapped her on the shoulder.

"What?" She deigned to half turn my way.

"You're in my seat."

"Don't got your name on it."

Where was John-John? He'd point out that'd always been my seat at the bar. "I just stepped outside for a minute."

"Tough shit. You leave, and the space ain't yours no more."

I tapped her shoulder again. I'm nothing if not persistent.

"What the hell do you want now?" she snarled.

"To tell you to get your bloated ass off my seat."

Then she and all her three hundred pounds loomed over me. "Or what?"

"Or"—I grabbed a handful of her oversprayed hair and yanked, turning her sideways so I could chicken wing her arm—"I move you myself."

"Ow. Stop. You're hurting me."

"That's the point." I tried to make her body parts touch, jerking her head back and her arm up. "Sit. Somewhere. Else. Understood?"

"Yeah, yeah. Let go of my arm."

I released her. Stupid mistake on my part. She threw a haymaker that clipped me in the lower jaw. Before she could throw another wild swing, I ducked, backtracked, and swept her feet out from under her.

She bounced on the dirty floor.

I left her there and returned to my seat.

But John-John shook his head, and I followed his gaze to where Muskrat helped the rotund one to her feet.

"That's it, Mercy, you're outta here."

"What? You're throwing *me* out? Why?"

"Because it's not okay for you to just beat the shit out of Clementine's customers whenever the hell you get an urge."

"But—"

"No buts. I used to let it slide with you, but no more. You know better than to throw your weight around."

I opted not to point out my opponent would've crushed me like a bug had she chosen to throw *her* weight around.

"You're banned, Mercy. I better not see your face around here for a month."

The bar had gone quiet, like the patrons were anticipating additional fireworks or some firepower from me. I looked for my sister.

But Hope was too busy glaring at John-John to look at me.

He lifted a brow. "Got something to say, *cousin?*" The last part with more sarcasm in it than I'd ever heard from my friend.

"Yeah, you're a dick. You were a pompous prick to me even before I married Jake. You've had a bug up your ass about Mercy since we walked in. So go ahead and ban me, too. Your *unci* ain't gonna be happy about this, *cousin.*"

John-John's face turned a darker shade of red. "Muskrat. Get them outta here."

Muskrat was smart enough to obey John-John, and to know not to touch me when he escorted us to the door.

I was too pissed off to be drunk, so I snatched the keys.

She sighed. "I'm sorry, Mercy. I didn't mean to screw that up for you."

"You didn't. I've been in there one time since I got back from Quantico. And it isn't like my phone's been ringing off the hook with calls from John-John to hang out." Now that I thought about it, had John-John called me at all?

No.

And he had acted paranoid when he spoke of me working for the feds.

Screw him. I'd accepted him for who he was. He could return the favor.

"Well, there's one thing we can check off our bucket list." She gave me a sly look. "Getting kicked out of a bar together. Only next time? Let's get really, really drunk first."

"Deal."

6

When the headlights from Dawson's truck bounced up the driveway right after dusk Sunday night, my belly jumped as if I'd swallowed a live fish.

Humbling, being cowed by an eleven-year-old boy.

The dogs went crazy, and Dawson let loose a shrill whistle to quiet down the barking. Setting my beer on the counter, I grabbed the spare Carhartt jacket from the coat tree and ventured out onto the porch.

Shoonga and Butch had Lex pinned against the passenger door. I shot a look at Mason, unloading bags from the backseat of his deluxe club cab.

"Shoonga! Butch! Get over here." The dogs raced up the steps, tails wagging, tongues lolling. "Sit." Butch obeyed immediately. Shoonga jumped up on me. Damn dog needed obedience school. "Shoonga. Sit." Whine, whine. I stood my ground. "Sit." He dropped his rear onto the porch. Then he gave me the where's-my-treat? look. *Nice try, pooch.* I patted him on the head with a "Good boy" and offered the same praise to Butch as I watched Mason struggling with the luggage while Lex gawked.

"Lex?" Mason said. "Wanna give me a hand here?"

"Oh. Sure." He grabbed the biggest duffel and threw the strap over his shoulder, then he paused, waiting to follow his father up the stairs.

I cautioned the dogs to stay and held open the screen door.

Mason stopped, smiled, and kissed me before walking inside.

Lex was too busy eyeing the dogs as he passed by to pay attention to me.

They clomped upstairs, and the floor creaked as they entered Lex's room. The acoustics in this house allowed me to hear, "This is your room. You can put your stuff away later." The floorboards creaked as they moved down the hallway. "This is the bathroom you can use."

"Where's your room?" Lex asked.

"Downstairs. Come on, I'll give you the tour."

I rested my behind against a kitchen chair and waited for them to return.

Mason draped his arm over my shoulder and kissed my temple. "Mercy, meet my son, Lex. Lex, this is Mercy."

I held out my hand. "Lex, it's great to finally meet you. Welcome."

"So this is your ranch?" he asked, taking my hand in a firm hand-shake. I didn't answer right away, as I was too busy gaping at Mason's mini-me.

Holy crap, did Lex look like his father. Same wavy hair—about twelve different shades of blond. Same vivid green eyes. Same wide-lipped mouth and stubborn chin. Lex's size was where the comparison ended. Mason was a big guy, six feet three, broad across the shoulders and chest, whereas Lex was small and scrawny, all arms and legs.

"Yes, it's my family ranch. My sister, Hope; her husband, Jake; and their baby, Joy, live in a trailer down the road. They come and go as they please, so you'll meet them tomorrow." I glanced at Mason, who couldn't seem to take his eyes off his son. As if he couldn't believe the boy was really here.

If I hadn't loved him before, I would've fallen head over heels for him right then.

Which made me a total fucking sap.

"Come on, I'll show you the rest of the place." Mason looked at me. "Unless you want to do it?"

"No, you guys go ahead. I'll get supper on the table."

"What're we havin'?"

"Roast. Mashed potatoes. Corn. Biscuits. Chocolate cake." Yeah, maybe I'd gone to some trouble to make a decent meal. But not because I was trying to impress the kid, or anything.

Dawson kissed me. "Mmm. We'll make it a quick tour."

Didn't take long to see the main floor. Then they donned coats and headed outside, much to the delight of the dogs. Just as I was filling my great-grandmother's gravy boat, they returned, laughing, cheeks bright red from the icy air, eyes shining. When I said, "Wash up," I was thrown back in time to when the kitchen was my mother's domain and Dad and I would have just come in from the cold, anxious for Sunday night roast and *The Wonderful World of Disney*. Made me a little misty-eyed.

Jesus. When had my emotions turned me into a live Hallmark card?

Lex was a watchful kid during supper, taking his behavior cues from his father.

Neither Dawson nor I were the type to blather just to hear ourselves talk. We were comfortable with silence. If Lex expected more conversation at dinner, he didn't mention it, nor did he ask a billion questions. The kid had a big appetite—two helpings of everything. Sophie would be in heaven.

After cleaning up the kitchen, I lingered in the doorway, seeing them engrossed in a Broncos game. I debated on retreating to the office and dinking around with my computer, but Dawson motioned me over to the couch. The instant I sat, he pulled me close. "I know how much you hate watching football, but hang out with us for a bit, 'kay?"

"Wake me up if I start to snore."

He pecked me on the mouth and smooched my forehead before he switched his focus back to the game. He didn't care that Lex was covertly studying us.

Since Mason had moved in and we'd gone public with our relationship, he didn't hide his affection for me. Now that I knew how much his affectionate side was an innate part of his makeup, I also understood how hard it'd been for him to keep it under wraps during our clandestine phase. Still, this constant touchy-feely, kissy-face stuff took some getting used to.

I dozed. The next thing I knew, Dawson poked my shoulder. "Hey, sleepyhead, go to bed. I'll be there in a sec. I'm headed upstairs to make sure Lex is all right before he hits the hay."

I squinted at the dark living room with the flickering TV lights. Shadows danced across my vision. This was the worst possible light condition for my eye injury. I squeezed my eyes shut, reopened them, hoping—like always—that my vision would clear. But it remained murky.

In the bedroom I stripped to a camisole and underwear and slipped between the sheets. Dawson spooned me just as I'd hit the peaceful state right before sleep overtakes all conscious cognitive thoughts. But the tension rolling off him kicked me back to full alert. "What's up?"

"I missed you last night." His rough-skinned hand skated up my arm from my wrist to the curve of my bicep.

"Okay. But spending one night apart when I was away for months isn't what's bugging you. Wanna talk about it?"

"I don't even know where the hell to start." He sighed. "I knew Mona had moved again. But I hadn't known it was to an even seedier area, if that's possible. When I asked her about it, she immediately got surly with me. Lex tried to smooth things over, but Mona didn't like Lex sticking up for me. She called him all kinds of names, then pointed at his bags and told him to get out."

I rolled over and rested my cheek on his chest. "That was it? That was how she said good-bye to her son?"

"Yeah. The kid was trying so goddamn hard not to cry . . . and I know that shit can eat you up inside if you don't let it out, so I told him to let 'er rip. I told him I wanted him to be honest with me about everything, the ugly stuff, the embarrassing stuff, the stuff he couldn't tell his mom or anyone else. And he lost it, Mercy. Had a complete, blubbering meltdown in the front seat of my truck. Christ. Big talk on my part. I didn't know what the hell to do.

"When he calmed down, I asked him about getting kicked out of school. He said he did it on purpose so he could come here to live with me, because Mona threatened she'd send him away for good if he screwed up again."

"Again? He's eleven. How many screwups can an eleven-year-old have?"

"Not many. And he's not a bad kid, not like he's dealing drugs, or doing drugs, or jacking vehicles, or stealing electronics, or hacking into computers. He gets into fights at school. A lot. Mona had to go to the school every time it happened. Deal with the teacher, the principal, the counselors, and the other parents. Evidently, one of the last counselors suggested Lex spend more time with me, when Lex mentioned being unhappy that Mona limited my visitation. She refused to consider it, and Lex kicked up his antagonism to the point where he got suspended."

I listened to him breathe. Listened to what he wasn't saying. He agonized over the fact he hadn't been there.

"Mona's always had a pretty good stranglehold on him. Now that he's old enough to think for himself, maybe he'll understand you were always trying to be part of his life."

"I hope so. When I offered to continue paying child support even if Lex lived with me, she jumped at the offer. And she didn't argue when I told her I expected we'd draw up an official custody agreement."

"Any idea why she's had a change of heart?"

"Who knows? I think she's relieved to be rid of him, and that's so freakin' wrong. Jesus. He's just a boy."

I let my fingers trace the muscles bunched in his jaw. "So Lex might be here permanently?"

"Maybe. Sounds stupid, huh? Being as he's only been here four hours." He made a soft groan when my fingers delved into the muscles knotted in his neck. "But here's the kicker. When we were driving here, and I was talking about my expectations for him in school? He blurted out that he wanted to register as Lex Dawson, not as Lex Pullman."

"Whoa. Really?"

"Yeah. Shocked the shit outta me. He wants everyone to know he's my son, and I can understand that because he needs something to feel he belongs here. Then he asked how long it'd take and how much it'd cost to have his name changed permanently."

Whatever it cost, I knew Mason would pay it. I just hoped his kid wasn't dicking with him. "Are you okay with that?"

"Like I'd say no. Christ. I've been after Mona for years to let me get his name changed."

Another thing I hadn't known. "Guess that means I'll have to stop calling you Dawson, since there'll now be two of you."

"I know I've asked you a couple of times, but be honest. Are you *really* okay with all of this?"

I don't know. "When haven't I been honest with you?"

He brushed his lips across my brow. "With work stuff. I can tell you're . . . agitated about some things that are going down at G-man central. But I suspect you can't talk to me about it or you would have." His lips started moving farther south. When he reached my belly button, he looked at me. "I'm done talkin'. You?"

"Uh-huh. But feel free to keep using that mouth."

I woke up late the next morning, so the kitchen was full of people when I sought out my first hit of caffeine.

Dawson and Lex. Sophie and Hope. Jake and Joy. Even TJ and Luke were sipping coffee. Damn good thing I hadn't strolled out in my thong.

Hope smiled at me. "Good. You're up. You can help us plan this thing."

"What thing?"

"A welcome-to-South-Dakota dinner party for Lex."

I almost choked on my coffee. "What? When?"

"Tonight."

I glanced at Dawson, who was ignoring me, the traitor. Or maybe this was his idea. "So who all are you inviting?"

"Our neighbors. Geneva and her family."

"I'll invite John-John and Muskrat. And of course Devlin will come," Sophie added.

Hope scowled and exchanged a look with Jake.

"Penny will be there, too. It'd do her good to get out of the house." She pointed at her grandsons, Luke and TJ. "Better be inviting your families, too, eh?"

"Yes, *Unci*," they said in unison.

"The sheriff's friends and coworkers." Hope cocked her head. "Do you wanna invite that guy you work with in the FBI?"

Hell no. "I'll ask if I see him today," I lied.

Dawson stood. "Come on, Lex. Let's get you to school."

TJ and Luke headed out, their coffee break over. Jake handed Joy to Hope and kissed them both on the cheek before he followed his cousins outside. Their workday had started hours ago.

Lex smiled at Joy and curled his hand around her shoe. "She's cute."

"Thanks," Hope said, smooching Joy's dark head.

"A woman in our building had a baby girl. Sometimes if the mom had to run to the store, I'd watch her. So, if you need anyone . . ."

"That's very thoughtful, Lex. Thanks," Hope said softly.

Okay, that was pretty sweet. And seeing the sheen of tears in Hope's eyes, I know she was thinking of Levi.

Mason handed Lex his coat. "Go on out to the truck. I'll be right there." He pointed to the living room, and I followed him. He put his mouth to my ear. "Just so you know, the party wasn't my idea, but I went with it, okay?"

"This is freakin' bizarre. Anyone who knows us knows we're not Hey-let's-have-a-dinner-party type of people."

"Agreed, but Lex seemed excited."

I hadn't seen that reaction. I poked Dawson in the chest. "You'd better be here, buster. No I-have-to-work-an-extra-eight-hour-shift cop excuse."

"Same goes, Special Agent Gunderson."

As I watched him walk away, the words *a party* kept ricocheting in my brain. What was next in my life? Joining a bridge club? Dawson and me buying matching club jackets?

God. I hoped this party had plenty of booze.

I made a quick detour to the Q-Mart for a cup of coffee. I had a craving for one of those Old Home fruit pies: a sugar-glazed crust filled with sweet, thick artificial filling. A snack laden with lard, sugar, and empty calories that would make Mason frown.

The clerk, Margene, gabbed on her cell phone while she rang up the young woman in front of me. When she turned to get money from her purse, I recognized her.

"Hey, Verline. I usually don't see you in here."

"I needed milk. And a pack of smokes."

She gave me a haughty look, as if she expected me to chastise her for her nicotine habit.

I held up my cherry-filled fruit pie. "We all have our vices." After I paid and headed to my pickup, I saw Verline lounging against the side of the building.

She walked toward me. "I, ah, forgot the other day when you stopped by. I wanted to say thanks for the basket of baby stuff. That was really cool of you and Hope."

"You're welcome. How are the kids?" I couldn't for the life of me remember their oddball names.

"Tiring. Seems like I don't ever get a break."

I felt sorry for this girl, even when I understood that her choices had put her in this situation. I surprised myself and her, when I said, "We're having a welcome get-together for Dawson's son tonight. Around six or so. You and Rollie should come if you don't already have plans."

"Plans?" She choked on a stream of smoke. "We never do nothin'. Can I bring the babies?"

"Absolutely."

"Maybe we'll see you there."

My workday consisted of paperwork. Turnbull was strangely subdued. He didn't ask about my weekend, so I returned the favor and didn't ask about his.

Midafternoon, I mustered the guts to ask Shay to meet me in the conference room. Director Shenker would be in the Pierre office this week.

The other agents were at various locations in western South Dakota. Which left no one to witness the massive ass chewing I was in for.

He was shuffling a sheaf of papers as he walked in. "Why the summons, Agent Gunderson?"

"I have to tell you something, but I don't want you to rip me a new one because it was an honest mistake."

Turnbull growled, "What did you do now?"

"I found out the name of the mysterious guy Arlette was supposedly seeing."

"Who?"

"Junior Rondeaux."

"As in Rollie Rondeaux, Jr.? The son of your friend Rollie Rondeaux?"

"Yes. Remember the no-show teenage girl the other day—Mackenzie Red Shirt?" I relayed the conversation we'd had in the parking lot. Then, that I'd stopped at Rollie's and Verline had said Junior didn't live with them anymore. I followed up with my run-in with Junior in Clementine's parking lot.

Special Agent Turnbull gave me the silent treatment for, oh, about fourteen seconds before he exploded. "And you didn't think I needed to know any of this immediately after it happened?" His eyes turned accusatory. "Are you protecting the Rondeaux family? I know about Rollie's tendency to collect favors. How many do you owe him? And just how long has he been your source?"

I stayed calm. "First of all, last Friday you were pissed off. You hung me out to dry in front of all the other agents, because I had the audacity to ask you questions on a case we're *both* working. When I brought up information I'd dug up on my own that might pertain to that case, you put no credence in my findings. Then you just let Shenker assign me shit work.

"I didn't ask Junior to approach me at Clementine's when I was having a night out with my sister. But if I hadn't used the sources at my fingertips, people I've known most my life, then I wouldn't have found out that Junior is somehow working for Saro."

Both Shay's eyebrows rose.

"You didn't know that?"

He shook his head.

I paused and poured a glass of water. Was I supposed to throw all my theories out there for Shay to shoot down? Just so he didn't think I was keeping information from him? Or should I wait until I had solid leads, evidence, whatever?

"Look, Mercy, you know we're less rigid in this office than other FBI offices. You and me? We're not officially partners. But we're both on this case. That means sharing all information, whenever that information is uncovered."

"So you're saying I should've called you Saturday night, after I talked to Junior."

"Yes. And instead of running out of here on Friday like a scolded pup, you should've taken me aside and explained exactly why I was flying blind, and that you'd talked to another witness with new information."

"Scolded pup?" I repeated. "Sir, I didn't leave on Friday, I was *dismissed* by Director Shenker. Which was a good thing, given that you'd made my trigger finger awful goddamn itchy during that meeting."

His lips twitched. "So noted. Anything else you want to tell me?"

"Case-related? No." I paused. "But as long as we're in disclosure mode, you should know that as of last night Dawson's eleven-year-old son, Lex, is living with us."

"For how long?"

"I'm pretty sure for good."

"Huh." He eyed me over his cup of coffee. "You up for the challenge of parenthood, Mama Mercy?"

That sounded weird. "Hell if I know."

"At least you're honest."

Not really. I hadn't been totally up front with Mason. It'd feel like betraying him if I confessed to Shay that I wasn't sure how this situation with Lex would work out. A happy outcome mattered to Dawson, but it gave our relationship, which was still new, a different dynamic. As much as I claimed I wouldn't be the boy's mother, in effect, I would have a part in raising him. Didn't that define parenting?

Shay gathered the papers he'd spread over the desk.

"Can I have those to make copies? Since I won't be back in this office the rest of the week?"

"Sure." He handed me the stack. "You really think you'll find correlating cases, or events that should've been designated federal cases that have been overlooked?"

"I don't know. But I'm on this assignment until Director Shenker releases me." I could tell Turnbull wasn't happy. He also knew he had only himself to blame. "Have a good week, Shay."

I'd made it to the door when he said, "Mercy. Wait."

I didn't turn around.

"If you need something this week, just call me. I can be there in an hour and a half."

"I'll keep that in mind." I almost relented and asked if he wanted to come to the party tonight, but I bit my tongue and went to make copies.

7

I wasn't sure how this dinner party stuff was supposed to work. Since it was at my house, was I expected to act as the hostess? Would I be in the kitchen while other folks mingled?

Someone had parked in my spot at the ranch. But I shoved that annoyance aside and watched Lex playing fetch with the dogs. I wandered over to the old barn. Shoonga raced circles around me, but Butch had his eye on the prize.

Lex let the ball fly, and Butch was off like a shot. Shoonga gave chase. I shoved my hands in my pockets. "Hey, Lex. How was school today?"

He shrugged. "Okay."

"How do you like your teacher?" *Lame, Mercy.*

"She's all right."

"That's good to hear. Do you have homework?" Lamer yet. *Why don't you just put him on the spot and ask if he made any new friends today?*

"I already did it."

"Great. So you up for this par-tay?"

He whipped the ball after Butch dropped it at his feet. "I guess. One of the kids in my class is coming. Doug . . . I don't know his last name."

"Illingsworth. He's my friend Geneva's son."

"So you really don't got any kids?"

"Nope, I'm not able to have children."

Lex's eyebrows lifted. "Ever?"

"Ever."

"Huh. So you and my dad won't have more kids?"

I hadn't considered that might concern him. The displaced-by-a-new-baby issue that Levi had struggled with after he found out his mom was pregnant. "Guess it's just you."

I thought I heard him mutter "No pressure" as he whizzed the tennis ball again.

A beat passed before he faced me. "So who's the teenage kid in the pictures around the house?"

That sense of loss punched me in the gut. "My nephew, Levi. He was Hope and Jake's son."

"Was?" He blinked. "Oh, wow. He's dead?"

I nodded. "Last year."

"How'd he die?"

How did I know he'd ask that? "He was murdered."

His cheeks paled. "Really?"

"Yeah. So you can imagine it's hard for us to talk about, but if you hear us mention him, at least you'll know who we mean." I offered him a wan smile. "Shoonga was Levi's dog. But we all sort of share him."

Lex didn't say anything else, so I took a deep breath and entered the Gunderson/Dawson party zone.

Not as much chaos as I expected in the kitchen. Sophie stirred a pot on the stove. Her daughter Penny arranged sliced veggies on a silver platter. Hope organized disposable plates, cups, and silverware on the table with Joy cocked on her hip. I said a quick hello and went to my bedroom to ditch my gun before Hope had a meltdown.

I really needed thirty minutes to myself, either pounding the gravel as I ran, or working out the day's stress on my yoga mat. But mind-clearing exercise wasn't a possibility, so I donned party duds—my rhinestone en-crusted Miss Me jeans, a long-sleeved Rockies blouse the color of lilacs, a Nocona belt dotted with silver conches, and my Justin clogs.

Dawson and I passed each other in the hallway. He gave me a quick kiss and vanished into our room to stash his gun.

Some women might have an issue with other women taking over their kitchen. Not me. Mostly because the kitchen had always been Sophie's domain. So no one gave me a strange look when I asked, "What can I do?"

"Keep an eye on Joy, now that you're unarmed," Hope sniffed, shoving the squirmy baby at me.

I checked out her party clothes. The little jeans I'd bought her with butterflies on the butt, and a pink sweater with a carousel horse and GIDDY-UP! emblazoned on the front. I kissed her chubby cheek and whispered, "Lookin' good, Poopy." Then I just happened to glance over at Sophie's daughter, Penny.

Holy crap. She was not looking good. Not at all. Thin to the point of emaciated, she wore a burgundy bandana to hide her bald head. Her brown eyes held that expression of chronic pain, an expression I'd heard my father wore during the last month of his life.

She caught me staring at her. "Thanks for invitin' me to the party, hey. I doan seem to get out much these days, 'cept for goin' to the doctor and stuff."

I sat across from her. "I'm happy you're here. Now I've got a witness to back up how much your mom picks on me."

The air behind me moved as Sophie flapped her dish towel at my head. "*Shee*. I ain't started to pick on you yet. Lucky thing you're holdin' that sweet baby, or I'd start right now."

Penny smiled at Joy.

Joy fisted her tiny hands in the tablecloth and yanked with a happy shriek. "Hey, troublemaker, you're not quite up to Criss Angel's level with the old pull-the-tablecloth-off-the-table trick yet." I stood before she did any real damage.

"I love babies. I would've liked to've had grandkids."

John-John, being gay, wouldn't ever have kidlets. And his sister, Penny's daughter Christina, had died in a car accident before Sophie came to work for us. My fleeting thought that such tragedy just seemed to befall some families was squashed when I realized most folks in Eagle River County thought the same thing about the Gundersons.

Devlin Pretty Horses, Sophie's freeloading son, swooped in and grabbed a handful of veggies. "Grandkids ain't all they're cracked up to be, trust me."

I'd never liked Devlin. A guy pushing sixty, who'd always lived with his mother? Pathetic. It'd be one thing if Devlin ever did a damn thing except sit on his ass and watch TV. Sophie made excuses for his lazy ways—excuses I'd stopped listening to when I was in high school. I slapped on a polite smile. "Devlin, I didn't know you were here."

"Been keeping an eye on the score. I got money ridin' on this game."

Another reason I disliked him. I wondered how much of Sophie's salary fed his gambling addiction.

"Got any beer?" Devlin asked.

"Devlin, you promised no drinking tonight," Sophie half pleaded. "You're driving us home."

"Relax, old woman. One beer won't put me over the limit."

"There's beer in the cooler on the front porch," Hope said helpfully.

Sophie scowled at Hope.

Devlin stood there for a second, as if he expected his mother to fetch it for him. Muttering, he headed out the door.

"So are John-John and Muskrat coming tonight?" I asked Penny.

"Just my son. Muskrat has to keep an eye on the bar." She pushed a line of carrot sticks closer to the sliced radishes. "I could use a stiff drink."

Sophie turned and frowned at her daughter. "It'll just make you sick."

"And since I feel sick ninety-nine point nine percent of the time, I can't see why I shouldn't have one. 'Cause it ain't like it's gonna kill me."

The woman had cancer. Why would anyone begrudge her a drink? "I'll make you one."

Penny gave me a grateful look.

I could knock back a shot or two of Wild Turkey, but since I'd been saddled with Joy, booze was off limits for me. I wondered if that'd been my sister's intention.

The door opened and disgorged a group of people. John-John. Geneva; her husband, Brent; and their large brood. Kiki, in uniform, although my eagle eye noticed she'd also ditched her gun. Bernice from the sheriff's office. Our hired hands, TJ and Luke Red Leaf, and their wives, Lucy and Ruby. I wouldn't have thought it strange that they clustered together, instead of gathering around Penny, Sophie, and John-John, if I hadn't recently noticed the tension between the Red Leaf and Pretty Horses relatives. Our neighbors, Tim and Kathy Lohstroh. Our other neighbors, Mike and Jackie Quinn.

Ten thousand kids ran in and out.

Dogs barked.

Hope plucked Joy from my hands as Rollie and Verline strolled in, sans kids.

Sophie harrumphed and gave them her back. John-John whispered something to his mother. And she shook her head vehemently.

Appeared I was the only person who intended to welcome them. "Hey guys, glad you could come. Can I getcha something to drink?"

"Anything with booze for me," Rollie said.

Verline stuck close to Rollie, which didn't seem to make him happy.

I poured the whiskey and water, one each for Rollie, Penny, Dawson, and Geneva, and a double for myself. After I handed them out, I heard Dawson yelling for me. I drained the shot and cut through the crowd that'd spilled into the living room. The last time we'd had this many people in the house had been after Levi's funeral.

Dawson stood in front of the TV with his hands on Lex's shoulders. He motioned me to stand by his side. "I'd like to thank Hope and Miz Red Leaf for surprising us with the idea for a party welcoming my son, Lex, to South Dakota."

I caught Geneva's eye and she mouthed "Sucker" to me. Mature, not to stick my tongue out at her or flip her off.

"As of this morning, Lex is enrolled in Eagle Ridge Middle School in sixth grade for the entire school year."

Clapping.

"Son, anything else you want to add?"

Lex's face turned a darker shade of red, and he shook his head.

"Ain't gonna be able to get away with nothin' with your dad as the sheriff, boy," Devlin shouted out.

Laughter.

"That didn't seem to keep Mercy outta trouble, though, when Wyatt was sheriff," Tim Lohstroh said dryly.

More laughter.

"Thanks, everyone, for coming. I believe it's time to eat, so help your-selves. The food, as always, will be excellent, again thanks to Miz Red Leaf and Hope."

Kiki offered her hand to Lex. "I'm glad you're here, and I imagine we'll be seeing you at the sheriff's office."

Lex nodded. His shyness with adults surprised me.

Geneva approached next. "Lex, I'm Doug's mom. I hope we'll see you at our place soon." She winked. "Always plenty of chores to do."

"My dad said I'd have chores to do around here."

When Geneva said, "It builds character," I rolled my eyes. We'd made fun of our folks endlessly for saying those exact same words to us at that age.

I stood close enough to Dawson that I heard his stomach rumble. I looked up at him and touched his arm. "Skipped lunch again today, Sheriff?"

"Got a little busy."

"You're starving. You guys get in line."

"You comin'?"

"In a minute."

Geneva smirked at me after they headed for the kitchen. "Aw, lookit you, worrying for your man's appetite and well-being."

I whispered, "Fuck off," in her ear.

She laughed. "You are so freakin' easy to tease, Mercy. And I'll admit, being domesticated and in love suits you. You look . . . happy. For a change."

Much as I hated the word *domesticated,* I couldn't deny I was happy.

"At least your job with the FBI hasn't put you two at odds. Yet. Can you tell me anything about the murder that happened on the rez?"

Of course Geneva put a disclaimer on my happiness—not to be mean, but because she knew me well. I'd mentally done the same thing.

"You know I can't comment on cases, except to say, it was a hellish week."

She lowered her voice. "And in addition to that stress, you're okay being mommy to Dawson's boy?"

"(A) I'm not his mommy, and (b) yes, without giving you more ammunition, I'm glad Lex is here because Mason is so happy about it."

"It's all about making your man happy. Stroking his . . . ego."

"Jesus, give it a rest."

But smart-ass Geneva went ahead and made kissing noises anyway, so I elbowed her in the gut.

"Not fair," she wheezed. "But fine, I'm done. I'll admit, with your friends and his . . . there's a weird mix of people here." We both glanced at John-John fussing around his mother. Devlin on his knees in front of the TV. Then Rollie and Verline exchanging harsh words in the corner. Sophie moved around, but without her usual hustle. "How is Sophie holding up?"

"Look at her. When I suggested she might want to slow down, she acted like I was firing her on the spot." I shot Geneva a sharp look. "And yes, I offered to keep paying her salary while she took a leave of absence to be with her daughter, but she said, and I quote, 'I won't be takin' no one's charity, hey.'"

"Stubborn woman. But not surprising. I think that's where you learned it." Her focus shifted. "Excuse me, but I have to make sure Krissa eats more than cookies for supper."

Somehow I ended up holding Joy again, who wasn't happy because she saw food and didn't have any. I plopped her into her high chair, right by Rollie and Verline. When Joy shrieked and pounded her fists on the plastic tray, Rollie made a disgruntled noise and left. Verline didn't follow him.

I tossed a couple of animal crackers on Joy's tray, because my food-nazi sister had specific dietary restrictions for her daughter. I'd gotten my ass chewed for introducing my niece to the deliciousness of chocolate ice cream.

I studied Verline. She was so damn young. A little on the plain side. Still carrying a few extra pounds from her last baby. When she tucked a hank of hair behind her ear, I noticed a discolored spot on her cheek, now faded to yellowish green.

A bruise. On her face.

I froze. Had Rollie hit her? This young girl who'd borne his children? No other plausible reasons for a facial bruise surfaced.

Could I get Verline alone to get to the bottom of it? And if I found out Rollie had caused that mark? I'd . . . I wasn't sure what I'd do. But I sure as shit wouldn't let it slide.

I mingled. I chatted. I let liquor soothe me. The crowd made short work of the sloppy joes, chips, molasses cookies, calico baked beans, and Sophie's famous radish-and-pineapple coleslaw.

When I saw Verline snap at Rollie and then storm outside, I followed her. She'd cut into the sheltered area between the two barns. The bluish glow of the yard light illuminated the darkness, so I wasn't completely night-blind.

She fired up a smoke and inhaled deeply, resting her shoulders and one foot against the outside barn wall.

"Verline? You all right?"

She didn't seem annoyed at my presence. "I'm fine. Just takin' a smoke break. Didja need something?"

"I wanted to tell you thanks for coming tonight."

Her eyes zoomed to me, my back pressed against the opposite barn wall. "You came out here in the cold to do that?"

"No. I came out to ask you what's going on with you and Rollie. You both seem tense."

"He's bein' a dick, so I'm bein' a bitch. That about sums it up."

Her words weren't laced with venom, as I expected, but sadness.

"Why? Has he said somethin' to you?" she demanded.

"No, but I've run into him a couple of times in the last week, and he's been grouchy."

Verline snorted. "Fucker is beyond grouchy." She inhaled and tipped her face to the sky as she exhaled. "He's pissed off we have another kid. Ain't like I can do anything about it now."

I didn't respond.

"He bitches all the time about bein' too old to be around babies. He don't want nothin' to do with them. Pisses me off because I thought he was different than other men. Makes me sick that he . . ." Her chin trembled, but she firmed it and smoked angrily. "I won't keep my babies in a place they ain't wanted. I know what that feels like."

"Is that how you ended up with Rollie?"

"Maybe. Met him when I was thirteen. Started chasing after him when I was sixteen. He never seemed old to me. He was a real man. Not like the mean men I'd been around. Drunks. Losers. Druggies. Wannabe gangbangers. Rollie talked to me. He listened to me. He didn't treat me like a stupid little girl. He treated me like I mattered."

I schooled myself against commenting on Rollie treating himself to sex with a young thang who had a serious case of hero worship.

"I moved in with him when I was seventeen. Thought since he'd done such a good job takin' care of me that I could return the favor." Verline puffed on her cigarette and blew out a stream of smoke. "Within two months I was knocked up. He wasn't upset, but all his kids that speak to him 'cept for Junior were majorly pissed off."

"Why?"

"They think Rollie's got money, and when he dies the pie's gonna be grabbed by another grubby fist. They oughten be thinkin' that way at all. No wonder he don't want nothin' to do with any of his kids or his ex-wives." Verline tilted her head and stared at me through the smoky haze drifting from her mouth. "He likes you. Respects you. I think he kinda wishes I was more like you. Tough." She shrugged. "But he don't want you the way he wants me."

Thank God. "I'm not blowing smoke up your skirt when I say Rollie's always spoken of you with . . ." Shit. Why was I getting in the middle of this?

Her eyes narrowed. "With what?"

My brain urged me to lie. But my tongue had been dosed with truth serum. "Exasperation. And affection. Does that make sense?"

She smiled. "Yep. If you'da said he spouted his undying love for me, I'da called bullshit. But seein's I recognize that scary-ass, don't-ever-fuck-with-me look in your eyes that I see in his? Well, I ain't gonna tangle with you. I ain't dumb."

There was my opening. "So are you dumb enough to let Rollie beat on you, Verline?" I pointed to the side of her face. "I saw the bruise, so don't lie to me."

Her sausage fingers skimmed the surface before her eyes met mine. "That's one thing Rollie ain't never done. Hit me. Truth is, Taj had a tantrum and smacked me in the face really hard with a metal fire truck." She laughed and coughed at the same time. "Even I know how lame that sounds. But it's true. And Rollie was pissed because I was holding the baby at the time, and he thinks Taj is a hellion. At sixteen months. Give me a friggin' break. He's a baby." She tossed her cigarette to the ground and crushed it beneath the toe of her athletic shoe. "Rollie was so sweet to me after that. Funny. Like my old Rollie, not like this angry old man version of him that I don't even know."

I believed her. Rollie had a violent streak as wide as mine. Granted, I'd never seen it, but that didn't mean I wasn't aware it was there.

"It's confusing as hell. When it's good between us, I don't wanna leave. But when it's bad . . ."

"Where are your kids tonight?"

"My sister is watching them. I wanted to come, even when I knew Rollie wouldn't. So I didn't tell him where we were goin' until after he got in my car."

That would've gone over well.

"I've heard about this place. Rollie talks about your mom sometimes. Course, I knew your dad when he was sheriff. So knowing all that . . . I was curious to see if your family is as fucked up as mine."

"What conclusion did you draw?"

"No contest. Your family is the friggin' Cosbys compared to mine."

Pounding footsteps echoed. Lex; Doug; TJ's youngest kid, Clay; and Luke's youngest kid, Dirk—they all skidded to a stop as they came between the buildings. "Oh, sorry, we were looking for . . ." They didn't finish the sentence, just raced off.

We started back to the house.

"Ain't you gonna whip out some advice?" Verline asked. "Or give me a pep talk about how all of this will blow over and get better?"

I faced her. "Nope. You'll figure it out, or you won't. Besides, if I gave you advice, would you take it?"

"Hell, no."

"That's what I figured. But I will wish you luck."

Three men were arguing in front of the steps. I jogged over when I saw Dawson wasn't around. "What's going on?"

"You're the same sneaking lying bastard." Devlin sneered at Rollie, ignoring me. "That shit ain't gonna help her."

I looked at John-John. He sported a look of hatred I'd never seen before.

Rollie crossed his arms over his chest. "I'm not such a bastard when I'm lending you money, Devlin. She's runnin' out of options, and so are you."

"Shut up."

"How much are you into Saro for?" Rollie calmly asked Devlin.

Devlin shot John-John a look before he glared at Rollie. "You don't know what you're talkin' about."

"I know you got debts all over the place. I know you ain't got a pot to piss in to pay off them debts. I know them guys ain't as patient as me." Rollie looked at John-John. "You gonna bail him out again?"

"Not your concern," John-John snapped.

"It is a concern to me because it's my business. My money. That money wasn't a gift; it was a loan. You ask him how much he owes me. Then you see if you've got the right to be uppity with me, *winkte*."

I'd watched the exchange with my mouth hanging open.

"Enough."

Now we all looked at Penny Pretty Horses as she slowly moved down the steps.

"Mom, what are you doing out here without a coat?"

"You afraid I'll catch my death of cold?"

I bit back a laugh.

But John-John heard the noise and whirled around to glare at me. "You think this is funny? She's dying of cancer, and you're laughing?"

Whoa. That was all kinds of bitchy.

Penny patted his arm. "Better to be laughing than crying, eh, Mercy?"

Like I was gonna answer that.

"And you two." Penny pointed to Devlin and her son. "Leave Rollie alone. I don't care about your business with him. I can talk to whoever I want and do whatever I want."

Rollie took a step closer to Penny. "I don't need you sticking up for me."

"Jesus, Rollie, don't be such a dick," Verline said, grabbing his sleeve and pulling him back. "She's dying."

"You shut up and stay out of this," Rollie warned.

"Yeah, why don't you take your sniveling jailbait girlfriend home and stick a pacifier in her mouth. It's probably past her bedtime anyway," Devlin said.

"You didn't think I was too young when you were grabbing my ass at the WIC offices, you fuckin' pervert," Verline retorted.

Rollie got in Devlin's face. "You touched her?"

"Every time I see him, he tries to cop a feel," Verline added.

"Don't act like you don't like the attention," Devlin sneered. "You'da blown me for five bucks, like all the other whores your age on the rez."

"For Christsake, that is enough." I stepped between them. "Either beat the shit out of each other so I can jump in and throw a few punches, or knock it the fuck off. All of you."

Silence.

"We're goin'." Rollie took Verline by the arm, and they argued the entire way he towed her to their car.

"Thanks for the drink, Mercy. And the hospitality. It's been nice seein' you." Penny spoke sharply to John-John. "I'm ready to go home now."

"About damn time. You shouldn't have come," John-John said to his mom. "None of us should be here. I knew this was a bad idea." He gave me another dark look.

What the hell?

Penny pointed to her brother. "You bring Momma home. No stopping anywhere. No causing trouble. And you keep your comments to yourself, understand? Momma don't need your bullshit tonight. Understand?"

"Yeah," Devlin grumbled, and went inside the house.

Then I was alone, more confused than ever.

"Well, it ain't really a dinner party with the Red Leaf and Pretty Horses family until someone shoots off his mouth or starts throwing punches. At least no one was bleeding. Or overtly drunk."

I turned to the sound of Jake's voice. "Have you been hiding in the shadows the whole time?"

"Yep. Been there, done that with them more times than I can count, and I know better than to get involved."

"You wanna tell me what's going on with your family?"

"Nope. 'Cause trust me, Mercy, you don't wanna know."

People streamed out of the house so I stayed put to say my good-byes. After the last vehicle started down the driveway, I trudged up the steps.

I stopped just inside the doorway. The kitchen looked like a scud missile had hit it. Food everywhere. Plates and garbage everywhere.

Guess I knew where my place was in the dinner-party hierarchy. Cleanup crew.

8

hree buildings, built close together, made up the Eagle River Reservation tribal seat of power. The tribal police station on the right, which also housed the jail, was the largest building. The tribal services building in the middle contained a mishmash of service offices, including the Bureau of Indian Affairs—BIA, WIC, Department of Social Services, Social Security Administration, energy assistance programs, and the two rooms the FBI rented for victim specialists. The third structure on the left side was the Eagle River Tribal Headquarters building. It housed several different entities, all involved with the business of running the tribe. The top floor was devoted to the tribal court system. The second floor held the tribal council's business offices and meeting spaces. The entire first floor, which was actually the basement since all three buildings had been built into the side of a hill, was devoted to tribal archives. Everything from the official tribal rolls to the newspaper archives—since the tribe owned the newspaper—to storage of closed cases, open old cases, police logs, and arrest reports from the tribal police were down there, plus historical documents dating back to when the tribe had taken the land offer from the U.S. government and became part of the reservation system.

I took the stairs and found the door locked. I had to use a buzzer to gain admission. "Yes?" echoed through the intercom.

"Special Agent Mercy Gunderson, FBI. I've been cleared with the tribal police through the tribal council to access certain archives."

No human response, just the buzzing click that signaled I could enter the inner sanctum. I almost felt like I needed to wear a hooded robe and spout Latin as I opened the door, especially when I caught a whiff of the musty air.

Although this floor was identical to the floors above it, the layout was completely different. The main section was similar to the reference area at a library: rows and rows of periodicals, a gigantic desk covered with computer equipment and ringed with filing cabinets of all shapes, sizes, and colors. I didn't get a chance to peer down the hallway, as the man behind the desk was headed toward me.

He offered his hand first. Depending on how traditionally they were raised, some Indian males shook hands with women and some didn't, so I never assumed. "Special Agent Gunderson, what a pleasure to see you again. I'm Sheldon War Bonnet, manager of the archives. I don't know if you remember me, but I helped you when you filled out the tribal registration form."

I didn't remember him. "Nice to see you again, Mr. War Bonnet. The FBI appreciates your cooperation."

"Please, call me Sheldon." He gestured to a sitting area I hadn't noticed. "Coffee?"

I didn't want to make idle chitchat with this guy, but since I'd be here all week, I smiled. "That would be great." I picked the overstuffed chair that faced the door—a ridiculous superstition given I was in a locked room. But me 'n' Wild Bill Hickok had the same phobia about sitting with our backs to the door, and Wild Bill's ignoring his gut reaction had gotten him killed.

"Cream or sugar?" Sheldon asked.

"Black is fine."

"A woman after my own heart." He handed me the coffee and eased into the chair opposite mine. "I didn't get a chance to mention the one time you were in here that I knew your father. He was good for the county. A great sheriff."

"Thanks," I mumbled into my coffee.

"Pity you lost the election."

"The better man won, that's for sure."

"I suppose only time will tell."

I covertly studied Sheldon as I sipped my coffee. He appeared to be in his late fifties. A full-blooded Indian. His thick glasses gave off a wicked reflection in the fluorescent lighting and I couldn't see his eyes, but I assumed they were brown. He wore a high-necked white T-shirt under a loose-fitting gray caftan with a split neckline. His khaki pants bagged everywhere, and his feet were behind the ottoman, so I couldn't determine whether he wore beat-up Birkenstocks or dusty hikers. He definitely held that old-hippie vibe—long black hair pulled into a ponytail, soft-spoken voice, his gentle demeanor that put us on even footing from the start.

"So what brings the FBI here?"

I had to tread lightly. During training we learned to share the least information about a case and how to redirect. And, if necessary . . . to lie. But I tried to stay within a realm of truth. "What I'm looking for would fall under classified information. But since I'm here as sort of a managerial punishment, the truth is I'm not sure where to start."

His eyes widened beneath his glasses. "Managerial punishment?"

"Off the record? Being the newbie agent in the office, I made the . . . ah, mistake of spouting off a theory to the big boss, and now I've been relegated to research said theory."

"That sucks. For you." He smiled. "Of course, I'm the type who prefers doing research to anything else. I assume you have parameters, so I can at least direct you to the correct archive?"

"That would be great. The cases I've been sent to research deal with a broad spectrum of fraud and sexual violation involving minors."

"Still a pretty broad definition." Sheldon frowned at his coffee. "How far back?"

"Does that make a difference in which area I'll start in or end up in?"

"No, just trying to be helpful. I assumed you'd begin with the police case files."

I drained my coffee. "Between us? This is busywork. So I don't care where I start. Especially if you, as the expert, believe I'll have better luck in a different area."

Sheldon preened a bit at the word *expert.* "Since I don't know specifics on what you're looking for, I suggest sticking to the police case files." He set his mug on the coffee table and unclipped a key ring from his belt loop. "I'll get you started in this room."

Looking at the precisely organized boxes of case files, it was obvious that the tribal PD could take organizational notes from Sheldon.

I'd compiled a list of obituaries I'd found online. Hard not to feel overwhelmed. I took down the first box, dated five years previously, and went to work.

Damn depressing that I found over a dozen instances of unexplained deaths of young women, including suspicious car accidents, assumed domestic violence, and drug overdoses. But for nearly every single one of the cases, information from the tribal police had been scant, at best, so I kept looking for more.

A loud rap on the door frame startled me, and I glanced up.

Sheldon said, "You have an incredible attention span. You haven't moved for three hours."

"Really?" I switched my head from side to side to alleviate the stiffness in my neck. "I attribute that more to stubbornness than anything else."

"I usually close up at lunchtime for an hour."

"Oh. I don't suppose you could let me stay in here?"

"Afraid not. Tribal council rules prohibit anyone besides me being left unattended in the archives." He smiled. "And I'm betting the break will do you good anyway."

I shut my notebook and shoved it in my purse. I gestured to the files. "It's okay if I leave these out? Since I'm coming right back?"

"Sure."

Once we were out in the entryway, he punched the button for the elevator, and I booked it up the stairs.

I thought about snagging a microwave sandwich at the grocery store, but fresh air would help clear the sad facts from my mind. I drove a couple miles out of town to the casino. I'd heard the tribal cops talking about the lunch specials, and now I had an hour to kill.

I'd been in this casino once before and had ended up tangling with a pickpocket. Glad to see they'd improved security measures since my last visit.

The same kid still worked at the front of the restaurant at the host stand. He grinned. "Hey! I remember you. You're with the FBI."

"I remember *you*. You said the tribal president was your uncle. But I didn't catch your name."

He held out his hand. "Hadley DeYoung."

I shook it. "Special Agent Mercy Gunderson."

"Table for one, Agent Gunderson?"

"Yes."

"This way."

After I'd ordered an Indian taco salad made with ground buffalo, I glanced around the space. The decor was typically Native American themed. The acoustics were such that I could still hear the *ding ding* of electronic gambling machines even in this enclosed area. There weren't too many people eating lunch. I'd bet with the nightly steak and crab special the restaurant did the bulk of their business at dinnertime.

Hadley stopped at the end of the table. "You out catching bad guys?"

"Nope. Just on my lunch break." I leaned back in the booth. "So Hadley, how are you related to tribal president Elk Thunder?"

"My mom was his sister."

"Ah. You weren't related to Arlette Shooting Star?"

"Nope."

"Did you know her?"

He looked down at his hands. "Not really. She hadn't been here very long."

"You didn't see Arlette on holidays or at family get-togethers?"

"What family get-togethers?" he scoffed. "My uncle doesn't have nothin' to do with our family anymore. It's all about Triscell's family. Since they've got money and stuff." He smirked. "But I sure like telling people he's my uncle. Makes 'em look at me differently. Know what I mean?"

I nodded. "My dad was sheriff when I was your age. But that back-fired on me. Most people thought I'd tattle on them to the law."

He laughed, and it reminded me of Levi.

"Can I ask you kind of a strange question?" He nodded. "Did it bug you that Arlette got to live with your uncle and you didn't?"

He thought about it for a few seconds. "Maybe a little. After my mom died, my dad got married again, and then he died a few years later, so I lived with my stepmom until she kicked me out. Never crossed my uncle's mind to give me a place to crash, even for a little while." He shrugged tightly. "But in some ways, I felt sorry for Arlette. 'Cause I know Uncle didn't want her living there any more than he wanted me."

Hadley had just confirmed Naomi's observation about the tribal president's attitude about his wife's niece. "Did you guys know each other at school?"

He shook his head. "I dropped out when I was sixteen. Needed to get a job. Been working here since it opened." He talked about his responsibilities until my food arrived, then left me alone to eat.

The food wasn't bad, and the portions were huge. After I ate, I still had twenty minutes before I could return to the gloomy basement, so I opted to wander through the casino.

Not many gamblers were trying their luck at the one-armed progressive jackpot win today. I wandered to the blackjack tables. Only one table had players. And one of those players happened to be Devlin Pretty Horses.

Just my bad luck I'd seen him two days in a row. Was there truth to Rollie's comment about Devlin owing money all over town? Surely the casino wouldn't advance him a loan?

I watched from behind a video poker machine as the trio at the table played several hands. Devlin's pile of chips was mighty small. It amazed me how fast the games went and how quickly chips vanished.

Devlin said something to the dealer. The dealer shook his head. An angry Devlin leaned closer, smacking his hands on the table to get the dealer's attention.

The dealer signaled to security.

Immediately, a strapping guard came over and escorted Devlin out of the building.

Interesting.

I watched the dealer talking to a guy I assumed was the casino floor manager. The suit-and-tie wearing guy nodded a lot at whatever the dealer said. After five minutes, I wandered outside and saw Devlin on his cell phone.

The instant he noticed me approaching him, he ended the call.

"Hey, Devlin, I thought that was you."

"Mercy, whatcha doin' out here? This ain't your normal hangout."

You would know. "I'm working at tribal headquarters this week, so I came out for lunch. What are you doing here?"

"The same. I'm about to have lunch with a buddy. He's running late. I'm just waiting out here for him."

Liar. "Have a nice lunch. The taco salad is good."

"Thanks. See ya."

As I drove back into town, I wondered who I could ask to get the truth about Devlin's gambling problem. Rollie? No. He kept secrets better than anyone I knew.

Maybe Penny. She'd seemed more than a little exasperated with her brother last night. I could swing by Sophie's house tomorrow on my lunch hour when Sophie wouldn't be there. I hated to go behind Sophie's back, but these family issues were taking a toll on her, and I couldn't stand to see her hurting.

I parked in the tribal headquarters lot. Although the lunch break had done me good, it was almost worse now, knowing I'd have to go back inside.

Wednesday was more of the same in the archives department. Sheldon and I chatted and had a cup of coffee before I locked myself in the newspaper archive section.

At Quantico we'd learned how to load the film into the microfiche machine. The damn movies made it look so easy, when in actuality, it sucked.

Sheldon refreshed my memory on the process before I selected a roll.

Then I began the arduous process of separating out articles specifically regarding women, looking for any information on car accidents, suspicious deaths, missing persons, reports of suicide, and fund-raisers—which were usually for a health-related issue.

Residents of the Eagle River Reservation had a high mortality rate. This wasn't one of those situations where a prescription for Lopressor or adding more fiber to a diet would change those stats.

I focused on young women between the ages of fifteen and thirty-five. In a one-year span, forty women died, which didn't seem significant until I reminded myself the entire population of Eagle River was ten thousand residents. And I was looking at only a twenty-year age span for victims. The only age group that had it worse than women of that age group? Babies.

I'd been damn glad to go home, because this assignment really was beginning to feel like punishment.

So yeah, I'd dragged ass, getting to tribal HQ on Thursday morning. Lex hadn't been thrilled I'd been tasked with car-pool duty again. Especially since Mason had had to work late the last two nights, which left me to ask Lex if he had his homework done.

I stopped by Sophie's house to talk to Penny. I half expected Devlin would answer my knock, but no one came to the door. I gave up in case Penny was resting and told myself not to get pissy when I noticed John-John's El Dorado was parked across the street.

Instead of going directly to the archives, I stopped in at the tribal PD. While Fergie didn't have any news on the case—not that she'd tell *me* anyway, since Turnbull was in charge—she told me a funny story about her most recent night in a patrol car. I realized since I'd joined the FBI, Dawson no longer shared stuff like that with me.

It was almost nine thirty when I hit the call button to be let into the archives department. Five minutes passed with no response. But every minute I wasn't in that room looking at sobering statistics was a happy minute. Still, I hit the call button again.

Sheldon finally answered and seemed annoyed to see me.

"Morning, Sheldon. I know I'm a little late—"

"Yes, you are. I understand you don't punch a time clock, Agent Gunderson, but I do. Tuesdays and Thursdays are the only days the archives are closed to the public so I can catch up on my work. Except today, I have to open up at ten since we'll be closed tomorrow. I wasted a half an hour this morning waiting around up front because I expected you earlier, and now I'm behind. When I get in the back rooms, I cannot hear the buzzer."

"I'm sorry. I didn't mean to add to your workload when you've been so helpful to me." I followed him to the desk. "You're closing tomorrow?"

"Yes. I'm taking a much-needed personal day."

I curbed my disappointment there wasn't coffee. And I knew I had to make nice. This would be a test, making nice without the benefit of caffeine. "Lucky you. Do you plan on doing something fun?"

Sheldon stared at me, as if gauging the sincerity of my interest. "I'm going hunting."

I gave him a big smile. "Really? That's great! Where?"

"Near Viewfield. A friend lets me hunt on his place."

"Good thing you've got permission. I tend to shoot hunters who trespass on our land."

He didn't find my attempt at humor funny. "You can't possibly catch all the trespassers, hunters or otherwise, with the size of the Gunderson Ranch."

"True, but that doesn't mean it's not fun *trying* to catch them."

Another dour look. "What about the Sheriff? Does he bring his buddies or his family to hunt in such a prime location?"

Sheldon was pissy today, but I doubted it was due entirely to my late arrival. "Dawson hasn't asked specifically that we open it up to his friends from Minnesota or his colleagues in the sheriff's office. There are a few local families that've been hunting on Gunderson land for years. They follow the rules, or they lose the privilege."

"Do you hunt?"

"Oh, yeah. I haven't done it for years since I've been gone during hunting season. We scored antelope buck tags this year and both bagged ours last weekend. Usually I hunt alone, but luckily the sheriff and I have complimentary hunting styles." I paused, wondering if I was blathering. "What tag did you end up with?"

"Deer tag for does. I put in for the elk lottery every year, but I've never been chosen."

I shrugged. "Elk are too freakin' big to pack out. And guaranteed, the damn thing is deep in the forest when you track one. I'm not that crazy about elk meat anyway." I smiled. "But I'm all over getting to use a bigger hunting gun."

Sheldon finally smiled back. "I wouldn't know." He sighed and ran a hand through his hair. "Sorry about being snappy. I know this doesn't seem like a stressful job, but it is."

"Understood. And I *am* sorry I was late."

He glanced at the clock. "Do you know where you'll be working today?"

"With police logs and cases."

"That room is unlocked. If you'll excuse me, I have three things to finish before I open the doors."

It surprised me how many people came in through the course of the day. I hadn't paid attention yesterday, since I'd been in a room off limits to the general public. Evidently, the reference section was better than those at the high school or the Indian college.

Sheldon and I both worked through lunch. When four o'clock rolled around, I put away all the file boxes and microfiche rolls. I pawed through the extensive military history section while I waited until Sheldon finished helping an elderly woman with her genealogy questions.

"Leaving so soon?" he asked.

"Yes. Thank you so much for all your help. You went above and beyond, Sheldon, and I appreciate it."

"You did find the information you needed?"

"I think so. I'll have to compile my findings and present everything to the boss to see if it gets my ass out of the hot seat."

He smiled. "You know where to find me if you need anything else."

"Good luck with the hunt tomorrow." I wondered if he took offense when I practically skipped out of the dungeon.

Although Director Shenker wasn't in the Rapid City office, Turnbull asked to see what I'd found, so I spent Friday morning at home putting all the data together before I headed into town.

"All right, Special Agent Gunderson. Wow me."

No pressure. I looked at him. "You realize this report is raw. I haven't had time to create flowcharts, graphs, timelines, or any of that fancy shit."

"Yes. I get it."

"I backtracked five years and focused on deaths of women in that initial age group." My lists referred to the women as numbers, which I hated, but it appeared more concise on paper. "And between us? Not fun information to compile."

"If we were in a bigger FBI office, you could've passed that tedious job onto an intern." Shay looked at me expectantly. "Bottom line. Any validity to your theory?"

"Yes. And no."

"See? If nothing else, you're getting the hang of writing government reports."

"Ha-ha. What I found is a lot of deaths. Mostly explainable. But each year for the past five years, there have been three or four deaths in a short period of time that weren't explained or investigated." I pointed to one report. "All with a . . . theme. If that makes sense. Three years ago, all three victims were killed in car accidents. Strange car accidents with no rhyme or reason. No witnesses. No other passengers in the car. And all the cars were found in remote areas."

Turnbull frowned.

"Then two years ago, all the women who died had been documented former drug users."

"Not unheard-of. The relapse rate is pretty high around here," he pointed out.

"I understand. But these three women were all found outside in the elements. Not in their homes or their cars, where they could crash after shooting up. One was found in a ditch. The next one was found in a field, and the third one was found by a set of railroad tracks a mile outside of town. And the tribal police didn't order an autopsy or blood work, or work the cases at all—including calling in the FBI. They assumed cause of death was due to drugs. Which is just so fucking . . . lazy, I can't believe it."

"How long was the time frame between victims?"

"For the alleged ODs? One month. For the alleged car-accident victims? One month."

"So these situations, for lack of a better term, took place regularly over a three-month period?"

"Yep. And when I looked at last year's victims, women who'd at some point been involved in violent domestic situations, the time spread was also one month. And again, the women were left outside. No need to take blood samples when the woman was gut shot and died, or when the woman was nearly decapitated and died, or when the woman was stabbed repeatedly and died. Each year I found a couple of cases that could go either way, as far as fitting the pattern, but I left them out of this. For now."

"Why?"

"Because of what Agent Flack pointed out. No need to investigate when it appears to be a cut-and-dried fatal domestic. There were six other cases like that in the last two years."

"Jesus. I can't believe no one noticed this." He glanced up at me. "I know getting this information sucked, Mercy, but this really is outstanding work."

"Thank you. Last thing. I'm pretty sure Arlette is the first victim this year."

Shay nodded. "But there's no discernable pattern yet, so we've got no way of knowing what type of woman the second or the third victims might be."

"Right. What I didn't have time to check was the tie between victims in previous years. Besides the surface similarities in the manner and timing of death. So my question: Do we consult a profiler? See if they've got theories on the type of person we're dealing with?" I paused a beat too long, and Shay glanced at me sharply.

"What else?"

"Or maybe they'll tell me that, as a newbie agent, I'm completely off my rocker. That I'm seeing conspiracies where there are none. That maybe this is all coincidence."

He sighed. "You brought up the same points Shenker will when we take this to him. We've been on this Shooting Star case over a week, and we've got more questions than answers."

"Speaking of the case . . . out of curiosity, why wasn't Latimer Elk Thunder brought in for a formal family interview? Arlette was his niece. And doesn't it strike you as odd that we found out more about Arlette from her friends than from her aunt?"

"Now that you mention it, I expected he'd make a much bigger deal about the murder, given how quickly he bypassed tribal PD and came straight to the FBI."

"Think Arlette's death was a warning to him? He realized that too late and now he wants to shove it under the rug? By enforcing a no-contact-with-the-family edict? Hoping the FBI will go away? Because we've learned that Arlette was more of a nuisance in his life than a beloved family member. I heard that from more than one source."

"Are you saying you think the tribal president had something to do with his niece getting staked?"

I hedged. "If the murderer's intent was to rattle the new tribal president, it didn't work."

Shay removed a slip of paper from his stack of folders and slid it to me. "We're thinking along the same lines. I made a list of Elk Thunder's most vocal detractors."

I scoured the short list. Rollie Rondeaux. Terry Vash. Arthur "Bigs" Bigelow. Bruce Hawken. Penny Pretty Horses. Not surprised to see Rollie's name, but I was surprised to see Penny's. "Are these names in any special order?"

"Contributors to Roger Apple's campaign for tribal president and his staunchest supporters." He tapped on Penny's name. "I know you're surprised to see her. But remember, she worked for the tribal council for the last twenty-five years. She had a strong opinion on who should lead the tribe."

I whistled. "Arlette was found on Terry Vash's land."

"I picked up on that, too."

We looked at each other.

My cell rang. The ID read LEX, and I noticed the time. "Shit. I was supposed to pick Lex up from school. Twenty minutes ago." I answered with a cheery, "Hey, Lex. No, I didn't forget." *Liar.* "I got waylaid in Rapid City." I waited while he hotly contested that response. "Don't do that, I can call Hope or Jake to come get you. They'll be there in fifteen minutes tops. It'll take me an hour if I leave right now." I briefly closed my eyes. "Fine. Call him and ask him if you can walk to his office. Just text me and let me know what I'm supposed to do." He hung up on me.

I would've hung up on me, too. Dammit.

"Problem, Mama Mercy?"

"Yes. I screwed up and now—"

"Prince Dawson and the king will make you pay?"

"Oh, bite me. I'm still adjusting to this family-scheduling stuff." Mason would be more understanding than Lex about my lapse. I hoped. "I've gotta go." I gathered my papers.

"I'll need a copy of those. I might get a chance over this long weekend to look at them."

I frowned. "Long weekend?"

"Veterans Day, remember? The office is closed on Monday."

"Damn. I forgot." That meant school would be out, too.

Shay smirked. "You seem to be forgetting a lot of things lately, Sergeant Major. See you Tuesday."

9

Tuesday morning, Turnbull's number flashed on my cell phone screen just as I'd left my house. "Gunderson."

"Agent. We've caught a case."

Best to save my breath asking questions. He wouldn't tell me anything over the phone anyway. "Where are you?"

"In your neighborhood. I'll meet you in the parking lot at Besler's grocery."

"I'll be there after I drop Lex off at school."

"Is Dawson punishing you for your oversight last week? He has you working as a kid's taxi service?" Turnbull said with a hint of snark. "What's next? You'll swap the FBI for the PTA?"

I shot a look at Lex, his Broncos winter hat pulled almost over his eyes. He stared straight ahead, his jaw set in the same stubborn manner as his father's.

"Who pissed in your corn flakes this morning, Agent Turnbull? Jesus. Have another cup of coffee and quit being an ass. I'm on my way." I hung up.

Lex looked at me, shocked.

"What?"

"Ah, nothin'." He turned and stared out the passenger's-side window.

Talk about awkward. And I was a little annoyed that Dawson's phone call a half hour ago had allowed him to run out, leaving me to take Lex to school.

Oh, and to try to explain that barging into anyone's bedroom without knocking isn't ever a good idea.

In the short amount of time we'd been living together, we were used to being alone in the house—at least in our bedroom, even if the kitchen seemed to be full of people in the morning. I'd sweet-talked Mason into a quickie before we started our day. Being lost in the moment, neither of us bothered checking to see if we'd locked our bedroom door. Lex burst in and saw me riding his dad like a jockey.

So how did I handle this? Tell him when two people loved each other . . . nah. Lame. I'd give it to him straight: I was crazy in lust with his father, and yes, even old people like us got it on at every opportunity. Nah. That was way too much information.

"Lex, look. About what you saw this morning—"

"I didn't see anything," he said way too fast. "And my dad already lectured me enough."

"I wasn't going to lecture you."

He shrugged, as if to say he didn't care. "Who's picking me up today?"

"I assume your dad. Why?"

"I need some school supplies. For a report. Stuff they don't have in Eagle Ridge."

"If you've got a list, I could pick the stuff up since I'm probably headed to Rapid at some point today."

"We're getting the list in second period. I just wanted to make sure *someone* wouldn't forget to take me."

Nice shot at my lapse in parental time management. Rather than defending myself or continuing the small talk, I reached over and turned up the radio. A catchy Keith Urban tune filled the truck cab, and I resisted the urge to sing along, a fact Lex probably appreciated.

Lex bailed out as soon as I pulled up in front of the middle school, before I could pep him up to have a good day and to study hard. I didn't leave immediately, wanting to see if friends would hail him. I remembered from my childhood in this small town that being the new kid didn't always translate into instant popularity. Geneva's kids exited the bus, and Doug yelled for Lex to wait. Relieved, I whipped a U-turn and headed to the meeting point.

Turnbull wasn't standing beside his Blazer when I pulled alongside his vehicle in Besler's lot. He was on the phone and motioned for me to wait before he rolled down the window.

"What's going on?"

"Follow me, and I'll explain when we get there."

Turns out we didn't have to go far. Just a mile on the other side of the city limits by the dump.

That's when my stomach dropped. Picking up a case at the dump couldn't be good. After we cleared the gate, a rusted-out scrap of metal with one hinge that hadn't been closed in years, I noticed a half-dozen vehicles. Mostly emergency and law enforcement—including Dawson's patrol car.

Yippee.

Then I bristled. Had his abrupt departure this morning been related to this case? He couldn't have warned me? I huddled in my coat after I slid from my pickup and waited for Turnbull. He'd parked in a vacant spot up closer to the action. He jogged back to me.

"I take it you've already been here?"

He nodded. "I got the call from the tribal police about this early."

I squinted over his shoulder but couldn't see anything beyond the cars besides patches of dead grass and a hillside dotted with litter. "What's the sheriff's office doing here?"

Shay studied me. "Dawson is pissing circles on the ground, bellowing about jurisdiction."

"That sounds about right."

"As soon as I saw the scene, I knew this was connected to our case, and I—"

"Took over." Connected case meant one thing. "There's been another murder?"

"Yeah. But before we head that way, you should prepare yourself."

Another gruesome scene. Good thing I'd had only coffee for breakfast. But something in his tone keyed me in. "Prepare myself? Why? I know the victim, don't I?"

"Yes."

"Is that why Dawson is here, too?"

"No." Shay moved a fraction closer. "You okay, going head-to-head with him on this?"

"I'll be fine, Turnbull. You seem to've forgotten I've spent most of my life in a male-dominated profession, shielding those closest to me about specifics of my job. This is no different."

That placated him, and he relaxed slightly. "Well, this case is gonna hit you from another side."

I braced myself. "Who's the vic?"

"Verline Dupris."

Shit. "Who reported her missing?" I couldn't imagine her disappearance would go unnoticed. I scanned the vehicles for Rollie's crappy pickup. Why hadn't Rollie called me when she'd gone missing?

Maybe because of your reputation as being a bloodhound for the newly departed. But I hadn't discovered a dead body in months, so I was hoping my debt to the universe had been marked PAID IN FULL.

"That's the thing. According to both the tribal police and the sheriff's department, she hadn't been reported missing."

My gaze snapped back to his. "How is that even possible? She has two little kids. One is a baby."

Turnbull sighed. "I have no idea."

"Who found her?"

"A guy who'd decided to dump his refrigerator just before dawn broke. He almost ran over her."

It'd been only a week since Verline had been at my house. She'd given off a vibe of unhappiness, and young, unhappy people sometimes did impulsive, stupid things. If she hadn't been reported missing . . . "You sure this wasn't a suicide?"

"I'll let you judge for yourself."

I'll admit I paused at the edge of the crime scene before I allowed my eyes to focus fully on the horror in front of me. My brain didn't want to process the images.

Verline. Naked. Just like Arlette Shooting Star. Her body precisely arranged, also like Arlette's body. But unlike Arlette, Verline hadn't been staked.

I squinted at the object resting on her stomach. It took a second to register that the object was Verline's hand. But that hand wasn't attached to her arm. Her hand had been cut off at the wrist and placed on her lower belly. The fingers curled into a claw, as if those bloodied and dirty nails intended to dig into the flesh of her abdomen.

Definitely not a suicide.

Trying to maintain clinical detachment was hard when faced with such an atrocity. Huge purple bruises dotted Verline's body. Rope burns crisscrossed her ankles from being bound. Her knees were scuffed up, as if she'd been kneeling on a concrete floor. My gaze skimmed her thighs and quickly moved over the dismembered hand. I glanced at the other wrist and saw more rope burns dug so deep into her flesh that the wounds had bled.

Had she been awake when this sick fucker had chopped off her hand?

I fought the surge of anger and forced myself to focus. Verline's chest was awash in blood, which had congealed into black goo. That's when I noticed her throat had been slit. With the funky angle of her neck, even lying down, I suspected Verline had been upright, tied to something when the fatal blow had been dealt. I glanced at Verline's face. Her eyes were closed. Lines of blood had poured from the corners of her mouth and over her lips.

What made no sense to me was the neatness of her hair. Not a snarled mess, no hair sticking up like I'd expect from a woman who'd been tied down and had thrashed about. Especially since she'd struggled hard enough against her bonds that her wrists and ankles were bruised and had bled. Her hair was neatly fanned out above her head.

There was little blood on the ground beneath her. She'd been killed someplace else and dropped here.

Why here?

To reiterate the point Verline was a piece of garbage?

To guarantee she'd be quickly discovered?

I looked at the skiff of snow covering the ground. Perfect timing on the killer's part. Dumping the body before the snow fell. No footprints. No tire tracks.

More white flakes drifted from the sky. My gaze connected with Shay's. "Has Rollie been told?"

"Not by any official agency."

Which wasn't to say he didn't know. Rollie had the reputation for having his ear to the ground. But if it'd been only an hour since the discovery of Verline's body, he might not be aware.

And I sure as hell didn't want to be the one to tell him. Part of me hoped that responsibility would fall to one of Dawson's officers.

I finally caught my first glimpse of Dawson, bearing down on us like a freight train.

"Agents," he said brusquely, "an update on jurisdictional status would be appreciated."

Turnbull said, "You want to claim the case for the county? Go ahead. But I'll warn you, you'll have it less than twenty-four hours and it'll be right back in our hands."

Dawson scowled. "So noted."

I didn't say anything. Two dogs in a pissing match was enough.

Officer Spotted Bear approached us. "Agent Turnbull?"

"Yes?"

"Rollie Rondeaux just arrived. What should I do with him?"

All three men looked at me.

I shook my head. "*No.* No. Fucking. Way."

Turnbull spoke first. "We all know it'll be easier for him to deal with someone he knows, and doesn't loathe, and we all know that ain't me or the sheriff."

"Nothing about this will be easy, Agent Turnbull." I looked at the scene. "Where's Carsten?"

"On her way. She should be here any time."

"Then I'll wait for her."

Turnbull shook his head. "This should be done now."

Dammit. "Exactly what will *you* be doing while I'm with Rollie?"

His expression didn't change.

I looked at Dawson. His face held the same stoicism.

Then I knew. The knot in my belly tightened. "You both intend to watch him for signs of guilt when he sees the woman he lives with, the mother of his children, carved up like a pumpkin? That's your big professional, investigative play? Jesus." I whirled around and took several deep *uji* breaths before I tracked down Rollie.

He sat in his pickup with the door open, puffing on a cigarette.

I waited in silence for him to say something.

Rollie dropped to his feet with a soft *uff,* shut the door, and ground out the red ember of his cigarette butt with the heel of his cowboy boot.

When our eyes met for the first time, it hit me how old he looked. The wrinkles lining his mouth became more apparent when he frowned. "So's it true? About Verline?"

"Yes, I'm sorry." I knew I shouldn't ask the question, but I did anyway.

"Did you find her, Mercy? Since you . . ." He gestured vaguely.

"No. How long had she been missing?"

"She wasn't missing." Rollie's tired eyes darted to the scene just beyond our line of sight, then back to mine. "I see your confusion, Mercy. Me 'n' Verline had a fight a few days ago. She packed up the boys and took them to Nita's. I ain't heard from her since, but that's the way it goes with her. She gets mad at me and takes off. Sometimes for as long as a week."

"Who's Nita?"

"Verline's mom. I ain't surprised Nita didn't call the police neither. Woman's got a serious distrust of tribal cops."

"More than you?" tumbled out before I could stop it.

"Uh-huh. I doubt Nita would be worried anyway. Even when Verline is staying there, she bounces from place to place."

"With the kids?"

Rollie shook his head. "Nope. She leaves 'em with Nita. After a couple days Nita calls me to bitch about getting stuck takin' care of 'em again. She hasn't called me this time." He paused for a second. "But I did get a call about this."

He wouldn't reveal his source, so I didn't ask. "I assume you're here to identify her?"

He nodded. Then he asked, "It's bad, huh?"

"Yeah, Rollie, it is. I'm sorry."

Any color he'd had in his cheeks drained away. He closed his eyes, bowed his head, and twisted his gnarled fingers around the beads on his horsehair necklace. His lips moved, but I couldn't make out the words. When he looked at me again, the coldness on his face and in his eyes chilled me to the bone.

"Take me to her."

Without a word, I led him to the scene.

All forensic activity stopped when we reached Verline's body. Rollie walked around her until he reached her head. He stared down at her for the longest time. I suspected he assessed every body trauma. I wondered why I hadn't stopped him from seeing this atrocity, the way I'd stopped Triscell Elk Thunder.

Because I knew Rollie could handle it?

I chanced a look at Turnbull and Dawson. Both men had donned shades.

A yelled warning had my focus zipping back to Rollie.

He'd dropped to his knees. His hand stroked Verline's arm, and his lips brushed her forehead. I watched as he pulled out a knife and sliced off a chunk of Verline's hair.

Officer Spotted Bear jerked Rollie to his feet.

"Let him go," Carsten said sharply. "And back off." She strode over to Rollie, ignoring everyone else. They spoke in low tones. Rollie nodded a lot.

Carsten patted his arm and made her way to us, her eyes flashing fire, her voice low and clipped. "He is a grieving man. Respect him in this moment."

Color me impressed. I'd worked with Carsten before, but the petite blonde always struck me as the observant rather than the active type.

She stood on the tips of her boots and got in Turnbull's face. "This is your scene; you're responsible for all law enforcement agencies. You know protocol in Indian Country."

"Always happy to have a victim specialist tell me how to do my job."

"Do your job properly, Agent, and I won't have to remind you."

Awkward. But Carsten had a point. There were many superstitions and death traditions within the Indian community. Turnbull should've kept a tight leash on Officer Spotted Bear—and the Indian officer should've known better anyway. It just made me think he had it in for Rollie as much as Turnbull and Dawson did. It also reminded me of how little I knew about some of those Sioux death rites and rituals.

Rollie looked at all of us. "You think I could've done this to her?" Then he spoke to Officer Spotted Bear softly in Lakota, guaranteeing few would know what the hell he said.

Spotted Bear remained stoic after Rollie had said his piece.

"Are you finished so we can process the crime scene?" Turnbull asked Rollie.

I thought Carsten might punch Shay in the mouth. I'd offer to hold her coat.

Rollie's eyes blazed at Turnbull. "Verline is not a 'crime scene' to me. You best remember that, boy."

"Mr. Rondeaux, we appreciate your cooperation, and we're sorry for your loss," Carsten said, stepping between the two men.

"But we'll need you at the tribal police station so we can ask a few questions," Turnbull added.

"When?" Rollie asked Carsten.

"As soon as you're up for it. Today."

"I'll be there." Rollie pointed a shaking finger at Turnbull. "Feel free to tell Verline's mother about this *crime scene*," he said sarcastically. "It ain't my place to overstep my bounds and let her know that another one of her daughters is dead." He turned and shuffled off.

The crime scene techs shooed us away to finish.

Carsten's phone rang, and she disappeared.

Turnbull, Dawson, and I gathered by Dawson's patrol car. Dawson rested his hands on his hips. "I'll be honest, Turnbull. We all know this body is in my county and not on the rez. The problem I have right now is lack of manpower. We're running double shifts until I get approval of the deputy applicant's paperwork from the county board. So I'll hand off the case to the feds, if you can guarantee that we will not be kept out of the loop. That if I ask for a progress update on this case and the one tied to it, *you'll* give me as much information as you're able to so I can use that information to protect the residents in my county."

That was the first I'd heard about how far Dawson had gotten in his deputy search. I knew he'd been taking applicants, but not that he was to the hiring stage. And it was a perfect example of how well we were able to keep our personal and professional lives separated.

Turnbull nodded. "That's fair. Thank you. So far I don't have the BIA and the DEA telling me the agencies I can share information with, which is a relief."

They talked about the two murder cases, and I probably should've been listening, but I tuned them out. My mind drifted to Rollie and the upcoming changes in his life. How would he raise two small children at his age? Or would he just permanently dump them with Verline's mother? I clicked on a comment my father had made years ago, about Rollie's disinterest in any of his offspring, regardless of which woman had borne that child. And come to think of it, I'd met only one of Rollie's adult progeny. Did his other kids live around here? Did I know any of them, not knowing Rollie was their father? The way Indians passed on surnames never made sense to me, so Rollie's kids might all have different last names.

"Gunderson?" Turnbull prompted.

"Sorry. What did you say?"

"Given Nita Dupris's hatred of the tribal police, especially those with native blood, I'm sending you and Officer Ferguson to notify her about her daughter."

I suspected it was more a choice of gender than skin color. "Isn't that something Carsten should do as a victim specialist?"

"Carsten is not in charge of this case, I am."

Man. Pissing contests all the way around this morning. Turnbull was my superior, and I would follow orders. "I'm assuming you'd like us to leave now, before this situation becomes common knowledge."

"Yes. I'll clear with Officer Spotted Bear to have Officer Ferguson accompany you, but I doubt there will be a problem."

"And afterward? Where am I expected?"

"At the tribal PD." Turnbull smirked. "I'll leave you and the sheriff to discuss your private business. Coordinating day-care pickup, supper plans, and such."

Jerk.

Dawson sighed. "Indian Fabio giving you grief about my kid?"

Given where we were, I couldn't even crack a smile at Dawson's nickname for Turnbull. "You think I can't handle myself with him?"

"With who? Lex? Or Turnbull?"

"Either."

"I've no doubt Turnbull is the way he is around you, or around us, because he doesn't know what to make of you, or us."

Was he purposely being vague? "I'm pretty sure your son doesn't know what to make of me after the situation this morning," I muttered.

Dawson discreetly reached for my hand. "I talked to Lex about it—as much as he'd let me. We'll just have to remember to lock our bedroom door. I definitely don't want that part of us to change just because we've got an eleven-year-old living with us."

"Me neither." I squeezed his hand before letting mine drop away. "Text me later."

"Good luck with the rest of your day. You'll probably need it."

10

Officer Ferguson dropped her vehicle at the tribal HQ and hopped into mine. I didn't ask if she was familiar with Nita Dupris's address or whether she'd had to look it up.

The Dupris house was a trailer that'd been added on to in several places. Four cars were parked on the yard. A baby-blue, free-form swimming pool, the edges collapsed in, squatted next to a molded plastic playhouse. Broken toys were strewn everywhere. Tonka trucks and plastic guns, swords and Happy Meal figurines. Naked dolls that eerily resembled forgotten babies. Frozen to the ground were white lumps that looked like piles of snow but were discarded diapers.

I knew nothing of Verline's family, but what I saw outside this house told me everything I needed to know.

Fergie sighed. "You taking the lead on this?"

My pride didn't allow me to admit I'd never before been the bearer of bad news, in an official capacity. "Sure. I've got a whole pocket full of zip ties."

She didn't crack a smile.

"Let's get it done." I beat on the siding six times, hoping the noise would cut through the cartoons I heard blaring on the TV.

After two minutes passed with no response, I pounded again.

The inner door swung open, leaving the torn screen hanging between us.

An Indian woman of indeterminate age barked, "What?"

I asked, "Are you Nita Dupris?"

"Yeah. So? Who are you?"

"I'm Special Agent Gunderson with the FBI." I gestured to Fergie. "This is—"

"I know her," Nita said crossly. "What do you want?"

"We're here"—a beat passed as I struggled for the appropriate words—"to talk to you about your daughter, Verline Dupris."

"I ain't seen that little shit for three days. So whatever she's gone and done, I don't know nothin' about it." Her harsh gaze settled on Officer Ferguson in her uniform. "And if she's in jail, she knows better than to ask me to bail her dumb ass out."

"Actually, Verline isn't in jail. She was found at the landfill a couple of hours ago."

"Landfill? What was she doin' . . . ?" Nita's lips flattened. "She hurt or something?"

"No, ma'am. She's dead. I'm sorry."

Nita didn't break down. Nothing in her face or her posture softened. "You're sure it's her."

"Yes, ma'am. She was positively identified."

"By who? That fucking lowlife Rollie Rondeaux? Or by his loser son, Junior?"

Before either of us could answer, another Indian woman, about thirty, holding a toddler, sidled beside Nita in the doorway. "Momma? What's goin' on?"

"Your sister Verline has gone and gotten herself killed."

"What?" The sister glared at us. "That's why these asshole cops are here? To tell us Verline's dead? Where the hell were you when—"

"Maureen. Enough. They don't care."

What were we supposed to do? Protest that we did care? Ask to be invited in so we could witness their grief to make sure *they* cared? Because I sure as hell wasn't seeing any sadness.

Don't judge.

Jesus, I wished Carsten was here. She'd do a much better job.

Another Indian woman, who looked identical to Maureen, bulled her way up to the door. "What the fuck do the cops want, Momma, and why ain't you throwed them off the steps yet?"

"Hush, Carline, you'll wake the babies."

"They say Verline's dead," Maureen said.

Carline was the first to show any upset about the news. She gasped and covered her mouth with one hand. "My baby sister is dead? How?"

"That's what we're trying to determine," I said.

In the background kids shouted. The diaper-clad baby in Maureen's arms wailed.

"Momma," Maureen started, "we gotta tell—"

"I know what we gotta do." Nita glared at us. "You done what you came to do. Now get the hell away from us."

"This is a difficult time," I said with as much empathy as I could muster, "but we'll need to ask questions and get statements from all of you. As soon as possible."

"Where? At the cop shop?"

I nodded.

"Fuck that," Carline spat. "I ain't gonna do it. You can't make me neither."

"True. But I'd think you'd want us to catch the person who killed your sister, and to do that, we'll need more information than we've got now."

"I can tell you exactly who killed her," Maureen snapped. "Rollie Rondeaux. Check that motherfucker's alibi."

"Yeah," Carline piped in.

"Look, I'd like to give you time to process this tragedy, but time is important. So we'll expect to see all of you at the tribal police station. Before three o'clock this afternoon."

"And if we don't show?" Nita asked me.

"Then we'll think one—or all—of you have something to hide. We'll write a warrant for each one of you to appear at FBI headquarters in Rapid City. It'll drag the process out for months. You'll be as tired of seeing cops on your doorstep as we'll be of showing up here, forcing your cooperation so we can prove that we do care, that we intend to lock up whoever murdered Verline. So put a lid on whatever issue you've got with law enforcement and trot yourselves down to the tribal police station before three o'clock today. If for no other reason than you owe it to Verline."

I gave them my back and stomped on the debris littering the ground as I strode toward my truck.

Doubtful that Carsten would've approved of that outburst, even if it was a tame response from me.

Officer Ferguson didn't have anything to add and didn't speak until we'd returned to the tribal PD parking lot. "Well, that was fun."

I pocketed my keys and faced her. "I take it that wasn't the first time you'd landed on Nita's doorstep."

She shook her head. "Far from it. We get several calls during the year with reports of domestic disturbances. Usually the neighbors call it in, and we're obliged to check it out. And even if one of them is beat to hell and bleeding? No one ever presses charges."

"Who's involved in the domestics?"

"Nita's daughters, never the same one. And I have a helluva time keeping them straight."

"How many kids does she have?"

"Nine. Two boys and seven girls. Ten years ago, her teenage daughter—I think her name was Arlene—died in a hit-and-run, and the family blamed the cops for some reason. Five years ago, her daughter Eileen was killed in a car accident. Both her sons are in the state pen. Now she's lost another kid." Fergie shook her head. "It's sad. No matter how much we wanna help them, nothin' changes. My understanding is that Nita got smacked around all the time by her kids' assorted baby daddies. For a while, rather than allowing her kids to get placed in foster care, they were shuffled among family members. But since her first daughter died, Nita has kept most the family together. Including her sons' kids and most of her grandkids. I've been told almost two dozen people live in that trailer."

And that information, while appreciated, sent off a warning that Officer Ferguson knew way more about the Dupris family than just gossip. She must've read my expression because she blushed.

"I only know all that because I busted Nita's daughter Doreen two years ago for possession. She did ninety days in jail. None of her family came to see her. As soon as she got out, she packed up her two kids and moved to Rapid. So she *is* trying to break the cycle. I just hope when she comes back here—"

"She doesn't get sucked in again."

She nodded.

"Me, too. Let's see what other shitty tasks the boys have lined up for us."

The tribal police station was surprisingly quiet. But before I snagged a cup of crappy coffee, Turnbull hailed me.

He waited outside a closed door to a room I'd never been in. "What's up?"

"The tribal president is here, and he wants an update on where we are on the Shooting Star case."

I frowned. "You're the senior agent. Why didn't you handle it?"

His golden brown eyes held suspicion. "You tell me, Gunderson, because he specifically asked for *you*."

"Me? Why?"

"Because I assume he's tired of seeing my ugly mug."

"Ugly," I snorted. "Right, pretty boy."

Shay leaned a fraction closer. "Seriously. No postulating, no wild theories, just the facts we know, okay?"

"Fine. But we'd know a helluva lot more if we'd been allowed to interview him."

"I think so, too. But watch your step with him."

I pushed open the door to the office.

Latimer Elk Thunder finished his cell phone conversation and rose, thrusting his hand across the table. "Special Agent Gunderson. Good to see you again."

I shook his hand. "Likewise, President Elk Thunder."

"Please. Have a seat," he said. "Could we get you anything to drink?"

"No. I'm good." Rather than make small talk about the weather or ask if he regularly took over the tribal police chief's office, I said, "So I understand from Special Agent Turnbull that you want a status report on your niece's case?"

"Only in how it relates to the other young woman found murdered this morning."

I felt Turnbull's quizzical gaze but didn't acknowledge it. "To be honest, sir, I've barely had time to catch my breath this morning, let alone look at the possible correlations between the cases."

His eyes narrowed. "I was under the impression there was already a suspect in the Dupris case."

I didn't bother to mask my reaction. "Your impression—your information—is wrong. We've brought no one in for questioning. And we just informed Verline Dupris's next of kin of her death. So I'm suggesting you allow us at least a couple of days to proceed with this investigation before we start checking to see if there are similarities."

He leveled a cool gaze on me. Expecting I'd crack under the weight of his disapproving stare? I'd have been offended if his puffed-up attempt at intimidation wasn't so laughable—and predictable. I studied him with equal aloofness.

Latimer Elk Thunder dressed to impress. His hair was neatly trimmed, his face mostly smooth, save for the wrinkles on his forehead and bracketing his mouth. I might call him a distinguished elder, but that seemed premature. Far as I knew, he'd done nothing to earn that honor.

"Well, Agent Gunderson. I'll admit I'm disappointed in your verbal report. I'd hoped bringing the FBI in on this would result in much quicker . . . results. But I appreciate your taking the time to explain the reason why there's been little to no progress."

For fuck's sake, Mercy, bite your goddamn tongue.

"Let my secretary know when you have new information, and she'll schedule an appointment."

Dismissed. Thank God. I booked it out of the room, Turnbull on my heels. I didn't stop moving until I pushed through the door to the stairs. When I looked at Shay, he was grinning in a way that annoyed me. "What?"

"Well done, grasshopper."

"I've been dressed down by generals. I know how to placate the brass on the fly, even if it's not what they want to hear."

"Good to know." He rested one shoulder against the wall. "Anything notable happen at the Dupris residence?"

"Not really. I told them to come in for questioning today and threatened a warrant if they didn't show, so we'll see if they do."

"Not a bad morning's work. Now if you'd only gotten to pull your gun."

"It ain't quitting time yet."

He laughed.

"Glad I amuse you." I held my hand to my stomach when it growled. I didn't feel like eating, but my body didn't care. "I'm gonna grab some coffee. Do a little research over at the tribal HQ. Ping me when Rollie and the Dupris family arrives." I squinted at him. "I am sitting in on the interviews, right?"

"Yes."

"Is Carsten?"

He scowled. "Yes."

"What's your problem with her?"

"Why would I have a problem with a privileged, know-it-all white girl who landed a job with the FBI because she wants to right the wrongs inflicted upon Native American people?"

"She said that?"

"No, but that's her attitude, and it pisses me the fuck off."

"With all due respect, sir, I hope you don't expect me to play referee between you two."

Shay bristled. "I can handle Carsten just fine."

I suspected that might be part of the problem. He'd like to handle the very attractive VS in a wholly different and unofficial manner.

I headed down the stairs and out the back door. So much for thinking that cutting behind the buildings was easier than going through the front entrance. I'd never realized how spread out the buildings were; the angle from the front created the illusion they were closer together. Plus, being built on top of a hill, entrances were actually on the second floor, not the first floor.

Since this was the first time I'd been at this vantage point, I'd never noticed the first level of the tribal HQ had an asphalt driveway running behind it like it'd once been used as a loading dock.

Steel doors bookended each corner. I wandered closer to the first door. It appeared to have been painted shut. Dead weeds lined the cracks in the faded blacktop. The width of the building was more than I'd initially gauged when I reached the second door. This one had been opened recently. I tried the handle, on the off chance that it was open and it'd save me a trip around the front of the building.

But it was locked.

I started around the corner and hoofed it up the hill, reminding myself to ask Sheldon about the back doors and what they were used for.

At the front entrance, I took the stairs down to the first floor and rang the intercom.

"May I help you?"

"It's Agent Gunderson."

The buzzer went off, and I opened the door.

Sheldon greeted me. "Mercy, I wasn't expecting you today."

"I wasn't expecting to be here, either, but I've got a break, so I figured I might as well tie up some loose ends. Mind if I have coffee?"

"Help yourself."

I poured a cup and let it warm my hands as I inhaled the aroma.

"So you've been released from your punishment and the drudgery of research?"

"No official word from the higher-ups, but I've been involved in field-work."

"That's what all agents want, right? To be out doing something instead of shuffling paperwork inside?"

"That's what I thought I wanted," I muttered.

Sheldon refilled his cup. "I heard another body was found."

I lifted a brow. "Bad news travels fast."

"Yes, the rumors reach into the bowels of the basement." He blew across his cup. "Are the rumors true?"

"Yes."

"I can't imagine preferring finding dead bodies to sitting behind a desk, Agent Gunderson."

"It's worse when you know the victim."

"I imagine it is. Sounds like your week has already started out on a sour note."

I exhaled slowly. "Yeah."

"Has the victim's name been released?"

"Verline Dupris."

His eyes widened beneath his thick glasses. "I knew Verline. Well, I didn't know her, but I knew who she was. Wasn't that long ago she'd registered her baby with the tribe." He sipped his coffee. "Such a shame. She was so young. Do you have any suspects?"

That direct question earned him an abrupt subject change. "Not only was I unprepared for fieldwork first thing this morning, but I left my notebook with my research notes at home. I hate to be a pain, but do you have paper and a pen I could borrow?"

"Of course, I'll set it in the police case files archive room for you."

I gulped my coffee and poured another cup in his absence. When he returned, I said, "Thanks, Sheldon."

"Just doing my job." He shuffled back to his desk, his gait slow and measured, as if he was in pain.

I felt like a jerk for being so brusque. For the most part, the man worked by himself day in, day out. It wouldn't kill me to visit with him for a bit. I wandered over to his desk. "Been a rough day all around."

He seemed surprised I was talking to him. "I can't imagine dealing with all you do in the FBI."

"So far it's not nearly as bad as what I dealt with in the army."

"Your dad mentioned you were in the military. The man was awful proud of you."

"How'd my military service come up in conversation?" I asked suspiciously.

"He saw my military certificates." He pointed to his desk. "I was full time in the National Guard."

"Oh. How long were you in?"

"Twenty. I opted out, figuring they might freeze retirement by the time my next option came around. I was a little gimped up anyway."

"So when did you come home to Eagle River?"

"Six years ago. My uncle Harold . . . he's my only living relative. He's getting on in years, took me in after my folks died, so I owe him. Know what I mean?"

"Yeah." I thought of Sophie. "I've got someone in my life like that, too."

He smiled and adjusted his glasses. "Luckily, I'd been in office work in the guard for years, so I was qualified to take over this job, managing the archives. It made it easier for my uncle to retire, knowing this place was in good hands."

Would my father have felt relief if he'd known I was on my way back to the ranch as he lay dying in a rented hospital bed?

"Mercy?"

I glanced up at Sheldon. "Sorry, I didn't catch that."

"I said I'm trying to get my uncle to start a hobby."

"I'm too old to start a hobby now. I can't imagine trying to tackle one twenty-some years from now."

Sheldon cocked his head. "Don't you have any hobbies?"

I doubted drinking counted as a hobby. "I run. Practice yoga. Hunt. Some people in my family call me a hobby rancher." By the expectant look on his face, I guessed he wanted me to ask him about his hobbies. "How about you?"

"Oh, nothing too exciting. I'm a history buff. Amateur photographer. I told you I do a little hunting. I'm interested in traditional native herbal remedies. And I'm an avid ornithologist."

I frowned. "You're an orthodontist?"

He laughed. "You are a funny one. I said I'm an ornithologist. A bird-watcher."

Jesus. Seriously? He was into bird-watching? That's where I drew the conversational line. I pushed back from the desk. "I probably better stop yakking and get some work done."

"No problem. I'm running behind schedule myself. Let me know if you need anything."

I did an Internet search for Arlene Dupris. I found a ten-year-old obit—she had died from injuries sustained in a hit-and-run. My gaze moved to the police case files. Since the place was über-organized, it didn't take long to find the right box with the file. I flipped though it and read it where I stood.

Ten years ago, Arlene Dupris was struck down a mile outside Eagle River. By the time she was discovered in the ditch, she was already dead. The tribal cops tried to pass the investigation to the Eagle River County Sheriff's Department, who'd passed it right back. No investigation at all, just shoved aside by two law enforcement agencies.

No wonder the Dupris family had an issue with cops. I wondered why my dad had just filed this case. How many other times had he done that? Curiosity got the better of me, and I started looking through random case files.

My phone rang, and the caller ID read DAWSON. "Gunderson."

"Hey, babe. How's it going?"

Babe. So much for professionalism. "It sucks ass, *cupcake.*"

He laughed at my term of endearment.

"I'm wishing you would've pushed harder to keep the case within the purview of the Eagle River County Sheriff's Department, Sheriff."

He snorted. "Right. Then Fabio wouldn't get to play tough FBI mentor to impress you."

That sounded almost like . . . jealousy.

"The reason I called is because I'm getting off so I'll pick Lex up today."

I glanced at the computer clock. Almost two hours had passed. Crap. I probably needed to get back to the police station. "Good thing. I'll be in interviews the rest of the day. Lex mentioned needing to go to Rapid for school supplies."

"I'll get him there. Since Sophie won't be here, you want me to cook supper?"

"Depends on what you plan to cook."

"How about antelope?"

"Didn't we decide to turn all that meat into jerky?"

"Nope. I kept the backstraps."

"Of my antelope meat? Or yours?"

"Does it matter?"

"It does only if you're bragging to Lex about how studly you are in putting meat on the table."

"Smart-ass. You want me to confess to my son you're a better hunter than me?"

"It'd be the truth, because I am a *much* better hunter than you."

He groaned. "Don't remind me."

"But you can process a kill faster."

"Such a sweet talker, Sergeant Major. I'll see you at home."

I returned everything to its proper place. I deleted the history on the computer in case chatty Sheldon got snoopy. I ripped out the two pages of notes I'd jotted down and set the notebook on Sheldon's desk. "I've gotta run. Thanks for your help today."

"Happy to assist. And you're welcome back here any time, Agent Gunderson."

I didn't remember to ask Sheldon about the weird doors I'd seen on the backside of the building until I was inside the tribal PD.

All hell had broken loose, and I forgot about it entirely.

11

Yells of outrage and flailing arms greeted me when I entered tribal police headquarters.

Verline's family members were attacking Rollie with their fists and their voices.

Several tribal cops stepped in to stop it, but there were five Dupris women and three cops. Bad odds.

So I jumped into the fray. I kept my back to Rollie, figuring he wouldn't take a swing at me. But someone did land two blows to my head in rapid succession, directly on my ear. The immediate burst of pain caused me to lose my balance.

That pissed me off.

And it didn't seem like the officers intended to restrain anyone, so I did.

Grabbing a zip tie from my pocket, I snatched somebody's arm midblow. I jerked the wrist; the body attached lurched forward. I saw a surprised look on Maureen Dupris's face a split second before I spun her around, immobilized her hands, and shoved her to her knees.

Another zip tie, another flailing arm, and I put Carline in the same position as her sister.

Nita glared at me as Officer Orson restrained her. I faced the other women I didn't know; I assumed they were more of Nita's daughters. "You will back off right now, or I will throw all of you in jail for attempted assault on a federal officer, understand?"

The women aimed defiant looks at me.

Nita sneered, "Try it."

Without breaking eye contact with Nita, I said, "Officer Orson, cuff her."

Protests rang out around me, but I ignored them.

Once Nita was cuffed, I stepped back. "Put her in interview room one."

"What about him?" Officer Ferguson asked of Rollie.

"Put him in interview room two."

"You can't just leave us out here like this," Maureen complained.

"I can put you in a holding cell, if you'd rather," I offered.

"We need to be with our mother. She's grieving. She's . . . not thinking straight."

I suspected Nita was the one who had sucker punched me. "Her grief hasn't seemed to affect her aim, so she stays in cuffs until she calms down." I looked at each one of them in turn. "We'll interview you separately, so make yourselves comfy on that bench."

I'd left my purse in my pickup. So much for popping a couple of Excedrin to stave off a headache. I was rubbing the spot between my eyes when Turnbull blocked my path.

His gaze roamed over my face and stopped at my reddened ear. "You always seem to end up in the line of fire."

"Story of my life. I don't suppose you've got any aspirin?"

"I'll track some down." Turnbull threw a look over his shoulder. "The tribal police chief is insisting on sitting in during the interviews."

I groaned. "More jurisdictional bullshit?"

"Yeah. And without you thinking I'm sexist, I believe the best division of labor is for you to question the Dupris family and I'll question Rondeaux."

There was more to it than that. "And we don't want anyone questioning whether I was impartial with Rollie, since I have a personal relationship with him."

"Exactly. But I want to observe your sessions and I want you present when I talk to Rollie. Okay?"

"Fine."

Turnbull opened the door to interview room one.

Nita Dupris stood beside the window. She turned and bestowed another lovely look of hatred upon me.

Tribal Police Chief Looks Twice entered after us, followed by Officer Ferguson and Carsten.

She raised a blond brow at me. "Is it necessary to keep her cuffed?"

I looked at Nita. "Do you plan on taking another swing at me?"

She shook her head.

I signaled to Officer Orson to remove the cuffs. On his way out the door I said, "Would you keep an eye on the daughters?"

We sat around the conference table. I inhaled a deep breath and let it out slowly and silently. "Miz Dupris, this is not a formal interview. You are not being charged with anything. Do you understand?"

A fuck-you look, but no response.

"I will need a verbal confirmation from you that you understand why you're here."

"Fine. I know why I'm here. Get on with the questions."

"Did your daughter Verline live with you permanently?"

"No. She's been livin' with Rollie Rondeaux for the last three years. But she and her babies had been staying with me."

"For how long?"

"About five days."

"Was she in your residence for the majority of those five days?"

"No. She took off the morning of the third day, and she ain't been back."

"And this didn't concern you?"

She shrugged. "Verline . . . well, she's young. She's got two little ones and an old man who don't care about her or them babies. She needs a break once in a while. She hangs out with her friends a few days and then she comes back."

"Who are her friends?"

"She don't tell me."

"Where does she go?"

Her lips flattened. "She don't tell me that neither."

"What's the longest you remember her being gone?"

"Five or six days."

"Do you have any idea where she spent those days?"

"Nope."

"So you weren't concerned when you hadn't heard from her?"

Nita shook her head.

"She doesn't even call you to check on her children when she takes these breaks?"

"Not usually. She knows they're better off with me than with Rollie." Nita leaned closer. "I ain't gonna let that old man have them. He ain't any more a father to them than the police chief is. And now they're all I'll have left of my baby girl—" Her voice broke.

Carsten poured her a glass of water and spoke in low, comforting tones.

When she'd settled, I resumed the questions. "Had Verline mentioned any threats against her?"

"Only the ones from Rollie. He said he'd throw her ass in the street if she got knocked up again."

That sounded like a Rollie bluff.

"Rollie also said that he'd kill her if he ever found out she was fucking around on him. He'd kill her and not lose a wink of sleep over it. I heard him say that one time when they were fighting on the phone."

No mistaking that as a bluff.

"Did she owe anyone money?"

Nita frowned. "I don't know."

"Had she been accused of taking something that didn't belong to her?"

"I don't know. Why does that matter?"

Because her hand had been chopped off like a thief's. "Was she involved in any illegal activity? Like selling drugs?" I sensed Carsten's displeasure with the question, but she didn't object.

"Verline didn't do drugs, and she stayed far away from people that sell them and do them."

I asked a couple more questions, but it was becoming apparent Nita was just a babysitter, not Verline's confidante.

"Can you think of anything else that might help us?" I asked.

"That sly bastard Rollie Rondeaux had something to do with her getting killed. Even if he didn't do it, he somehow made it happen. He wanted to be rid of her. And he knows I will fight him tooth and nail on getting permanent guardianship. I've done it with my boys' kids, and I'll do it for Verline's babies, too."

"Thank you, Miz Dupris. We'll be in touch."

I scribbled in my notebook as Carsten walked out and brought in the next family member.

The interviews with the sisters were short. None of them had seen Verline during the missing days, but all of them were convinced Rollie Rondeaux had killed her. None could offer proof, but they all believed it.

The last sister to come in was Doreen. She asked if her answers would be confidential, and I had a glimmer of hope that she could provide new information. When I asked if she had any idea where Verline might've spent those missing three days, she said most likely with Junior Rondeaux.

There was our first lead.

Shay, Carsten, and Officer Ferguson left to escort the Dupris family out of the station, leaving me with the tribal police chief. I said, "No love lost between the Dupris family and Rondeaux family?"

"Ain't just the Dupris family that takes issues with Rondeaux."

I shut my notebook before I met the police chief's eyes. "You've known Rollie Rondeaux a long time. You've been a cop on this reservation for years. Do you think Rollie could've done that to Verline?"

Tribal Police Chief Looks Twice fidgeted. Then he sighed again. "I honestly don't know. But I do know we've been making the man wait for over an hour. I'll be surprised if he hasn't left."

The five of us paused outside the other interview room. Turnbull handed me three aspirins and a bottle of water before leading the way inside.

Rollie was hunkered down in his chair and appeared to be sleeping. But as soon as we gathered around the table, he looked up.

His red-rimmed eyes made my heart hurt.

"Thanks for waiting, Mr. Rondeaux," Carsten said.

"I don't suppose you can tell me anything Verline's family said about me, hey."

"Afraid not," Turnbull said brusquely. "So let's get started. When was the last time you saw Verline?"

"Five days ago."

"And was everything all right between you?"

Rollie shook his head, and the braids by his temples swayed.

"Care to elaborate?" Turnbull asked curtly.

No response, which annoyed Turnbull.

"It's okay, Mr. Rondeaux," Carsten said softly. "Take your time."

Finally, Rollie said, "We had a big fight. Same old, same old. She's young, I'm not. She wanted more than just bein' my live-in, and I wasn't about to put a ring on her finger."

"What happened after the fight?"

"Again, same old, same old. She packed a bag, shoved the kids in the car, and took off for her mom's place."

Shay tapped his pen on his pad of paper. "How often did that happen?"

Rollie scratched his chin. "I reckon once every two or three months. First time it's happened since she had the last baby. But that didn't change the way she acted. Verline don't call, she stays away until she works her mad off. By that time she's sick of stayin' with her mom, so she comes back to me."

"Were you ever worried when you didn't hear from her?"

"Worried to the point I file a missing-persons report? Nope."

"Didn't it bother you when she took off with your kids and dumped them at her mom's house?"

"Course it bothered me. Nothin' I could do about it. She wasn't gonna listen to me. She was young. And as she pointed out, I ain't got no claim on her."

"Did you have any idea what she was doing and who she was doing it with when she disappeared for a few days?"

Rollie went very still. "I heard rumors. Never confirmed or denied."

"Would any of those rumors ever cause you to become violent with Verline?"

"Huh-uh."

"How would you describe your relationship with the two children you and Verline have together?"

"No different than the relationships I've had with my other kids. They're both babies. Attached to her teat. Alls they care about is her. They don't need me for nothin'."

I got the impression that that didn't particularly bother him.

Turnbull wrote in his notebook. "You didn't want more kids? Were you mad that she got pregnant?"

"Having more babies at my age wasn't something I wanted. It was something Verline did."

"So you didn't threaten her?"

"Nope."

"Do you know anyone else who might've threatened her?"

Rollie just stared at him.

Tension thickened the air.

After a minute or so, Shay prompted, "Mr. Rondeaux?"

"I have many enemies, Agent Turnbull. But none have been so bold as to threaten my family, let alone act on it. But perhaps that's what this is about, eh? To prove a point to me?"

Why hadn't I thought of revenge on Rollie as a motive for killing Verline? Rollie was well connected, but that didn't translate into well liked. Plenty of folks would love to see his intricate web of favors dismantled. What better way to do that than to put him under police suspicion that he'd killed his estranged lover?

When Rollie's gaze connected with mine, I saw nothing in his eyes. My stomach roiled, and my heart nearly stopped. I'd existed in that black vortex for years, and I recognized that blank look in him; I saw it in my own eyes in the mirror after I'd snuffed a life. And for the first time, I realized that my friend . . . might be guilty of murder. Or more than one murder.

"What about your son?"

"Which son?" Rollie asked Turnbull, tearing his gaze away from mine.

"Junior. He lived with you and Verline for a while. Why did you kick him out?"

He said, "My prerogative," and nothing else.

For the next four questions, Rollie gave one word answers.

I knew he was done cooperating, the chief knew he was done cooperating, but Turnbull didn't stop—until Carsten interrupted.

"Thanks for coming in and answering the agents' questions, Mr. Rondeaux. But I believe that will be sufficient for today. It's been a tiring day for you; I can't imagine you'll get much sleep, but you should go home and try. Someone from Victim Services will be in touch in the next few days. We're sorry for your loss."

Rollie nodded. It took him a beat or two to push out of his chair, again reminding me how old he'd started to look. Carsten escorted him out. Chief Looks Twice and Officer Ferguson followed.

Shay's voice was cutting. "Did you see how he shuffled out of here like an old man? Trying to leave the impression that he's harmless and helpless?"

I kept my mouth shut. Shay wasn't asking for a response. Just thinking out loud. I was more than a little confused. More than a little heartsick. I wanted to go home and try to put this day behind me. I interrupted his muttering. "Are we done here, Agent Turnbull?"

He aimed a cool gaze at me. "You are, I suppose."

"What do you have to do?"

"Paperwork on another case. Might as well finish while I'm here."

I stood. "Are we in the Rapid City office tomorrow? Or here?"

"Rapid City. Unless you hear otherwise."

"See you." I found my coat in the employee breakroom, although I had no recollection of putting it there.

I popped the collar around my ears when the wind sideswiped me. Huge snowflakes swirled, the effect strangely magical set against the black backdrop of the night sky and the foggy beams from the parking lot lights. I was so entranced by the sight that I didn't notice the hooded figure lounging against the SUV next to my truck until I reached the driver's-side door.

My hand automatically went to my holster. People always ask me why I leave my coat unbuttoned: I'd rather be cold than have buttons keep me from immediate access to my gun. "If you're armed, drop it. Slowly. Hands in the air."

My voice startled him and he leaped back, throwing his arms above his head. "Jesus, you scared the crap outta me."

"Who is that?"

"Junior."

"Are you alone?"

"Yeah. And *shee*, why you always pointin' a gun at me, hey?"

"Why you always sneakin' up on me, hey?" I held my stance. "Why are you lurking in the parking lot?"

"Waitin' for you."

"Didn't you tell me you'd be dead if Saro caught you here?" I snapped.

"I . . . can I put my damn hands down?"

I nodded, keeping my gun on him. "Why were you waiting for me?"

"I wanted to ask you about . . . Verline." Junior lowered his hood, and I saw misery etched on his face.

I had a bad feeling about this.

He tilted his head toward the sky and closed his eyes. Snowflakes landed on his cheeks and melted immediately, sliding down his face like tears. "I can't believe she's dead."

I let my gun fall to my side. "When was the last time you saw her?"

"Four days ago."

"Where?"

"My place. She'd been staying with me since she'd left Rollie. We were trying to figure out what to do."

Oh no. He wasn't insinuating . . . ? Because that would be a total clusterfuck. "What do you mean, what to do?"

Junior looked at me then with such an expression of desolation that my breath caught. "I loved her. She loved me. We . . . were together, but I wanted it to be more. She did, too, I think. Although I know she still wanted to be with Rollie."

Fuck, fuck, fuck. "How long has this been going on?"

"Started after she found out she was pregnant, less than two months after she had Taj. Rollie didn't want nothin' to do with the first baby, and she knew it'd be more of the same with the second. She hid the pregnancy from him as long as she could. Then when Rollie found out? He stopped going home. She needed someone she could count on." He glanced at the ground. "That was me. I took her to the hospital when she went into labor a month early, and I was with her in the delivery room. Those boys are more mine than his. I, at least, wanted them. And her."

Despite my reluctance to dig deeper into this bizarre love triangle, I knew I didn't have a choice, given what Nita had said about Rollie threatening to kill Verline if he found out she was cheating on him. "Did Rollie know you and Verline had feelings for each other? Is that why he kicked you out?"

His head snapped up. "No. He was pissed about me working for Saro. Pissed when he found out I'd been seeing Arlette Shooting Star. But the only reason I did that—"

"Was so he didn't figure out you and Verline were sleeping together."

He nodded. "I also wanted to poke Rollie, about me being friends with Arlette. When he let me move in with him two years ago, he was such a dick about who I could and couldn't hang out with. Entire families on the rez were off limits. Such old-fashioned bullshit, the grudges he kept."

"Did Rollie know about you and Verline?"

"I don't know!"

I called bullshit on that. Rollie was too astute not to see what was right in front of him. "Any idea what Rollie would do if he found out?"

"He'd probably kill her."

We both froze.

Junior didn't retract the statement. He continued to stare at me with some weird kind of childish hope I'd assure him that his father couldn't possibly have murdered Verline.

But I couldn't assure him because he'd just given me exactly what I hadn't wanted: Rollie's motive for murder. This insight from Rollie's son would convince Turnbull of Rollie's guilt. It'd definitely give him a reason to bring Rollie in for an official interrogation. And knowing Shay like I did, he'd do it tonight. Hammer away at Rollie until the wee small hours.

Rollie needed time to grieve.

Or did he need time to come up with an alibi?

I stilled. Where had that thought come from? As much as I'd like to deny it, the logical side of my brain insisted I consider Rollie a suspect in Verline's murder.

I had to do my job. I shoved my gun back in the holster. "You need to listen to me very carefully. I'm a federal officer. What you just told me is crucial information on a homicide case. I cannot ignore it. I cannot pass this on to my supervisor as secondhand information. You will have to come in, either to the FBI office in Rapid City, or here to the tribal police station, and answer a few questions."

He started to back off, and I regretted putting my gun away. "I can't. I told you what Saro would do to me."

"Saro's power is negligible. Mine is not. I can issue a warrant on you. I can actually arrest you for obstruction of justice if you don't cooperate." I kept edging closer to him. "Remember one very important thing, Junior. You didn't tell me this information because we're friends." I did question whether Junior had told me this because he wanted to put the screws to his old man.

"But—"

"You told me because you want justice for Verline as much as I do. If you loved her, you wouldn't hesitate. In fact, if you *really* loved her, you would follow me back into the station right now so I could take your statement."

He pulled his hood over his head. "Lemme think about it, okay?"

"I'll give you twenty-four hours. If I don't see you or hear from you before then, I'm bringing out the big guns."

He nodded and slipped into the darkness.

12

Dawson and Lex weren't home, which was probably a good thing. Sadness had lodged itself deep in my gut at what I'd witnessed today. Violent death. Grief. Hatred. Suspicion. Family rivalries. Add in my questions about Rollie's guilt . . . and my brain was fried.

A five-mile run followed by a full hour of yoga would be the healthiest way to push my body into the same exhausted state as my brain.

So why had I headed straight for the liquor cabinet?

I knocked back two generous slugs of Wild Turkey before I put away my gun, or even took off my coat. I carried the third glass with me into the bedroom. Once I'd stripped to nothing, I took it into the bathroom, draining the whiskey before I climbed in the shower.

Steam, water, heat, and a slight buzz took some of the edge off. But didn't stop the images from flashing in my mind. Verline's body. Rollie's tender farewell kiss. The Dupris family's angry accusations. Junior's tears. Junior's accusations. Junior's stubbornness.

Wet hair braided, lotion applied, I left the bathroom stark naked and heard the kitchen door open. I ducked inside my bedroom. I needed to get into the habit of wearing a robe so Lex wasn't traumatized by my naked body. I pressed my back into the bedroom door. Had it been only this morning Lex had walked in on us? Seemed like that'd happened a week ago.

As much as I fantasized about crawling into bed with a bottle, I dressed and joined father and son in the kitchen.

Two pizza boxes sat on the table. "I thought we were having antelope?"

"We were starved, and it'd be at least another hour to cook the steaks after we got home, so we'll save those for another night when we're not so rushed."

Mason walked to me and curled his hand around my face, locking his gaze to mine. "So it's Wild Turkey therapy, not yoga, for your rough day?"

I nodded, appreciating he didn't pass judgment.

He pressed his mouth to mine, giving me a sweet kiss as his thumb gently stroked my cheekbone. He pulled back and murmured, "I believe I'll join you in that drink."

I noticed Dawson had bought spinach salad as a side dish. The man had healthy eating habits, much to Lex's dismay. I wondered if the kid had ever tasted a fresh vegetable before coming to live with us.

After we dished up, I asked, "So the school project supplies are purchased?"

"Yep, Lex can start on it tomorrow after school."

"What's the subject?" I asked Lex.

He gave me a look like he couldn't believe I cared, but I needed something to take my mind off murder and lies.

Lex launched into an explanation. It was encouraging that he was taking an interest in his classes, given he'd been pulling straight Ds at his previous school. His cell phone vibrated on the table. He ignored it.

Mason picked it up and slid it next to the pizza boxes. "It's your mother."

Lex scowled. "I don't wanna talk to her."

"We've had this discussion, Lex. You can't just blow her off. She cares about what's going on with you."

"Only so she can use it against me. And use it against you."

"I don't follow."

"If she finds out I like living here, she'll make me go back to Colorado. I just know it."

"Son, that won't happen."

"You don't know her like I do, Dad. She's already mad I'm using your last name. She's said when I go see her for Christmas that maybe she won't let me come back here. I don't understand why I have to spend Christmas with her. I've *never* gotten to spend Christmas with you. She doesn't care about me. She just doesn't want me to like you better than her."

Dawson was agitated; Lex was miserable. And the phone kept ringing. I picked it up. "Hello?"

"Who's this?" Mona demanded. "Why are you answering my son's phone?"

"Hey, Mona, it's Mercy. I see Lex left his phone on the counter again."

"Where is he?"

I looked at Lex. "He and his father went to town for supplies for a school project. They should be back in a couple hours. Would you like me to give Mason a message?"

"No, but tell that kid to call me tomorrow since I'm on my way to work." She hung up.

"Crisis averted." I slid the phone to Lex. "You're supposed to call her after school tomorrow. Let's hope she's in a better mood. Now finish your spinach so your dad will let us have cookies."

Dawson had Lex clean up the kitchen. I'd just poured myself another drink when the house phone rang. "Gunderson."

"Mercy? Is it true? About Verline?"

"Hope, hang on a second." I took the cordless phone into the office away from Lex's curious ears. "I'm sorry to say it is true."

"That's so horrible. Who's taking care of those poor babies? Rollie?"

"No. Verline's mother."

"Oh." I heard her juggle the receiver. "Joy is just Little Miss Grabby Hands. Jake, take her for a sec." More phone-clunking noises, then a sigh. "Now we can talk."

"About what?"

"Sophie."

I was not in the frame of mind to hear Hope complain or whine. "What about her?"

"She . . . wants to quit."

Okay, not what I expected. Good thing I was sitting down. "Really? Why?"

"Penny is being difficult, I guess."

"So Penny's gotten worse?"

"No, that's the thing. Penny is actually improving. I mean, not like she's in remission, but some of the natural herbs and stuff have helped her. She's back to walking every morning. She's eating. Her spirits are better."

I took a long sip of my drink. "That sounds like good news. Not like Penny is being difficult."

Hope sighed. "That's what Jake and I think, too. But you know how stubborn Sophie is. She has it in her head to spend every waking moment with Penny while she can."

"I take it Penny doesn't want that?"

"No. She told Sophie to worry about doing her job."

"Which caused Sophie to quit that job." I swirled the amber liquid in my glass. "How do you feel about her quitting?"

"Jake is worried she won't be able to live on just her Social Security checks."

My little sister wasn't very good at evasion. "That's how Jake feels. How do *you* feel?"

When Hope hesitated, I braced myself, anticipating she'd break down. Her curt response shocked me. "Look, I love Sophie. But after Levi . . . and during my pregnancy, she smothered me. I thought that after Jake and I moved into our own place, she'd keep working at the ranch like she always has and give us a chance to be a family. But she comes over here every day. Tells me how to do things. She basically tries to run my house. I can't even watch the TV shows I want. And I can't really talk to Jake about this stuff because she *is* his grandmother. So to be honest, I'm glad she's quitting." Another pause, and I could almost see Hope biting her lip. "Sounds horrible, doesn't it?"

I tried to wrap my head around this side of my sister. Hope had never wanted to do things for herself.

Or maybe she had. But our dad and Sophie wouldn't let her. They made her think she was incapable.

"Do you think I'm an awful person?" she whispered.

"No, sis, not at all. I'm just surprised. Sophie got pissy with me when I asked if she'd considered retiring."

"That's because it wasn't *her* idea," Hope retorted.

"When did she talk to you about this?"

"Today. And before you get all up in my face that she didn't talk to you, she told me you're under a lot of stress with Lex living with you."

"Lex is one of the least stressful aspects of my life."

"I'm happy to hear that. He's a sweet boy. I like him. I liked Levi a lot at that age, too." She cleared her throat. "Anyway, a couple afternoons when I've been over there doing books, he's kept Joy entertained."

Had I been so wrapped up in my day and making sure Mason's needs were being met that I'd forgotten Lex was part of my life, too? Probably permanently. I needed to stop treating him like a guest and start thinking of him as part of my family. "Thanks. Sometimes I get the feeling he's disappointed Mason and I won't have other kids."

She laughed. "That's not true, trust me. He likes being the sole focus of his father's attention. Anyway, I hear Little Miss screaming, but I wanted to run one last thing past you."

"Shoot."

"Sophie has asked for the rest of her yearly salary and her year-end bonus. Is it okay to cut her a check for fifteen grand?"

I whistled. "We can afford that?"

"Yeah. But . . ."

"Spit it out, Hope."

"I think Devlin may be pushing Sophie to get the money. I overheard him in the background coaching her. She'll probably give it all to him. And he'll blow it all at the casino."

Dammit. I'd gotten so busy I hadn't dug into Devlin's gambling issues. "Does Jake have any idea who Devlin owes money to?"

"No. He don't wanna know. I don't, either. And you should stay out of it, too."

I'd heard Rollie mention Saro, but I wouldn't get within a mile of that psychotic motherfucker if I could help it. Asking John-John wasn't an option. The tribal cops probably knew who on the rez was in the business of loans. Maybe I could discreetly get the information.

"Mercy? You still there?"

"Sorry. Been a rough day. Nothing you can do but write the check. What Sophie does with it after that . . . out of our hands."

"I hate that."

"Me, too. Thanks for the heads-up. Give Poopy a kiss for me."

"Stop calling her that," Hope huffed, and hung up.

I returned to the kitchen and topped off my drink.

Everything in this kitchen had Sophie's touch. The arrangement of the dishes in the cupboard. Where the utensils were placed in the drawers. Where the kitschy objects hung on the walls. The positioning of refrigerator magnets. The style of the tablecloths and the place mats. I didn't remember much from when this space had been my mother's domain.

I'd changed only one thing in this room in all the years I'd lived in this house—I hated the frilly, moth-eaten curtains that blocked the great view of the ranch, so last month I'd yanked them down.

Sophie had thrown a hissy fit, claiming she felt naked without the coverage the curtains provided. But I'd held my ground. And she'd backed off.

Even though she hadn't been here every morning recently, she was around often enough. I couldn't imagine Sophie not being here at all. Would I ever see her? Would she stop by to chat? Would she call me? Would she welcome me into *her* home? Or would the relationship end like every other working relationship I'd had? Where she'd become part of my past? Where she'd be gone like she'd never been there at all?

That thought sucked the air from my lungs. I'd already dealt with so much loss in my life. I couldn't stand losing Sophie, too. But I couldn't push her to stay. That would be awfully damn selfish.

"Mercy?" Mason yelled from the living room.

"Yeah. Coming."

Apparently, this was our family bonding time: watching the boob tube together. I sat on the couch next to Mason, and we chuckled through an episode of *The Simpsons.* Then the Xbox came out, and father and son became embroiled in World of Warcraft.

Belly full, warmed by the booze, I allowed my eyes to drift shut. The sounds of Mason and Lex talking smack while doing battle faded into the background.

I stood on a hillside in the last dark moments of night before dawn teased the horizon. I wore combat fatigues. An M60 strapped over my shoulder. On patrol, on the prowl, but where was my partner? We weren't allowed to go over the fence alone.

My feet wanted to pace, but I remained still. Watchful. I inhaled and got a nose full of the putrid, raw-sewage stench of Iraq. I glanced down to see sand blowing across my boots. The wind whipping against me didn't cool my body. How could it be so hot at night?

A hum of approaching vehicles reverberated in the distance, and I automatically lifted the rifle toward the sound.

There, at the top of the hill. Three Humvees. They clicked their headlights on, blinding me. I squinted, my eyes watering at the searing light. I held my hand up and noticed what those lights illuminated.

Bodies.

The first set of headlights shone on Arlette Shooting Star. I could hear her screaming for help. Before I could move toward her, a javelin sailed through the air and pinned her to the ground, piercing her heart.

The headlights above her went out.

The second set of headlights shone on Verline. She was on her knees begging for help. Before I could move toward her, a red slice appeared across her neck. She reached up to stop the flow of blood and with another slice across her wrist, her hand fell to the ground.

The headlights above her went out.

The third set of headlights shone on Levi. I wanted to run up the hill toward him, but I looked down to see my boots mired in sand. My ankles disappeared, then my calves, then my knees. I screamed, helpless, wanting to save Levi from what I knew was coming. I glanced up but it wasn't Levi on the hillside, dead. It was Dawson.

Shot through the head. Eyes blank. His light just . . . gone.

I put my hands on the ground in front of me, trying to maneuver myself out of the sinkhole before it swallowed me. But my hands kept slipping. Lifting them to the light, I saw they were covered in blood. Rivers of blood from the three bodies poured downhill toward me like a red mudslide. I used my last breath to scream when the bloody sand engulfed me.

My eyes flew open, and I realized I'd screamed out loud. The front of my shirt was soaked, and I reeked of whiskey. I still clutched the empty crystal glass.

Deep shame burned, and I didn't want to see Lex's expression or hear Mason have to explain what'd happened. Why I was such a freak.

But as I reached to set the glass on the coffee table, Mason's strong hand was right there, taking it from me. I looked at him, and the worry etched on his brow seemed to shame me further.

Without breaking eye contact with me, he said, "Lex, turn that off and give Mercy and me a few minutes, okay?"

The sounds of gunfights and explosions ceased abruptly.

I thought I heard Lex mutter about us leaving our clothes on, and I might've smiled if I hadn't been vibrating head to toe from the shocking effects of the nightmare.

Then Dawson hauled me onto his lap. He draped an afghan over us and tucked my face into his neck, tightening his arms so I couldn't move.

He knew what I needed. He'd been through this with me before. When the shakes wouldn't stop, he whispered against my hair. "It's just us here. Let it go. It wasn't real." He kissed my crown. "Please, sweetheart, let it go."

I did, but not with big gasping sobs. Not because I was ashamed to cry in front of him. I'd cried in front of him plenty. I sat and let his warmth, his scent, his strength bolster me.

After he recognized I'd calmed and returned to myself, he loosened his hold and eased back to peer into my face.

"Bad?"

I nodded.

"Wanna talk about it?"

I shook my head.

"You sure?"

"Uh-huh."

"It might help."

We'd had this exact same dialogue a dozen times since we'd been together. Mason never pushed me. He'd hold me and distract me with sex to bring me back to a happy place.

"I don't suppose you can drag me off to bed and make me forget about it?"

Mason smiled. "We've already been busted once today. Let's not push it right now, okay?"

"Okay." I rubbed my cheek along his jawline. "I love you."

"I know you do."

Him tossing my usual response back at me made me smile. "I need to change out of the whiskey-soaked clothes. Then I might crawl in bed and put this day behind me."

"Sounds good. I'll hang with Lex and be there in a bit."

I smooched his mouth. "Don't forget to lock the bedroom door tonight."

The next morning I let Dawson sleep in and took over kitchen duties.

Not even the scent of cooking bacon roused Lex, so I knocked on his door. "Lex? Time to get up and start the day."

No answer.

I knocked louder. "Come on, kiddo. Rise and shine."

The door opened a crack. He rubbed his eyes. "Man, you're even more annoying than my dad in the morning."

"There's a compliment."

He mumbled something and shut the door in my face.

But he was dressed and downstairs in five minutes. "What's for breakfast?"

"Waffles and bacon. Help yourself."

"Cool." Lex loaded his plate.

I poured him a glass of milk.

"Thanks, Mercy."

"You're welcome."

He ate. I drank coffee. I finally noticed his plate was empty, yet he still dragged his fork through the puddle of syrup.

"If you're still hungry, I can make another waffle."

"I'm full." Lex looked up at me and wore the same contrite expression I'd seen on his father's face.

"Something wrong?"

He blurted out, "I'm sorry."

"For what?"

"For playing World of Warcraft in front of you. It's just a game to me, and I didn't know it'd bring back bad memories of being in war and stuff. I won't play it anymore."

Such a sweet boy. Like his dad in so many ways. I wanted to hug him, but that'd probably freak him out. So I reached over and messed up his hair. "Thanks. The bad dreams usually stem from something that happened at work. But not always. It's kind of a crapshoot. I never know when they'll pop up and knock me flat."

"There was a guy in my apartment building who'd been in Vietnam. Some days he'd be great."

"It's those not-so-great days that are scary."

Lex nodded. "One time he was sleeping in the hallway, and I accidentally woke him up. He tackled me. I had to hit him in the face to get him to leave me alone. Then he got really embarrassed, and I didn't see him for a while."

"I know the feeling."

Mason ambled in. "Mornin'." He helped himself to coffee and looked around. "Where's Sophie?"

"She's not here."

"*You* made waffles?"

"I am not entirely helpless in the kitchen, Sheriff. Besides, you'd better not insult my cooking since I'll be doing a lot more of it." I sipped my coffee. "Sophie quit."

"She did? When did this happen?"

"Hope told me last night. I guess it's effective immediately. She wants to spend more time with Penny before she . . ."

Dawson frowned. "Is Penny worse?"

"No." I explained what I'd been told the night before.

"That's good news anyway. And I have some more good news." He focused on Lex. "I talked to Phil Beecham, the bus driver for this area. He said if you're down by the main highway by twenty-five before the hour, he'll pick you up and take you to school. Won't that be great? Getting to know the kids from around here?"

"I guess." Lex left the table without picking up his plate.

"Huh-uh. Get back here. You know the drill."

"Sorry, Dad." He looked at me. Firmed his chin. "Is Sophie quitting because of me?"

"No. Why would you—" Had the kid taken the blame for everything at his mom's house? "To be honest, Sophie is getting on in years, and it's gotten harder for her to do all the things she used to do. It doesn't have anything to do with you. In fact, she was pretty excited when she heard you were coming. More cookie recipes for her to test out."

"I never knew anyone who had a housekeeper and a cook," Lex said.

"Sophie's more than just a housekeeper to me. She's sort of filled in since my mom died when I was a kid."

"Oh." Lex hustled off after a warning from his father about being late for school.

Dawson wrapped himself around me while I rinsed the dishes. "I know you'll miss her. I'll miss her, too. But this is probably the best for everyone."

I disagreed.

And in my mind, this was a temporary situation, anyway. Sophie would be back.

13

We probably should've been at the tribal police department getting the tribal officers' input on the case. But instead, I found myself at home base—the Rapid City FBI office—in the conference room, alone with Agent Turnbull.

And it seemed a bit . . . official. Instead of the brainstorming session Shay had hinted at.

"We're in agreement that the Shooting Star and Dupris cases are connected?"

I nodded. "Any reports back from the crime lab?"

"Yep. Verline also had high levels of digitalis in her system." He rapped his pen on the blank sheet of paper in front of him. "So now, how about if we start with a list of possible suspects." Then he looked at me pointedly.

"What? You want me to go first?"

"Yep."

Damn. "Junior Rondeaux."

"Why?"

"He'd been sneaking around with Arlette, effectively pissing off both his father and Verline."

The *tap-tap-tap* of Turnbull's pen sounded on the table as he studied me. "Why would Verline be mad if her live-in's son was making time with the tribal president's niece?"

I'd get a browbeating for not immediately telling Turnbull about Junior Rondeaux cornering me last night. It'd be entertaining to watch steam blow out of his ears—if not for the fact all that steam would be directed at me. "Before you have an aneurysm, I was in shock after yesterday's events when Junior waylaid me in the parking lot at the tribal PD."

"Why didn't you bring him into the police station? He was right fucking there. I was right fucking there."

Yep, Turnbull was really pissed if he used *fuck* in the office. "He took off, and I didn't think 'by any means necessary' was appropriate use of force in this case. Yes, I could've shot him in the leg. But I figured it'd be counterproductive, since he'd end up in the hospital, unable to answer our questions anyway."

Angrier, faster tapping with his pen. "What exactly did Junior Rondeaux tell you?"

I relayed the conversation to the best of my recollection. When I reached the part where Junior told me of his fear of Rollie's threats to Verline if he found out she'd been cheating on him, I hesitated. And Mr. Intuitive G-man caught it.

"No editorializing, Agent Gunderson."

"Fine. Junior said Rollie would kill her."

Silence.

His handsome face was a total blank.

I tossed out one of the two other theories I'd been kicking around. "What if Junior killed Verline to protect her? If Verline had a hormonal moment, especially if Junior had been telling Verline about spending time with Arlette to make Verline jealous and force her into a decision about leaving Rollie. Verline could've offered Arlette a ride, claiming to know Junior, drugged her, and staked her."

"So you think Verline picked Arlette up from school that day?"

"It's a possibility. Arlette was keeping Junior a secret so she wouldn't tell Naomi about her lunch plans."

"Where would Verline have obtained digitalis?"

I said, "From Rollie," without thinking. "He and his family are into all that native natural herbal stuff."

More pen tapping. "Go on."

"Let's say . . . Junior knew Verline killed Arlette, and he also was starting to suspect that Verline wouldn't leave Rollie, no matter how much she claimed she wanted to. Junior knows Rollie is an unfit parent. He also knows that if Verline turns up dead, the cops will be looking hard at Rollie for the murder. So he'd frame his father, make sure Verline's kids are taken care of, and protect her crime."

After I finished, I had the strangest feeling Turnbull was holding back laughter.

"You done?"

"No." I crossed my arms over my chest. "I haven't even mentioned Saro."

That brought him up short. "What would Saro's part be in this?"

"Junior works for Saro in some capacity. If Rollie is in jail for Verline's murder, his business is kaput. Getting rid of a business rival plays into Saro's hands. Not to mention, Saro is obsessed with finding Verline's cousin, Cherelle, for her part in his brother Victor's murder. Maybe Verline took something from Saro, and Saro made an example out of Verline by whacking off her hand as a warning to others on the rez who might think about crossing him."

"After you left to talk to the Dupris family, we also discovered at the scene that Verline's tongue had been cut out."

"Jesus. But that makes sense if Saro is involved. If Verline had talked out of turn, or *wouldn't* talk, Saro would remove her tongue as another example."

"And Saro's reason for killing Arlette?"

"He's sadistic. He may've done it for kicks. But I heard grumbling in the tribal PD that the new tribal president has demanded tribal cops put the smackdown on drug dealing. They're not even supposed to let a single prescription pill pass hands. There's no way the cops can police it. Maybe Saro voiced his displeasure with Latimer Elk Thunder's edict by killing his niece. There was no way of knowing how little Arlette meant to her uncle."

No response but a cool stare.

"What?"

"I find it interesting, and maybe a little disturbing, that you didn't mention Rollie Rondeaux as a possible suspect. Even his own son thinks he's guilty."

I said nothing.

"So along those lines . . . do your job. Don't discount anything. Don't discount anyone. Get me some proof to back up either of your theories. Within the confines of the law."

I stood. "Don't insult me, Special Agent Turnbull. I'm a team player. I know what team I'm on. *Rah-rah! Go FBI!* and all that shit."

"You're a drumroll short of nailing that punch line, Agent Gunderson."

Everyone was a comedian. I slipped on my coat, shouldered my purse, and walked out.

Junior Rondeaux's twenty-four hours were almost up.

Verline's sister had told us where Junior lived—a shack on someone's property. Looking at it now, I doubted the place had running water. Maybe it had electricity. The windows were boarded over.

I parked on the street and backtracked to the door, which wasn't completely closed. Loud noises—moans and groans—came from inside. Was Junior hurt? I pulled my sidearm, kicked the bottom of the door with my boot, and said, "FBI. I'm coming in."

First thing I saw? A naked ass. Then a naked back. The girl on the bouncing mattress screamed when she saw me. She shoved Junior so hard he flew out of bed and landed on that naked ass. She yanked the covers up but not before I got a glimpse of her pendulous breasts.

Fucking awesome.

She yelled, "Don't shoot! It's not his fault! I told him I was eighteen!"

Jesus. Seriously? She thought the FBI was on underage nookie patrol?

Junior scrambled to his feet and threw his arms in the air. He knew the drill. "Christ, don't shoot! I'm not armed."

"I can see that."

"What are you doin' here?"

I kept my gun trained on him and did not allow my gaze to drop below his chin. "I heard noises. And since you're involved in a federal investigation, I suspected you might be in distress. I announced myself before I came in."

"Yeah? Well, I didn't hear you because we were a little busy!"

"A federal investigation?" the girl repeated. "You didn't tell me you were part of that."

"But baby, I'm not. Listen to me."

From the corner of my eye I could see the girl scrambling to get her clothes on.

"So much for mourning your true love, Verline, huh, Junior? She's been dead, what, a day? And you're already bumping uglies with someone else?"

Junior shook his hair out of his eyes. "I ain't got a gun in here, so do you mind putting that thing away?"

"I'll put mine away if you put yours away." I lowered my gun but didn't holster it.

He whispered to the girl, and she pushed back, slipping on a hoodie—but not before I noticed she had hickeys all over her neck. She was on the plump side, as well as the illegal side. I practiced my hard-cop stare as she shuffled past me.

Then I glanced at Junior. He'd pulled on a pair of boxing shorts and a long-sleeved shirt.

"Didja hafta bust in right then? You couldn't have waited another five minutes?"

"Just be goddamn thankful I'm not having you arrested for statutory rape when I haul your ass into the tribal PD."

His eyes rounded. "What?"

"I gave you twenty-four hours, which are almost up. You need to give an official statement about why you believe Rollie had sufficient motivation to kill Verline Dupris." I gestured to his feet. "Put on some shoes."

"But I can't—"

"Yes, you can. You're riding with me. And if you pull any bullshit moves, I'll shoot you. Understand?"

"Yeah. You're kinda violent and trigger-happy for a fed."

"That's why they hired me."

No issues getting Junior to the cop shop. Officer Ferguson was on duty, and she snagged an interview room.

For all his blustering about not wanting to talk to the cops, Junior spilled his guts pretty good. Nothing he'd said was new information to me, but I was relieved to have it on record. As the interview wound down, one thing occurred to me. "I know your uncle Leo and Rollie both practice Native American herbal medicine. It seems to be a family thing. Have you ever shown an interest in it?"

"You mean has Rollie ever taken me out to gather plants, twigs, berries, flowers, and shit? No. That old-way stuff don't interest me. That's where me and Arlette were alike. We liked reading about it, not doin' it."

"How's that?"

"Her aunt did all that natural herb stuff, too. Made her own home remedies. Every Indian has a different recipe, and they still claim theirs is *traditional*. It's a buncha crap. But some folks, white folks especially, will pay big money for it."

Fergie and I exchanged a look.

"Thanks for coming in, Junior." I held open the conference room door. "You're free to go."

He snorted. "Like I had a choice. How am I getting home? You brought me here."

"I could get a patrol car to drop you at your place," Officer Ferguson said sweetly.

"I'd rather walk."

After I shut the door, I noticed Fergie's perplexed look. "Does everyone else at the tribal PD think Rollie is guilty?"

"To be honest, we haven't discussed it. Not like you feebies do. Diagramming the problem from every conceivable angle. Keeping your findings to yourself. But I'll admit all agencies missed the herbal angle with Triscell Elk Thunder."

I let her opinion of *feebies* slide. "True. I believe I'll have a follow-up chat with her. You busy right now?"

Fergie raised her pale red eyebrows. "You plan to just show up at the tribal president's house?"

"Yes. Why? Do they discourage drop-by visitors?"

"Do ya think?"

"But it would be for official business. Not like I'm expecting them to serve me a cocktail and appetizers or anything."

"As an FBI agent, you can get away with dropping by—even with the no-contact order. Me? No way. The tribal president can put pressure on the council to put pressure on the tribal police to ax me. So I'll give you the address, but I'll be right here, safe in the office, by my computer, typing up this interview for the case file."

I grinned. "Sounds good. Will you fax a copy to the FBI?"

"Sure."

Before I headed out, I remembered one other thing I'd forgotten to ask Junior, so I posed the question to Fergie. "This is off the record. But if a person needed money because he had, say, a gambling problem, who's in the moneylending business on the rez? Besides Saro. I know Rollie dabbles in it. But there's got to be more than those two."

Officer Ferguson fidgeted.

"This is not for an FBI case. I'm not looking to borrow money. I'm just asking; hypothetically, if I needed extra cash, who I could ask?"

She opened her mouth. Snapped it shut.

That gut feeling told me I wouldn't like her answer. If she answered.

Officer Ferguson looked around guiltily, and then leaned forward. "You did not hear this from me. Promise you'll keep me out of it?"

"Absolutely."

"You're already going to the right place."

I frowned. "I don't follow."

"Latimer Elk Thunder owns the gas station. But do you think that's where he got all his money? No. He's got a loan business on the side."

"No kidding." I wondered if the feds were aware and forgot to mention that small factoid to us. Or maybe they assumed because I was an enrolled member of the tribe I already knew about tribal shit like this. Dammit. I'd really hate it if I was the only agent in the dark. "How long has this been going on?"

"My understanding is he took over the gas station from his father-in-law about five years ago, after the man had a fatal heart attack. That's when he expanded the moneylending portion of the business. Part of the appeal for borrowers is he doesn't demand cash as repayment. He'll take anything of value, which is why people go to him. And if repayment isn't made fast enough, he'll expect those who owe him to perform a task."

Sounded very much like Rollie and the favors he bargained for. "What kind of task?"

"I'm not sure. But one guy I picked up for public intoxication a few months back begged me to arrest him. He wanted a place to sleep, even in jail, where no one could harass him."

"After Elk Thunder got elected, was law enforcement worried that he'd overstep his bounds and ask the tribal cops to turn a blind eye to his activities?"

"Yes. No one in this office was happy he won the election. Our old tribal police chief, Darwin Swallow, requested early retirement. Then he moved to Arizona."

"How did Elk Thunder win?"

"Members of the tribe want to believe things would get better. There would be new jobs. There would be new houses. Better health care. Better opportunities for young people. Elk Thunder played on that, without promising it. He's pretty charismatic." She shrugged. "He didn't win by much, but it was enough."

"Any other high-profile tribal members resign a position after Elk Thunder took office?"

"Not that I'm aware of."

"I appreciate your candor, Fergie." I slipped on my coat.

"Will any agents be around tomorrow?"

"Probably not here. But if somebody races in and confesses to the murders, give Agent Turnbull or me a call at the Rapid City FBI office."

I recognized the street address Fergie gave me as being in a newer development on the outskirts of Eagle River. The Elk Thunder abode was one of the nicest houses: a brick ranch style, with a two-car garage and a circular driveway in front. A chain-link fence ran down both sides of the house, keeping critters and trespassers out of the backyard.

I parked in the circle and admired the landscape as I walked up to the front door. I rang the doorbell twice.

The door flew open, and Triscell warned, "I told you kids not to—Oh, Agent . . ."

"Gunderson," I supplied.

"Obviously, I wasn't expecting you."

"Sorry to bother you, Mrs. Elk Thunder, but I was on my way home, after an interview regarding Arlette's case, and I realized I hadn't done a follow-up interview with you."

"Do you have any leads on who killed Arlette?"

"Not yet. Your husband asked the same question." I inched closer to the door, wanting a peek at the presidential palace. "Is he home?"

"Yes, but he's on the phone. Tribal council business. It can take hours."

So much for my testing the water and hitting him up for a loan. "Ah." I stared at her long enough that she realized she hadn't invited me inside.

"Sorry, come in."

I suspected I wouldn't make it off the tiled foyer. But I could see the room beyond the fake marble arches. No colorful Indian artwork or decor anywhere in the living area. The entire room—from the couches to the end tables to the carpet to the walls—was white: hues ranging from pristine white, to off-white, to vanilla, to cream. I wondered what Rollie would say about that. "You have a lovely home."

"Thank you. We've worked hard for it. No one knows how much energy it takes to own a business."

I made appropriate affirmative noises.

"So are you here because that other girl was found dead?" she asked. "And are the cases connected?"

"That's what we're working on." I blathered about some random, pointless procedural stuff until I sensed her impatience. Then I pulled a Columbo, smiling before I apologized for rambling. "Oh, one more thing before I let you get back to what you were doing. I understand you're an herbalist, using traditional Native American herbs?"

"I dabble. Why?"

"I have friends who dabble, too. It seems there'd be a lot of different things to store and to remember. What ingredients can be mixed together, and what cannot be mixed together. Do you have a special area where you work?"

She leaned against the wall, more at ease. "No, I work in the kitchen. There's really not that much to mix, since I make small batches for my own use."

"Small batches of what?"

"Facial products. Natural ointments for sore muscles."

I nodded. "I love arnica gel. Did Arlette ever use any of your natural products?"

"No."

"Nothing? That's unfortunate. I hope your husband takes advantage of your herbal expertise."

She smiled. "Oh, he does. He knows just as much about herbs and cures as I do."

Bingo. "Do you concoct herbal teas? I know Sophie was always trying to get me to drink her rose hip and marshmallow root tea." *Such a liar, Mercy.*

Triscell's smile faded. "I don't see how that's relevant."

I'd hit a nerve. But for teas? "It's probably not. Well, except for the fact Arlette had poison in her body. Digitalis? Ever heard of it? Nasty stuff."

"Are you accusing me of poisoning my niece? Because if that's your assumption, I can assure you that your commander at the FBI will get—"

"No, ma'am, I'm not accusing you of anything. I'm just asking. This information didn't come up until after you'd been in the tribal PD, and we've not had a chance to speak to you or your husband about it, since he slapped us with a no-contact order where you're concerned."

Her eyes turned frosty. "Latimer did that? Well, I certainly had no knowledge of it. And I wouldn't have agreed with his decision. Death is too common around here, and you can ignore it until it happens to your family." She straightened her spine. "So ask your questions, because I've got nothing to hide."

Maybe she didn't, but I'd bet her husband did. "Since our findings indicated the poison was in something Arlette ingested, we want to cover all avenues. Especially with teens putting crazy stuff in hookahs and smoking it. Or mixing up more potent energy drinks." I paused. "Arlette didn't show an interest in learning traditional natural herbal remedies from you? Or would that be something she'd try on her own? And maybe she'd accidentally screwed it up by using the wrong herb?"

"I don't keep foxglove on hand just for that reason."

"Oh, smart."

"Not that it matters. If food didn't come prepackaged, or wasn't full of fat, salt, and sugar, she wouldn't eat it. Arlette had an aversion to anything natural."

I wondered if this woman had made her niece feel fat, or like a freak. In that moment I had a pang of sorrow for Arlette and Verline. I took two steps back. "Thank you for your time, Mrs. Elk Thunder. If you have any questions how the case is progressing, don't hesitate to contact Carsten McGillis, your FBI victim specialist."

Agent Turnbull wasn't in the office the next day, so I couldn't share my interesting findings about Latimer's business practices and Triscell Elk

Thunder's herbalist skills. And because I'd already been reamed for not sharing information in a timely manner, I tried calling him, but he didn't pick up. I learned from Frances that he was stuck in court.

The following day, I'd had several cases to follow up on that weren't related to the murder cases in Eagle River. One involving a wiretap of an alleged member of a biker gang and his threats against a judge. Another involving the placement of a witness in protective custody with the U.S. Marshals Service in preparation for testimony in a federal case.

By the time I caught up with Turnbull in the conference room right before lunch, I wished I'd steered clear of him. Talk about manic highs and lows. I found myself biting my tongue so as not to ask if he'd taken his bipolar meds.

When I tried to relay what I'd pieced together, Shay waved me off. "None of that matters now."

"None of the work I did on these cases for the last two days matters? Really? Even if it changes the course of the investigation?"

His eyes narrowed. "Did you get a confession from someone?"

"No, but—"

"Then like I said, your busywork doesn't matter."

Busywork? Man, he was a total asshole today. "So?"

"*So,* is Rollie Rondeaux on your suspect list?"

"No, but that's—"

"The problem. Rollie is your friend, and he played you, Mercy. Don't you see that?"

Shay's arrogance kicked my belligerence into high gear. "By telling me about the string of suspicious deaths that'd gone unnoticed by the tribal police? That's playing me? Because I consider the initial information Rollie provided crucial to this case. No one in the tribal PD or the FBI connected the dots—"

"Until *he* told you to look for the connection," Shay snapped. "He told you there'd be more deaths. And doesn't that strike you as odd, Agent Gunderson? That Mr. Rondeaux, a man who's made no bones about his hatred for law enforcement on any level, was suddenly helping us? Then the next victim just happens to be his domestic partner? Coincidental and convenient, don't you think?"

Turnbull's implication was wrong. I'd witnessed the look on Rollie's face after he'd seen what'd been done to Verline. He'd masked it quickly, but that type of horrified anguish couldn't have been faked.

I dropped my hands behind my back so Shay couldn't see me clenching my fists. "So you still believe Rollie killed Arlette to throw everyone off, just so he could get rid of Verline? Bullshit."

"Do you have any proof besides your gut instinct, Agent Gunderson?"

"I'm not discounting the tribal president as a suspect. Too many tribal members don't like him, which makes me wonder if the election was rigged because the margin was so close. I can't fit it all together yet, but he's too slick. He didn't miss a beat after Arlette was found dead, and he was far too eager to pin his niece's murder on Rollie Rondeaux *before* Verline's body had even cooled."

"So the tribal president . . . what? Offed his niece because she was a nuisance? Then he aced his political rival's lover to throw suspicion onto Rollie for *both* murders? Huh-uh. Not buying it."

"What about the fact Verline's body was found at the dump? Is it coincidence that Bigs Bigelow owns that land? And he supported Latimer Elk Thunder's opponent for tribal president? This is the second body with that common thread. You're saying it's just a coincidence?"

"Maybe it's *too* coincidental." Shay studied me. "How much do you know about Rollie's background in the marines during Vietnam?"

"Enough to know that he did what he had to do to survive war. He did what he was ordered to do, no different than the rest of us who took orders from Uncle Sam. Besides, how do *you* know anything about his background? Military service records are sealed." I'd always suspected Shay had accessed mine, and when I saw the brief gleam in his eye, I knew that checking up on Rollie wasn't the first time he'd crossed the line.

He gave me that cool-eyed stare.

"Okay, Special Agent Turnbull, why don't you tell me your suspects? Since you've exhausted and discounted all of my theories."

Shay poured himself a glass of water. He drank, jotted something in his notebook, and then turned it toward me.

Two words were on the paper, in bold letters:

ROLLIE RONDEAUX.

"He's my only suspect. He had a twofold purpose in killing Arlette. To prove to his son that when he gives an ultimatum about family rivals and alliances, he expects it to be followed. And to dick with Latimer Elk Thunder.

"You told me Rollie warned there would be other dead women on the rez. And a week later his young girlfriend is dead? He doesn't have an alibi. He suspects his son was sleeping with his girlfriend. He cut off her hand as a symbol of biting the hand that feeds you. He cut out her tongue because she knew that he'd killed Arlette and he suspected she'd blab. And you told me that Rollie is familiar with native herbal medicine. Verline had far more marks from being restrained than Arlette did, which indicated she struggled harder, which I attribute to her being intimately acquainted with her attacker. In each instance, Rollie had means, motive, and opportunity. That puts a check mark next to every single thing on my list, which confirms him as a suspect." He pointed at me with his pen. "See, Agent Gunderson, you let your personal feelings for him color your judgment."

"And you let your hatred for him color yours."

That comment caught him off guard. "I don't hate him. But I don't trust him. I know he's been on the wrong side of the law for years, and everyone always looks the other way. He's not some harmless old man, Mercy."

"I never claimed he was." My frustration with Turnbull's refusal to consider other suspects definitely put starch in my tone. "While I'm looking elsewhere, you'll be building a case against Rollie?"

"No need to look elsewhere. Rollie Rondeaux is guilty. I've already built the case. We've got enough probable cause to ask the assistant U.S. attorney to take this case to the grand jury."

My mouth dropped open. "How can we possibly have enough evidence to ask for an indictment?"

"We'll ask for this to be presented to the grand jury for investigation. That way we can serve a warrant to Rollie's son, Junior Rondeaux. We'll serve a warrant to the tribal president, Latimer Elk Thunder. We'll use your testimony regarding what he told you after the first murder victim was discovered but before the second victim turned up. Rollie has firsthand knowledge of herbal medicine, and we can obtain a search warrant for his residence. That should be enough for an indictment and his subsequent arrest to stand trial."

My stomach acid turned my morning oatmeal into sour mash. I'd have to give sworn testimony against Rollie.

"We're taking this to the assistant U.S. attorney after morning court adjourns."

The action had already been decided before I'd entered the building.

Shay's cell phone pealed. "Turnbull. Yes. What? No, you're kidding, right?" Pause. He stood abruptly. "When? How the hell is that even possible? No, fuck that. What are our options . . . Sorry? Yes, sir. No, sir. I understand. Yes, I appreciate the call."

Shay hung up. He stalked to the window and squeezed his cell phone so hard that cracking plastic echoed in the room.

"What's going on?"

"Director Shenker was just informed by the Eagle River tribal PD that they arrested Rollie Rondeaux last night on a charge unrelated to our cases. They're holding him in the tribal jail."

Confused, I asked, "Which means what?"

"He's locked up tight. A tribal member, accused of committing a misdemeanor crime on tribal land, falls under the jurisdiction of the tribal court system, not the federal system. We can't forcibly extradite him until he's faced a tribal judge and been convicted or acquitted. It's within the tribal police's purview to keep Rollie incarcerated until he's brought before a tribal judge. And since there's no due process in the tribal court system, Rollie is out of our reach. Indefinitely."

A jurisdictional pissing match. How fun. "But Rollie has to stay in the tribal jail, right? It's not like he can post bond and roam around free on the reservation?"

Turnbull gawked at me like I had a screw loose. "That's hardly the point, Mercy."

"*You're* missing the point, Shay. Rollie is locked up, out of society. If he is guilty of a couple of gruesome murders, then he won't be committing any more from behind bars. The residents of the reservation are safe from him and his murderous ways."

Another arch look from him.

"Is this just about you wanting the collar? Putting another feather in your federal cap so you can get the hell out of this two-bit FBI office and back to a real division office where you belong?" I taunted him.

He meandered toward me, snakelike. I held myself very still, half expecting to see a forked tongue before venom-tipped fangs ripped a chunk out of me.

"Be smart, Gunderson. Be a team player. And if you haven't figured it out? It's very much us versus them when it comes to tribal politics and jurisdiction. They're more than willing to take our help, but they rarely extend the same helping hand. This is a slap down. The tribal police are proving they've got all the power."

I'd hoped I'd left this political jostling behind when I'd left the army. "So what now?"

"Now we see if we can assist Flack and Mested with their sex ring case, involving interstate trafficking of minors, child pornography . . . You think reading obituaries for a couple of days was bad? What you see and read today will make you question why you became an FBI agent in the first place."

Too late. I was already questioning it. "Lead the way. Beings you're the senior agent and all."

Another scowl. "Give me a minute to find my—"

"FBI-mandated anger management course materials?"

He flashed his teeth. "Back the fuck off, Gunderson. But if you wanna see me in a killing rage? By all means, stick around."

I'd had enough of his male posturing. I poked him twice on the chest, right below his snappy turquoise bolo tie. "You don't scare me. You never have. So don't even fucking try."

Evidently, the guys in conference room two had heard our exchange. They were mighty quiet when we entered the room.

Good.

14

I didn't share my after-work plans with Turnbull. He'd argue. Blather on about the FBI's role, and mine.

The sporadic bouts of snow on the drive home were irritating. Just enough of the white stuff fell from the sky to cover the ground, but not enough to mask the barrenness of winter fields.

The jail was on the bottom level of the tribal PD building. The space wasn't much different from any other jail I'd been in, with the exception of the Iraq prisons, which were little more than latrines.

A harried woman around my age inspected me. "Visiting hours ended at five."

I slid the lanyard bearing my federal ID into the metal tray.

Her gaze dropped to my right hip. "You're not carrying, are you Special Agent Gunderson?"

"No, ma'am."

"Sign in, please. Who are you here for?"

"Rollie Rondeaux."

"Mr. Rondeaux has requested no visitors."

"He'll see me." I smiled. "I'll wait over here until I'm cleared through."

The pamphlets in the waiting area shouldn't have amused me, but they did. How to cope with having a loved one in jail. The importance of family during a prisoner's incarceration. Advice on how to support the person behind bars, while disapproving of the crime committed.

I circled the coffee table, piled with magazines, and stopped in front of the map that detailed the borders of the Eagle River Reservation.

"Agent Gunderson?"

I whirled around. "Yes?"

"Mr. Rondeaux will see you. At the buzzer, enter on the right."

A loud buzz, and then the sound of locks disengaging.

I stepped into a small room with a state-of-the-art full-body X-ray machine. A voice instructed me, "Feet shoulder width apart, arms at your sides, take a breath and hold it."

Beeeep.

"All clear. Exit through the rear door, Agent Gunderson."

Another buzzing sound and more locks disengaging. I found my-self in one of those rooms like on TV, where individual cubicles were separated by pegboard walls. A Plexiglas wall divided the two spaces. A phone hung on the right on each side.

The dingy gray-walled opposite room was empty.

A steel door opened, and a guard led an orange-jumpsuit-wearing, handcuffed Rollie into the room.

The guard pointed at the center section, and I sat.

Rollie plopped into the chair across from me. The guard didn't undo his handcuffs. He didn't leave after he'd handed Rollie the phone, either, but took the chair by the door and leafed through a magazine.

Surprisingly, Rollie didn't look bad.

"Wasn't expecting to see you, hey," he said.

"That's my goal in life. To defy expectations."

He snorted.

"Dare I ask how you are?"

"Been better." He rested his elbows on the counter, hunching over like an old man. That was the only way he could hold the receiver in both hands. "They spent a couple hours goin' over the rules. But it ain't like I got freedom to make any choices, so it was kinda pointless. I scrubbed the bathrooms upstairs in the cop shop. Guess that's my daily duty. I also gotta mop in here tonight and clean the windows." He paused.

"What?"

"Which Mercy am I lookin' at right now?"

"Do you mean am I here as a fed? Or as your friend?" I noticed his grip on the receiver tightened. "I'm here as your friend, old man."

Rollie nodded. "Don't got many of them."

"So what did you do that landed you in the tribal jail?"

"Ran a Stop sign. Didn't realize I had a cop behind me for about two miles, 'cause I ain't got a rearview mirror and the side mirrors are cracked. Got me for evading arrest. When I got here, they made a big stinkin' issue about my parking tickets."

"How many tickets are we talking?"

"Fifty-seven."

"Seriously? You were issued that many tickets in a year?"

Rollie shook his head. "Been a coupla years. They ain't all mine, but they're for cars registered to me. Or stolen from me." He shrugged. "Ain't my fault, but there's nothin' I can do. Tribal cops been waitin' to get their hands on me for a while, so I'm pretty sure they're gonna let me rot in here."

That's when I realized Turnbull's suspicions were somewhat correct. Rollie's arrest *was* to keep him on the reservation and out of federal hands. It wasn't even a power play on the part of the tribal police; it was Rollie's. Smart move. It didn't convince me of his guilt in not wanting to be brought up on federal charges for killing Verline and Arlette.

"Who arrested you?"

"Spotted Bear. That power-hungry bastard."

How long had Officer Spotted Bear owed Rollie a favor?

Rollie tipped his head back, and I saw a cut on top of a bruise right under his jawline. "He even punched me. Course, he's telling everyone I *slipped.*" He snorted. "The whole department had a good laugh at me on my knees today, scrubbing their shit from the toilet."

"I honestly don't know what to say to that."

His brown eyes turned shrewd. "Does Turnbull know you're here?"

"No, I had to flash my badge to get in, since I missed visiting hours."

"You gonna be in trouble, Mercy girl?"

"Probably. Nothin' I can't handle."

"I'm sure he's brought up some of the bad things I did over there a long time ago. I'm not that same gung-ho marine kid, following orders.

I'm an old man." Agony and sadness flitted across his face. "I didn't do that to Verline. I don't even know what was done to the other girl, and they think I was responsible."

If I'd entertained—however briefly—any serious thought that Rollie might've killed Verline, it ended in that moment. I recognized that grief, where the numbness of shock would be preferable to the sharp-edged feeling of constant pain. I *knew* in my gut, in my bones, and in my soul that he wasn't guilty.

"Rollie," I said his name softly so he looked at me. "I never thought you did it."

"Then you are the only one. Even my son . . ." He held the phone away and coughed. Like he had a bad taste in his mouth. "Sorry. That kid. Always working an angle. I'd be proud of him if he wasn't so stupid."

"What's up with the no-visitors rule?"

"Ain't nobody I wanna see. And unless I refuse to see everyone, then they can make me see anyone who shows up."

"Anyone in particular you're avoiding, besides Junior?"

Rollie studied me. "Ask the question you came here for, hey. You know this dancin' around the subject stuff just ticks me off."

I smiled at the flash of grumpy Rollie. Now that I knew in my gut Rollie was innocent, I could move on to the other reason I'd come. "Devlin Pretty Horses owes you money."

He nodded.

"I heard you say he also owes Saro money."

Another nod.

"Did he borrow money from Latimer Elk Thunder, too?"

A cold stare. "Ain't smart messing in this."

"I don't have a choice. I have to sort what's relevant and what isn't. Are you and Latimer in competition for loan customers?"

He shook his head. "I ain't gonna claim to be altruistic, but my customers don't use the money they borrow from me for gambling."

"So Devlin didn't blow the cash you lent him at the casino?"

"He assured me the money was for specialized cancer-treatment drugs for Penny. I believed him. It was a way of helping her because . . ." He cleared his throat. "That part don't matter. I found out he'd lied to me that night at your place."

"How'd you find out?"

"From talking to Penny. She asked if I had herbal remedies that'd stop the queasiness. I suggested a couple of mixes, including . . . ah, peyote. She said the peyote Devlin had bought for her didn't help much, and he'd smoked it all anyway."

My mouth dropped open. "*That* was Devlin's specialized cancer-treatment drug? Po—peyote?"

Rollie's voice dropped another octave. "And who is the peyote distributor around here?"

Saro.

"I don't like lookin' like a chump. But Latimer don't mind, 'cause he's still handing Devlin money any time he asks. Something is up with that, but I can't figure it out. Part of me don't wanna know because it ain't pretty where my thoughts have gone. Saro got paid for the goods he provided Devlin. But Devlin owes him cash from before Victor got whacked. John-John's bailed Devlin out with Saro before."

"He has?"

"Yes. Why do you think Saro started showing up at Clementine's all the time? Because he could."

Jesus. My head was spinning. How could I have not known *any* of this?

"Saro is a dangerous man. But don't discount Latimer. Saro don't pretend to be something he's not. Latimer is just as much a thug as Saro. He just uses more snake oil to look polished. And Saro ain't got nothin' on Latimer when it comes to dealing out payback."

Neither of us said anything for a minute or two.

I considered changing the tone of the conversation, filling the dead air with talk of Dawson and Lex. But it seemed trite.

"Mercy."

I glanced up from staring at the bottom of the partition. "What?"

"You gotta find out who killed her."

"That's what we're trying—"

"Don't feed me that federal-line bullshit. They stopped lookin' for the killer after they made up their minds it was me, huh?"

Took about ten seconds, but I nodded.

"I didn't tell you about the deaths of women on the rez before Verline was killed for any reason besides you are observant in a way most folks ain't. You see things others can't. Or won't."

I'd take his compliment. My most important lesson in sniper training was taking time to observe everything around me. To be patient. To be aware of the obvious, but to become a student of the obscure. But it wasn't like him to dole out positive reinforcement, so I was immediately suspicious. "Rollie, if you know who's responsible and you're keeping it to yourself for some scorecard or to go vigilante—"

"I'm not. I'd tell you if I knew. I'm too damn old to take on someone that smart. Because, mark my words, whoever is doin' this is one smart SOB. If you find this person? Then you and me? We're square."

I'd wondered what it would take to clear my markers with him. Working for him hadn't done it. And I'd be glad to have the debt erased because I didn't like owing anyone anything.

The guard pushed to his feet, and I knew our time was over.

Rollie said, "Be careful, Mercy girl. But be ruthless. That's all this twisted fuck knows. Don't hold nothin' back."

"Take care, Rollie."

I probably should've gone home. But I wanted a drink and a chance to clear my head before I had to slap on a happy face for Mason and Lex.

Clementine's was off my list of watering holes. I understood Penny's health issues were adding pressure to John-John's life, but if I'd behaved like him, he would've read me the riot act. Maybe this was an indication that our friendship had always been one-sided.

It was a quiet night on the road between Eagle River and Eagle Ridge. Perfect road conditions to make my Viper go fast. The one time I'd taken the dust tarp off her after I'd returned from Virginia had nearly resulted in Dawson arresting me. That thought made me smile.

I pulled into Stillwell's. Last time I'd been in the joint I'd ended up in a bar fight. Not my fault. But trouble trailed after me like a forsaken lover.

But I wasn't drowning my sorrows tonight. I'd have one drink, a bowl of pretzels, and I'd take time to reflect on the information I'd just learned from Rollie. I chose to sit in a booth in the back. After I received my beer, I took a healthy gulp and closed my eyes.

The gut feeling the FBI told me to discount got stronger. I'd been distracted by several incidents over the course of the last two weeks—but my gut instinct hadn't ever failed me.

"Mercy?"

I opened my eyes and saw Sheldon War Bonnet at the edge of the table. Of all the people to run into tonight. "Sheldon."

"You drinking alone?"

Like that was a bad thing. "No, I'm meeting someone."

"I'll keep you company for a bit. I'm meeting someone myself." And bold as brass, Sheldon just slid across from me with his drink.

I tried not to gulp my beer, resigning myself to making polite chatter for at least two minutes. Five tops.

"I haven't seen you in here before." Sheldon groaned. "That probably sounded like a cheesy pickup line."

It did. Creeped me out a little. "I don't come in here much. Used to be my dad's hangout. Clementine's is more my speed. Although I don't have nearly as much free time as I used to."

"Working in the FBI isn't a nine-to-five job?"

I shrugged. "Some days. It's all still new. Still trying to put the training theories into practice."

Sheldon smiled. "Kind of like being in the military. They train you to be prepared for all contingencies, but not all soldiers get to put those skills into practice."

Hah. Wrong. I had a chance to use damn near everything I'd been taught and then some. "Remind me what service branch you were in again?"

His smile tightened. "Army National Guard. Seventy-second CST out of Lincoln, Nebraska. I handled internal communication."

"Oh." I scrambled to find something positive to say. Because an internal communications clerk with a guard unit and a black-ops soldier were light-years away in skill sets. "CST. Stands for Civilian Support Team, right? So I'll bet your unit didn't see any action?"

He shook his head. "We had heavy training for four years in order to receive the CST designation, and all positions within the company were frozen. No new members signed in, none were allowed to sign out. Basically, by receiving the CST, we were permanently grounded as a unit."

"That's the way it goes. We finished one tour—expecting we'd get a four-to-six-month reprieve stateside—but four weeks later, we were eating sand in another desert hot spot. Not fun."

"Some of us would've given a left nut to see any action." He sipped from his bottle of Michelob Ultra. "Did you get to use what they taught us in basic training?"

"I was in transportation, so I saw my share of IEDs."

"I meant, did you get to fire M60s at hostiles? Engage in small-arms fire?" He paused. "Sorry. For a second I forgot the army's directive about keeping women out of combat roles. You probably had to hunker down in your truck and ride out any firefights, right?"

Trying to get a rise out of me by bringing limitations of gender into the conversation? Combat jealousy was a reality with National Guard units that hadn't been called to serve in any overseas capacity during war. I forced a laugh. "Hunker down and ride the storm out. Yeah, something like that."

"Is this loser bothering you?"

I did a double take at seeing John-John at the end of the table. Then I did another double take when I realized that the loser in question John-John meant . . . was me. What the hell? I'd had enough of his insults. I drained my beer before I was tempted to toss it in his face.

Sheldon said, "Watch the insults, John-John. Rumor is, Mercy is one tough chick."

"I take it you two know each other?" I asked.

John-John said, "Can't get nothin' past you, Miz FBI Bloodhound. Sheldon and I went to high school together."

Whoa. I never would've guessed that. Sheldon looked at least a decade older than John-John.

"I'm surprised you two are drinking buddies," John-John said, his gaze winging between us.

"We're not. I've spent time in the tribal archives over the last couple of weeks. I was waiting for Dawson to show up, and Sheldon joined me. What are you doing here?"

"On my way to my mom's. *Unci* don't let her drink, which is dumb, since Mom's got cancer, so I hafta sneak her a bottle. I remembered halfway to the rez I'd forgotten it at the bar. I pulled in and noticed your truck in the lot. Was gonna point out how easily you change your loyalties."

"I've been banned from Clementine's for a month, as you'll recall. It'd serve you right if I found a new place to drink," I retorted. "And *they* have happy-hour specials here."

"I'd be over the moon if you found a new place to fight," John-John shot back. "Lord, Mercy, most of my regulars haven't been in the number of bar fights in their lifetimes that you have been in the last year."

"Most of those fights came when I was working for you, *winkte*."

We locked gazes, daring each other to take this argument one step further, because we always did. But were we really going to cross the next line?

"John-John, I was sorry to hear your mother has cancer," Sheldon said, breaking the ugly silence.

John-John tore his gaze from mine. "How'd you find out?"

"Eagle River is a small place, and I worked with her at the tribal HQ, remember? To have this happen right after she retired?" Sheldon shook his head. "Sad, man. I heard she's had a rough go of it."

"It was bad for a while there, but it seems to be getting better. Her appetite is back. She's even getting some exercise."

"So she's not flipping you and Sophie the bird?" I asked jokingly.

"Reminding you that she's lived her life on her own terms and she'll die on her own terms, too?"

"That's really not your business, now that Sophie don't work for you, is it? None of us hafta worry that *Unci* is blabbing family secrets to folks that ain't family." John-John stepped back. "I gotta get."

Whoa. He'd taken that completely wrong. I scooted out of the booth. "Looks like my man stood me up, so I'm gonna go home—"

"And pick a fight with him?" John-John supplied with a sneer.

"Piss off."

We walked through the door that separated the bar side from the package liquor side.

John-John ordered a bottle of raspberry vodka and inspected me, from my ponytail to the tips of my hiking boots. "You look more like a cop every time I see you."

"I'm not a cop."

He shrugged. "FBI. Deputy. Highway patrol. BIA. Tribal police. MP. Different names, but all types of cops."

"And what? We can't be friends now because of my job? That's why you've been such a dick since I got back from Quantico? I don't ever hear from you. Not a word, John-John. And when I do see you? You're rude, insulting, or looking for an exit sign. So I wanna know what gives."

He slid a twenty across the counter, waiting until his order was packaged before he spoke to me. "I've been busy."

"I don't doubt that. But that's not it. And you're not one to back down from speaking your mind."

"You're right." His eyes went cold and flat. "You want it straight up? Or sugarcoated?"

"When have I ever needed a fucking spoonful of sugar?"

"Fine. Right after you got back, I had a vision."

"About what?" I paused. "Me? And I'm in danger or something?"

"No. *I* am."

"I don't understand."

"According to this vision, being around you puts me in danger."

My mouth dropped open so far it almost hit my chest.

John-John stared at me. "So you can see why I've kept my distance."

"Bullshit. I can see you've used it as an excuse to blow me off."

"Can you blame me?" John-John shot back. "Given you're always stumbling over dead bodies?"

"Are there dead bodies in this vision?" I demanded, fighting a burst of anger and embarrassment. My curse, or whatever the fuck it was, hadn't manifested itself for months. I hated he'd thrown it in my face because he knew how much the discovery that I had some *woo-woo* mystic Indian shit inside me had freaked me out.

"Yes. More than one body, Mercy."

"You've always said visions were subject to interpretation."

"Not this time."

"What is this horrible vision? I bust into your bar with an AK-47 and unload? Kill you and all your customers? Then sit on the bar chugging free whiskey, singing 'Don't Worry, Be Happy' while admiring my killing spree?"

He rolled his eyes. "Overly dramatic much?"

"Overly evasive much?" I countered.

That pushed his buttons. John-John didn't get in my face like I expected. He gave me a sneering once-over. "You're not in the vision. You *are* the vision. A heavy black cloud that descends over everything. Over everyone I care about. Muskrat, Mom, *Unci,* Uncle Devlin . . . Black means death. There's no misinterpretation. Even Sophie couldn't argue with it."

I felt like he'd whacked me in the stomach with a two-by-four. It all made sense now. Muskrat steering clear of me. John-John banning me from the bar. Sophie's abrupt departure.

I'd jokingly called myself a pariah. Now I was one.

Or was he blowing smoke?

John-John's eyes continued to bore into me. "You think I'm lying?"

"No. I just want to make sure the heavy black cloud you're seeing is me, not a shadow of someone else."

"Like who?"

I paused for effect. "Like Saro."

His intense gaze darted away.

"You know, I'd wondered why he picked Clementine's, almost out of the blue, as his new hangout. But I thought I'd probably just missed something in my drunken haze after Levi died." I got in his face. "Did you really think there'd be no repercussions after dealing with a psychotic fucker like Saro? Even if you were doing Devlin a favor by paying off his debt? No wonder you kicked me out of your bar and cut me out of your life. You're embarrassed because Saro owns you now."

"No one owns me," he snapped. "And this high-and-mighty I'm-an-FBI-agent attitude is why I don't want you around, Mercy. Go ahead. Convince yourself you're not the danger to my family. But I know better."

"Do you? Because the most dangerous person to your family right now is not me."

"It's Saro?" he asked sarcastically.

"No, it's Devlin."

Without another word, I turned and walked off. My hand shook so hard I dropped my keys before I could get my truck unlocked. Resting my forehead on the window of the driver's-side door, I forced myself to take long, deep breaths.

The drive home was a blur.

At least the dogs were happy to see me. I must've stayed outside a long time, because Mason came looking for me. But he didn't crowd me, demanding the affection he usually did, so I must've been giving off some dark vibes.

I'm just the little black rain cloud of death.

I whipped the slobbery tennis ball as hard as I could.

"Rough day?"

"Yeah."

"I heard about Rollie getting locked up."

"I'm probably in deep shit with Turnbull since I went to see Rollie at the jail."

Butch bounded back with his prize, nearly bowling me over with his doggy pride. Shoonga, not to be outdone, hip checked me with his head. Damn dogs could always make me smile, even when I didn't want to—but not today.

"What's really going on? Something with your job?"

"No, and I'm not just saying that because it's something I can't talk about. It's . . . really stupid, probably, but it's been digging into me like a burr, and now it's beginning to fester."

"Tell me what it is, or I'll nag you like Sophie did."

"Ironic that you should mention Sophie. She's part of it." I told him about John-John's vision. I hated how my voice wavered, so I added some profanity that'd make a SEAL blush. But I got it all out without breaking down.

He let me wallow for a minute after I finished. Then he trapped my face in his hands and forced me to look at him. "Fuck him. You bring happiness and light into my life, Mercy. Into a lot of other people's lives, too. If they wanna believe that *woo-woo* Indian bullshit, let 'em. But you don't have to buy into it. You don't need a friend like that."

"Thank you."

Dawson pulled me into his arms. "That said . . . since you're running low on friends, does that mean you're gonna marry me pretty soon? 'Cause people are starting to talk. They're saying that you're just using me for sex."

I smiled. "You're gonna be shocked as hell one of these days when I actually say yes and demand a huge freakin' diamond, Dawson."

"Nah. The real way to cement the deal is to buy you a huge freakin' gun." He kissed me with that combination of sweetness, steadiness, and total acceptance that I craved. "How long's it been since you target shot?" he murmured. "Take some time tomorrow with your favorite guns and a whole pile of ammo. That'll cure what ails you."

The man knew me so well.

15

It was a long week at work, because we hadn't turned up any new information on either case and Shay and I were both on edge. Turnbull hadn't said *boo* about my visit to my jailbird friend last Friday.

I returned to the reservation Thursday night to attend Verline's wake. The church was packed, and I scooted into the back pew.

Nothing could've prepared me for what unfolded.

Drums pounding. Sage burning. Verline's family breaking into spontaneous tremolo—similar to a male's war cry but more sorrowful. It didn't feel like a church service. Kids running in and out and shouting in the aisle. The constant hum of adult conversation. People laughing. People wailing. People passing objects around. All four corners of the room had some activity. If alcohol was legal on the rez, I imagined there'd be a bar.

Four poster boards with pictures of Verline, the edges decorated with vibrant artificial flowers and pieces of hair, were on easels in an arc around the sparkling white casket. A closed casket. People would wander up to look at the pictures, move to the next set. Maybe a friend or a kid would join someone in the progression. They'd hug. Laugh. Cry. Then move on.

If I gleaned anything from this event, it was the move-on attitude. So Verline was dead. Death happens. I couldn't decide if that was a healthy attitude or a callous one.

It bothered me that Rollie couldn't be here. He'd stare down the haters. He'd ignore Verline's family and his own children, and focus on what mattered: honoring Verline in his own way.

I was still in the minority believing in Rollie's innocence. Where Shay saw similarities, I saw coincidences that seemed off—almost staged. Maybe if I broke protocol and talked to Dawson, he could give me the insight I was lacking.

All of a sudden everyone got up and started clapping. Pie tins were passed around as noisemakers.

What the hell? Had I been transported to a Baptist revival?

With the loud voices, the cloying smell of Indian tacos, and the scent of greasy fry bread floating up from the basement, the screaming kids, the noisemakers, and the heat from too many bodies in too small a space, I felt a panic attack coming on.

Not now. Not when I wasn't near anything that could serve as a talisman to ground me—like a bottle of Wild Turkey, a yoga mat, a long stretch of road, or Dawson. I was pushed and jostled as I forged a path to the red EXIT sign above the door. I thought I caught a glimpse of Junior, but he vanished in a sea of mourning revelers.

Shoving open the door, I sucked in lungs full of crisp air, using the quiet and the cold as my calming influence.

Every time I attended an event on the reservation, whether it was a powwow or a funeral, I had a serious sense of discomfort about my Indian heritage. I'd never considered myself Indian. Not out of shame, but out of ignorance. During my childhood, my mother's Minneconjou Sioux ancestry wasn't mentioned in our household. From what I'd remembered of her physical appearance, she'd never looked Indian, not the way Sophie, Jake, and Rollie looked Indian. Now, enrolling in the tribe seemed like a farce. I had no freakin' clue what it meant to be *part* Indian.

Had my mother's dismissal of her heritage meant I'd missed out on knowing an essential part of who I was?

You can't miss what you never had. And definitely not what you don't understand.

Halfway across the gravel parking lot, weaving between cars, I heard footsteps behind me. I turned around.

No one. Just my paranoia.

I quickened my pace, relieved to reach my pickup. Relieved—until

I found my face smashed up against the window and some douche bag twisting my arm up my back.

"I hear you've been talkin' shit about me."

Saro.

Despite the immediate panic flooding my body, I managed a terse, "Let me go."

He laughed that high-pitched girlish laugh that chilled my blood. "Say please."

I threw my head back at the same time I rolled my shoulders into his hold, and kicked the side of his knee. I didn't knock him down or bust his nose, but I got him to release me. I spun around and faced him, crouching into a defensive stance.

Another laugh. "I don't fight women. I fuck them. And a feisty bitch like you ain't my type." His gaze zeroed in on my mouth. "Although . . . seeing a chick bleed does add appeal."

Lucky me. I wiped the blood from my lip. "What do you want?"

"Same thing you do."

Your head on a spike and your teeth on my key chain? Nah. "Which is what?"

"The murder cases solved."

"I'd be happy to take you to the tribal PD if you want to talk to someone about your concerns for your personal safety."

"Think you're funny, doncha? I don't think it's funny that the feds are here on the rez all the time. The BIA sends a new rep, then the DEA wants to know why the feds and the BIA are sniffing around. Makes it hard for a man to do business."

"Yeah. Scaling back on selling drugs to kids is a real bitch, ain't it?"

His eyes were flat black pools. "I've got a blade, and you know I ain't afraid to use it."

Yikes. I tamped down the sarcasm. "So here's my question, Barry. Did you use that sharp tanto blade to hack off Verline's tongue and hand after you killed her?"

"Why would I waste effort killing her?"

When I pressed my back into the door of my pickup, Saro edged closer. His looming presence and deadly stare were intimidating, but not as frightening as when he'd held a knife to my throat. The scars he'd left were faint, but I knew they were there. And he knew they were there. "Because Verline and Cherelle were cousins. Maybe Verline lied to you about something regarding Cherelle. Or maybe Verline stole something from you. Chopping off body parts seems your style." Crap. *No sarcasm, remember, Mercy?*

He gave me a lunatic grin. My insides quivered with fear. "Efficiency is more important than style. People find what I want them to find. Only a fuckin' amateur would be so blatant, so don't insult me by assuming I had anything to do with them two little bitches getting sliced and diced. And ain't Rollie Rondeaux in jail for the murders?"

"He was arrested on unrelated charges."

"Why am I on your personal suspect list?"

I wondered who'd told him: Junior? John-John? "Because you have motives for wanting both Arlette Shooting Star and Verline Dupris dead. The tribal president is pushing the tribal cops to crack down on drug deals on the rez. Killing Elk Thunder's niece sends a message the new crackdown doesn't make you happy."

"Don't matter what the tribal prez wants, or what he thinks he can tell them cops. They ain't dumb. They know who to make happy."

Meaning no one messed in Saro's business. Was that why the tribal cops refused to consider Saro a suspect? "Why did you hire Junior Rondeaux?"

"Don't push me. I don't answer your questions, you answer mine." Then Saro slammed the back of my head into the window. My vision wavered. His hand clutched the side of my face, and he dug his thumb into the cut on my lip.

Stupid church rules that wouldn't let me attend services armed. I could've shot this ass wipe twice by now. But instead, I had to play helpless because I had no way to defend myself.

"Do the feds know where Cherelle is?"

"I don't know."

He pushed harder into my bloody lip. "Don't. Lie."

It'd be difficult to speak since he wouldn't move his hand, but I wouldn't ask him to move it. "I'm not lying. DEA is handling that case. Not us." The intimate press of his body against mine kicked in my gag reflex.

"You shot the bitch who killed my brother." Not a question.

"Yes."

Saro released me. "If I wanted to prove a point to the tribal prez, I'd turn his niece into a drugged-out whore, not kill her. That way, she's making me money and shaming her family. Win-win for me."

A Sumo-looking guy, whom I assumed was Saro's henchman, appeared from out of nowhere. He glared at me, and Saro slipped away into the darkness. Then Sumo dude disappeared as well.

My mouth bled. I hated that I'd started to shake. I hated him. I yelled, "Great talking to you, Barry."

No answer. Not even Saro's stupid girly laugh echoed back to me.

You're an idiot for taunting him after you escaped with just a bloodied lip this time.

Footsteps on the gravel had me reaching for my sidearm, only to come up empty again. But it wasn't Saro sneaking up on me from another angle. It was Shay Turnbull.

He reached for my hand. "Come on."

I allowed myself to be led, mostly out of shock that Turnbull was here. Standing in the shadows watching while a psycho, murdering, drug thug pushed me around. I jerked my hand. "Let go."

Shay stopped, too. "What?"

"Is there a reason, Agent Turnbull, you just let Saro rough me up?"

He shrugged. "You had it handled."

"Handled?" I pointed to my mouth. "I'm bleeding, asshole. Couldn't you have arrested him for assaulting a federal officer or something?"

His eyes narrowed. "Jesus, Gunderson. Why are you shaking like that?"

"Because Barry Sarohutu is deranged. And the last time I crossed paths with him? He cut me. Six slices across my neck. Oh, and then he jabbed a knife into my chest, while taunting me about carving up my family members, before he choked me out. So yeah, be glad I'm just shaking and not fucking screaming."

Shay muttered, grabbed my wrist, and dragged me along behind him until we reached his Blazer; he deposited me in the passenger's-side seat.

I fumed.

He fumed.

A snap. Rustling. A tearing sound. Then a terse, "Look at me." I faced Shay, and he said, "Hold still." He dabbed at the cut with a Wet-Nap.

"Shit, that stings," I hissed.

"Suck it up, Sergeant Major. It's an antibiotic wipe. Who knows what diseases a vermin like Saro is carrying."

I closed my eyes and tried to calm myself while Shay gently cleaned me up. I felt ridiculous for letting him tend to me. I was perfectly capable of patching myself up. I opened my eyes.

"That oughta stop the bleeding and keep you from catching—"

"Asshole-itis? Douche-bag-ism?" I supplied.

Shay permitted a quick grin before he became serious. "No bullshit, Mercy. Tell me when Saro did that to you."

I looked away. I didn't ever want to relive that night.

"Maybe this will help loosen your tongue."

I glanced back to see Shay waggling a silver flask. "Really, Turnbull?"

"What? Don't all injuns carry firewater? For medicinal purposes?"

"I wouldn't know. I'm not really Indian, or so I've been told." Still, I grabbed the flask and drank deeply. Ooh. That went down smooth. No burn to this stuff. I took another swig before I handed it back. "That's definitely not Wild Turkey."

"Life's too short to drink cheap whiskey." He knocked back a slug and said, "Start talking."

I told him everything from that night.

Shay didn't respond for the longest time. Finally, he cleared his throat. "I know sorry won't cut it, but I am sorry you had to go through that.

If I'd known, I sure as hell wouldn't have let him . . ." He snatched the flask and drank. His eyes shone with fury when he looked at me. "We're not partners, but as much as we're working together we might as well be. This is something I needed to know. I can't mentor you, or do whatever this is, unless you're up front with me."

I understood where he was coming from. But there'd been no reason to mention the incident with Saro until now. I said as much.

Brooding Shay returned briefly. "Does Dawson know what happened with Saro?"

I shook my head. "Two days later I killed Anna, so we both had plenty to deal with."

"Are you going to tell him what happened tonight?"

"Probably not."

We didn't speak for several long moments.

I finally said, "What are you doing on the rez tonight?"

"Thought I'd check out Verline's wake to see who showed up."

"Aren't you convinced Rollie murdered Verline?"

"Yes, but it's looking less like he murdered Arlette Shooting Star. And the real kick in the pants? My original suggestion that the cases aren't connected would still make the most sense, if not for the digitalis found in both victims."

"I hadn't completely discounted Saro, but after tonight, he's fallen farther down the list."

"I have to agree."

"What do you know about the BIA sending a new lawman rep?"

"Nothing. I'd like to know where Saro is getting his information. Although the BIA has a presence in Eagle River, it doesn't maintain a permanent law enforcement agency. But they're quick to point out under federal statutes they can, at any time, change that."

"Awesome."

"Are you all right to drive home?"

I rolled my eyes at his insult and his abrupt dismissal. "It takes more than a couple of sips of whiskey to affect me."

"I'll remember that when we go out drinkin'."

Not if, when. Bizarre, imagining Shay and me tying one on together. "Now that you've introduced me to the good stuff, Turnbull, I won't be nearly the cheap drunk I was."

"Cheap is a state of mind. Need me to walk you to your car, Sergeant Major?"

"Need me to kick your ass?"

He snickered.

"See you tomorrow."

Dawson had left the porch light on for me.

I trudged up the porch stairs, not out of breath, but the exertion had me trying to remember the last time I'd gone for a run. Not since before the Shooting Star case. The thought of hauling my ass out of bed at five a.m. in the dark to run in the cold . . . made me shudder. But I'd rather be tired than out of shape.

When I glanced up from wiping my boots on the rug, I saw Dawson had files spread over the kitchen table. Since he didn't start gathering them up, away from my prying eyes, they weren't confidential.

He helped me take off my coat. When I looked at him, his gaze was on my swollen lip. "Don't ask."

Mason placed tender kisses all around the area. Twice. When he eased back, I said, "That was way better than a Band-Aid."

"I'll get some ice."

The house was quiet. "Where's Lex?"

"In his room."

I lifted a brow. "By choice?"

"Nope. He got mouthy. I'd had enough shit from others today, and I didn't need it from my kid. So I sent him—"

"To bed without any supper?"

"No. Smart-ass. I sent him to his room after supper. After he did the dishes, after he fed the dogs, after he took out the trash, after he vacuumed the living room, and after he cleaned the upstairs bathroom."

I whistled. "Hard-ass dad came to town."

He placed the ice pack on my mouth. "Do you think I'm too easy on him? Too buddy-buddy?"

"Not at all. He'll see how much he can get away with. Even if it's not major. Lex is a good kid, but good kids have bad days, too."

He rested his forehead to mine. "Thanks. What's on your agenda tonight?"

"A big tumbler of whiskey and a couple of episodes of *Top Shot*."

"I'll join you as soon as I finish this paperwork."

"Anything I can help you with to speed things up?"

The sheriff lifted a brow. "Really? An unsolicited offer of help?"

"I know we're not supposed to talk about our jobs, but I want you to know you *can* talk to me, if you need to."

"Same goes." Dawson returned to the table, and I noticed he had on his running clothes.

I sat across from him. "So what are you working on?"

"Double-checking incident reports. The county board has had a complaint that the ambulance crew is taking too long to respond to emergency calls. I'm compiling the data from dispatch about call time and the data from the ambulance crew about the on-scene arrival time."

"Why don't you have jiggly Jilly doing this? Or does her enormous rack get in the way of reading the paperwork on her desk?"

He grinned. "You really don't like my secretary."

"No, I don't. She's stupid. If I try to call your direct line? *Oops.* She disconnects me every time. On purpose, I'm sure." I wasn't jealous of the big-chested, blue-eyed platinum blonde. She just annoyed me with her frosted lipstick, and the frosty manner with which she treated me. "She isn't doing her job if you're bringing work home, Mason."

"So noted." He passed me a stack of folders. "Write down the pertinent deets. Call time, location, time of arrival. Reporting EMT."

I'd finished half the stack when I reached an incident report that disturbed me. A call had been placed by someone at the Diamond T about a possible domestic disturbance with injury. A woman was stumbling around, bleeding, before she collapsed in the middle of the road. My eyes widened when I saw the victim's name.

Verline Dupris.

I scoured the date on the report. Two weeks before Verline and Rollie had shown up for the dinner party. Officer Jazinski reported that no charges had been filed and that Verline blamed her injuries on falling down the steps and her confusion from dehydration. No mention of Rollie. No mention of Junior, but I'd bet money one of them had been there.

"I recognize that pissed-off look," Mason said, startling me. "What did you find?"

"An incident report regarding Verline." I looked at him. "A few weeks before she died. Why didn't you mention this to Turnbull or to me at the scene when Verline was found?"

"Because it's confidential information."

"That's crap. It directly affects our case."

"Then the FBI should've issued a subpoena for any reports of domestic violence from the Eagle River County Sheriff's Department involving either Verline Dupris or Rollie Rondeaux. But no one in the FBI bothered to follow up." Dawson held up his hand when I opened my mouth to protest. "This is a perfect example of why when our jobs intersect we're better off keeping to the nondisclosure rule."

I angrily tapped my finger on the file. "Is this why you thought Rollie was guilty?"

He nodded.

And then I knew. "This isn't the only incident report or domestic-violence call involving Verline and Rollie, is it?"

"No."

"How bad does it get?"

He just stared at me.

I wanted Dawson to tell me everything. But I knew he wouldn't. I respected that about him as much as it pissed me off. I shut the file and shoved the stack back at him. "It's best if I don't do this. I might find out the Eagle River County Sheriff's Department knows exactly who murdered Arlette Shooting Star and Verline Dupris, but God forbid that information is freely shared between agencies, due to protocol and rules of nondisclosure." I stood.

"Mercy—"

"Save it. This feels less like you're protecting the privacy of the residents of your county and more like you're getting back at Turnbull for slapping a gag on your department earlier this year."

Then Dawson was right in my face. "Bullshit, Agent Gunderson. It's not my fault the FBI didn't follow through. And if you want total honesty? If I would've told you about the previous domestic calls, you wouldn't have told Agent Turnbull anyway. Not only because you don't believe Rollie is guilty, but you know it would've been a breach of trust between *us*."

I fumed, mostly because he was right.

He shoved his hand through his hair and then stormed off. He came back thirty seconds later wearing a windbreaker.

I stopped him at the door. "Where are you going?"

"For a run. And no, I don't want you to come with me."

The door slammed behind him.

Awesome end to my day.

16

Special Agent Gunderson?"

"Yes. Who's this?"

"Officer Orson. From the tribal police. Remember me? We—"

"Yes, I remember you. What's up?" *Why was he calling me on a Sunday?*

About fifteen seconds of silence filled my ear. Then he said, "You asked me to let you know if anything weird happened that might be related to the case."

"And it has?"

"Well, I don't know. Maybe. About an hour ago two people came in and reported a missing person. To be honest, that happens all the damn time; then the missing person rolls back home after a couple of days being on a bender."

"Is the missing person female?"

"That's the thing. Yes, she's female, but she doesn't fit the pattern of the other two victims. First, she's older."

I paced. "Like how much older?"

"Old enough to be the other girls' grandmother. And the other thing? You know her."

I froze. "Who is it?"

"Penny Pretty Horses."

"She's missing? Who filled out the report?"

"Her mother. Sophie Red Leaf? Who, I understand, used to work for you. And her son. John-John Pretty Horses? Who, I understand, you used to work for at Clementine's?"

"Yes. How long since anyone last saw her?"

"According to the report, they waited twenty-four hours." Officer Orson sighed. "Look. I'm not supposed to do this, but do you have a fax number where I can send this report? I'm not sure if it has anything to do with the Shooting Star and Dupris cases because . . ."

Rollie Rondeaux was in jail. Even Officer Orson believed Rollie was guilty.

"You can send them to my home fax, and then if I think the FBI needs to get involved, I'll talk to Agent Turnbull."

"Thanks. I didn't want to overstep my bounds, but I also didn't want the feds to accuse us of dropping the ball again."

"So noted." I gave him the fax number.

I'd forgotten Hope was in the office working on the books. She glanced up expectantly as I came in. "A fax is coming through for me."

She returned to her calculator.

A minute later the fax machine beeped and spit out paper. I skimmed the part about name, age, etc., and skipped to the last-known whereabouts section.

Evidently, Penny had gone for her noon walk and hadn't returned. Sophie hadn't immediately panicked because Penny had a tendency to go where the road took her. Sophie claimed she hadn't kept too close tabs on her daughter because Penny was easily upset if she was treated like a child.

When Penny hadn't returned by noon the following day, Sophie contacted John-John. They called her friends and checked the hospital, but no one had seen her.

"Mercy?" Hope asked. "What's wrong?"

"Have you talked to Sophie recently?"

She looked at the papers in my hand and then back at me. "Not since she picked up her final paycheck. Why?"

"This can't go any further than us, but I just got word Sophie and John-John reported Penny missing a couple hours ago."

Hope's face paled. "What do you think happened?"

"I don't know."

"Maybe we oughta just call Sophie and ask." Hope picked up the phone.

"Don't. I'm not supposed to have this information."

Hope looked at me. "Well, obviously, I won't ask about that. But Sophie might tell me something if I call to see how she's doing."

I straddled the chair opposite the desk as she dialed.

She drummed her fingers on the desk, and it struck me how . . . confident she acted.

"Devlin? Hey, it's Hope." She frowned. "Jake's wife? Yeah." She listened for a minute or so before she said, "Is Sophie around? Oh. No. Don't wake her. Just tell her . . . I miss seeing her, and I wanted to know how she was doing. Okay. Bye." She scowled at the receiver. "Devlin is such a shithead. I've never liked him. He acted like he didn't know who I was. Anyway, Devlin claimed Sophie was taking a nap, but I could hear her and John-John talking in the background."

"But he didn't say anything about Penny being missing?"

"Nope."

I stood. "I think I'll take a drive."

"I'd offer to go," Hope started, "but I want to get this done while Jake is taking care of Joy."

Made me happy Hope could let go of her mama responsibilities, even for a little while, just to do the ranch books. "That's okay. I've had my fill of domestic stuff. A little alone time will be good for me."

Things had been tense in the Gunderson/Dawson household since our little blowup, and so far we hadn't kissed and made up. Mason had a rare weekend off, so he and Lex had been inseparable and underfoot. Every day had been the same. First they'd watch a movie—a loud movie. Then they'd play video games—loud video games. All of which required popcorn, pretzels, and peanuts—loud snacks.

Earlier that morning, when I'd needed a break, I'd gone outside with a couple of guns to keep up with my shooting skills. Practice had almost become an addiction for me. With nothing better to do after supper while I was at Quantico, I spent at least two hours at the shooting range every night. Four hours on the weekends if we weren't tasked with other training.

But my target practice session had been short-lived. Mason and Lex had decided to throw a football around. Then a baseball. When I was tempted to shoot their balls out of the air, I knew I needed to go. I'd spent the rest of the day inside.

Now I would've liked someone's company besides the radio.

Jake called on my way into Eagle River after he'd heard from John-John that Sophie was so distraught over Penny's disappearance that she'd gone straight to bed.

He advised me to turn around.

I kept right on driving.

The shades were drawn at Sophie's house. There weren't a bunch of cars on the street. Was no one here supporting them? After all Sophie had done for her grandkids?

John-John wouldn't let me past the front door. "She doesn't want visitors, Mercy."

"But I'm . . ." *Family.*

Wasn't I? Sophie had been an enormous part of my life, seen me through some bad times, and I wanted to return the favor.

The raw anger on John-John's face indicated I'd be wasting my breath, trying to convince him to let me in.

"Fine, I'll go. But you'd better tell her I was here."

He looked off into the distance, his jaw set so rigidly the tendons in his neck stood out. Then he nodded and closed the door in my face.

On my way to work Tuesday morning I'd just turned off the gravel onto the blacktop when I saw Shay standing beside his vehicle, parked on the shoulder.

What the hell? I threw my truck in park and jumped from the cab, clenching my teeth against the wind slicing through my clothing. "You have an aversion to my ranch? It's just three miles up the road."

Shay wore dark sunglasses. "Couldn't chance slurping coffee with the people in your household, Mercy."

People, meaning Dawson. "This couldn't wait until I got to the office?"

"We're not going to the office." He shifted his stance against his car, which was one of Shay's few tells.

Bad news. My stomach dropped to the tips of my boots. "Tell me what's going on."

"Another body. This one ID'd by Officer Spotted Bear as Penny Pretty Horses."

Blood whooshed in my ears. "What? When?"

"An hour ago."

"Does Sophie know? John-John? Devlin?"

"Not that I'm aware."

I blinked at him. Cocked my head as if I'd misunderstood. "Are you serious?"

"Yes. And since, for all intents and purposes, you're related to members of the Pretty Horses and Red Leaf families, you'll have to ride with me to the scene and refrain from using your cell phone."

That chapped my ass. "You think I'm gonna . . . Why would I want to call Sophie and give her this shitty news?" This would destroy her.

His agitation was laced with sadness. "Just get in, okay?"

I fished my cell phone out of my front pocket, shut it off, and tossed it to him. "You know it's the only cell I've got. Keep it to assure yourself that I'm not making any unauthorized calls. But no way in hell am I riding with you, Agent Turnbull. I need some time to get my head on straight."

Shay couldn't argue with that logic. He climbed into his vehicle and pulled a U-turn, I followed him.

Penny Pretty Horses. Dead.

Then it occurred to me that Turnbull hadn't said anything about it being a murder. Only that they'd found a body. So maybe Penny, in her drugged-up state from cancer medication, had wandered off. Or maybe she'd gotten tired of the pain and the looming death and had decided to take matters into her own hands. End her life where and how she wanted.

That fit with the arguments Sophie had been having with Penny about treatment—or the lack thereof.

Still. It made me sick. Poor Sophie. Poor John-John.

I hoped I wouldn't be tasked with telling them the news.

Frosted bits of white swirled in the air as the sky tried hard to snow. The wind picked up, and I had to hold tight to the steering wheel to keep from blowing across the damn road.

I hated days like this. Gloomy, with just enough water in the air to turn the normally dry air humid, but without enough precipitation to make snow.

Tumbleweeds the size of compact cars drifted and bounced across the highway. The yellow metal sign warning of slippery road conditions twisted in the wind like a piece of cheap cardboard.

Mentally bitching about the weather kept my mind off what I'd be facing. Turnbull's vehicle hung a right at the last residential street on the rez. There'd be no jurisdictional issues this time. Several emergency vehicles already lined the street.

Turnbull waited, and I noticed he'd added a heavy jacket over his clothing, the back emblazoned with FBI in enormous white letters. Before I had an attack of jacket envy, he handed me an identical coat.

"Thanks."

"No problem. I hope to hell we aren't out here long. I'd really like to get the body down soon."

I looked at him. "Down?"

"The scene is behind the house. Mostly hidden from the street."

I rounded the corner and stopped in my tracks.

I squeezed my eyes shut. Counted to ten and reopened them.

But the same grisly sight greeted me.

Penny. Naked. Hanging upside down from a tree branch. A meat hook jammed through both her Achilles tendons and chains secured around her ankles.

Just like an animal kill.

Dried blood trailed down the backs of her calves and thighs.

I forced my eyes to travel the length of her naked torso. Her arms hung down like misshapen animal limbs. Her wrists had been slit, and blood pooled in the dirt beneath her in irregular splotches. As if the wind had blown her around as she'd bled to death. Or like she'd been moving, trying to get away, trying to stop her lifeblood from slowly dripping out.

The turbanlike covering she'd worn to hide her bald head was gone, leaving her skull bare, showing where her hair had started to grow in and the patches where it hadn't.

That turned my stomach. Penny had been so self-conscious about being bald. For her, having her head exposed would've been worse than being naked.

And the indignity went on.

I wanted to look away, but I forced my gaze to stay on . . . this. On what some sick bastard had done. Killed a woman with cancer. Stripped her, humiliated her, and hung her up like a prized kill. Slit her throat and left her to die.

Rage filled me. Then sorrow. Then a combination of both that lodged in my throat like a logjam.

Another hour passed before the members of the Emergency Response Team arrived from Rapid City. They were thorough. Which equaled slow.

A crowd gathered. The tribal cops were doing their best to contain it.

Then I heard that awful noise. One I recognized. A howl of outrage, pain, disbelief, shock, and grief. But I'd never before heard that sound coming from my friend John-John.

I heard it again, this time from Sophie. The word *no,* followed by a long wail. Over and over.

If I heard that sound in the wild, I'd find the animal and put it out of its misery. But I could do nothing but stand there and bear witness to their sorrow.

After five minutes of mournful keening, I looked at Shay. "How fucking much longer are you gonna leave her up in that goddamn tree?"

"Agent Gunderson—"

"Get her down or build a damn barricade around her. No one should see this. Least of all her family."

"That's the first smart thing I've heard from the FBI since we got the call," Chief Looks Twice said.

He and Shay conferred. Then Shay finally motioned for his crew to take her down.

Because Carsten wasn't on scene yet, I went to deal with the family.

The family. Like they weren't my family. Like I could keep professional distance in this situation.

Sophie sat on the ground, rocking back and forth and wailing in a low-pitched tremolo, nearly catatonic in her grief.

John-John also sat on the ground. His face was stoic through the tears streaming down.

Devlin wasn't overtly grieving. Devlin was mad. As soon as he saw me, he stomped over.

"This is your fault," he spat.

"Devlin, I'm sorry. We're doing everything—"

"But it'll be too late for her, won't it? Penny is dead. Murdered. Fucking slaughtered. Just like was forecast in John-John's vision. And just like in that vision, here you are in the thick of it. Pretending you care—"

"I do care."

Devlin screamed obscenities at me.

I let him.

But Shay wasn't having any of it. He got in Devlin's face. His eyes were the coldest I've ever seen, and his voice cut through the bullshit spewing from Devlin like a scythe. "Stand down. Now."

Devlin's mouth snapped shut.

"I understand you're grieving. But just because you're personally acquainted with Agent Gunderson—"

"It's her fault my sister is dead!" He pointed to me. "Look at her! She's acting guilty because she knows it's true."

"One more word, Mr. Pretty Horses, and I will have you forcibly removed from the scene and locked up in the tribal jail. Don't tempt me on this." Shay motioned to Officer Ferguson. "If this man speaks, cuff him. If he resists arrest, use whatever level of force you need to ensure he cooperates. Understood?"

"Yes, Agent Turnbull."

Turnbull herded me toward the street. Then he loomed over me. "Say something, Gunderson."

I couldn't.

"How long would you have allowed him to dress you down?"

I looked over at Sophie, rocking and crying. Then my gaze moved to John-John, staring through me, his eyes vacant with shock. I met Shay's gaze again. "I don't know. I just . . . froze."

"There's something else going on with them. Tell me."

Turnbull and I had seemed to be on a sharing kick—at least from my end—since the night of Verline's wake, so I told him what I knew of John-John's vision. Penny's death. My presence as the little black rain cloud of doom.

If I believed Shay wouldn't discount it, well, I was wrong.

He towed me behind the ambulance. Then he stepped in front of me, blocking me from everyone's view. His strong fingers circled my wrist, and he lifted my own hand in front of my face. "You see this? Is there blood on it?"

"No."

"Did you string up your former housekeeper's daughter like a hunting trophy?"

"No."

"Then you can't shoulder the blame."

I blinked at him.

"A vision is no more relevant than a dream, Mercy. No one can assign real meaning to it. And those who claim they can have usually been smokin' too much peyote, or hitting the firewater too hard."

"But you're the one who told me—"

"About your tie to the spirit world?"

I nodded.

"Not the same thing. I can understand why they didn't call you when Penny went missing. But your tie doesn't have a damn thing to do with someone else's vision."

Numb, I mumbled, "Thank you."

"This is gonna be hard. But you can handle it."

"Because I'm a good agent?"

Shay curled my hand into a fist before he released it. "No, because you're a good person."

I watched him walk away. Then I forced myself to seek out Sophie. I sat in the dirt next to her, at a loss about how to help her.

Wasn't long before she was leaning on me. Just her head on my arm. She stopped rocking. Her tears continued to fall.

So did mine.

Finally, she wiped her nose and her eyes on her sleeve. "I'm tired, Mercy." Her voice was a breathless rasp of defeat.

"I'm sure you've spent the last day without getting much rest. You want me to take you home?"

"No, John-John will need to. It'll help him if he can fuss over me."

"What can I do?"

I sat very still as Sophie's back straightened and she looked me in the eyes. Her lip wobbled. She firmed it and bit off, "Find who did this to my daughter."

"I will. I promise. And if you need anything . . ."

"I'll let you know." Sophie touched my face, almost absentmindedly, the way she used to when I was an awkward teenage girl. "How is the Sheriff?"

"Well, he hasn't left me yet."

She tsk-tsked. "You're strong, Mercy. But I like that you don't have to be so tough with him. You're a good match. Now with Lex living there . . . you have a family of your own. You need that more than you know."

This woman I should be giving comfort to . . . was trying to comfort me. More tears fell down my face. "I miss you."

"Ah, I miss you, too. You and your grumpy ways."

I blurted, "Then why did you quit?"

She patted my cheek. "Because I thought it was my job as Penny's mother to make her last few months bearable. As much as she claimed she was getting better and the herbal medicine eased her pain, I only had to look in her eyes to know she was lying. She was dying. I just can't believe it came to this . . ." She briefly closed her eyes, then those sorrow-filled black pools were back on mine. "I never put much stock in the way John-John interpreted that vision. I want you to know that had nothin' to do with me leavin', no matter what he says, hey."

I held my breath.

"I believe the reason he saw the darkness surrounding you was because you're the only one to make this right. But you'll need to return to that dark place it took you so long to get out of, *takoja*. Don't let the blackness swallow you up again."

My skin became a mass of goose bumps.

Then Sophie was on her feet, shuffling away.

John-John spoke to her before heading toward me.

I stood and waited, my head so fucked that I felt I'd drifted to another plane of existence.

"*Unci* doesn't blame you, but I do."

And . . . I crash-landed right back down to earth.

"She didn't have the vision. *I* did. I won't put a rosy spin on it."

"I will figure out who did this to your mother. Not because I need to prove that your vision painting me the big, bad monster is wrong. You seem to have forgotten *I'm* the good guy. Go ahead and use your anger, John-John. You're entitled to it. But don't direct your anger toward me. And keep one thing in mind."

"What?"

"This may not be the end to your family troubles, but the beginning. You might not like what I turn up when I really start to dig."

"Don't get dirt on my grandmother. Stay away from her. Don't call her. Don't stop by. Don't send her flowers. Don't bring her food. Don't do nothing. Leave her be. It's my job to protect her. Even from you. Maybe *especially* from you." His trench coat made a dismissive flapping sound when he whirled around.

Took a long minute before I could move. Before I could breathe.

Ironically, I found my cool detachment in his heated words.

For the first time I noticed the crowd.

Gawkers were a part of crime scenes, something I hadn't really paid attention to or understood until I took a psych-ops class at Quantico. The crowd was a comfort of sorts. It allowed humans to connect after a tragedy, letting them show sympathy while at the same time allowing for the thank-God-it-wasn't-me sense of relief. But all too often with a violent crime, the orchestrator of said crime came to the scene and fed off that shock and horror.

I took a more in-depth look at the dozen and a half people milling about. The crime-scene photographer discreetly snapped photos of the crowd. Probably wouldn't mean much as far as comparing this case to the other two, since this scene was public while the others had been off the grid.

Another round of sorrow rolled through me as Penny's body was loaded into a black bag and lifted into the ambulance.

Shay ended his phone call and ambled toward me.

"That was Director Shenker. Given your close association with so many members of the family—"

"He's pulling me off the case?"

"No. Take a deep breath, Gunderson. We think it'd be best if Carsten and I handled the family interviews this afternoon. Shenker's requiring you to take the remainder of the day off, but he expects you at the VS offices on Eagle River tomorrow at the usual time."

I went home.

Dawson was working.

Lex was at Doug's house doing yet another school project.

I went for a ten-mile run. I could've run another ten.

Sweaty, cranky, and carrying an armload of mail, I didn't hide my annoyance when Jake pulled up next to me as I walked down the driveway.

He rolled down the window. "You busy?"

"Yes."

He shook his head. "Nice try. Come on, you need to clear your head. You ain't been out and about on the ranch since you got back from Virginia."

I squinted at him. "Did Hope send you over here?"

"Yep. When we heard about Penny . . . Hope knew you had to deal with it, since that's your job, and she wanted me to make sure you were okay."

My sister's concern touched me. So I hopped into the passenger's side of the truck . . . and hopped back out when we reached the first gate. We bumped along the existing truck tracks. I opened three more gates. Just as I began to get annoyed, Jake stopped at the top of the rise and parked instead of cutting to the left and following the ridge down to the closest pasture.

I climbed out and avoided stepping on a clump of cactus. The soil was sandy and dry enough to support that type of vegetation. I didn't understand how those flat and barrel-shaped succulents survived the winter months, when the wind on this plateau blew a million miles an hour and a heavy crust of snow covered everything.

The cactus would be here long after I was gone.

I skirted a pile of scat—it appeared rabbits enjoyed the view here, too—and stood on the remaining chunk of a butterscotch-colored rock. Most of it had cracked and tumbled away down the steep incline, leaving a chalky white trail of sun-bleached shale.

Wrapping my arms around myself, I faced the wind. Not bitterly cold like this morning, but with enough bite to remind me night would be approaching soon. I gazed across the expanse of the valley. Skeletal trees followed the path of a dry creek bed.

The right side of the ridged plateau curved sharply, appearing flat until it fell away into nothingness. Stand too close to the edge in spring-time and I would feel the earth's pull, the ground shifting beneath my feet. Wanting me to tumble down the hillside like the hunks of red dirt and jagged rocks scattered and broken before me.

I'd walked this ridge more times than I could count. Always marvel-ing at the topographical variances, from summertime lush grazing areas down by the creek to the wooded section that rimmed the bowl on the left. Everything I could see from this vantage point was Gunderson land. My father had said it often enough, with pride, that I'd loved coming here as a kid to look and lord over my domain. Knowing it'd be mine someday. And wanting that ownership in the worst way.

Now the vastness humbled me. As did the responsibility of being steward to this land for as long as it owned me.

Jake walked up and stood beside me. I wondered if he saw this the same way I did. Or was his view more calculating? Hoping, come spring-time, the creek would run high, the grass would grow tall, and Mother Nature wouldn't be the bitch, trying to test a human's resilience.

He handed me a can of beer.

I looked at him and managed a smile. "Thanks."

He cracked open a Coors, and we drank in silence. Not rushed. Not uncomfortable. Not pregnant with words that needed to be said but that neither of us wanted to speak.

Despite our past issues, Jake and I understood each other.

At least today.

That thought made me smile.

We each finished our cans of beer, but neither of us made a move to leave.

After a bit, Jake said, "Not everyone in my family believes John-John's visions are gospel, Mercy."

His comment surprised me. "Why do I think the Red Leaf family was . . . I don't know if *supportive* is the right word, but maybe . . . ac-cepting of his talents?"

"It ain't like we got much choice, to be real honest." He sighed. "*Unci* is hurtin' about Penny. That don't give John-John and Devlin the right to take their pain out on you. Sophie ain't happy about that."

"You talked to her?"

"Of course. She's . . . this whole thing rips me up inside, mostly for her. For all her faults, loving too much ain't one of them. With all that's gone on in the past few weeks, and since you were gone for months . . . I know you're questioning your place with her, Mercy. Don't. She *does* consider you her family. Both you and Hope."

A shard of pain lanced my heart that the woman who'd been a surrogate mother to me was emotionally eviscerated and I wasn't allowed to comfort her.

Before I let that thought weigh me down more, Jake handed me another beer. I gave him an odd look. "Two beers in one day, Jake? Really? You got some bad news to tell me?"

"Funny. Not bad news. But something you oughta know. Something you shoulda been told a long time ago."

Jake wasn't a guy prone to drama, so the fact he'd brought me out here in the middle of the ranch to talk to me set off all my warning bells.

"This is something you can't tell anyone, Mercy. I ain't kiddin'. Not Dawson. Hope don't even know. And you cannot let on that you know of this, to any of the people who are involved. I gotta have your word."

"You've got it."

Jake took another gulp of beer. "You asked about the bad blood between the Red Leaf family and Rollie Rondeaux. It don't got nothin' to do with us. Mostly, it's between the Pretty Horses family and Rollie. It started with Penny, Rollie, and Sophie." He paused with the beer can in front of his mouth. "Because Rollie is John-John's father."

Shocked, I gaped at Jake for almost a solid minute before I could speak. "Are you serious?"

"Yep. Short version: Penny and Rollie had a fling while Rollie was married. Penny got knocked up, had John-John, but wouldn't give him the Rondeaux name. Rollie refused to support her or the kid unless she did. Sophie got pissed off and said she'd tell everyone—including Rollie's wife—about John-John's parentage. Rollie made a threat—I have no idea what—and everyone involved clammed up. Most secrets don't stay that way for very long, but in this case? It's one that's been kept for years."

"How'd you find out?"

"Wyatt told me." Jake crumpled the first beer can. "When he figured out that Levi was my son. I'm pretty sure your dad meant it as a warning, since John-John hates Rollie's guts. He didn't want that to happen between me 'n' Levi when I told the boy I was his biological father. Not that it happened before Levi . . ."

I squeezed Jake's arm. I sometimes thought he suffered the most from Levi's death. He had the loss of what might've been. "Who all knows this secret?"

"The obvious ones: Penny, Rollie, Sophie, John-John. I'm sure he told Muskrat."

"Devlin?" I asked, and then said, "Of course he doesn't know. Devlin can't keep his mouth shut. So how'd my dad find out?"

"He swore from the first time he saw John-John that the boy was a dead ringer for Rollie. Wyatt had no love for the man, after what happened to your mother, so he confronted Sophie and she told him the truth. She said she'd quit if he told anyone or treated John-John different."

My dad had been pretty indifferent toward John-John, but I'd always chalked that up to the disturbing vision he'd had about my mother—a year prior to her death.

"John-John and me, for bein' cousins, well, you know we ain't never been close. Same goes with Luke and TJ."

"Why? I've never understood that."

"Just one of them things. When I found out this secret, around the time John-John opened Clementine's . . . fifteen years ago, I showed up for a drink to support him. John-John wouldn't serve me. Said he wasn't gonna have his ragtag relations hanging out in his bar."

"Because Clementine's is so classy," I said dryly.

Jake smiled. "That's what I said. Then I did a dumb thing. Opened my mouth and asked if his father would be welcome. John-John punched me. Damn near knocked me out. He said if I ever told anyone, he'd cut out my tongue and watch me choke to death on my own blood."

"He said that? Holy shit." I had that bad gut feeling again. Verline's tongue had been cut out. Had she somehow discovered that Rollie was John-John's father? Had she threatened to spill the beans? Or maybe she wanted money to keep quiet about what she knew?

No, John-John couldn't have killed Verline any more than Rollie could have.

But this was getting a little too coincidental and spooky for my liking.

"So now you know why none of the Red Leaf family is allowed to drink in his bar."

"God. Jake. I'm absolutely . . . stunned. I never suspected. I mean, Rollie has been such a smart-ass about John-John over the years. When I think of all the shit he said . . ." Now I wondered if my dad had been trying to tell me something when he said Rollie didn't give a shit about any of his kids, no matter who their mothers were. Stupid me, I hadn't bothered to ask him what he'd meant.

"You can't let on to Sophie or John-John or Rollie that you know the truth," Jake warned.

"Trust me, I won't. You know how good I am at keeping secrets."

"Yes, I do." He threw his beer can in the back of the feed truck. "Now that we're done gossiping, let's get them cows fed before dark."

When Dawson brought Lex home a few hours later, he found me on the floor in our bedroom, sitting amid my guns, as I cleaned out the gun safe.

He leaned against the door frame and raised an eyebrow. "Should I be worried?"

"No."

"I remember a few months back when you pulling a gun on me was considered foreplay. So if you wanna go ahead and whip out that Glock, feel free."

I smiled. "We already reminiscing about the good old days, Sheriff?"

He crouched down next to me. "No. But the last couple days haven't been very good."

"True." Without looking at him, I said, "So you heard about the case we caught today?"

"Yeah. But I wasn't talking about that."

I looked at him.

"I'm sorry."

"For?"

He touched my face. "For the way it's been between us."

"Me, too." I leaned into his touch, needing a connection to something. Ever since I'd talked to Jake, I'd felt untethered. Not even being surrounded by all my beloved firepower had grounded me. "Thanks."

"Anytime." He continued to gently stroke my cheek. "Are you okay?"

"Not really."

"I can tell. It's been so tense around here that even Lex is worried about you."

"He is? Why?"

"In the last couple of days, you haven't asked him even one time if he has his homework done."

"I haven't yelled at him for leaving his dirty socks on the couch, either."

"I'll remind him of that," he said dryly. "But my son also has suggested that I do something . . . impressive to make up for my dickish behavior. His words not mine."

"Like what?"

He grinned like he had a big secret. "Well, I know you've got a thing for bull riders, so Mad Dog is coming out of retirement this weekend to compete in the annual Sheriffs Association Fund-Raiser, which just happens to be a rodeo."

"Really?"

"Yes. You impressed yet?"

The nickname Mad Dog had stuck during his bulldogging and bull-riding days. I'd tried calling Mason that right after we'd first met, but the name didn't fit him now. Still, I'd be lying if I didn't admit I'd imagined seeing him in all his glory on the back of a bull. Or more accurately, that I'd fantasized about seeing him in a pair of fringed chaps, tight jeans, a championship buckle, and a black hat. It appeared I'd get to see the real deal. "Okay, I am impressed."

"So it's a date? You'll watch me ride Saturday night?"

"Yep, I'll even be your very own buckle bunny."

Dawson hauled me to my feet. Then he pulled me into his arms. I thought about protesting for a split second, but I wanted this. I'd missed this—how he and I were together. I finally felt some of that peace I'd been looking for today. I wrapped myself around him, buried my face in his neck, and sighed.

Mason murmured, "That was a happy sound."

"That's because I *am* happy."

"Even when we occasionally piss each other off?"

"Yep. The best part of fighting with you is always the making-up part. We are about to make up, right now, aren't we?" My hand slid down his body until it met the hard flesh pressing against his zipper.

He growled, "I think it's past Lex's bedtime. Don't go nowhere, I'll be right back."

I laughed softly.

It seemed for the first time in years, my personal life was on a happy plane. And I'd be damned if I'd spoil the feeling by worrying about when it'd end.

Thursday afternoon, Director Shenker singled out the cases that Turnbull and I were working on at the biweekly meeting. He shuffled through his notes. "Three female victims, ranging in age from twenty to sixty-two. None of the murder methods are the same. The victims were not related. Nor were the victims well acquainted. The commonality is the victims had digitalis in their systems." He looked at Shay. "The family requested immediate release of the body within twenty-four hours? Why? Wasn't this last victim in the final stage of breast cancer?"

"Yes. She had a living will, and she'd filed paperwork requesting no religious ceremony. She was cremated yesterday."

That caught me by surprise. I'd heard nothing about it from Hope or Jake.

Shenker sighed. "I guess it doesn't matter. Have either of you made *any* progress? We've got no suspects . . . on *three* first-degree murder cases?"

Shay and I didn't make eye contact. As the senior agent, he should jump in with a progress report.

He didn't. Why? Was he afraid he'd get spanked by the boss? I wanted to cluck at him for being such a chickenshit.

"Agent Gunderson."

Shit. I felt all eyes in the room on me.

Now who's clucking? "Yes, sir?"

"Did you find anything in your research at the tribal archives to substantiate your earlier theory? About previous deaths of women on the reservation being overlooked, unsolved murders?"

I decided to let fly. I'd gotten smacked down by the boss before, and I probably would get it again. "Yes, sir. Over the last five years, at least three women died in a similar manner, and those deaths weren't investigated by the tribal PD. Rural car accidents. Domestic abuse turned fatal. Former drug users found OD'd. The pattern was there, but I do understand—to some degree—how the cases were overlooked. Like in these most recent cases, the previous victims were women of varying ages. They were each killed a month apart, over a three-month span. And because the death situations were . . . close enough to be believable for the victim's lives, not even their families raised a stink about the cases not receiving proper investigation from the tribal PD. The women who died in mysterious car accidents? All had long records of serious traffic violations and accidents. The women who were found stabbed or sliced up? All had many documented instances of domestic violence. The women who OD'd? All had long histories of drug addiction. The assumed suicides? Those women struggled with depression and had made previous attempts at suicide. So there is a pattern."

Shenker nodded. "So how do these latest victims fit? Because the pattern has been altered. No one-month lag time between murders. Do you have a theory on why?"

"Before, the killer was content, probably smug, in the knowledge he was getting away with it. But his method has gotten more disturbing. That's a point of pride for him now. Some initial theories within the tribal PD and the FBI were that Rollie Rondeaux killed Arlette Shooting Star as a screen so he could get away with murdering his live-in, Verline Dupris, a week later.

"It might've initially served the killer's purpose to throw suspicion at Rollie Rondeaux. Then Rollie was arrested and placed in tribal jail. This is where his need for attention has come in. Now he's afraid Rollie *will* get credit for his kills. So he kills again, in a very brutal and very public place. This time the killer wanted everyone in law enforcement to know that Penny Pretty Horses wasn't a copy-cat murder."

Silence.

"Thank you, Agent Gunderson. I appreciate the legwork on this." Shenker peered over his bifocals at Agent Turnbull. "It appears it was a good thing Mr. Rondeaux was placed in tribal police custody before we went to the assistant U.S. attorney to ask for a grand jury investigation."

Turnbull remained stoic.

"But we are still looking at three first-degree murders and no suspects." Shenker frowned and pulled out his BlackBerry. "Sorry, I've been waiting for this call. Take ten, people."

Chairs creaked as everyone got up, but I stayed put, figuring this would be the quietest place. I closed my eyes, wondering if I could get in a quick ten-minute combat nap.

But there was always the possibility I'd drift into a combat nightmare.

"Great job laying out the cold cases' facts, Mercy."

I opened my eyes and looked at Shay. "Thanks."

"You pulled my ass out of the fire, because guaranteed, Shenker was holding a blowtorch."

"You would've deserved it."

"Definitely." He grinned. "I might make an FBI agent out of you yet, Sergeant Major."

I leaned closer and whispered, "Fuck off. Sir."

Shay laughed. "Any issues with the Red Leaf and Pretty Horses families?"

"No. In fact, I had no idea the family had requested early release of the body."

"It's been a long week." He paused. "Do you have plans for the weekend with the Dawson boys?"

I must be giving off friendly vibes for Turnbull to ask about my personal life. "Mason is riding in the Sheriffs Association charity event Saturday night."

Shay lifted a brow. "Riding? Like, motorcycle? A poker run or something?"

"No. It's a rodeo benefit, so he'll be bull riding."

"Better him than me, I guess."

With all the tragedy and drama that'd gone on in our lives recently I was looking forward to a night at the rodeo. "What are you doing this weekend?"

"Working."

"Why?"

He grinned at me again. "Someone's gotta figure out what's going on with these cases while you're off jerking on Dawson's . . . rope."

17

If Dawson was nervous about riding a bull, he hid it well.

Lex peppered his father with questions. Dawson answered in the measured tone I'd started to think of as "daddy speak," where he showed loads of patience, and rarely allowed his explanations to venture into pure lecture territory. I was still trying to find my balance with Lex. Dealing with Dawson's son wasn't the same as dealing with my nephew.

"So when was the last time you rode a bull?" Lex asked, leaning over the back of the seat from his place in the middle of the club cab.

"A couple of months ago at a bull-riding expo at the Eagle River pow-wow."

My head swiveled toward him. "Really? How come I didn't know that?"

"Because you woulda chewed me out and reminded me I'm too old," Dawson said with a grin.

"You *are* too old," I retorted sweetly.

"Probably. But I managed to stay on eight seconds, and that's what counts."

"I don't think you're too old," Lex offered, sending me a scowl.

Talk about a case of hero worship.

You were exactly the same way with your father at that age.

Dawson snatched my hand off the seat and kissed my knuckles. "I didn't tell you because I didn't want you to worry from a million miles away in Virginia."

Mollified, I let him hold my hand. I gazed out the window, tuning out their conversation and trying not to think about Penny's body dangling from a tree. Trying not to think about the pain in Sophie's eyes. Trying not to chastise myself because we weren't any closer to catching the murderer than we had been the day Arlette Shooting Star turned up dead.

Billboards zoomed by as we hit the outskirts of Rapid City, and then we were among grocery stores, fast-food joints, secondhand stores, and car dealerships.

I hadn't taken in a rodeo since I'd gotten out of the army. Stepping through the arena doors, the unique smells of sawdust, dirt, manure, livestock, and cotton candy blasted me in the face, the scents carried on the hot air blowing from the heaters. I glanced over at Lex, who was wrinkling his nose.

The seats in the Pennington County Events Center weren't even half full. A horse trailer display took up a good chunk of the entryway. We skirted the high-end rigs and paused between the concessions and the ramp leading to the stands.

People milled about. Friends greeted one another with handshakes and heartfelt slaps on the back. Cowboys and cowgirls of all ages stood in groups, drinking beer and laughing. Kids dressed in jeans, boots, and hats raced by at full throttle. The loudspeaker boomed with announcements. A 4-H Club sold raffle tickets for a quilt. A small western tack store, pegboard walls laden with ropes of every color, material, and length had cropped up between a real estate broker's table and a FFA booth.

Despite the number of years that'd passed since I'd been around rodeo culture, nothing had changed. An odd sense of comfort filled me, and I felt silly for it. I'd merely been an observer in this world—a role that was the norm for me.

Dawson stopped in front of a corridor of metal fencing that led to the area marked for contestants. "I'll see you guys later."

"But . . . why can't I come back and help pull your rope?" Lex asked.

The kid had studied up on bull riding, I'd give him that much.

"Thanks for the offer, son, but they're pretty strict about who goes behind the chutes. I'll meet you at the contestant's gate as soon as I'm finished, okay?"

"Okay."

Dawson sidestepped his son and loomed over me. "Need money for snacks? The kid eats like a horse."

"Nah, I've got it covered." I stood on tiptoe and pressed my mouth to his. "Promise me you'll be careful, old man."

"I will." He draped his equipment bag over his shoulder and headed to the back of the arena.

Neither Lex nor I moved until Dawson was out of sight.

"What you hungry for first? Popcorn or nachos?"

"Nachos."

After we loaded up on junk food, we found seats in the middle section and settled in to watch the show.

This was a charity event put on by the South Dakota Sheriffs Association, but rodeo standards never changed. A young girl belted out "The Star Spangled Banner," and all the men and women in the place removed their hats without being reminded. That was followed by recognition of all the veterans in the arena. We were asked to remain standing while the crowd gave us a resounding round of applause for our service to this country. On the outside, I might've looked like a stoic combat survivor, but on the inside, I wept for what war had taken from all of us and felt immeasurable pride that my years of service meant something. Having these strangers acknowledge our collective dedication always moved me; it never seemed staged, just sincere. And these days, no one did a double take at seeing a woman standing with the men.

Lex started shoveling in nachos, but that didn't keep him from talking with a mouthful of food. "I'm gonna join the marines when I get outta school, just like my dad did."

I shot him a glance. Last week the kid wanted to be a cop. This week he wanted to be a soldier. Next week he'd probably want to be a bull rider. I tried to remember if I'd changed my mind about my future occupation every week when I was his age. Had I ever dreamed of following in my father's footsteps? Maybe. But the one thing that'd stayed constant was the resolve that my career would involve guns.

"Why does the guy ridin' saddle bronc have that thing behind his head?" Lex asked, with a cheese-covered chip pointing at the rider. "If they're worried he's gonna hurt the horse, then how come they make the riders wear spurs?"

"It's rider safety gear, and it's meant to protect the rider's neck and head from injury, not the horse. And the spurs they wear are designed not to cut into a horse or a bull."

"Oh." *Crunch-crunch.* "Did you ever do rodeo stuff?"

"Nope. Only in the stands as a fan."

Lex finished the nachos, a big bag of popcorn, a large Diet Dr Pepper, and a package of licorice. He left to go to the bathroom twice, which entitled me to tease him upon his return. "Are there cute cowgirls by the concession area?"

He scowled. "Why would you ask that?"

"Because you've been popping up and down like a jack-in-the-box."

Another scowl.

"Anyone you know from school here tonight?"

"No. Jeez, why are you acting like you care? My dad's not here."

Ouch. I hadn't wanted to horn in on Dawson's time with his son, so I'd hung back, which evidently made the kid think I didn't like him. I needed to change that, but I wasn't sure how to do it.

We watched the calf roping. And the team roping. When the bull-dogging started, Lex stood. "I'm thirsty. Can I have money for pop?"

I shook my head. "There's a drinking fountain by the bathrooms."

"But my dad—"

"Said nothing about allowing you to drink unlimited quantities of caffeine. He'd say no, and you know it. Take your cup and get some water if you're so thirsty." I looked at him. "And think about the fact you're only nice to me when you want something."

Lex's cheeks colored. He snatched up the cup and stomped off.

Yeah, it appeared they'd removed the mothering genes when they'd taken my uterus.

The pouty preteen plopped beside me and heaved a world-weary sigh. "How long before bull ridin' starts?"

"It's next."

Like the other events, the entrants were a mix of current pros, old pros, and amateurs. The "places" were largely symbolic; the sponsors were donating the prize money to the association's charity, a summer boot camp for kids on the cusp of juvenile delinquency.

Finally, the speeches ended, and the bull riding began. The first six guys got thrown off. The next two rode. Not prettily. They hadn't skimped on the rough stock for this charity event.

"Next up in the Conrad Electric bucking chute, Eagle River County sheriff Mason Dawson. Sheriff Dawson hails from Minnesota, and in his younger years, competed in bulldogging and bull riding on the Midwest Circuit. He consistently placed in the top ten, but chose to trade in his bull rope and piggin' string for an M16 in the marines. Sheriff Dawson has drawn the bull Dark Dream, from Jackson Stock Contracting."

I leaned forward, my elbows on my knees, surprisingly nervous. Not much of Dawson was visible except the top of his hat.

"How long does it take for him to get ready?" Lex asked.

"Depends on if the bull fights in the chute. Depends on how long it takes to wrap his hand and get a good seat. Meaning, where he feels he can hold on for eight seconds. Have you ever watched bull riding on TV?"

"A couple times, after Dad told me he was a bull rider."

I smiled, happy to see that Lex's worship of his father appeared to be genuine. "When your dad nods his head, the guy standing outside the gate will open it."

"Then he's out in the dirt, staying on for eight seconds."

"Let's hope."

When Dawson and the bull left the chute, Lex and I both clapped and shouted encouragement. Dawson looked awful stiff on the bull, almost as if he held on by sheer will. But when it comes to a two-hundred-pound man versus a fifteen-hundred-pound bull . . . in a battle of wills, the spinning, kicking, jerking bull tended to win.

And Dark Dream was a kicker. The hind legs came up on every hop.

He'd spin and jerk his back end, sending Dawson sliding sideways. Dawson didn't have much chance to spur; he was too busy hanging on.

He stayed with the bull jump for jump, but when the bull went into a spin, that's when I knew Dawson was about to eat dirt.

The bull's last attempt to toss his rider on his ass happened in slow motion. Dark Dream went nearly vertical, throwing Dawson forward. His head connected with the bull's skull.

That contact immediately knocked Dawson out, but his hand was still tied into his bull rope.

We watched, horrified, as Dawson's limp body was flung around like a slab of meat as the bull tried to get rid of him.

The bullfighters raced in quickly—although it seemed like an hour passed while we stood helplessly in the stands. One bullfighter freed Dawson's hand while the other bullfighter distracted the bull.

Dawson hit the ground face-first and didn't move.

The bull trotted off, tail twitching angrily.

By then both the bullfighters were on their knees, blocking any view of what was going on.

Two guys from the medical team jogged out and crouched beside Dawson's motionless form.

Lex leaned into me. "Mercy? Is he okay?"

"I don't know. Let's just give them a minute to check him out."

My hand had somehow found Lex's shoulder, my fingers curling into it, when two more guys brought out a stretcher.

The announcer said, "How about a hand for our bullfighters and our medical team for their quick response time?"

When they carried Dawson out of the arena, I could tell he still wasn't moving. That's when panic set in. That's when I knew if I'd been here by myself, I would've jumped the metal corrals and raced across the dirt to see what was going on. But I did nothing.

Lex's scared voice jolted me out of my inertia. "Mercy? Where are they taking him?"

"Get your coat and let's go find out."

Everything in the arena seemed too bright, too loud, as we walked past the concession stand. Past the booths selling trinkets. Past the teenagers laughing. The corridor leading to the back of the arena seemed to lengthen to the size of two football fields as Lex and I started down the tunnel.

When I saw the lights of an ambulance bouncing off the walls, I began to run.

The guy in charge of keeping out casual spectators didn't give us any grief. "You Sheriff Dawson's family?"

I nodded because my mouth seemed stuck shut.

"The medical team is over there."

Just as we reached the makeshift medical tent, the ambulance sped away, lights swirling. I didn't hear the siren kick on until they were on the street.

The man I'd seen race out after the bullfighters and call for the stretcher was talking on his cell phone.

The gate man tapped him on the shoulder, and he faced us, holding up one finger. After he finished his call, he ambled over.

I scrutinized his clothes, looking for signs of Mason's blood.

"I'm Dr. Grant. You're Sheriff Dawson's family?"

"Yes."

"He's on his way to Rapid City Regional Hospital. As I'm sure you saw, he's suffered a serious blow to the head."

"Did he regain consciousness?"

The doctor shook his head. "He already had swelling, so we got him out of here as quickly as possible. I just got off the phone with a neurosurgeon. He's headed to the ER." He patted my upper arm. "The sheriff will be in good hands. Dr. Jeffers is excellent with sports-related brain trauma."

Brain trauma.

The doctor's eyes met mine. "Will you be all right driving to the hospital, or do you need someone to take you and your son?"

Strange to hear Lex called my son. I realized that he and I were holding hands. "Thank you, but I'll be fine to drive."

As we started to leave out the back door, I heard someone yell, "Mrs. Dawson?"

That stopped me in my tracks. I turned around. "Yes?"

A cowboy hustled toward me. "Here's the sheriff's equipment bag."

"Thanks." I reached for it, but Lex grabbed the handle before I could.

"No problem. If there's anything any of us at the Sheriffs Association can do, please let us know."

"I will."

I'd expected Lex would pepper me with questions, but we made the drive up Fifth Street to the hospital in complete silence. In the ER parking lot, I snagged the equipment bag and set it on the seat. I rooted around for Mason's wallet.

Lex frowned at me, like I was picking his dad's pockets.

"I'll need his insurance information."

He stuck to me like a tick as we entered the hospital through the ER doors.

I checked in with the nurse. Gave her my name and was told to have a seat.

About ten minutes later the receptionist handed me a clipboard to fill out the basics of Mason's information. I knew his height, his weight, his birth date. I filled out the insurance section after finding the Blue Cross/Blue Shield card in his wallet. But I didn't know his blood type. Or the date of his last tetanus shot. I only realized he was an organ and tissue donor when I looked at his driver's license. I had no idea who his next of kin was besides me, and technically, I wasn't supposed to be handling this medical shit because I had no legal rights as Mason's domestic partner.

Frustrated and scared shitless, I handed over the paperwork and looked around for Lex.

The kid was trying to peek in the windows of a set of double doors leading to the actual ER.

"They'll let us know when we can go back," I said, lacing my fingers through his to tug him away.

He scowled, so much like his father that I had to bite the inside of my cheek. But he didn't let go of my hand. "You want a soda or a snack?" I asked.

"You told me no more soda tonight," he said sullenly. "Or candy."

"Suit yourself." I plunked the money in the vending machine and stared at the choices. The brightly wrapped packages blurred as I blinked back tears.

Then Lex stood beside me, staring into the rows of candy, cookies, chips, and nuts. He leaned his head into my arm.

I about lost it then. I put my hand on his shoulder and pulled him closer. "Wanna split some M&M's?"

He nodded.

"Plain or peanut?" I asked, hoping for plain.

"Peanut," he said.

I ended up buying both kinds. I must've eaten mine, because when I glanced down, the wrapper was empty.

Lex was too big to sit on my lap. When his eyes began to droop, I moved us to a bench seat, rolled my coat up as a pillow, and set it on my lap. "Lay your head down. I'll wake you up as soon as anyone comes out to talk to us."

"Promise?"

"Promise."

He snuggled in without another protest. I stroked his damp hair away from his face, almost absentmindedly.

He said, "Mercy?"

"Mmm?"

"Why's it been such a long time?"

"I don't know."

"I'm scared."

"I know, Lex. Me, too."

Five minutes later, Lex was asleep. I glanced at the clock. Midnight. We'd been here over three hours without any idea what was going on. Had they taken Mason to surgery? Was he alone, wondering why I wasn't by his side, as he'd been by my side all the times I'd needed him in the last year?

Was he . . . ?

No. *Fuck* no. I wouldn't think that way. I couldn't.

I watched people come in, wait around, and leave. Sick babies and worried parents. An older woman with a hacking cough that sounded like pneumonia. A couple of drunks who'd done stupid things and were bleeding all over the tile.

The clock ticked from midnight, to one o'clock, to two o'clock. I tried like hell not to freak out that I hadn't seen a single medical person in five hours.

I closed my eyes, letting my head fall back against the wall. I wondered if anything was going through Dawson's mind right now, or if it was blessedly blank.

I'd had my share of concussions. The worst one had happened as a fluke. Our elite squad was supposed to be in Fallujah only overnight, long enough to sneak in and eliminate our target. But the assassination infuriated the locals, and they stepped up their aggression. We had no choice but to stay and return fire until reinforcements arrived.

The shit vehicle we were assigned for patrol had no protective combat panels. It was an open jeep with a turret rifle mounted in the back. I was in full battle rattle, manning the turret, scanning the area for sniper activity. Then we were so busy trying to return fire that the driver didn't see an IED until the front tire hit it.

The last thing I remember was flying through the air, in slow motion, like in a scene from *The Matrix,* before I smacked into a concrete wall headfirst and the lights went out.

The combat helmet saved my life, but I'd hit hard enough to crack it in half like a walnut. The impact knocked me out cold. Because they weren't sure if my brain would swell, the medical personnel kept me out and under observation for twenty-four hours. I freaked out when I woke up in a flimsy hospital gown, with a severe headache, smelling like dirt, antiseptic, and unwashed gym socks.

My smart-ass teammates had taken my cracked helmet and strung the two broken pieces together with cord, gluing dead brown weeds and sand on the outside, turning it into a gigantic coconut bra.

I must've dozed off because a hand on my shoulder gently shook me awake. "Mrs. Dawson?"

I blinked groggily at the nurse in blue scrubs. "I'm Mason's fiancée. Mercy Gunderson."

"The doctor would like to speak with you." She glanced at Lex, who sat up and rubbed his eyes. "Do you want me to stay out here with your son while you go back?"

"No, he's coming with me."

"That's fine." We followed her. She coded in a number on the keypad and swiped her ID. The big doors opened.

It was eerily quiet in the ER. I expected people to be yelling and machines to be beeping. Nurses and doctors racing about. But the action seemed to be centered on banks of monitors. The overhead lights were dim. I caught sight of medical personnel with their feet up on the desk, heads back, taking a nap in the lull. One person wearing vibrant purple scrubs dotted with horses restocked a medical supply cabinet. Another person changed the physician's name on a white dry erase board.

Along the corridor were rooms with curtains drawn and rooms with doors shut and rooms with doors open; empty gurneys lined the hallway. So much to look at I nearly ran into the back of the nurse as she let us into a tiny cubicle-like office.

The man offered his hand. "I'm Dr. Jeffers."

"Mercy Gunderson, Mason Dawson's fiancée. This is Lex, his son."

"Have a seat. I know it's been quite a few hours since Mr. Dawson was brought in, but we needed to observe him before we decided on a course of action."

"Has he regained consciousness?"

Dr. Jeffers shook his head. "That's not necessarily a bad thing. Here's why: the impact with the bull caused massive swelling in his brain."

I felt like I was going to throw up right on his neatly ordered desk.

"At this point we have no idea if there's brain damage. In the first hours he was under observation, the swelling increased significantly."

"What does that mean?"

"We needed to take immediate action to stop the swelling. We gave Mr. Dawson an IV with Mannitol, a chemical compound that helps suck water out of the brain and reduces intracranial pressure. This procedure alleviated some of the pressure. Then my colleague, Dr. Masters, an anesthesiologist, recommended Propofol, a sedative used during surgery, to put Sheriff Dawson into a medically induced coma."

"Coma?" Lex repeated.

I gently squeezed his shoulder.

"There is some controversy surrounding choosing this method, but I spoke with colleagues after our first corrective attempt didn't produce the hoped-for results. We believe a medically induced coma is the best course of treatment because Sheriff Dawson is young. He's in excellent physical condition. Putting him under allows an opportunity for the brain swelling to recede, which limits the amount of brain tissue that can be permanently damaged." Dr. Jeffers gave me a considering look. "Do you want to hear all this now? I know it's late, and you've been here for hours."

"I'm fully awake, so fill me in."

"The benefit of this type of treatment is that the coma is reversible. We can adjust the amount of Propofol entering his system and bring him out of it at any time. Naturally, we want to do that only when his brain has had a chance to heal. During a brain injury, the metabolism of the brain is altered. With drugs that put the brain at rest, we can try to keep it from shutting down other important body functions. But because the main effects of the sedative are outside the brain, that also means he's on medication to keep his blood pressure up and to keep his heart pumping. He's also on a respirator, so we can mechanically control his respiration rate. We are closely monitoring his EEG—his brain waves. Any questions so far?"

About ten million. "Any idea how long he'll be under?"

"There is no set time. I've dealt with this situation before, and if I had to hazard a guess at this point, I'd say we're looking at around six to seven days. Obviously, we want Mr. Dawson brought out of it as soon as it's safe because of the other potential health issues associated with his being in this state."

"What other health issues?"

"Pneumonia. Blood clots. Muscle paralysis. All conditions that stem from patient immobility during the coma and that could linger after he regains consciousness."

I closed my eyes. So many thoughts racing through my head. Would Mason ever be the same? And if he wasn't . . . would he push me away? Would he think I couldn't handle him being less than perfect?

"I understand it's a lot to comprehend, Miz Gunderson. And the 'wait and see' diagnosis is never ideal, but it's the only one I have right now."

"Thank you. Thanks for . . . working to save him." That sounded lame, but I really didn't know what else to say.

"You're welcome. I'll be monitoring his condition personally. And I'll keep you as up-to-date as possible." He looked at the chart. "This cell number is the best way to reach you? Do you have a work number during the day?"

"I'm a federal agent with the FBI, but that number is your best bet for reaching me at any hour of the day or night."

His eyebrows rose, and he looked at me a little differently after I disclosed my occupation.

Lex blurted, "When can I see him?"

"He's in ICU," the doctor started. "It's been a long night, and maybe if you come back tomorrow—" Dr. Jeffers stopped speaking when I shook my head.

"We need to see him. If only for a minute."

After a couple seconds he nodded. "I'll arrange it. But you should pass on the 'no visitor's' policy to other family members."

"His coworkers, too?"

He nodded. "The slightest infection is deadly for him. So if either of you develop even a case of the sniffles, you'd best stay away."

"Understood."

"I'll take you up to see him right now. That way I can answer any questions."

"Sounds fair," I said to Lex. "I know you'll make your dad proud and follow all the rules, right?"

Dr. Jeffers talked to Lex, trying to put him at ease. He led us out of the ER through a maze of hallways until we were at a bank of elevators, a different set than the ones I'd used before.

We stopped on the fourth floor and took a left. The doctor spoke briefly to a nurse, and she directed us to an area where we put on protective clothing. Surgical masks. Latex gloves. Plastic gowns. Once we were suited up, Dr. Jeffers stopped in front of room 406.

I froze outside the door, waiting for courage to muscle past my fear. Waiting for Dawson's gentle hand to touch my face, urge me to open my eyes and reassure me that this was just another bad dream.

Come on Mercy, wake up. It's me. It's just us here, remember?

But the hand clutched in mine was small. The doctor had tried to prepare Lex for what he might see once we were in the room, yet I'd in no way prepared myself.

I couldn't do this.

The hiss of a breathing apparatus echoed like a steam radiator, jarring me when Dr. Jeffers opened the door.

I inhaled a deep breath. I clenched my teeth together as I exhaled out my nose.

I couldn't do this.

"Come. *On.*" Lex dragged out those two words. Not even his impatience spurred me. He tugged at me until I followed him.

We both stopped at seeing the big man lying in a hospital bed. The gown he wore left his body uncovered from midthigh. I had the overwhelming urge to cover him, knowing he'd hate being so exposed. His feet were encased in socks. I wanted to yank them off. He hated wearing socks to bed.

I didn't want to look higher than his feet, but I did.

Mason was hooked up to machines and IVs, and I heard the respirator's sucking, wheezing sounds as the machine breathed for him.

"You can come closer," the doctor said softly.

Lex had to jerk hard on my arm to get me to move.

A bunch of apparatuses surrounded his head, so I knew he was there, but I couldn't actually see his face. His hands were by his sides. Even in sleep Dawson's big hands were curled into fists. Or his hands were on me. They were never like this. Flat. Posed. Pale. Artificial-looking. Lifeless.

Don't even fucking think that way.

"Dad?" Lex said. "I know you can't talk, but I wanted you to know I'm here. Lex. And Mercy."

The surgical mask muffled the words, but not the earnestness in them. *Stay strong. For fuck's sake, stay strong for this kid.*

I held myself together even when everything inside me was starting to fracture.

"Mercy?" Lex said. "Don't you wanna say something to him?"

I swallowed before I asked the doctor, "Can I touch him?"

"Briefly."

My feet felt encased in cement as I closed the gap to the hospital bed. I ran my latex-covered fingers over his knuckles then up his wrist and thick forearm, stopping when I reached the sleeve of his hospital gown. I leaned forward. "I love you. And if you don't want the wrath of a crazy woman on your head, you will pull your stubborn ass through this. You will not leave me alone, goddammit. You will not—" My voice caught. Only through sheer will did I manage not to throw myself on him and weep.

I turned away. The doctor had left and a young nurse stood beside Lex. She looked at me. "I'm sorry. You have to go."

Lex shook his head. "I can stay and talk to him. And when he wakes up, I'll be able to run right out and let you guys know."

That's when my tears fell.

The nurse squeezed his shoulder. "That's real sweet of you to offer, but the very best thing you can do right now? Allow your father time to heal."

"But they say on TV that people in a coma can hear and stuff. I don't wanna leave him here. I don't want him to think that no one cares about him."

I tugged Lex against my side, and he burrowed into me. "He knows we care, Lex. I promise, if I thought the doctors were wrong, we'd be bunking in your dad's hospital room."

"Really?"

"Really."

18

I thought I might have problems staying awake during the drive to the ranch, but I focused on the sunrise. The purple horizon morphed into pink—hues ranging from bubblegum to salmon to cotton candy—finally bleeding into the orange and peach tones of dawn.

First thing we did after stumbling out of the truck was feed the dogs. Strange to beat Jake to that morning chore.

Then I started making calls.

Lex stayed beside me as I gave Deputy Moore the lowdown about Dawson's condition. She didn't say much. I realized I probably should've called her earlier so she could have filled Mason's shift. I shut off Dawson's cell phone and put it in his T-shirt drawer.

Next I called Hope. I pleaded exhaustion and promised to let her know when we woke up.

I called Shay last. I needed his gruff demeanor more than sympathy.

Lex was damn near falling asleep on his feet, so I marched him to his room. He let me tuck him in.

Too damn wired to sleep, I paced. I sorted laundry. Geneva called to inform me that she'd be over later with food.

Word got around fast in Eagle River County, and the home phone began to ring off the hook. I appreciated that the sheriff garnered such genuine concern, but it was emotionally draining to have to repeatedly explain what had happened.

I checked on Lex and finally crawled into bed myself.

I woke a little after three, not refreshed but grateful for dreamless sleep. I'd left the door unlocked and saw food piled on the table. As I contemplated snatching a cookie, a knock sounded. Shay let himself into the kitchen. Looking around, he took off his coat and draped it over the chair.

The words *Make yourself comfy* dried on my tongue.

I leaned against the doorjamb separating the kitchen and the living room, still in my pajamas.

His eyes met mine. He seemed at a loss for what to do with his hands. Finally, he said, "Jesus, Mercy. I'm so sorry."

I didn't move. He came to me. Standoffish Shay hugged me. Surrounded by warmth from his body, I hadn't realized I'd been so cold until I started to shake.

Once I started, I couldn't stop. Still, I didn't cry. Mason would've swept me into his arms and held me until the shakes stopped.

But Shay wasn't Dawson. He held on to me as long as he could stand it. Then he settled me on a chair, poured me a glass of Wild Turkey, and tersely said, "Drink."

I drank. As soon as the glass was empty he poured another.

At some point I realized Shay had taken my hands while I stared at the second glass of whiskey. One night last year I'd done shots, determined to keep track of how many I could handle before I passed out. Fifteen. It wouldn't take that many belts right now. Tempting, to test that theory.

"Mercy?" Shay's voice snapped me out of my imagined alcoholic stupor. "What have you been doing?"

"Pacing. Sleeping. Wondering how I'll get through the next week."

"That's how long . . ."

"They're keeping him sedated? Yeah. It sucks."

"I bet."

I told him about the limited visiting hours. Five minutes an hour. "It sucks."

"I'm sorry."

I told him about the "wait and see" diagnosis. "It sucks."

"Hanging out with an eleven-year-old boy hasn't done your vocabulary any favors."

"*You* suck."

He smiled softly, and then it faded. "Talk to me."

"I will go crazy one minute at a time if I don't have something to take my mind off this." I'd already felt myself slipping into that deep pit of despair. Questioning why I ever thought I could be happy for any amount of time because something bad always happened and ruined it.

"What can I do?"

"Put me to work. I can't stand around for a week and wring my hands."

"I'll see what I can do."

"Thank you." I inhaled. Exhaled slowly. "Did you work on the cases this weekend?"

"Some."

"Did you get anywhere?"

"Not really."

"I got to thinking that I hadn't told you about Penny's son Devlin and his gambling problem. He owes money all over the place, including to Saro, Rollie, and Latimer—"

"Mercy, stop."

Confused, I looked at him.

"Your focus needs to be elsewhere this week. Not on the cases."

"But—"

Shay shook his head and squeezed my hands. "Don't try to bury yourself in work. It won't help. Trust me, I know. You've got more important things to deal with."

The stairs creaked, and Lex raced into the kitchen, stopping upon seeing Shay sitting so close to me, holding my hands, while I was in my pajamas.

I eased back. "Hey, Lex, you remember my coworker Shay Turnbull?"

He shook his head. "Have you heard any news about my dad?"

"No, I promised I'd wake you up if I did."

"So when can we go to the hospital?" His gaze landed on my empty lowball glass. "You haven't been drinking all day, have you?" He stepped closer, sniffled the air like a human Breathalyzer.

"I'm fine. We should both eat something before we go."

Lex's mouth turned mutinous. "I'm not hungry."

"Well, I *am*. So park it. As soon as we eat, we'll go."

"Is he coming with us?" Lex asked suspiciously.

"Nope. No visitors, remember?"

Shay took that as his cue to leave.

I walked him outside. "I appreciate your driving out. I . . ." I wanted to ask him to stay longer and felt stupid for it.

"Hey." He grabbed my hand, forcing my attention. "Anything you need. Anytime, day or night. Call me. Okay?"

"Okay."

He retreated. "I'll see if I can arrange for you to help Carsten at the VS office in Eagle River this week."

"Thanks." I watched his Blazer disappear down the driveway before I returned inside.

I microwaved two helpings of Geneva's chicken pot pie. Lex finished his in approximately three mouthfuls and was out the door, waiting in the truck, before I swallowed my last bite.

Usually, I didn't mind the silence between us, but at this moment, it was choking me. About halfway into town, I asked, "Do you miss your mom?"

Lex squirmed. "Sometimes. But I like it here better."

Another silent void filled the cab. Then the boy started bouncing his feet. He leaned forward, burying his face in his knees and wrapping his arms around his calves.

"Lex. Are you gonna be sick?"

A muffled, "No."

"Do you have to go to the bathroom?"

"No."

"What's wrong?"

He raised his head. "Why did you ask about my mom? Is it because if my dad's not all right, you'll make me go back to Colorado to live with her?"

I hadn't thought of that.

"Because if he's in a wheelchair, I can take care of him and stuff. I promise I would be a really big help."

Don't cry. "I know." I set my hand on his shoulder. "I guess we'll have to wait and see."

Monday morning Lex looked up from his bowl of Cookie Crisp cereal when I entered the kitchen. I paused in front of the empty coffeepot. Mason made coffee in the morning. It was just another pointed reminder that he wasn't here.

I snagged a Coke from the fridge. I turned around to see Lex frowning at me. "What?"

"Will they let you wear a gun at the hospital?"

"No, why?"

"So why do you have it on?"

"Because I have to go to work today, and you have to go to school."

His spoon clattered into his bowl. "What? No way. I'm going to the hospital to stay with my dad."

"There's nothing you can do at the hospital."

"I can talk to him. You heard that nurse saying he can probably hear us. I want him to know I'm there."

"Which is why we'll visit him after you're out of school this afternoon."

His green eyes, identical to Mason's, narrowed, and I recognized the look—ass chewing ahead.

"So you're just gonna go to work today and forget about him like nothing happened?" Lex demanded. "What if he dies?"

"Don't say that," I snapped. "Don't you *ever* say it, let alone think it, do you hear me?"

Lex dropped his tear-filled gaze.

Goddammit. I didn't know how to do this. I probably should've hugged him—done anything besides yell at him. I counted to twenty. "Look, Lex, we're both on edge because we're worried about your dad. But there's nothing we can do at the hospital today except get in the nurses' way. We can only see him for five minutes at a time. He isn't just gonna wake up, and honestly, that wouldn't be a good thing anyway.

He'd want you in class. He'd want me to go to work and do my job. And we'll stay at the hospital as long as you want tonight."

"You promise?"

"I promise." I knocked back a big swig of soda, hoping the fizz would dissolve the lump in my throat. "Now get cracking so you're not late."

He bailed, leaving his bowl on the table. Mason would've made him come back and pick it up, but today, I let it slide.

Dawson's condition hadn't changed. Each day passed in a blur. One day. Two days. Three days. Four days. Lex and I visited him every night. And every night I felt myself slipping deeper into depression.

I made Jake remove the booze from the house. It was too great a temptation.

Other things got moved around. Pictures. Clothing. Kitchen items. I snapped at Lex about putting things back where he found them. Hope intervened. I snapped at her, too, ignoring how irrational it was to lose my cool because I couldn't find a fucking spatula.

Carsten tried to get me to talk. If I could've talked to anyone, it would've been her. She was a genuinely thoughtful and kind person, not a pushover—Turnbull had pegged her completely wrong.

But talking to her meant I had to consider that my life might change drastically in the next week. I refused to give voice to "what ifs" about Dawson.

A few people stopped into the Victim Services office to ask me about Dawson's condition. Sheldon War Bonnet. Tribal Police Chief Looks Twice. Officer Orson. Fergie. It bothered me a little that I hadn't heard from Sophie because I knew she was fond of the sheriff. I blamed John-John. If nothing else, blaming him made me feel better.

So I was surprised when Latimer Elk Thunder ambled into the offices on Thursday afternoon.

"Agent Gunderson, I just heard about what happened to Sheriff Dawson. What a shock. I came over right away to tell you how sorry I am."

"Thank you."

"If there's anything you need, anything I can do, don't hesitate to ask."

Here was my opening. Hopefully, if the FBI got wind of this, they'd chalk up my nosiness and crap attitude to stress. "Does that offer include lending me money for hospital bills? I heard you're the go-to guy around here for a short-term loan."

He stiffened briefly, then smiled. "You heard right. Sadly, banks aren't an option for many of our tribal members in need . . . So I fill the need. It's not like I'm getting rich for providing this service."

Bullshit.

"Are you in a financial bind, Agent Gunderson?"

"No, I'm more concerned for a family friend. Devlin Pretty Horses owes you money. I'm betting not a small amount, either."

"I don't normally discuss my business, but I can assure you that I'm not worried. Devlin is good for it."

"How can that be? He doesn't have a job. He lives with his mother. Devlin has nothing of value."

Latimer parked his behind on the corner of my desk. "Now that's a harsh judgment. You can't possibly know *everything* about the Pretty Horses family or their financial situation, current or future."

I fought the urge to stab his casually swinging leg with a letter opener. "And you do?"

An indulgent smile. "Of course. I'm in a position where I have full budget oversight for the tribe. We have several well-pensioned employees, and it's my job to make sure our financial experts stay on top of the employees' investment portfolios. Penny worked for the tribe for over twenty years. She had a better-than-average wage, so she had a better-than-average pension, too.

"And she had decent health insurance coverage, thank goodness. Although aggressive cancer treatment will eat up that lifetime maximum pretty fast. But it doesn't appear to me that Penny's family will have outstanding medical bills, which is a plus in this horrible situation." He shook his head sadly. "Imagine getting such a dire cancer diagnosis one month before retirement."

He wore an expectant look, like he wanted to keep talking. And I realized, as he alternately smirked, preened, and showed sympathy, that his ego would be his downfall. Latimer Elk Thunder needed to prove to me that he was smarter than me.

Rollie's warning popped into my head: *Mark my words, whoever is doin' this is one smart SOB.*

Not only was Elk Thunder smart, he was slick. So I had to ask him the right questions so he would feel he was doing me a favor as well as putting me in my place. "It is sad. No one can prepare for something like that."

"True. But between us, Penny was better prepared than most. The tribe provides a great benefits and retirement package to employees, complete with 401k, disability insurance, and life insurance."

A life insurance policy.

Whoa. Why had he specifically mentioned that?

Because it mattered that Penny had a life insurance policy now that she was dead.

Penny would have had to name a beneficiary.

But who? Not Sophie. Before the cancer diagnosis Penny probably assumed she'd outlive her mother. Plus, Sophie would call a financial windfall from death "blood money."

Would Penny name her son the beneficiary? Most likely. But John-John ran a successful bar, and he'd have the same attitude about the money as Sophie.

That left one other family member.

Surely Penny hadn't been dumb enough to list Devlin as her beneficiary?

John-John and Sophie would both feel too guilty to take the money from Penny's life insurance policy. But Devlin wouldn't feel the slightest bit guilty. He'd snatch that cash like it was his due.

The tribal president knew how much Penny's life insurance policy was worth. He also had to have known that the long-term outlook for Penny's cancer survival hadn't been good. So he could lend Devlin the face value of the policy. He'd know exactly when the insurance company cut the check to Penny's beneficiary. He'd make sure he collected every dime, plus whatever astronomical interest fee, before the ink on the insurance company check was even dry.

Something truly awful occurred to me. If there was a double indemnity clause on the life insurance policy? Then Penny's getting murdered would double the cash payout.

"Agent Gunderson?"

I refocused. "Sorry. I'm just—"

"Understandable." He patted my hand like I was a child.

Which pissed me off. "So did Arlette have life insurance? I mean, as your ward she would fall under your health insurance policy."

He stilled.

"I'm also curious as to why you didn't come into the tribal PD for an official interview. It looks a little suspicious, don't you think? That the tribal president, who was all fired up to have the FBI in on a missing-persons case, who was also worried about impropriety, wouldn't make himself available for questions."

"What are you implying, Agent Gunderson?"

"I'm not implying anything, Mr. Elk Thunder. Just stating a fact. I have to wonder just how long you'd hold the position of tribal president if some of the facts in this case were made public to the members of the tribe." I ticked the points off on my fingers. "Arlette's body was found on your political rival's land. Verline's body was found on your political rival's land. Penny Pretty Horses's body was found on your political rival's rental property. One might draw . . . conclusions. Especially when it's revealed that Arlette was secretly seeing Junior Rondeaux on the sly. And isn't it ironic the next victim, Verline Dupris, was living with Rollie Rondeaux, who backed your rival's campaign for president? As did the next victim, Penny Pretty Horses?

"What if it was also disclosed that you benefit from all three deaths? You never wanted your wife's niece to live with you, so you're rid of her *and* you receive a death benefit payment. With Rollie Rondeaux in jail, you're probably picking up some of his loan customers. Now that Penny is dead, her brother can collect on her life insurance policy and make full restitution for the money you lent him." I stood and loomed over him. "Think you'd survive the political storm if any of this was leaked to the press?"

He laughed, but his eyes were nearly black with anger. "Oh, Agent Gunderson, I'm not the one who should be worried about surviving. The reservation is a dangerous place for feds. And women, apparently. Since you're both? Well, *waiscu,* watch your back."

Waiscu. The derogatory Lakota name for a white girl. "Are you threatening me, Tribal President Elk Thunder?"

"Just stating a fact." He pushed up quickly from the desk, surprising me and literally knocking me off balance.

I stumbled over my chair and into the wall.

He gave me a scathing once-over, bit off something guttural-sounding in Lakota, spun on his heel, and left.

Goddammit.

Rather than letting my anger send my blood pressure to stroke level, I sat in my chair and furiously wrote down my thoughts. After that display? Latimer Elk Thunder jumped to the top of my list as the killer. Part of me thought he wouldn't sully his hands; he'd hire someone else to do it for cash—or as a task to settle a loan. But part of me also believed he'd take pride in getting blood on his hands and doing the job his way.

But then . . . my theory about the past murders disguised as random deaths wouldn't hold water.

My thoughts raced back and forth until I was nearly dizzy.

I had no one to talk to about any of this.

In that moment I missed Dawson with an ache so acute I had to put my head between my legs to stop the pain.

Focus, Mercy.

I breathed.

That's all I could do: take one breath at a time.

I was still in that addled and agitated state of mind when I headed to my pickup. As I messed with my key fob to unlock the door, I saw a manila envelope taped to my steering wheel. Immediately, my gun was in my hand as I spun around, scanning the area. I didn't see anyone. I shoved my gun in my holster and tried the door handle.

Unlocked.

Good thing I hadn't left any guns in my truck.

I slid in and shut the door. The envelope hadn't been sealed. There were no markings of any kind. I tipped the envelope, and pictures spilled onto my lap.

The first picture had been shot through my living room window. I had Joy on my hip, and her head had been crossed out with an X in red marker. The next picture was Hope in her car, backing down the driveway of her house, her head crossed out. The third photo of Jake had been snapped while he rode his horse, his hat-covered head crossed out. The fourth shot showed Lex waiting for the school bus, his face inside his hoodie marked with a red X. The last picture was of Dawson standing beside his patrol car out in the middle of nowhere, talking on his phone, his face also obliterated by a red X.

My lungs were absent of air for long enough that spots began to dance in front of my eyes. Somehow I gulped in oxygen and let it out. And did it again. I stared at the images, wondering what this sick son of a bitch had planned. To fuck with me? Gauging how homicidal I'd get? Or how scared I'd get?

I was already there—on both counts.

Anyone could've put these in my pickup.

What the hell was I supposed to do? Fight back? Take this to the FBI? I don't know how long I sat there, weighing my options and finding none viable because I was still flying blind. I had no one to talk to about this. One by one, I slid the pictures back into the envelope.

Two loud raps on my window made me jump. My head whipped toward the sound, and I saw Sheldon War Bonnet's shocked face through the glass.

Shit.

Casually, I set aside the envelope and cranked down the window. But I couldn't muster a smile.

"Agent Gunderson? Are you all right?"

No. Thanks for asking. Now go away. I cleared my throat. "I'm fine. Why?"

"Oh, no reason. I came out to grab something from my car, and I noticed you sitting in your vehicle. And on my way back inside, I see you're still here. You sure everything is okay?"

"Just got lost in thought. For longer than I realized, apparently."

Sheldon nodded. "It happens. Especially after all you've been through lately. Any change in Sheriff Dawson's condition?"

I shook my head.

"Any idea how long you'll be working in the FBI's VS offices?"

"Probably just through tomorrow."

"Then you'll be back at the FBI offices in Rapid?"

What a snoopy fucker. "Yeah. The need for our services is over at this point, unless new information on any of these cases surfaces."

"Well, I liked having you around. Even if you didn't enjoy having to do research." He smiled. "Don't be a stranger, Mercy."

I couldn't lie. I couldn't smile. I just said, "Take care, Sheldon."

"You, too. See you soon." He limped around the front end of my truck. Then he stopped, waved, and cut through the cars toward the building.

A phone call from Lex prompted me to get going, because, once again, I was late picking him up.

19

When my stomach rumbled after I dropped Lex off at school the next morning, I realized I'd skipped supper the night before and breakfast this morning. Without Sophie nagging me to eat, I forgot.

I missed her. Not just her cooking, but her offbeat comments. Her bossiness. Her nosiness. I missed how she always seemed to know when I needed a hug or a sharp word.

My life had big holes in it. I couldn't do anything but fill the one in my belly.

I slid into my favorite booth at the Blackbird Diner.

Mitzi hustled over with coffee. "Mercy. Hon, how you holding up?"

I'm about to crack into a million pieces. Thanks for asking. I scoured the menu even though I had it memorized. "I'm taking it day by day."

"We're all praying for Sheriff Dawson. He's a good man."

"Thank you, Mitzi. We appreciate it." I pointed to the rancher's breakfast—eggs, toast, bacon, sausage, hash browns. More food than I needed, but I ordered it anyway.

"Coming right up."

Maybe it was petty to wonder if pity had kept her from demanding that I remove my gun.

We'd been allowed to stay with Mason for a half hour last night. I'd held his hand while Lex had talked. And talked. About guy things. About things Lex wouldn't tell me. It had hit me, then, how much Mason meant to his son and how quickly it had happened. What would Lex do if his father wasn't the same?

Which inevitably led to the question: What would *I* do if Mason wasn't the same?

I'd held it together until we'd gone home. I held it together through the TV shows Lex asked me to watch with him. I held it together until I crawled in bed and Mason wasn't there.

The sheets smelled like him. I'd crushed his pillow to my chest and couldn't hold it together another second.

Tears are never cathartic for me. I understand that holding them in and never crying is a type of avoidance. There had to be a better coping mechanism for fear and sadness than one that resulted in red-rimmed eyes, Rudolph's nose, and a wet, puffy face.

But I'd promised not to revert to my recent outlet for frustration—a bottle of whiskey—so tears won out. Pissed me off I hadn't felt the slightest bit better. Really pissed me off that I had no idea what to do with those damn pictures. I'd feel stupid running to the FBI.

Won't you feel worse if the threat is real and someone you love gets hurt?

I wasn't alone with my conflicting thoughts long, there in my little corner of the Blackbird Diner.

Deputy Kiki Moore joined me, sliding coffee-to-go on the tabletop. "It's automatic for me to buy two cups. One for me, one for the sheriff."

I understood her loss of the familiar, but I swore if she started bawling I'd slap her.

She looked up at me. "No change?"

I shook my head.

"Damn. Mercy, I'm sorry. This sucks all the way around. We were short-staffed before this . . ." She took a long sip of coffee. "I don't have the title of acting sheriff—I don't want it because I have faith Dawson will return—but I will tell you that I went ahead and hired one of the applicants for the deputy's job."

"Who?"

Kiki met my gaze. "Robert Orson. He's an officer with the tribal PD. You know him?"

"Yeah. When did he apply?"

"A month ago."

Interesting that Officer Orson hadn't told me he'd applied for the job before I'd suggested it to him.

"Dawson wasn't sure about hiring him, so he'd been dragging his feet, waiting to see if any of the other applicants passed the background check. Deputy Jazinski, Deputy Purcell, and I cannot work twenty-four/seven. Even with a new hire we're still a deputy short." She grinned. "That ain't the case with Orson. He's a tall guy. He'll probably just scare people when he climbs out of the patrol car."

I smiled because Officer Orson was about as scary as a kitten. "Probably."

Kiki scooted out of the booth after Mitzi dropped off my breakfast.

Between bites, I found myself looking for Rollie.

Or Shay.

Or someone else to butt in like usual.

But I ate alone and had that overwhelming urge to cry.

Either put on a fucking bib or quit being such a baby and eat.

I finished, paid, and was in my truck listening to Miranda Lambert singing about a dry town as I cruised to the rez. Tempting to drive straight past and play hooky. The weatherman had predicted a balmy fifty degrees for the day. Target shooting was a coping mechanism that might shake me out of . . . whatever this was.

Melancholy? Too tame a word to describe how I felt.

But I was definitely disturbed. Maybe a little unstable.

After I parked in the lot shared by tribal headquarters and tribal police, I stayed in my pickup and stared at the buildings, wondering what I was even doing here.

I appreciated that the FBI had assigned me close to home, allowing me to be available for Lex. My usual *Buck up, suck it up, don't fuck it up* mantra wasn't helping today. The last thing I wanted to do was kill time in the Victim Services office and answer phones. I decided to stop by the tribal archives first and snag a cup of coffee. Pretty pathetic if a conversation with oddball Sheldon War Bonnet held more appeal than sitting in the office trying to get to the next level of Angry Birds on my BlackBerry.

I trudged downstairs, but the archives department was closed. I rang the bell. Wasn't it supposed to be open on Fridays? Maybe Sheldon was on coffee break? I beat on the door. "It's Agent Gunderson."

Just as I was about to ring the bell again, a voice behind me said, "That doesn't help."

I whirled around and recognized the girl sitting there hidden in the shadows. Arlette's friend. "Hey, Naomi. What are you doing here?"

She scowled. "If you're thinking I'm supposed to be in class, my teachers excused me to do research for my project. I'm just waiting for Sheldon."

Sheldon? That seemed a little informal. "Has he been here today?"

"Not that I can tell." Naomi gave me a once-over. "What're you doing here?"

"Same thing you are. Using research as an excuse not to go to my job."

That brought a quick smile from her. "I'll admit, as I walked across the football field, I thought about ditching school for the whole day."

"We are on the same wavelength. Mind if I join you?" She shrugged, and I sat on the concrete floor across from her.

"You have to do research for your job?" she asked.

"Lots of it."

"So it's not all interrogating witnesses, finding clues, and arresting bad guys?"

I snorted. "Not even close."

She raised her chin a notch. "Well, it should be. Cops around here suck."

"Why's that?"

Naomi's gaze narrowed, trying to figure out if I was being serious or sarcastic. After coming to the conclusion I wasn't jacking her around, she said, "When my mom died? The cops said it was from a drug overdose. But she'd been clean for, like, six months. No relapse or nothing. Then she just disappeared and didn't tell my grandma or me where she was going. She *never* did that. Not even when she was really high. Three days later the cops found her dead in a ditch outside of town."

A strange sense of déjà vu washed over me. I'd read that file. I'd included it in my case report. "Did this happen about two years ago?"

Naomi straightened. "Yes."

"What was your mom's name?"

"Diane Jump."

I dug in my satchel and flipped open my notebook. I'd flagged three cases of assumed ODs. The first girl was young, only sixteen, but she'd been in rehab off and on since she was twelve. The second victim was a woman in her late thirties, with multiple arrests and time served in jail for various drug infractions. The last victim was older, in her early sixties, and she'd been a homeless addict for over twenty years.

Again, I'd written down that I hadn't found any lab reports in any of the individual case files. It was as if the tribal cops had looked at the body, made an assessment about it being a drug-related death, and closed the case.

"Did you find something?" Naomi asked.

"I'm not entirely sure, but there seems to be . . . a common thread linking some other cases around that time." I looked at her. "Did the police tell you they ran postmortem drug tests on your mom?"

She shook her head. "She'd been busted for drug possession so many times, they knew her drug of choice was smack. They assumed that's what killed her." She couldn't contain the hope in her voice: "Do you think the cops were wrong?"

I searched her eyes. "Why is this so important to you?"

"It's not important to me. Well, okay, it is. Like I said, my mom had been clean for the first time in her life. It'd mean a lot to my grandma to know that my mom hadn't been lying to us. That she'd really started to change." Her brown eyes were surprisingly defiant. "It ain't like we're gonna sue the cops or nothin'. We'd just like to know the truth."

That's when I did a dumb thing, even though it'd probably come back to bite me in the ass. "Here's the deal. I'll tell you what I suspect, but if you tell anyone I said this, I'll deny it. Just between you and your *unci*, okay? I think someone killed your mom and made it look like an overdose." I expected tears. Or outrage. Not a sad nod of acceptance.

"Thank you. That's what I thought, or maybe what I'd hoped . . ." She cleared her throat and glanced at my notebook as I shut it. "That's the type of research you're doing?"

"Yeah. It's kind of depressing."

"I'll bet Sheldon was a big help. He knows everything."

Again with the familiar use of *Sheldon*. "Does he help you with research?"

"He's usually super-busy, but there's a lot more reference materials for history projects here than there are at the high school. Arlette came down here all the time."

Why hadn't Sheldon mentioned that to me?

"She and Sheldon talked books. So after she quit hanging out with me, I started coming down here because I was missing her. I thought maybe . . ." She blushed. "I thought maybe Sheldon would discuss vampire books with me like he had with Arlette. He's easy to talk to, even if he does talk a lot."

How well I knew that.

"And man, didja ever notice he asks a ton of questions?"

"I had noticed that." I paused, not wanting to seem too eager. "What kind of questions does he ask you?"

"What questions *didn't* he ask me?" she half complained. "But it is kinda cool because no one at school cares what I think."

"High school pretty much sucks ass. That's why I couldn't wait to leave and join the army."

"Really? That's what I wanna do, too! Since Sheldon served in the military, he's been telling me what branch of the service I should apply to."

"I'd definitely tell you to join the army." I smirked. "What did he say?"

"Any branch besides the National Guard if I wanted to see any real action. With the way he kept grilling me about my interview with the police, I figured he'd probably been a military cop, so I was surprised when he said he was in communications. He wanted to know if I'd heard anything. If the tribal police had possible suspects."

That was really weird. Why would he care? To get a scoop on gossip?

"Come to think of it"—Naomi squinted at me—"he asked a lot of questions about you."

"Me? Why?"

"I dunno. He thinks the tribal cops are idiots, too. He said he was interested in how the big guns do it."

It was unnerving to hear that Sheldon had used my favorite phrase. How closely had he been monitoring me when I'd been working in the archives?

Paranoid much, Gunderson?

I stood. "Well, this big gun is gonna get in big trouble if she doesn't get something done today."

"I think I'll wait a little longer to see if he shows up."

"You don't wanna go back to school?"

She wrinkled her nose. "My next class is algebra."

"Keep your grades up," I warned. "The military recruiters look at things like attendance, and academic records. It'll help them choose where to place you after you're through boot camp."

"Oh, okay." She looked at me strangely, almost shyly. "Would you be willing to talk to me sometime about what it's really like being in the army?"

"Sure. And if you promise me you won't skip class anymore, I'll see if I can't put in a good word for you with the recruiter."

"That'd be so awesome!" Naomi scribbled in her notebook, ripped out a piece of paper, and handed it to me. "I won't call you because I know you're busy, but I got a new cell number, so you can call me when you get time."

"Why the new number?"

Another scowl. "Because Mackenzie posted my old one in the computer lab with a note that I was a snitch."

"Doing the right thing doesn't make you a snitch." I put the paper
in my notebook. "Now get to class and balance some equations." Her
laughter followed me up the stairs.

Lost in thought, I literally ran into Officer Ferguson when I walked
through the front door.

"Agent Gunderson. What are you doing over here? Hanging out with
your boyfriend?" she joked. Then her face paled. "Oh, shit. I'm sorry. I
forgot the sheriff is in the hospital. Sometimes I just open my mouth
and don't—"

"It's okay." I paused. "But I'm curious: Who'd you mean by my 'boyfriend'?"

"Sheldon. In the archives department. I think he's got a thing for you."

I frowned. "Why would you think that?"

"He always asks about you."

"You have lots of occasions to talk to Mr. War Bonnet, Officer
Ferguson?"

She shrugged defensively. "I usually bring boxes of case reports over.
Sheldon and I shoot the shit." Fergie looked over her shoulder and then
leaned in closer. "I've got a crush on him, okay? Not that I'd ever act on it."

"Really?" I didn't want to say eww, but . . . eww.

"I know what you're thinking. But last year we had about thirty boxes
to transfer here, and I wasn't sure if Sheldon wanted me to load them in
the elevator or bring them around back to the loading bay. When I got
down here, I found the outer door open, which never happens on days
the archives are closed. I poked my head in before I announced myself
and saw Sheldon hefting huge boxes over his head. Then he climbed up
to the top of the shelving unit like a monkey. He was wearing one of
those wifebeater-type shirts, and it rode up." She released a soft whistle.
"I thought six-pack abs were a myth, but Sheldon has them. Man, and
his arms are completely ripped. In fact, his upper body is really toned.
It's a shame he keeps it hidden under such baggy clothes."

Why would Sheldon hide his physique? I'd always seen him as a doughy guy. Something Shay had said about Rollie jumped into my head. *Did you see how he shuffled out of here like an old man? Trying to leave the impression that he's harmless and helpless?*

But it made no sense why Sheldon would want people to think he was gimped up. For sympathy? So people would assume it was from an injury he'd sustained in the service?

Fergie's voice pulled me out of those thoughts. "I didn't want to get caught gawking at him, so I ducked around the corner and waited a few minutes. Then I yelled real loud when I came in."

"Did he stand on a ladder so you could admire him in all his sweaty, muscled glory?"

She chuckled. "No, he'd put on a long-sleeved shirt at least one size too big. I assumed it was a hand-me-down from his uncle."

"Do you know his uncle?"

"He was in charge of the archives when I first started as a cop. Then Sheldon moved back to care for him and to take over the archives job. Harold is a sweet guy. Quiet."

"Do you ever see him?"

Fergie looked thoughtful. "No, he has health issues. But Sheldon talks about him. Harold is lucky that Sheldon lives with him so he didn't end up in a nursing home. Anyway, I have more boxes for him. I've been trying to dump them off for the last month, but he keeps telling me the storage area by the loading bay is full. I'm tired of getting my butt chewed by the police chief because we've got sensitive case files stacked in the hallway."

"How full can it be back there? What else does he use the loading bay for?"

"Between us? Nothing. I saw a cot back there one time, but I never let on that I noticed his little R and R corner. So what if he's made a little nesting spot to take naps? I don't care. I just want him to quit stalling and take these boxes off my hands."

Now that I'd thought about it, I'd never asked him about the locked door in the far back room. "Well, Sheldon isn't here today. Maybe he's taking his uncle to the doctor or something."

"Could be. He'll be pleased to hear you're concerned about him." She nudged me with her shoulder and grinned. "Sheldon is crushing on you big time, Mercy."

"Maybe the tribal PD should start drug testing, because obviously you've been smoking crack."

"Ha-ha. Seriously you wouldn't see it. Bet you also don't know your partner—I mean, your *coworker,* Agent Turnbull—has a big-time crush on you, too. As does *my* coworker, Officer Orson. Even Nancy in the jail told me you're da bomb."

What a load of horseshit. "I think you're mixing up annoyance and affection, Officer Fergalicious, at least when it comes to my coworker," I said dryly.

"Think what you want. But I know that Sheldon is mighty interested in you and your contribution to the cases. He's asked me everything, from what you say about your military service, to how good you are on the shooting range, to your family connections, to your relationship with Sheriff Dawson, to your hobbies."

Based on my former military position and the need to keep a low profile, a feeling of wrongness churned in my gut. "Huh. Well, I'm really not that interesting."

"Tell that to the guy who's carrying around a lock of your hair."

I went very still. "Excuse me?"

"Kidding, Gunderson. But I wouldn't put it past him to steal something of yours just so he'd have an excuse to ask if you lost it and could give it back."

"I hope you didn't give him my address."

"*You* would've given him your address when you enrolled in the tribe."

I remembered the day I'd registered as a member of the tribe, as I'd been suffering from a particularly vicious hangover. Hope was snippy with me because I'd insisted she and Joy come along to enroll. I'd had a sense of resentment that I couldn't put my real occupation in the army on my application.

My face flushed with mortification. Had I really written "insurgent removal specialist"—aka sniper—on my tribal enrollment form?

Holy shit. Holy, holy, shit. I'd be in huge fucking trouble if the army ever found out.

No wonder Sheldon showed interest in me. Question was—how much interest? Who else had he told? My gaze zoomed back to Officer Ferguson. "I gotta admit, I was really hungover the day I applied for tribal membership. I might've written down all sorts of lies and stuff."

"Whatever you wrote was fascinating enough that Sheldon asked a bunch of questions when you lost the election and took a job with the FBI."

"Maybe I should pay Sheldon a visit. See if he's all right. See if he'll let me write a retraction statement on certain areas of my tribal enrollment form, due to my, ah, liquid creativity." I paused when she laughed. "Do you know where he lives?"

A guilty look crossed her face.

I tried to keep it light. "Come on, Fergalicious, you already said you had a tiny crush on him. I'd think it was weird if you *didn't* know."

Fergie flashed me a sheepish grin. "When you put it that way . . . he lives about three miles out of town toward Crested Buttes. There's an owl sitting on top of his mailbox, and the entrance to his place is through a gate. I've never seen the house because it's behind a bunch of trees." She paused. "You really thinking of going out there?"

"Nah. Just yanking your chain, trying to make you jealous that *your* crush has a crush on me." I forced a smile. "I've got too much to do. The FBI is running me ragged trying to put something together on these cases."

"Good luck with that. I'll see you around."

20

Halfway to Sheldon's house I considered whipping a U-turn and heading back to the VS office.

But that little voice in my head and that gut feeling the FBI advised me to discount . . . were clamoring for attention. I had nothing else to do but fret about Mason, or count the hours until Lex was dismissed from school.

Or I could find a quiet corner in Stillwell's and drink.

Nah.

I drove past Sheldon's slowly, staking out the place, but with no traffic, it really didn't matter who saw what I was doing. Thirty yards from the turnoff was a steel gate. The front entrance was secured with a heavy chain and a lock. Talk about overkill. Usually, a security system around here was a neon sign to robbers. *We have something of worth that needs protection, please rob us.*

What valuables did Sheldon have that required such security measures?

Then I remembered he lived with an elderly uncle. If the man suffered from Alzheimer's, then I understood the need for extra precautions. I scanned the fence line. Sturdy fencing. KEEP OUT and NO HUNTING and NO TRESPASSING signs were attached at random intervals.

There wasn't a gravel road running along the backside of the property, so I turned around, debating my next move. Park at the gate and wander up the driveway, claiming I was worried when he hadn't shown up in the archives department?

Would that give him the wrong idea? Especially since Fergie was convinced the man had a crush on me?

Was there any logical reason for me to be here besides those niggling feelings that wouldn't allow me to leave it be?

No, a stealth entry would be my best option.

Leaving my vehicle by the side of the road might raise questions. At the next entrance to the adjoining field, I drove over a cattle guard and bounced along the field, hoping it wasn't a bull pasture. As soon as I reached the base of a hill, I shut off my pickup. I slipped on a camo Carhartt coat. I kept my gun on my hip and left the coat unbuttoned as I slid from the cab.

If I hadn't needed to blend, I wouldn't have bothered with the coat. The sun shone from a watery blue sky. A great day to be outside hunting, hearing the dried grass crunch beneath my feet as I followed the fence line.

Before I reached the shelterbelt on Sheldon's property, I scrutinized the fence for an easy-access point. I found two saggy, rusted-out pieces of barbed wire and stepped on the lowest section, yanking the upper section high enough to let myself through.

I crept along, on full alert. This stealth behavior was easier when I wasn't dressed in full combat gear or the restrictive garb of burkas or niqabs.

Approaching the house, I didn't see a vehicle. My gaze moved to the detached garage twenty yards away. No windows in the garage doors. I crouched and made a break from the shelterbelt to the side of the garage. I reached around and tried the knob. Locked.

Now I had no choice but to walk up to the front door and knock.

Making sure my gun was easily accessible, I stepped from the shadows and skirted a rusted-out metal drum. Very little other junk around the perimeter.

I casually strolled up the wooden steps to the front door. I knocked three times. Waited a solid minute before I knocked again.

No answer.

After one last series of knocks and a loud, "Hello? Sheldon? Mr. War Bonnet? Is anyone home?" I was certain the house was empty. I tried the door. Locked. I couldn't see in the windows—the shades were pulled.

Nothing here, Mercy. Just get in your truck and go home.

I turned around too fast. My right eye is pretty good during the day, but for some reason, I had a case of vertigo. I lost my balance and landed rather indelicately on my ass.

Glad no one was around to see that.

As I rolled to my knees, I saw something red beneath the wooden deck bench. Weird that Sheldon would have the same tacky ceramic mushroom yard ornament we had. I'd given it to Sophie as a joke, but she loved the damn thing. She'd moved it to the raised flower bed by the gazebo after I'd accidentally hit it with the weed whacker and chipped off part of the stem.

I reached for it and nearly dropped it when I saw the damaged stem.

Not exactly like mine . . . it *was* mine.

Shock warred with a burning sense of betrayal. What was wrong with this fucker that he'd show up at my house and steal something from me? Why had he been sneaking around?

Kind of like you're sneaking around his place right now?

Not the same thing.

I very carefully set the mushroom down and faced the door to Sheldon's house. I didn't have a lock-pick set with me—another handy tool I'd picked up in spec-ops training—and right now, I didn't have the patience to mess with a deadbolt. Chances were high his back door wouldn't have double locks.

Wrong.

The back door was more secure than the front door.

I jogged back to the front. I needed to get inside, but my options were limited.

Shooting off a lock doesn't work unless you're using a shotgun or a rifle. I wasn't entirely sure Sheldon's uncle wasn't inside. Randomly shooting the fuck out of something, while fun and cathartic, would be dangerous. I didn't have bolt cutters on me, and Sheldon's garage was locked up as tight as his house. Trying to kick in a door . . . not smart unless you used a battering ram to weaken the wood.

Looked like I was breaking a window.

If I got caught, I'd say I'd smelled smoke and believed the house was on fire. Since I knew an elderly man lived there, I had to get inside by any means necessary and verify that he was all right.

More than plausible. And enough probable cause to cover my ass if someone showed up while I was breaking and entering.

I slipped my left glove on. No reason to leave fingerprints. I threw an elbow into the glass, and chunks dropped everywhere.

Adrenaline surged through me. I used the butt of my gun to break the jagged pieces free from the window frame before I found the string-pull and jerked up the blind.

Good thing it wasn't a long drop through the window. I stepped into a small mudroom and kept my gun in my hand as I entered the kitchen and called out, "Sheldon? Mr. War Bonnet?"

No response.

I don't know if I expected Sheldon to live in squalor—many rez residents did. No judgment on my part. That state was the societal norm. But Sheldon's kitchen counter wasn't piled high with crusty, smelly dishes; empty frozen-dinner boxes; and beer cans. The dishes in the drying rack were clean. One cup, one bowl, one spoon. Odd. I peeked in the refrigerator. Not much fresh food. I opened the cupboards. Every one was filled with meals ready to eat. That was weird. Why would he willingly eat MREs?

The kitchen doorway opened into the living room. A decent-sized TV hung on one wall. One plaid couch. One coffee table without a single object on it. Rows and rows of books covered two bookshelves on the far wall. All military themed. Fiction. Nonfiction. Nothing too out of the ordinary.

I moved to the hallway. Four closed doors. Keeping my gun in my right hand, I wrapped my gloved left hand around the handle and opened the first door. A closet packed with junk.

Keeping with the room-clearing tactics I'd had drilled into my head, I shoved open the second door. A bedroom I assumed was Sheldon's.

One side resembled the barracks from basic training, but from a single soldier's view. One cot with an army-green wool blanket, one footlocker, pegs embedded into the wall for clothes. Christ. I could've bounced a quarter off the bed, it was so tightly made. He'd allowed a few concessions. A humidifier hummed in the corner. A gun safe abutted the closet. The gun safe was locked and the closet held work clothes.

The other side of Sheldon's bedroom had been set up like a military command office. A desk. A computer. Maps on the wall. Little army men in a Plexiglas container with tanks and equipment that could be moved around. Different topographical dioramas were stacked along the wall.

It looked like a movie set, staged and pristine. Nothing like a real command center in wartime with broken shit piled up everywhere.

The third door opened into a bathroom. Typical 1950s ranch house. White tub, white toilet, white tile. Mirrored medicine cabinet above the white pedestal sink. I opened and scrutinized the contents. Herbal concoctions in plain bottles. No prescriptions. For either Shelton or Harold. Did that mean he had to lock up Harold's medication?

The last door stood at the end of the stubby hallway. The lock on this door was an industrial padlock—on the outside.

Dammit.

I understood the necessity of a lockdown procedure if an elderly person tended to wander, but I hoped Sheldon hadn't locked his uncle in his bedroom while he'd gone to run errands.

I couldn't shoot this lock off. Couldn't bust down the door. I might look for a crowbar to remove the latch the padlock was attached to, if I had lots of time.

Or . . . I could look for a spare set of keys. Remembering the big key ring Sheldon carried at the archives, I knew he had at least one extra set. Where would I keep them?

In my office. In a place where they'd be clearly marked, but out of plain sight. I returned to Sheldon's bedroom and started opening drawers in his desk.

Bingo. In the back of a filing cabinet was a metal box containing keys. And score, they were all marked. I snagged the sets for the spare bedroom and the garage.

The padlock to the bedroom clicked open easily.

In hindsight, I wished it hadn't worked at all. Because what I found behind that door was beyond disturbing.

I'd kept my gun out and swept the room. At first, I thought I'd walked in on a sleeping man. Easy to do with a human shape stretched out on the bed with the covers pulled up. But something about the too-pale, too-still form resting atop the pillow bothered me. I stepped closer.

My breath stalled.

Not only was the guy on the bed dead, but he was mummified.

Mummified.

Holy shit.

I'd never seen anything like this.

The top of the head hadn't been wrapped in gauze, so graying black hair stuck up in dull tufts. The strands looked as if they'd disintegrate upon contact. It also looked like an entire can of shellac had been poured on the face and neck. The mouth was open, covered in gauze, in a parody of *The Scream*.

The star quilt had been tucked beneath the man's mummified neck, blocking the rest of the body from view. I knew I had to pull that quilt back. I studied the lump under the covers for a solid minute to make sure nothing was moving, like rats or mice feasting on rotten flesh and living inside a dead-body cavity. Critters that would shriek at me with high-pitched outrage that I'd discovered their secret snack and home combination.

Inhaling deeply, I grabbed the corner of the quilt hanging on the floor. I hesitated and felt like a total pussy for it. What was my problem? I had no issue dealing with soldiers whose innards were dragging in the dirt after being gut shot, so why was I hesitating when this guy was already dead?

Just jerk it back like a bandage.

So I did.

The rest of the body was wrapped in gauze. The arms were secured alongside the body, not wrapped separately. The legs were wrapped as one unit, too. The entire form held a shiny glaze, like this was a kid's art project. I half feared if I looked closely, I'd see glitter. But I knew it wasn't papier mâché crafted to resemble a human when I noticed the feet hadn't been wrapped. A greasy, soiled spot on the sheet gave the impression of decayed flesh beneath the skeletal bones.

Fucking nasty. I shuddered.

The body didn't smell like rotten flesh, but there was a sour herblike odor. I had no way of knowing how long this dude—who I presumed to be Harold War Bonnet—had been dead.

No wonder Sheldon kept his house locked up tight.

Why would he do this?

Some kind of loneliness?

No, Sheldon hadn't struck me as the sentimental type, if mummifying your relative's body could be considered sentimental.

Another thought turned my stomach.

He'd done this for money.

With no one the wiser about his uncle's death, Sheldon had kept collecting his uncle's Social Security checks and tribal pension checks after the man had died.

Another shudder rippled down my spine. What if Sheldon had killed his uncle? He could've done it five years ago, right after he'd taken over the archives job. Officer Ferguson mentioned she hadn't seen Harold War Bonnet for a long time.

Sheldon War Bonnet was one sick puppy. This creepy asshole had a lot more to answer for now than stealing a goddamn ceramic mushroom out of my garden.

I left the mummified body exposed and backed out of the room. No sense in trying to cover my tracks. I swept the perimeter of the house one last time for signs of a basement or a crawl space but found nothing. I unlocked the back door and left it wide open. Same with the front door. I shoved the token he'd stolen from my garden in my outside jacket pocket.

As I stood in front of the door to the garage, manipulating the lock, I tried to figure out a way to tell Turnbull what I'd found here and why I hadn't reported my suspicions right away.

Mainly because I hadn't had *any* suspicions about the man. The archivist hadn't been on my radar at all. He'd seemed the mild-mannered type, content with his (boring) role in life. Curious, but no more curious than Margene, the snoopy gossip at the Q-Mart. And I hadn't considered her a suspect, either.

Did I consider Sheldon War Bonnet a suspect in the murders because I'd found a mummified body in his house?

It certainly put him on my bring-in-for-questioning list.

I imagined my conversation with Agent Turnbull about the situation: *So . . . Fergie swore this Sheldon guy had a mad crush on me, so I thought I'd check it out. You know: Sneak onto his property. Break into his house to see if he'd penned love letters to me. Find out if, as an amateur herbalist, he'd been concocting a love potion that would make me fall madly in love with him. And during my search for those incriminating items, can you believe I found his uncle? Mummified.*

Yeah. That was a feasible and reasonable explanation.

Not.

The padlock opened, and I removed it from the latch. I turned the doorknob with my left hand, keeping my gun in my right.

Damn dark in here.

I paused and listened.

Nothing.

I patted along the wall until I found a light switch, then I flipped it on.

What I saw was beyond déjà vu.

Pictures were spread out on a long wooden bench. Random pictures—except they were all of me, copies of the ones I'd found in my truck yesterday. But there were more. Most photos were recent, but . . .

where had he found a picture of me in my uniform? I peered at it more closely and wanted to throw up. He'd taken this out of my dad's office.

Not only had he been sneaking around outside my house, he'd been inside. When?

Whenever he wanted—I'd forgotten to lock the doors since Dawson had been in the hospital. He could've dropped food off, just like my friends and neighbors had, the day after the accident. Word had spread fast, and if anyone had questioned him about who he was, he wouldn't have had to lie. I *had* been working with him.

When had this gone beyond crush behavior? Sheldon had always been too . . . earnest and helpful. And now I realized it hadn't been a coincidence when he'd shown up that night at Stillwell's, or when he'd just happened to be walking past my truck yesterday. He'd broken in and left an envelope of disturbing images, then he'd hung around to see my reaction. Why? In hopes that I'd confide my fears in him?

Fuck that. Fuck him.

I gathered all the pictures, methodically searching every nook and cranny for more. On the very bottom shelf, I found a photo printer with a memory card still in it. I took the memory card and the camera hidden behind the printer.

I'd really believed that Latimer Elk Thunder had left those pictures as a warning. If I was that far off base with him, how far off base had I been with everything else? What else was Sheldon capable of?

Maybe you don't want to know.

But I'd gone this far. I pulled back the heavy plastic curtain and stepped to the other side of the garage.

My gaze scanned the wall. A whole lot of dried herbs hung from hooks in the ceiling. How had I forgotten Sheldon had told me he was an herbalist? I had no idea what foxglove looked like, but I'd bet the ranch it was up there.

I squinted at the rafters and froze. Those hooks. I recognized them. It was the exact same type of hook used on Penny Pretty Horses. Yes, they were common hunting tools around here . . . but coupled with the herbs . . . I spun around and saw a collapsible cot. Leather restraints hung from both sides, top and the bottom. Bloodied restraints. Bloodied ropes.

Oh God. Oh sweet Jesus.

Freaked out by what I was seeing, I stumbled back into the shelving, knocking bottles loose, sending them crashing to the cement like glass bombs.

Clapping my hand over my mouth, I attempted to calm myself. But any chance at calmness fled when I noticed dark black blotches on the plastic curtain.

I knew what blood spatters looked like when they dried.

Just. Like. That.

I bit the inside of my lips to hold the bile down when I realized I'd stumbled into Sheldon War Bonnet's House of Horrors.

The floor had dark stains. Could be from oil, but I doubted it. The bloodstains on the plastic tarp could be from an animal kill, but I doubted it.

The entire hideous scenario flashed through my brain. Sheldon dragging the victim from his car, stripping her, and strapping her to the gurney. Letting her get thirsty and then offering a drink of digitalis-laced water. He could leave her out here for a day or two while he made his demented plans. That's why he'd planned the murders in the fall months. Not only was it hunting season, there'd be less chance of the body bloating in summertime heat, gathering insects and interest.

Sheldon War Bonnet was a serial killer.

I had no feeling of pride I'd found this information. Pure dumb luck on my part.

I had no feeling of accomplishment that this discovery would provide closure for the victim's families.

Right now, I didn't care.

Because someone in my family was next on his list.

21

When I reached my truck, I realized two hours had passed during my B&E at Sheldon's house.

I checked the camera for a memory card. Finding none, I threw the expensive camera out the window as I headed home.

Two things occurred to me: When Sheldon saw his house had been broken into, he wouldn't call the cops. But he'd know exactly who had done it when he saw the ceramic mushroom and the pictures were missing.

He could torch his house and his garage, erasing evidence of his psychotic ways. But he'd still be gunning for me.

I just had to outgun him. And that was something I was very, very good at.

On my way to the ranch, I called Jake. "Listen carefully. You need to pick Lex up from the bus stop and keep him at your house overnight. Tell him that the hospital called and said his dad can't have visitors tonight and that urgent FBI business came up and I'm away on a case. Take extra precautions with Hope and Joy. Do not trust anyone with information about me, except for Shay Turnbull. Do not let anyone in your house. Not even anyone you know. Hunker down until I give you the all clear. Okay?"

"Okay. What else?"

"Can you get your hands on a gun?"

"I've got one."

"Good. Keep it with you at all times."

"I won't ask what's goin' on, but I will tell you to be careful."

"Thanks." I lingered on the line, half wanting to say something sentimental for him to pass on just in case . . . but I slammed a lid on that mind-set and hung up.

I picked a hidden vantage point beyond where the bus dropped Lex off to make sure Jake didn't run into any problems when picking him up. I'd texted Lex an apology, an update from the nurse on his dad's condition—no change—and the promise we'd go to the hospital first thing tomorrow.

Lex's response? "'kay."

Daylight had started to dim when I pulled up to the house.

I rolled the pictures and shoved them and the memory card in my purse. I'd stashed the Carhartt behind the seat. In my haste to get home I hadn't put my other coat back on, so I shivered as I hustled up the porch steps.

In the kitchen I ducked down and put the pictures and the memory card in the oatmeal container, shoving it onto the back of the lazy Susan.

I grabbed a Coke out of the fridge. I turned around when a phone on the kitchen table, a phone I'd never seen before, started to ring. I went on full alert and answered it. "Hello?"

"Mercy. I hoped you'd be the type to pick up a ringing phone."

Sheldon War Bonnet was on the other end of this call.

Play it cool. "Sheldon? Why would your phone be in my house?"

"After I heard about the sheriff, I felt so bad for you and the boy that I dropped off some cookies. No one was around, and I assumed you were sleeping, so I just left them on the table. I only realized today that I must've left my phone there." He laughed. "Sort of pitiful, isn't it? That no one ever calls me and I just noticed it was missing . . . five days later?"

Such a liar. Did he really believe I wouldn't notice a cell phone on my kitchen table for almost a week? "Do you want to meet someplace so I can give it back to you? I'm not doing anything right now."

He said, "I know." But then amended it to, "But I wouldn't want to put you out."

My guts twisted when I realized he'd known exactly when I'd gotten home. He had to be someplace close by. "No, I insist. As a matter of fact, why don't you come out to the ranch and get it?"

Silence.

Then he sighed. "I hear the distrust in your tone."

"Well, it does appear you broke into my house. If you wanted to talk to me, you could've just called the house phone, rather than using this type of ploy."

"Technically, it wasn't breaking in since you didn't lock your door." He tsk-tsked. "Too bad you don't lock everything up as tight as your gun safe."

The bastard had been in my bedroom.

Before I could retort, he said, "Speaking of safe . . . have you checked in with your family? You know they're all alive, and well, and accounted for?"

A spike of fear lodged in my soul.

"Well, you know the sheriff is buttoned up tight in room four oh six at the hospital. Last I checked, roughly a half hour ago, your sister Hope and your niece were snug in their trailer. Along with the sheriff's son. Jake will return from feeding cattle soon. That takes care of the Red Leaf family. At least, that branch of the Red Leaf family. Have you talked to John-John lately? Probably not. I heard that bit of nastiness he said to you that night at Stillwell's about his stupid vision. He really is such a flaming faggot, you're better off without his friendship."

Faggot. I hated that word. "Sheldon, what do you want?"

A noise clunked against the receiver; then, "How about Sophie Red Leaf? When was the last time you spoke to her? When was the last time *anyone* saw her?"

Hope had told me yesterday she couldn't get ahold of Sophie. I'd intended to call her today, but I'd gotten sidetracked. Still, she was safe. Devlin and John-John were constantly around her, all of them grieving together.

"Mercy?" he asked with a sharper edge. "When was the last time you saw Sophie?"

"Last week."

"That long?" He tsk-tsked again. "Isn't the woman almost a mother to you? I'll bet if you called her right now, she wouldn't pick up. I'll bet if you marched up to her front door right now, she wouldn't answer. I'll bet if you broke the door down, you wouldn't find her at home. Where do you think she could be?" Sheldon laughed. "Ooh. I know exactly where she is."

Fear, outrage, and more fear built inside me—I was done playing dumb. "What the hell have you done with her? She's an eighty-year-old woman, you fucking sick bastard."

"Ah, ah, ah. I'd curb that tongue if I were you. Don't give me a reason to take out my frustration with you . . . on poor Sophie."

"Why are you doing this? She's done nothing to you."

"But she means something to you, doesn't she? I'll bet she means *everything* to you. I'll bet you'll do anything to get her back."

I paced. My heart raced, but my mind seemed sluggish. How the hell had he gotten to Sophie? "Tell me where she is."

"Tell you what. I'll give you a chance to win her freedom." Sheldon's tone mellowed to that of a lover. "But first, let's get to know each other better. Seems our talks were always interrupted. I hated that. Didn't you?"

That stopped me from pacing. "Why do you want to talk to me?"

"Because you're a fascinating woman. But before you do anything stupid, like try to use your house phone to ring up your federal pals, be aware that I cut the phone line. This is between you and me. No using your cell phone during our conversation. If I find out you've talked to anyone besides me or signaled them in any way . . . I will gut Sophie slowly and pull out her entrails while you listen. So continuing this conversation is entirely up to you. I'll give you a minute to think on it."

I had déjà vu for the second time today. This reminded me of the phone call from Theo the morning he'd taken Hope. The little jerk-off had called me, warning me about all the horrible things he planned to do to my pregnant sister if I didn't follow his instructions.

Oh, I'd followed his instructions. And then I'd killed him.

Did Sheldon know that, no matter how tough he played this, he was just as dead as Theo? No one threatened my family and got away with it. *No one.*

I looked around. When had he put my house under surveillance? I doubted he'd installed cameras in here—too obvious, too much money, and too time-consuming. Which meant right now, he was close enough to see into the house. I suppressed a shudder and steeled myself for a conversation with a madman. "Fine, Sheldon. I'm listening."

"Good. But I want you to ask me questions."

What the fuck was with psycho killers wanting to keep a running dialogue with me? Theo. Iris. Saro. Sheldon. Did I give off some trust-me-with-your-twisted-secrets vibe?

Maybe it's because like recognizes like.

No. No. No. I was not like any of them. Not at all. "What kind of questions?"

"Like how long I've been involved in this sideline?"

"I'm betting . . . about five years, since you first realized you could get away with killing women and making their deaths look like accidents."

"You really were doing your research in my archives, weren't you? I'm impressed. But you didn't know I was the one you were looking for, did you?"

"No. You had everyone fooled." I paced. "So why change now and kill Arlette in such a public way? No one knew what you were doing. You could've gotten away with it for many more years."

"I got bored. There's very little premeditated murder on the rez. Usually, it's one Indian killing another in a drunken fit at three o'clock in the morning. So I wanted to up the stakes. The death of the new tribal president's niece carried an air of political intrigue."

Political intrigue. In South Dakota? "So Arlette wasn't in the wrong place at the wrong time?"

"Give me a little credit," he said tersely. "One time I asked her about a book she carried around, so she assumed I was interested in her reading habits. She went on and on about the stupid world of vampires. Staking her was my own little slice of irony."

I ground my teeth at the pride in his voice. "How did you abduct her?"

"I didn't have to. That was the beauty of it. She'd skipped school to do a research paper. I knocked her out, put her in a big garbage bag, then drove up to the back door and loaded the garbage into my car. Even if anyone had been watching me, they'd never have suspected because I dump the garbage once a week."

"Handy. I wondered how often you used the doors. So with the political-intrigue angle, you intended for Rollie to take the blame for Arlette's and Verline's murders."

"Yes. Arlette went on about Junior. But I suspected something was going on between Verline and Junior when they came in to register the baby. What a sick love triangle, with father and son. Anyway, Verline was easy to get to."

"Why cut off her hand?"

"I figured that would send the FBI profilers into a tailspin." He sighed. "I overheard a phone conversation when you were in the archives, and I was very disappointed that you considered Saro a suspect. That man is a common thug. He has no imagination whatsoever."

"That's what you call what you did to Penny? Using your imagination?"

"Of course. I hadn't intended on Penny Pretty Horses to be part of this, but her valiant struggle with cancer and her going against her family's wishes to live on her own terms touched me. I had to do something to end her suffering. I picked her up on my lunch break when she was out walking. Instead of fading from people's memory as just another cancer victim, Penny Pretty Horses will be remembered a lot differently."

Let him feel superior. Let him ramble.

"Did you see me there? At the scene?" he asked.

"No, I was a little busy dealing with grieving family members and crime-scene containment."

"You really should be more observant. Then you would've figured out that *you* were supposed to be the third victim, not Penny."

"Me," I said dully. "Why me?"

"I saved the best for last. You're a worthy adversary. I'm done talking. It's time to discuss the rules of the game."

"You actually believe I'll play some game with you?"

His genial, albeit psychotic, demeanor vanished. "You will play. Look under the place mat."

I didn't want to. So help me God, I didn't want to. A ball of fear inched up my throat. I eased aside the quilted place mat and saw a stack of photos. Copies of the ones I'd taken from Sheldon's garage, different from the ones he'd left in my truck.

"I especially love the one of you in your bathrobe as you're feeding the dogs."

I'd especially love to feed you to the fucking dogs.

The last photo was of Dawson and me together, standing by his pickup in a private moment. It appeared as if the photographer had been within a few feet of us. Dawson's head was annihilated by an X, and red covered my face.

"The last one is my favorite," Sheldon said cheerfully. "Can you imagine how horrible it would be to feel your lover's warm blood coating your skin? Having bits of his brain matter and chunks of bone in your hair? Watching his life end as he falls to the ground like another bag of meat?"

My vision swam, and I squeezed my eyes shut against the gruesome images clogging my rational thought. Imagining Dawson dead.

Stay focused. He's distracting you from talking about what he did with Sophie.

"I know why the FBI was so hot to snap you up—other than the fact you're a woman, a vet, and a minority."

"Why's that?"

"You're a killer. See, that's where we're alike, Sergeant Major."

He had no fucking right to use my rank with such familiarity. No right.

"But you think you're better than me. I saw it in your eyes that night at Stillwell's. You think that because you went to war and I didn't, you know how to win a battle. I've studied thousands of offensives. I know ops inside and out. I'm your equal in tactical maneuvers. I'm your equal in everything. And I'll prove it."

"How?"

He paused. "I want to test your skill as a soldier against mine."

"And if I refuse?"

"You won't. After I kill Sophie I'll move on to your sister. I'd get her worked up by placing my gun against her temple. Maybe I'd put the barrel in her mouth. Or between her legs. I know how she feels about guns. She might be one I try to literally scare to death."

The blood coursing through my veins like lava instantly turned ice cold. "Fine, I accept your challenge. But I have a condition."

Sheldon sighed again. "I thought you might say that. What is it?"

"I want to talk to Sophie to make sure you haven't already tortured and killed her."

"Are you questioning my honor?"

"Honor, intent—whatever you choose to call it. I need proof."

"Or what? I'm holding all the cards."

"Not so. If you don't prove she's alive, then I've got nothing to fight for. I'll assume you're a liar. I'll assume you killed her. I'll call the Eagle River Sheriff's Department, the FBI, and the tribal police right now. I'll have my sister and our family in protective custody before you can touch them." I stormed to the kitchen window and looked out.

A laugh burned my ear. "Glaring out the window seems overly dramatic for you."

And he just gave himself away. He wanted me to know that he was someplace close and I still couldn't get to him. He had to prove he was aware of my every move.

It took every bit of resolve to turn away and act flustered. "You live on the rez. I'd send the tribal cops to your house first."

"You really think I'm stupid enough to hold her at my house?" he sneered.

"You really think I'm stupid enough to agree to your game without demanding proof of life? Tactical error on your part, Sheldon. It's always the first maneuver in a hostage situation. You should know that with all your book learning about military ops."

Silence.

I held my breath, wondering if I'd gone too far.

"Listen very closely." A pause. "Sophie? Say something to Mercy."

An inhuman wail burned my ear as the drawn-out word *no* echoed back to me. Had he hurt her to get that response? I didn't feel a sense of triumph. I just felt sick. Wait. Where had I heard that type of wail before? When Theo had Hope? Had she made that agonized sound?

"Satisfied?"

No, you vicious cocksucker. I won't be satisfied until your blood saturates the ground. "Yes."

"You agree to my game. My test of skills?"

"Yes."

"There's another envelope inside the bag of dog food on your porch. Get it and open it."

My skin crawled, as I could feel his unseen eyes on me. I snatched the envelope, folded back the metal clasp, and a sheaf of papers spilled out. Papers that looked like a fictional spy's dossier, something you might see on TV. Maps. Christ. The only thing he hadn't added was TOP SECRET stamped in red lettering on the front of the envelope.

"Anything look familiar?" he prompted. "Find the map marked A."

I didn't want to play his stupid games, but I had no choice. He'd printed out a topographical map and marked off an area with a red square.

"It's the upper section of the Gunderson Ranch. The area known as the mini-badlands. Bordered by forest on one side and a rocky canyon on the other. That part of your land, about ten square miles, isn't used for grazing or anything else, so we won't be interrupted."

"I don't understand."

"That's because I haven't explained the rules yet," he snapped. "To-morrow morning you can enter that marked-off section on the map from whichever side you choose. You'll have from sunup to sundown to find the six items at the six locations I've marked on your map. You'll need all six . . . *hints*, if you will, to figure out what bunker I've hidden Sophie in."

This guy had a massive chip on his shoulder about not being called to war. An elaborate ruse to prove his prowess? What a psychotic mother-fucker. I imagined he probably had a fake uniform decorated with fake medals. "What will you be doing while I'm gathering clues?"

"While you're completing your assigned *mission*," he corrected testily. "I'll be trying to stop you. By any means necessary. Just like in real war."

"If you capture me, will you kill me?"

"Not until you've exhausted my entertainment options."

"So if you win"—I hated saying that—"and you have me to keep you entertained, then you won't need Sophie. You'll let her go?"

"I'm a man of my word. If I say I'll let her go, then I'll let her go."

"If I win, in addition to your telling me exactly where you stashed Sophie, I'll expect to haul you in so you can stand trial for your crimes."

He laughed. "You're such a little do-gooder patriot. That's why I picked you for this challenge. You understand fair play. You'll follow the rules. Rest up tonight, Sergeant Major. You'll need it. This will be a physically demanding op."

Op. Fuck him.

"Last two items of business: Don't leave the house. Period. For any reason. And as soon as we're finished talking, destroy both cell phones."

But what if the hospital called about Dawson? No house phone, no cell phone—they'd have no way to get in touch with me.

"These are non-negotiable points. I will know if you disobey either directive." Mr. Chatty hung up.

He was really into reinforcing my paranoia.

Think, Mercy. I went with the assumption he was using one of those cone-shaped audio devices that required a physical presence within two hundred yards and a pair of binoculars. That'd give him eyes and ears on me.

I quickly and quietly slipped the battery out of my phone. I found a meat tenderizer and beat his disposable phone into pieces. I piled the busted phone on top of mine. Even up close, they both looked broken.

I paced for a good five minutes.

If Sheldon got bored watching me, he'd head home. That would fuck up everything. With his genial tone and excitement about his stupid challenge, he didn't know I'd broken into his house.

I had a small window of opportunity to turn the tables. Because I wasn't waiting around for Sheldon's elaborate plan for me to role-play The Most Dangerous Game. I didn't figure he'd play fair.

But I wouldn't play fair, either.

I'd do what I did best.

Go on the offensive.

It'd taken Sheldon days to come up with such an intricate and well-ordered strategy. By purposely choosing Gunderson land on which to carry out his game, he expected me to feel smug in my advantage over him.

But my advantage was op planning on the fly. *Change, adapt, execute.* Almost as much a part of my military sniper mantra.

I needed to draw Sheldon out and get him off balance.

So I'd blatantly break his specific rule to stay put. If my guess was correct, he'd be too curious to see what would make me break the rules, if only so he could throw it in my face and use it as an excuse to hurt Sophie.

Hopefully, Dawson's cell phone had enough juice after being shut off for a few days for me to make one call. I grabbed my notebook from my messenger bag and trudged to my bedroom, fished out Dawson's cell, and headed to the bathroom. I turned on the shower in case Sheldon aimed his listening device in this direction.

I dialed the number on the slip of paper and paced while I waited for her to pick up.

"Hello?" she answered warily.

"Is this Naomi?"

"Yes, who's this?"

"Mercy Gunderson. FBI. We spoke today?"

"Hey, why are you calling me? Am I in trouble?"

"No. How would you like to earn a hundred bucks for helping me?"

A pause, then she said, "For real?"

"For real. This is a top-secret FBI operation, so you have to keep it between us."

"Okay. What do I gotta do?"

"Do you have a vehicle?"

"Yeah."

"What kind?"

"A Dodge minivan."

"Is the gas tank full?"

"About half. Why?"

"I need you to drive to Besler's grocery store in Eagle Ridge. Know where that is?"

"Uh-huh. Then what?"

"Park close to the front doors. Leave the keys under the seat. Go in the store, get a cart, and pretend you're shopping. Take your time but don't talk to anyone. Don't look around, just act like you're buying groceries."

"Should I wear a disguise or something?"

"Just a winter scarf. Don't look for me. I will find you. Try to stay in the back of the store."

"You ain't pulling my leg? You're really gonna be there?"

"Yes. Look, it's really important you follow these instructions to the letter. Don't tell anyone where you're going. Don't text or talk on your phone, either in your car or in the store. Don't deviate at all."

"I won't."

"I'll explain more when you see me in about forty-five minutes." I hung up. Then I stripped and wrapped myself in my robe, exiting the bathroom and closing my bedroom door.

Keeping the lights turned off fucked with my bad eye, but I had no choice except to work in the darkness. I started adding layers of clothes.

A sports bra. A long-sleeved under-armor shirt. I yanked on a pair of jeans and slid on the super-thin subzero winter coat I'd saved from my Afghanistan tour. The light weight allowed me to move and kept me warm, but not too warm. For an overcoat, I pawed through the closet until I found my black duster. Two inside pockets, two deep outside pockets, long and sloppy-looking. Perfect.

Next, I needed hardware. Whatever I took had to fit on my person. The familiar smell of gun oil wafted up as I opened the gun safe. Pity there wasn't room inside the coat for my H-S Precision takedown rifle. But this op wasn't about stopping power. Not right away. I required firepower that used standard grade bullets. Nothing too big, nothing subsonic, nothing traceable. I wanted a gun that was light, concealable, and could be assembled in a snap.

I grabbed my AR-15.

At a little over eight and a half pounds, it was my lightest-weight semiauto. I'd had it sited with an Elcan day/night digital rifle scope and an IR flashlight, which served as an image intensifier for night shoots. I'd added a Gemtech suppressor—no more need for earplugs—and replaced the standard trigger with a three-pound Timney trigger for a no-jerk pull. The AR came apart with two easy clicks by pushing the pins from the left side of the aluminum receiver and pulling them out on the right side.

Click-click and the rifle was in two pieces.

Click-click and it'd be assembled. Snap in the clip, pull the charging handle, and it was ready to fire.

The nylon sling was still attached to the upper and lower sections. With the sling looped around my neck, even the sixteen-inch barrel and suppressor were hidden, dangling beneath my armpits.

That done, I slipped on my coat.

Next, I shoved the two magazines, each preloaded with fifteen .223-caliber bullets, into the pockets.

I balled up a nylon duffel bag and tucked it inside the largest purse I owned. I'd started keeping cash inside the gun safe, rather than the office safe, because it rankled having to explain to Hope why I always kept a significant stash on hand. I counted out the bills.

Almost done. I dropped a three-inch knife in a leather sheath, along with my black Merrill soft-soled hiking shoes into the purse. Last thing I grabbed was the monocular thermal-imaging device that had cost me an entire month's pay. But with the compromised eyesight in my right eye, especially at night, I needed—deserved—the extra advantage. I'd lusted after the thermal-imaging devices I'd used with my sniper rifle, but the army frowned on soldiers taking home a twenty-five thousand dollar piece of equipment.

During this rapid-fire preparation, I'd calmed. I'd reached the place I hadn't accessed since my nephew had been murdered. The black cesspool that held the memory of all bad things I'd done—without remorse. The dark spot inside me that would never evaporate completely. The hidden parts that were the truest part of me.

Methodical.

Ruthless.

Unstoppable.

Showtime.

I left the bedroom carrying my purse, letting dread slow my movements. I tugged on my gray wool cap with the ear flaps. Jammed my feet in snow boots.

At the kitchen sink I felt Sheldon watching me—no idea where he'd hidden himself outside—but I knew he was close by. I shuffled through the paperwork, several times. Turned the map sideways. Studied it this way and that. Made a disgusted noise and set the papers on the counter. I poured a glass of water, allowing myself to gaze into space. Allowing fear to show. I even gasped and clapped my hand over my mouth, as if trying to hold back tears.

Do you see me as a broken woman, you sadistic motherfucker? Is your sick head swimming with ways to torture me and break me completely?

Bring it.

Because it was on.

22

Sure enough, after I'd traveled about a mile down the gravel road, headlights appeared in my rearview. Most likely, that bastard had been spying from the barn, with the direct view of the back porch and into the kitchen windows. He could've parked on the other side of the house, and I wouldn't have seen his vehicle because I never drove past the ranch anymore. Not like when I'd lived in the foreman's cabin.

I hadn't been there since my return from Quantico. Maybe that's where he'd holed up and was keeping Sophie. It was close enough that he could keep an eye on both of us.

It took every bit of control not to spin a U-turn and play a game of chicken with him.

As I made the drive into Eagle Ridge, I went over the plan in my head several times, not knowing if it'd even work. But if this plan didn't work, the next one would. And if not this one, the one after that. The thought of Sophie tied up somewhere, grieving, scared, mad, hungry, crying, hurting, and cold—that's what would keep me going.

At Besler's, I parked in the space closest to the front entrance, but not under the streetlight. I tucked the keys under the mat, shouldered my purse, and strolled inside. Just another grocery shopper.

I grabbed a cart and headed past the produce section. I spied Naomi at the back of the pet-food aisle. She didn't acknowledge me when I moved past her and hefted three fifty-pound bags of dog food into my cart. Then I stood beside her, pretending to comparison shop between brands of kitty litter.

We were nearly shoulder to shoulder when I said, "Meet me in the women's bathroom in three minutes. Knock four times."

Luck was on my side because no one was using the restroom. Once inside the single stall, I ditched the trench coat and dug out the folded duffel bag. I snapped the AR-15 together, shoved it and the rest of my equipment into the bag, and zipped it shut. I'd just finished changing my shoes when I heard four knocks. I unlocked the door, and Naomi stepped inside.

"Thanks for doing this, Naomi."

"What am I doing?"

"First off, you should know this is a covert government operation. You've heard the phrase 'plausible deniability'? That's what'll happen if you ever tell anyone about this, understand?"

"Yes, you can trust me."

"Good. Here's the plan. We're swapping identities." I pulled off my hat and tugged it onto her head. "Next, coat and shoes."

As we faced each other, I had the first hope this switcheroo would work. We were close to the same height, and the buttoned-up trench coat would mask our physical differences. I wrapped the scarf around her neck.

"Here's the tricky part. Listen very carefully. Stay in the store for ten full minutes after I leave. Buy something simple. Once you get outside, keep your head down so your scarf covers most of your face; that way if my suspect has his binoculars on you, he won't know you're not me. Walk quickly, but do not run. Do not look around. Act like you've got something weighing on your mind and you cannot be bothered to pay attention to your surroundings. My truck is the black Ford F-150 parked in the center row, the second spot facing the exit. The keys are on the floor." I paused and studied her. "You all right so far?"

"Yeah, go on."

"Drive back to the rez. Go directly to Our Lady of Perpetual Help Catholic Church. Park as close to the front entrance as possible and leave the truck keys in the ashtray. There's mass tonight. First thing you do after you're inside? Find the coatrack. Hang up this coat and shove the scarf and hat in the sleeves. Then go into the bathroom and switch my boots for your shoes, and put on your coat, both of which will be stashed in this purse."

"Okay. What do I do with your boots and purse?"

"Leave them hanging on the back of the door hook in the bathroom stall."

Naomi nodded. "Then what?"

"Then you return to the sanctuary, sit in the back pew, and catch the last of the sermon."

She wrinkled her nose.

"After the service ends, you'll pin this folded note"—it read: *Find me before I find you*—"on the front of the coat and exit the church. Walk over to the Pizza Barn, order your favorite food, and take your time enjoying it." The note was the biggest gamble. Would he find it before someone else got snoopy and read it?

"That's it?" Naomi asked.

"Two other important things. You'll have to walk home after eating."

"Wouldn't be the first time."

Here was the trickiest part. "And in the morning? You'll have to report your car as stolen."

Naomi's mouth dropped open. "What? You didn't say anything about taking my car! I need it! It might be a piece of shit, but—"

I put my finger over my lips to signal for quiet. Then I reached into my purse and pulled out a stack of bills. "There's twenty-one hundred bucks here. After the tribal cops find your car, there's enough to get it repaired, or enough for you to buy a different one. You just need to report it missing. But not until morning."

She looked torn.

"If the maroon Chrysler out there is your van? Then I'm being more than generous in replacement cost."

"I know, but . . ." Naomi looked at me thoughtfully. "Is there a chance the cops will contact me tonight about my car?"

"Slim. But if that happens, tell them the last time you saw it, it was parked in the driveway or on the street or wherever you normally park it." My eyes searched hers. "And if you really want to be a dick, you can bring Mackenzie Red Shirt into the conversation as a possible suspect. She's been harassing you after you brought her name up with the Shooting Star case. Harassing you to the point you had to change your cell phone number. Officer Ferguson can back you up on that."

Naomi's eyes gleamed. "That would be sweet payback."

"Can you do that? But *only* if it comes to that?"

"Yes."

"Remember. This is a covert op. The tribal police have no idea what the FBI is doing, and we need to keep it that way."

"I understand."

"Good. Now run through this for me one more time so we've nailed down every detail."

She ran it down in perfect order, with the same type of clinical detachment I used. I knew there was a reason I liked this girl.

"All right. Let's do this."

Luck was still on my side that no one had moved my cart with the 150 pounds of dog food. I set the duffel bag in the cart and rolled the bags on top of it, hiding it completely.

I picked the young cashier I didn't know. When my turn came, I struggled to heft the first bag onto the conveyor belt. Since it was unwieldy, she didn't take the next two bags out of the cart, she just rang up the first bag three times. I paid cash, secured the scarf around the lower half of my face, and left the grocery store.

This was the test. I couldn't look around to see if Sheldon was waiting for the other me to exit the grocery store. Although I'd seen his headlights, I had no idea what kind of vehicle he drove. I unloaded everything in the back of the van. I didn't adjust the seat, didn't wait around. I took off and found a parking spot at Smith's Car Repair two blocks from Besler's.

I pretended to talk on the phone, in case somebody was watching me. Ten minutes later, Naomi sped past on her way to the reservation.

Less than two minutes after that, Sheldon followed in a dark green Dodge Neon.

Got you now, motherfucker.

No need to follow close and risk blowing my advantage, since I knew Naomi's end destination. I kept a Chevy pickup between our vehicles as we rolled down the blacktop to Eagle River.

The church was located in the center of town on the main drag. As I passed it, I saw Naomi walking up the stone steps, neither too fast nor too slow. Again, I couldn't take a chance and case the lot for Sheldon's car, so I kept driving.

At the three-block mark, I pulled onto a side street, ditched the dog food, and grabbed my duffel, placing it in the front seat. I drove four blocks and backed into a spot at an abandoned bank that had been turned into a private-sale car lot and was a block up from the church.

With binoculars I scoured the church lot for Sheldon's car, finding it in the middle, but I couldn't see any activity inside. Hopefully, Sheldon wouldn't enter the house of worship until after the service ended. I couldn't wait to see the look on his face when he realized I'd given him the slip.

Nothing happened in the next half hour. Once people started spilling out the main doors, I kept my binoculars focused on picking Naomi out of the crowd.

She hadn't left too soon or too late. She wore her coat. Her shoes. Carried her purse. No trace of my things on her person at all.

Whew.

Naomi walked with a young boy toward the Pizza Barn. Just another couple of teenagers, hanging out. Sheldon knew Naomi, but he wouldn't connect her with me.

Cars began to clear out. Even with a straight-shot view of Sheldon's vehicle, I couldn't tell what he was doing inside. Fuming, most likely.

I waited for him to get out of the car.

When only three cars remained, Sheldon left his car. He slowly spun a circle, casing the parking lot as he approached the steps.

I checked out his attire. Black combat clothing. Black hikers. Black wool skullcap.

What I didn't see? A bulletproof vest. Or a weapon holstered in his utility belt. Or his glasses.

A surge of rage stirred up my tranquil pool. Purposely misleading people into thinking he was physically disabled, both his body and his vision, was a coward's way of fighting.

I hated cowards.

Sheldon briskly scaled the steps, still looking around before he disappeared inside the church.

I smiled.

Three minutes later he left the building and paused outside the heavy, hand-carved wooden doors, his gaze on my pickup. Pretty quick sweep of the church. I refocused my binoculars. He had something crumpled up in his right hand.

Aw. He'd found my hate note.

I smiled again.

I wondered if Sheldon still felt on top of his military op.

Would he go home?

Would he return to my place?

Or would he go to Hope's and follow through on his threat?

Sheldon didn't make a move for several minutes.

Then he casually walked around my pickup. He pulled a knife out of the side pocket in his cargo pants. He stabbed the sidewall of my left rear tire. Satisfied the tire was flat, he strolled to his car, climbed in, and started it.

This was it.

My pulse didn't waver.

Not when he slowly pulled onto the road, heading toward Eagle Ridge.

Not when he passed by me sitting in this crappy decoy.

But my heart almost stopped when I saw Sheldon's taillights flash and his reverse lights come on.

Oh shit. As the rear end of his car came into view, I ducked and placed my shoulders on the passenger's seat, staring up at the dingy ceiling.

Gravel crunched as his car backed into the empty spot one vehicle away from mine. He'd settled in, waiting to see if I'd return for my pickup.

That surprised me, because it was a smart move. Strategic. Calculating. Not angry, hotheaded, and panicked.

I wanted him off balance.

See? We're alike, Mercy.

No, we aren't.

I closed my eyes and slowly breathed in and out. Sheldon wouldn't stay here long if I didn't show up. He'd be on the lookout for me.

Ironic I was sitting right next to him.

Breathe. Think. Plan.

I could get to the heart of this right now. I still had the advantage.

I could burst out of the car, gun blazing. Randomly shoot at him until he told me where he'd hidden Sophie . . . or until the tribal cops showed up at the sound of gunfire. Even they wouldn't ignore that.

Or I could come up on his six, knock him out, and tie him up. Drag him back to the foreman's cabin at the ranch and torture him until he told me where he'd stashed Sophie.

Then you are just like him, aren't you?

So?

Even as I created and discarded strategies, part of my brain refused to cooperate. The dark part that didn't want this man arrested. The dark part that wanted this man dead.

Evidently, Sheldon got tired of waiting. He started his car and pulled away.

I didn't have time to waste debating the morality of murdering a murderer.

Traffic was steady on a Friday night on the reservation, which allowed me to tail him discreetly. When the last car between us hung a left, I hung a right.

Parking along the road, I cut all the lights. I even unscrewed the interior light after breaking the plastic housing. Then I slipped on my night-vision goggles.

And no doubt about it, the hunt was on.

I returned to the road. The night-vision goggles would work perfectly if I didn't meet another car. The images were shadowy, as if everything had been dipped in liquid silver and spots had tarnished to black.

Damn quiet and dark on the road between Eagle River Reservation and Eagle Ridge Township. We hadn't passed a single set of headlights.

Would Sheldon lead me to where he was hiding Sophie? Or would he follow through with his threat to hurt my family?

Then he abruptly turned onto a gravel road that served as a cut across to the Viewfield Cemetery and also led to an abandoned camping area. The place had been developed over thirty years ago by Kit McIntyre, the snake who'd tried to buy my ranch, ironically enough, but it'd never become a hot spot for campers. In fact, I'd forgotten that it—and the cut across to the road running in front of our ranch—existed.

Which is why it made an ideal spot to keep a kidnapped woman. No one close enough to hear her scream.

The longer I followed him on this road the easier it'd be for him to spot me. When I figured we were far enough off the main drag, I put my plan into play.

I hit the gas and rammed into the back end of his car.

Sheldon's car fishtailed. He didn't overcorrect and jerk the steering wheel. But he did slow down.

Mistake.

I gunned it again, swerving so the front end of the van smashed into the left rear of his car with enough force that taillights shattered and the bumper went flying.

That hit sent Sheldon's vehicle toward the ditch on the right side of the road. He slammed on the brakes.

Mistake.

The car sat sideways.

After I threw the van in reverse and got far enough to build up decent ramming power, I dropped it into Drive and floored it. Spitting gravel, the engine whining, I made the last impact count.

Metal crunched, squeaked, and crumpled as I nailed Sheldon's trunk dead center, sending the car sailing forward. I saw a flash inside the car when the front end smacked into the upper edge of the ditch and the air bag deployed.

Steam hissed from the front of the van as I parked on the edge of the road and killed the ignition. I shut off my night-vision goggles and set them on the seat. Then I grabbed the AR and the extra clip, and slipped the cord connected to my handheld infrared around my neck.

The van door creaked as I opened it. I kept the rifle aimed at the back of Sheldon's car; the trunk was popped up, too mangled ever to close again, and I came around the left side.

The moment of truth.

But the driver's door was open. The airbag deflated from the deep slice across the center.

No sign of Sheldon. Pity, I didn't see any signs of blood, either.

Looked like we'd be playing a game of cat and mouse after all.

I crouched in the ditch, figuring out my next move as I listened for sounds. Shoes on gravel. Feet pounding through grass.

Nothing.

Not a hint of breeze stirred. The darkness was absolute. No lights from town. No nearby yard lights. No snow. No moon. Even the sky was overcast with thick black clouds, so it'd be very easy to disappear into the inky blackness.

Which way had he gone?

Had Sheldon climbed through the barbed-wire fence? Or had he run forward, through the ditch? Creating enough distance so I'd assume he'd gone through the field, and then backtracking?

I listened. I heard nothing but the clicking sounds of the car engines. Sheldon had no special-forces training. That's when I knew he wouldn't run away. He'd stick around and try to best me, like he'd initially planned. Rub it in my face that he was the superior soldier.

So what would I do if I had his advantage but not the special-ops training that taught me not to choose the easiest options?

Run to the closest place that offered a decent hiding spot. Get ahead in the trees and wait.

I knew he'd have a gun in his holster. But what would he be armed with?

Maybe he had a gun with a scope. Possibly even a night-vision scope.

But Sheldon had spent all his time preparing for tomorrow. I doubted he was prepared to fight now. My hunting gadgetry gave me the advantage. He'd consider using those gadgets to be cheating, thinking that a real soldier relied on skill and training.

Wrong. A real soldier took every advantage to annihilate the enemy. Building a better predator by whatever means necessary.

I crawled between the barbed-wire strands and stood, pausing to scan the immediate area with the infrared.

No red heat signatures.

Sheldon had already covered serious ground if the sensor hadn't picked him up yet.

I kept the infrared in my left hand and the rifle in my right as I continued to scan the terrain. This sweep of prairie began a gradual rise until it met the tree line. I assumed that was the direction he went. Easier to miss shots when distracted by the trees and shadows.

That's when I heard a twig snap.

Pinpointing the sound, I crouched almost parallel to the ground. My adrenaline kicked in, but due to my sniper training, I didn't get skittish. I became even calmer, breathing slowly, hyper-focused on waiting for my prey to give himself away.

The grass was timber dry and made a crunching sound with every hard footfall, encouraging light steps.

I heard nothing for several long moments.

Just when I believed I'd followed a deer, I heard the soft scrape of fabric on bark. I spun, pointing the infrared. A big red mass a hundred feet to my left at eleven o'clock.

Releasing the infrared, I raised the rifle, my eye on the scope, and in the split second it took to pinpoint his location I fired.

A loud hiss of air echoed back to me, followed by the rustling of grass. Bastard was on the move. Had I hit him? Nicked him? Or missed entirely?

I raised the infrared again and watched the red blob scurrying away. Slowly. Then it stopped. I took a perpendicular path to where Sheldon rested. I'd keep parallel to him as I moved, so when he bolted toward the tree line, I'd be in front of him instead of behind.

I heard a gun discharge, and then pain ripped through the outside of my left thigh.

Son of a bitch. That fucker had shot me.

Now I was really pissed. I knelt down and lightly touched the rip in my pants. My fingers came away wet. Gritting my teeth, I drew my finger across the spot more firmly, discovering it was only a flesh wound. Bled like a bitch, but I didn't have a bullet lodged in my leg. If I left it alone, it'd clot so I could finish what I'd started.

I heard pounding footfalls and looked up just as Sheldon rushed me. I rolled into him, instead of away from him, and he skidded face-first across the ground.

I bounced up and stomped my boot heel on his wrist, forcing him to release his gun while I placed the rifle muzzle on the back of his head. "Don't fucking move." I reached down and picked up his gun. A Glock. I ejected the clip, letting it hit the ground. "Tell me where she is."

"You cheated," he snapped, turning his head sideways to glare at me.

"Tough shit. What have you done with Sophie?"

"Tough shit," he mimicked. "I'm not telling you anything."

With the AR-15, I aimed for the dirt and fired at the ground next to his thigh. "The next bullet goes in that thigh. Where is Sophie?"

He laughed. "You're bluffing."

I shot him in the leg. Using his gun and the last bullet that'd been left in the chamber.

He screamed.

When he quit whimpering, I shoved his empty gun in my pocket and repeated, "Where is Sophie?"

"I'll die before I tell you."

"I doubt it, but I'm willing to test that theory. I've got two full clips, Sheldon. I can give you a whole bunch of two-twenty-three-cal piercings until you start talking."

"You're a cold bitch."

I shot him in the arm.

He screamed again.

When he quit whimpering, I placed the gun muzzle on the back of his neck. "Next bullet will be the start of your necklace."

A beat passed, and then he said, "I didn't take her, okay? I only told you I took her because you wouldn't know any different."

"Liar."

"I swear. The day before yesterday, Sophie and John-John came into the archives with Penny's death certificate to update the tribal rolls. I overheard them talking. John-John was taking Sophie to a weeklong sweat ceremony in Eagle Butte. They weren't telling anyone where they were going."

"Not even Devlin?"

"They said he was going to a poker tournament in Deadwood."

"Bullshit. You're lying."

"I'm not. I swear."

"Then how did you use Sophie's voice when I demanded proof of life?"

"Remember I told you I was at the crime scene? I had a mini tape recorder with me, and I recorded Sophie wailing. And John-John, too."

That's why Sophie's response had sounded familiar—I'd heard it live. "Why, you sick fuck?"

"Because I got off on hearing their reactions. Over and over." His voice dropped to that grotesque purr again. "I used the recording on you, and you fell for it. You really believed I'd kidnapped Sophie and hidden her away." Sheldon sneered, "It was almost too easy. You ain't as smart as you think you are."

This lowlife piece of shit had tricked me? Sophie *wasn't* in danger? I was stunned by that piece of information and so relieved that I relaxed my guard.

Probably Sheldon's intent. He rolled and knocked my feet out from under me.

I hit the ground hard but managed to keep hold of my rifle.

Then something connected with the side of my face, something that felt suspiciously like a boot.

I grunted from the pain, and my vision went wonky. The immediate ringing in my ears added another level of confusion, but I managed to duck, expecting another blow. But I heard footsteps fading as he raced away.

Now that I knew the truth, there wasn't any reason to continue this game of hide-and-seek.

My brain went to war with itself.

Catch him and take him to the Eagle River Sheriff's Department. Call Agent Turnbull. Turn all my information over to the FBI. Including Sheldon's confession to me over the phone about the killings. Point them toward the evidence at his house, supporting my claim about his murder spree. Plus, he'd committed fraud on a federal level for cashing his uncle's checks, not to mention that he'd murdered and mummified his uncle.

Letting justice take the proper course is what I'd sworn to do as an FBI agent.

But that wasn't what I wanted to do.

Sheldon's threats toward my family had sealed his fate.

I brought up the infrared again and scanned the vicinity.

Bingo.

He'd tried to hide behind a pine tree.

Rather than wasting ammo, I knelt down and felt the ground for a rock. I threw it toward the trees so it'd sound like I'd followed him and was flanking his left.

And Sheldon did exactly what I expected. He moved from behind the tree, out in the open.

I had my scope lined up on my target, and I pulled the trigger four times.

He crumpled like a bag of meat.

Keeping his body in the crosshairs of my scope, I stood and edged toward him. He wasn't moving much, so I thought I'd killed him.

When I was within five feet, he wheezed, "You shot me in the back."

"Yep."

"Lazy. Cheating. Not sportsmanlike."

"This isn't a sport."

"I can't move my legs," he said, panicked. "Or my arms."

"That's because I aimed for your spine. I severed it."

"I'm paralyzed?" Sheldon shrieked.

I rested the muzzle above his heart. "It's no worse than what you did to your victims."

"But they all died. I can't live like this."

I leaned closer. "Oh, you're not gonna live through this."

He closed his eyes and nodded. "Good. Thank you. Kill me. Now."

"No."

Sheldon's eyes reopened.

"I won't put you out of your misery because you deserve this pain." I slung my rifle over my back and grabbed onto the hood of his sweatshirt. Then I dragged him fifty yards into the brush.

"They'll know you did this," he said with another wheeze.

"How?" I removed his knife from the sheath on his utility belt. "Because of all the pictures you had of me in your garage? Pictures like the ones you left in my truck? Pictures you used to threaten me to play your stupid military game? Don't worry, I took them."

Understanding flashed on his face.

"Yes, while you were busy breaking into my house today? I was busy breaking into yours." I tsk-tsked, sounding patronizing—exactly like he had during his phone call. "You are one demented motherfucker, mummifying your uncle. You killed him and kept cashing his checks. So you've shown yourself to be a thief, a liar, and a murderer. While I just proved that I am the superior soldier."

Hatred brimmed in his eyes.

Using his knife, I slit the fabric of his cargo pants from ankle to crotch on both legs. The bullet hadn't left much of an exit wound on the front side of his leg. Careful not to leave fingerprints, I removed both his boots and his socks, then tossed them aside.

"Pity you won't feel the field mice eating off your toes. Or the birds pecking out your eyeballs. Or the coyotes snacking on your intestines." I sliced open his shirt and saw my first shot had clipped his right hip. I ripped off a clean strip of his T-shirt and wrapped it tightly around my thigh to staunch the bleeding.

I tossed his gun on the ground, just out of his reach.

I gave his face one last contemptuous look.

And I walked away.

Actually, I ran.

After I found the tape recorder and cell phone in Sheldon's car, after I determined nothing remained in his vehicle that pertained to me or my family, I left the door open and the keys in the ignition.

I broke down the AR and put it in the duffel bag. Next went in the night-vision goggles, the infrared, the tape recorder, and the cell phones. The van started. But it sputtered and died five minutes later on the road back to Eagle River.

I was still eleven miles from my truck and the reservation. The duffel bag had straps on the back side, allowing me to wear it as a backpack. After double-checking that I hadn't left a trace of myself in Naomi's van, I started out at a slow jog. Staying on the soft shoulder until I saw an approaching vehicle's headlights. Then I ducked into the ditch, catching my breath. When the coast was clear again, I returned to pounding the pavement.

Soldiers get injured during ops. I handled it the same way I always had. Shut down any emotion and focused on my training. Mind over matter. Keeping pain in a separate compartment to deal with later. Counting each footstep. Focusing on each breath.

I reached a sentient state of shock. Like everything I'd seen and done had happened to someone else. I slowed to a walk as the lights of the Eagle River Reservation came into view. I cut away from the main road and into the residential area. Two punks approached me then backed away when they caught a glimpse of my face. Or maybe it was my bloodied leg that sent them scurrying.

My truck was still in the church parking lot. On a whim I tried the church doors, expecting them to be locked up tight at midnight, like everything else. But the big doors swung open, welcoming me inside.

Trusting lot, these Catholics.

My boots and purse weren't in the bathroom, but my coat still hung on the rack. I slipped it on and felt a wave of comfort wash over me. I'd never been fond of this coat, but it might just become my new favorite.

After I changed the tire, I drove home. Still on automatic.

Once inside the house I cleaned my gun. I put everything away, almost methodically. I grabbed the envelope of pictures that had been left in my truck and that I'd hidden in the lazy Susan. I replaced the battery in my phone to check for missed calls. None from the hospital, thank God. I texted Jake that I was okay and told him to bring Lex home first thing in the morning.

I took the fake dossier file, the disposable cell phones, the tape recorder, and the pictures outside. Stacking everything into the burning barrel, I used a propane torch to light the papers on fire.

While watching the plastic melt, the photos bubble then curl into ash, I made one phone call. When Rollie Rondeaux's answering machine asked me to leave a message, I said, "Now we're square."

After the fire died, I returned inside. I stripped and cleaned myself. Red then pink water swirled around my feet as I poked the spot where the bullet had grazed my thigh.

I felt no pain, no shame, no remorse, no vindication.

I just felt tired.

I stretched out on the couch, turning the TV on for company.

If I thought I'd stare at the ceiling, unable to sleep as I relived the day's events, I thought wrong.

My body and my mind shut down, and I was grateful for the darkness.

23

I shouldn't have been surprised when Turnbull showed up the next morning.

So when I answered his knock—yes, the girl can be taught about the importance of locking doors—I'd already drunk half a pot of coffee. "Agent Turnbull."

"Agent Gunderson, you look like . . ."

"Hell. Yeah, I know. Help yourself to coffee."

He doctored a cup with cream and sugar before he faced me. "Rough night at the hospital?"

I shrugged.

"I tried to get ahold of you last night."

"My cell wasn't working."

"Neither was your house phone."

I shrugged again. "That happens sometimes, out in the middle of nowhere. Vermin biting through wires. I'll call the phone company on Monday to get it fixed."

Turnbull waited for me to say something else.

But I didn't. I couldn't. I'd said too much already.

Then he was right in my face. Studying the bruise that covered my left cheek, and then his gaze dropping to my swollen and bloodied lip. "What the fuck happened to you?"

Keeping things to myself was standard operating procedure in the army, even before I became black ops. I didn't owe my unofficial FBI partner anything because he could slap cuffs on me and throw me in jail for the rest of my life if he knew the truth. "It's nothing. I'm fine."

He placed his fingers under my chin and forced me to look at him. Then he touched the bruise, not with gentleness, but with enough force to make me wince. "What did you do last night?"

My gaze searched his, and I didn't back away from his firm touch or probing eyes. "It's no big deal. I heard a noise, went outside to check it out, and tripped over my bootlaces. I ran right into the barn door."

"Bullshit."

I jerked out of his hold and retreated. After refilling my cup, I rested my backside against the countertop. "Why are you here on a Saturday morning? Did we have a break in the cases or something?"

"No, I had a bad feeling about you."

"I thought we were supposed to ignore those gut *feelings* in the FBI."

But he wasn't looking at my face. "Jesus, Gunderson, why is your leg bleeding?"

I glanced at my left leg and saw red spreading across the gray sweat material. I waved off his concern. "No biggie. I cut myself shaving."

Then Shay was in front of me again, poking at the stain.

This time I yelped.

Mr. Intense was in my face. "Is that a goddamn bullet hole?"

"I just nicked the surface. You know how much those superficial wounds bleed."

"Let me see it."

"What? No." I tried to scramble back, but he put his hand on my thigh and squeezed. I snapped, "Jesus, knock it the fuck off, you sadistic asshole."

"Bathroom. Now. Or I call an ambulance. Your choice."

So I followed him into the bathroom.

He afforded me a quick once-over. "Sweatpants off."

I refused to blush when I peeled them down my legs.

"Get on the counter so I can make sure you don't have a damn bullet in there."

I knew better than to argue with that tone. I handed him a first-aid kit after he finished washing his hands.

"What will it take to convince you to talk to me about what happened last night?"

The poker face I'd mastered slipped. And for all the people it could've
happened in front of, just my luck it was Special Agent Shay Turnbull.
When I wasn't wearing pants. "I guess that depends on who I'm talking
to right now."

"Are you asking if I'm wearing my badge?"

"Yes, but I'm not just talking figuratively."

Shay locked his gaze to mine. "I'm more than the badge, Mercy."

"Still not hearing the reassurances I need, Agent Turnbull."

Indecision clouded his eyes. Then he said tightly, "Tit for tat, eh? My
dark secret for yours?"

I had so many secrets I wasn't sure if last night's events even counted
as the dark variety. "Fine. But it'd better be what I want to know, and
don't pretend you aren't aware of exactly what that is."

"Then tell me what *I* want to know. Were you shot last night?"

"Yeah. It's no big deal. I've been shot before."

"I see that." His fingers traced the ugly ridged scar on my other leg,
and the skin tightened with gooseflesh. Then he bent over the wound,
seeing blood oozing from beneath the bandage. "You say there's no bullet in there?"

"I already poked around in it."

"I'm gonna take a look anyway." Shay ripped off the covering quickly,
but it still hurt like a mother.

Blood gushed out and ran down the inside of my thigh.

He caught it with a piece of gauze. Took him a bit to speak. "You've
asked why I got reassigned to South Dakota. You assumed I was demoted. In a roundabout way, I was. I was reassigned because my partner
in the Minneapolis office allegedly committed a crime, and I refused to
be part of the federal hanging party." He sucked in a swift breath. "This
needs stitches."

"So I should ask Dawson's doctor if he could patch up a bullet wound
while I'm killing time in the waiting room? Wrong." I pointed at the

first-aid kit. "Use the butterfly bandages. I just couldn't hold the skin together and put the bandage on myself."

His eyes met mine. Not aloof like I expected but filled with concern. "I'll help you, but you have to promise if this gets infected you'll let a medical professional look at it."

"I promise. Now tell me what happened."

"This is gonna sting." He sprayed the entire area with antiseptic. "My former partner joined the FBI after college. Top of his class, he could've done anything. Even the CIA was sniffing around. But he was Ojibwa and wanted to stay in Indian Country to help his tribe. Part of the reason for his choosing a branch of law enforcement stemmed from his witnessing his mother and his sister brutally raped and murdered when he was twelve. He knew who'd done it. The cops had known, and nothing was ever done because the man was a DEA confidential informant."

My stomach twisted. "No one is untouchable."

"Trust me, this man was. Then we found out, through not entirely legal channels, that this monster had recently raped and killed another ten-year-old girl. But the crime had been covered up because the Indian girl was in foster care. And because the DEA needed this sick fucker's crucial information for a major drug op, they swept it under the rug." He pointed at my leg. "Pull the skin as closely together as you can and hold it."

I gritted my teeth and watched as he attached the butterfly bandages.

"The FBI and the DEA were convinced that my partner was the one who gutted the confidential informant like a trout a day before the man was supposed to deliver key information on a major drug shipment."

"What was your part in it?"

"Mine?" Shay's eyebrows rose. "None. The night this DEA snitch was killed, my partner and I were at a strip club sixty miles from the scene of the crime."

"Alibied?"

He dabbed at the pooled blood. "Ironclad. Corroborated by two men we'd gotten into an altercation with after the . . . female escorts they provided for us earlier that evening tried to double the agreed-upon price."

Four solid witnesses to alibi Shay and his partner's whereabouts. "And the feds?"

"No charges were filed on the criminal side, but my partner lost his job with the FBI for moral implications."

"That's fucking ironic."

"Tell me about it. I agreed to an immediate transfer out of the Minneapolis office, where I was third in line for the top slot. My ADA saw to it I was listed as a training agent for ICSCU. They sent me here. And I'm unofficially the DEA's bitch. No matter where I'm transferred. For as long as they deem it."

So many things made sense now. Including how Shay knew so much about Saro's organization. He'd been part of a task force keeping tabs on my friend Jason Hawley's criminal activities. Yes, he answered to Shenker, but he acted with a different vibe, as compared to other agents in our office. I'd chalked up those attitudes to male pissing contests—the new guy coming in and taking over. But it was more complicated than that . . . and a pointed reminder of how much I hated politics, in the office and in the military.

"Do you regret that decision?"

"No. I don't live my life as black and white as you seem to believe I do. I'm *Rah-rah! Go FBI!* and all that shit, ninety-nine-point-nine percent of the time."

But there was that teeny percentage . . . that wasn't completely aboveboard. Maybe we were more alike than I'd imagined. But I'd never seen those dark edges in him that existed in me.

"I know what you're capable of, Mercy. I also know you don't act unless you've been pushed into a corner." He handed me two large bandages. "Keep this covered until it stops bleeding."

"Aye, aye, Dr. Turnbull."

"Don't say that. It reminds me that my sister is the doctor in the family."

Before I could ask for more information, he said, "Get some pants on. I'll be in the kitchen waiting to hear about your night maneuvers, Sergeant Major," and he left the bathroom.

Night maneuvers. I almost snorted. But it was a strangely apt description. I slipped on a baggy pair of jeans and returned to the kitchen.

Shay stared out the window. Without turning around, he said, "Where can we talk?"

We'd have privacy if we used the office, but I couldn't tell him what I'd done in my dad's space. Paranoid and stupid, but some ghosts are difficult to shake.

"Let's go outside." Jake had taken the dogs with him after he'd dropped Lex off early this morning, so we wouldn't be hounded for attention. I shoved my phone in my back pocket and grabbed my coffee cup.

Another day of mild weather and no need to bundle up. But I shivered anyway as I curled my hands around my mug and stared straight ahead at the barn.

"Tell me all of it."

Easier to confess what'd gone down without making eye contact, even when I'd mastered the art of looking a superior in the eye and lying my ass off.

No lies this time. I told Shay everything.

It wasn't freeing. But it'd be hypocritical to expect absolution for guilt I didn't feel.

And Shay didn't offer it.

"You're sure no one saw you?" he asked after a bit.

"Leaving the area?"

"That, and carrying a duffel bag of death across the reservation."

I tossed my cold coffee over the porch railing. "I didn't see a single person on my solitary eleven-mile run in the dark. Nor did any Samaritan on the rez offer assistance when I changed my freakin' tire at midnight."

"Was that intentional on your part? Making sure this altercation happened on tribal land so you wouldn't have to deal with Dawson or his colleagues if you somehow got caught?"

"I didn't choose the spot. He did." The words *And I won't get caught* went unsaid.

Another beat passed. "How do you think this will play out?"

"The tribal cops will find Naomi's car first. I can hope, given what I've seen of their investigative techniques, that they'll chalk it up to rez kids taking a joyride and abandoning the ride after crashing the car."

"And Sheldon's car?"

"The tribal cops'll find that, too, I imagine, unless someone else finds it first, figures it's an abandoned car, and decides the finders/keepers rule is in effect." Which also happened frequently on the reservation.

"And if the tribal cops decide to look deeper?"

Deeper. I almost laughed. "Like bringing search-and-rescue dogs to the scene once they figure out Sheldon is missing? Well, *if* that happens, the dogs will find Sheldon's body. Or what's left of it. They'll find him full of bullets. A common-enough caliber of bullets."

"Will anyone report Sheldon missing?"

"Not until Monday or Tuesday when Sheldon doesn't show up for work. Once that happens and the tribal cops get to his house? It'll look like a break-in, and then they'll find his mummified uncle. Then they'll find Sheldon's instruments of torture in the garage. Blood from the victims on that plastic curtain. Digitalis. From that point, it depends on whether they find his body. They might just assume Sheldon fled. But if the body is found, then the tribal PD will look at the victim's family members as suspects. But Rollie is still in jail. John-John and Sophie were in Eagle Butte at a sweat ceremony."

Shay's gaze sharpened. "That leaves Latimer and Triscell Elk Thunder."

"What we know of the tribal PD? They won't seriously investigate the tribal president. They'll buy his alibi. They'll consider good riddance to Sheldon War Bonnet and act like the tribal police solved a case the FBI couldn't."

"You really did look at every conceivable angle."

I shrugged. "I had nothin' else to think about on my run. There's nothing linking me to any of this. No proof."

"No worries young Naomi will brag about her part?" he asked skeptically.

"She has limited information about what she believed was a government op. Plus, she mentioned a possible career in the military. I could provide her with a rec with the local recruiter, if she needs one. If she tattles, well, I'll go out of my way to paint her a liar."

"Jesus, Gunderson. I'm happy you're on my side."

I smiled. "Now that we're all open books for each other and shit, spill about your military service, Turnbull."

Shay gave me the slow, sexy grin that was inappropriate as hell and yet . . . somehow not. "I thought you would've guessed by now, Sergeant Major."

Then it clicked. "Fuck me. You were a SEAL."

"Yes, ma'am."

My eyes narrowed. "That's not all. You were a SEAL sniper."

"Guilty. But I was out of the teams by the time Operation Iraqi Freedom started. Basically, I was an Indian kid from South Dakota looking to see the world, and I ended up in navy intelligence. After a couple of years of that, I opted to try out for the SEALS. I stayed in the teams for almost a decade. Didn't reenlist after twelve years and immediately went to Quantico."

"Impressive." No wonder he had knowledge of my military background. But I felt a little smug that I outranked him.

"How do you plan to handle this?" he asked.

"I'll probably have to resign from the FBI. Not only for my, ah, night maneuvers, but if Dawson has a long recovery ahead of him, he'll need me to take care of him full time. As will Lex. My duties to my family have to come first."

"I'm not talking about the FBI."

I met Shay's intense stare head-on, and yet I had a frisson of fear that this would be the first time I broke an eye lock. "Then what are you talking about?"

"How that situation will affect you. Tracking and killing hasn't been part of your life since you got out of the service. Yet you've killed three people in less than eighteen months. Obviously, those kills are nothing compared to what you racked up as a sniper. But this time *will* affect you because it wasn't done in the name of God or country, or in self-defense. Maybe you won't see the aftershocks for a few weeks or months, but they will happen."

Rather than nod regretfully and blow off his armchair psychiatry, I held his gaze, giving him the honest answer that would haunt me more than leaving Sheldon War Bonnet to die. "You're wrong. I have no remorse. Nor will I ever wake up in the middle of the night filled with remorse—not in two hours, two days, two weeks, or two months. For a few hours I became that person I'd been trained to be. I did what I was very, very good at. Maybe it wasn't as easy to slip into that skin as it once was, but I was still able to do it. Then I shed that skin just as soon as I finished with it, just like I always have." The dark emotions inside me took a little longer to fade than the violent actions I'd taken, but portions had already started to blur.

He continued to stare at me, as if he didn't believe me. Like this was all an act with me.

It wasn't. This glimpse I let him see was the truest part of me.

"That bothers you, doesn't it? That I'm not wallowing in regret. That the reason I'd quit the FBI isn't out of guilt, but practicality. My life with Dawson is what matters most to me."

"The sheriff won't want you to quit, Mercy. We both know that. No matter what happens during his recovery." He turned away from me. "It'd suck if you quit."

I rolled my eyes. "Suck for who?"

"It'd suck for me because I'd get stuck with another newbie. Because of your military background, you're an above-average agent. And you put the pieces together on these cases when no one else could."

Man, he sucked at flattery. "But it wasn't because of great detective work. It was dumb luck. Or bad luck. And it's not like I can tell Shenker or anyone else how I did it or what the final outcome was."

He lifted a brow. "A good chunk of it was detective work. The rest doesn't matter. I'll know how capable you are. And you know it. That should be enough."

It should be . . . but would it be?

My cell phone buzzed in my back pocket.

I took it out and recognized the number from the hospital. My heart leaped into my throat. "Gunderson."

"Hi Mercy, it's Lisa from the ICU. I wanted to let you know that Mason is awake. The doctors started easing back on his meds about ten last night. By four a.m. he was conscious. He's been dealing with the neurologist and the physical-therapy folks. He's been telling everyone he just wants to go home."

Tears sprang to my eyes. "I'll be right there." I hung up.

Shay was in my face, his eyes that soft gold color I'd only seen a few times. "Mercy, goddammit, I'm so sorry."

"For what? Dawson is awake."

He took a step back. "He is? But you're—"

"Crying. I know. They're happy tears, Turnbull." I hugged him. "Thank you. For everything."

"I'll pass along the information about the sheriff's condition. Check in Monday and let us know when to expect you back to work."

Before I had formulated my response—*that might be never*—I watched him climb into his vehicle and drive away.

I ran into the house and up the stairs. "Lex? Get a move on, boy. Your dad is awake and we need to double-time it to the hospital."

I was nervous.

Dr. Jeffers wanted to meet with us ahead of time. To warn us of complications?

I'd seen far too many of those made-for-TV movies where the coma patient wakes up and doesn't remember anybody.

Or the coma permanently altered the patient's personality.

Or the patient had nerve damage that affected the physical condition of the body.

So I was grateful for Lex's chatter in the pickup on the way into town, although I processed it only as noise.

At the hospital the doctor informed us that there didn't appear to be any permanent brain damage. That, except for a few minor things, Dawson had come out of the coma better than expected. He'd make a full recovery.

All my life I'd heard the word *miracle* tossed around, but I'd never believed it until now.

Mason would remain in ICU for a day or two, but we didn't have to don protective gear to see him.

Lex practically bounced from foot to foot as we stood outside the door to room 406. The doctor went through a list of suggestions, which again, I largely didn't hear, due to my thundering heart.

Then the doctor opened the door.

My first glimpse was of Dawson sitting up in bed. Arms crossed over his chest as he scowled at the TV. His gaze snapped in our direction at the sound of Lex's shoes squeaking on the floor.

But his eyes were solely focused on me.

Lex raced toward him, only to come to a screeching halt.

Then he looked at Lex. "It's okay, son. I'll take a hug just as long as you don't squeeze my neck."

Mason's voice was a deep rasp, his words slower than normal. I hung back and let Lex entertain him, until Mason fidgeted and raised a questioning brow at me.

"What?"

"You're acting a little gun shy for bein' my *fiancée* and all."

I smiled and reached for the hand he'd held out. I threaded my fingers through his and brought his arm to my chest, wrapping my other arm around and giving his knuckles a soft kiss.

The doctor said to Lex, "The nurse mentioned ice cream. Let's have you pick some for you and your dad."

After they were gone, I said, "How do you feel?"

"Confused. My throat feels like I swallowed a pound of glass and chased it with a gallon of lemon juice. My head . . . hurts. My eyes . . . are happy to see you."

"Just your eyes?"

He smirked. "The one-eyed monster is happy to see you, too." Dawson tugged on my arm as a signal he wanted me closer.

I leaned close enough to feel his minty breath on my cheek before I lowered my mouth to his for a chaste kiss.

He murmured, "Kiss me like you mean it, woman. I damn near died." And he promptly blew my mind with a kiss so hot, yet so full of love, that those pesky tears filled my eyes again.

But I didn't stop kissing him. Couldn't, actually.

Finally, I eased back and peered into his face. "You ever scare me like that again, Mason Dawson, and the hurt I'll inflict on you will be ten times worse than any two-thousand-pound bull, got it?"

"Loud and clear, Sergeant Major." He frowned. "Your mouth is bleeding."

His enthusiastic kisses had opened the cut on my lip, but I'd ignored the pain. I grabbed a tissue and dabbed at the spot.

Then his focus narrowed on my face. "Jesus. Is that a bruise? What the hell happened to your cheek?"

"Would you believe I walked into the barn door?"

"No."

I forced a laugh.

"Are you okay?" he asked. "You seem a little . . . off."

You have no idea. "Been rough having my man in a coma. I'm better now that you're better." I let my fingertips brush the bristly growth on his cheeks and jaw. I just wanted to crawl in bed with him and surround myself with everything that was him.

"Mercy. What's really goin' on? Something happen at work this week?"

"Nothing that I can talk about." Not a total lie.

Dawson closed his eyes. "You want to know what woke me?"

If he said some kind of *woo-woo* shit, like he'd had a nightmare about me being in danger, I'd freak the fuck out. "What?"

"I dreamed about that weekend I visited you at Quantico. We hadn't seen each other in two months."

"And we didn't leave the room for the first twenty-four hours. After that we barely left the hotel." I remembered thinking the state's slogan—VIRGINIA IS FOR LOVERS—was apt. "Why do you think you dreamed of that?"

"Because that's when I knew."

"Knew what?"

"We were solid." His breathing slowed. "So you're really gonna marry me?"

"Yes, if you ever produce a ring."

"It's been in my sock drawer since the week you came home. If I'da known a head injury was the way to convince you to become my wife, I'da climbed on a bull a lot sooner."

I resisted my impulse to whap him on the chest. "I'm not changing my name."

"I don't care. Just as long as you don't change your mind."

"I won't."

"Good." A long pause. "I'm so tired."

"Rest." I brushed his hair back from his damp forehead. "I'll be here when you wake up."

Dawson and I were solid. It'd just taken a little trip over shaky ground to get me to believe it.

EPILOGUE

Two weeks later . . .

I woke to the smell of bacon frying.

What the hell? Mason was still asleep next to me. I squinted at the clock on the nightstand. I doubted Lex was up at 6:30 cooking breakfast for us. But then again . . . the boy had been so helpful since his father had come home from the hospital that I really didn't know what I would've done without him.

I slid free from being pinned beneath Dawson's leg and arm, patting his shoulder when he scowled that I'd somehow escaped his hold.

Pulling on my robe, I yawned and headed to the kitchen. "Lex, if you want help—"

But it wasn't Lex standing at the stove. It was Sophie.

Although her eyes were sad, she smiled at me, even when I continued to gape at her as if she were an apparition. "Good mornin', *takoja*. I'm thinkin' of whipping up some omelets."

I wanted to ask what she was doing here. But I just stood there, like an idiot, with my mouth hanging open.

"You're always grumpy until after you've had that first shot of caffeine. Luckily, I made a pot of coffee, eh?"

A few weeks away hadn't changed her bossy ways. I marched up to her and hugged her, ignoring her warnings about bacon grease splattering us. And I kept right on hugging her until she hugged me back and sighed.

Then she patted my shoulder. "I missed you, too, Mercy. Now sit."

I sat. Sophie brought us both a cup of coffee and took the chair across from mine. If she noticed the ruffled place mats were gone, she didn't mention it.

"How's the Sheriff?"

"Really good. He's working half days through this week. If his arm is more responsive to the physical therapy on Friday, he'll go to full shifts next week." The only lingering effect from the coma was Dawson's limited mobility on his left side. It frustrated him not being 100 percent. A feeling I was familiar with.

"He's lucky. I prayed to *Wakan Tanka* when I heard about his accident."

"Thank you. Every day I realized how blessed we are."

"I prayed for you, too, Mercy. I prayed you'd find peace. I prayed you'd discover the power in forgiveness."

Not likely. Especially since I knew she was talking about forgiving John-John. I lifted my cup to drink.

Of course, Sophie's sharp gaze focused on the diamond engagement ring on my left hand. "I'm assuming you finally said yes to the Sheriff?"

"He was being a pain in the ass about it, so I agreed to marry him just to shut him up." I set down my cup. "So you coming back to work for me or what?"

Sophie harrumphed. "Yes, you need a caretaker. I saw that you hadn't cleaned the laundry room at all while I was gone. I'm gonna need a bigger vacuum, hey, to get them dust rhinos under the couch cleaned up."

"So noted."

"I ain't gonna work full time. Mebbe just two days a week here. Hope and Jake don't need me meddling at their place. Jake said you took time off. Are you back to work at the FBI now?"

"No, I'm on personal leave until I know Dawson's recovery is complete." After that? Who knew? I wasn't sure if I expected Director Shenker and Agent Turnbull to beg me to stay, or if I'd feel relief if they let me go. Either way, I would have to make a decision soon.

Every day I read the paper and listened to the news, expecting to hear a breaking story about a bullet-riddled body found in the woods on the rez. But after two-plus weeks . . . nothing. The tribal police hadn't made a statement about what they'd discovered at Sheldon War Bonnet's house, either. Rollie's warning—*All the sick stuff most people, even the cops, on the rez turn a blind eye to*—had proven true. It was easier sweeping evil under the tipi. Or denying its existence altogether.

"You could always go back to work at Clementine's," Sophie suggested, pulling me out of my thoughts.

"I doubt that's an option, since John-John and I aren't speaking."

"He's sorry, Mercy. You have no idea how sorry he is."

"That is true. I have no idea how sorry he is, because I haven't heard from him or seen him at all," I retorted.

"He's grieving."

"I know. So are you. Just . . . don't make excuses for him, okay?"

Sophie lifted her stubborn chin. "My grandson *is* going to apologize. Mebbe the question should be: Will you let him?"

I shrugged. I'd believe it when I saw the whites of John-John's eyes. He'd have to come up with something pretty spectacular in the making-up department. Because after Geneva and I had our big fight? She'd brought me a bucket of kittens.

What could possibly top that?

A towel cracked next to my elbow, and I jumped.

Sophie cackled. "Go on, now. Get your man and your boy up to the table for breakfast. I ain't got all day. It's time things got back to normal around here."

My man and my boy. How I loved the sound of that.

Had I really complained only a few short weeks ago that my life had become mundane? After what I'd gone through in the past few weeks, I'd never complain again. I'd embrace waking up a cranky kid every morning. I'd send Dawson off to work with an affirmation of my feelings for him every day, even when it seemed silly and redundant. I'd let Sophie nag me about anything, just as long as she did it in person.

I'd take this new normalcy in my life for as long as I could get it.

ACKNOWLEDGMENTS

My editor, Megan Reid, is a rock star, and so instrumental in getting Mercy where she needed to be. I am so thankful for everything she's done.

The agents in the local FBI office have gone above and beyond in answering my questions, steering me in the right direction when I've veered off the path. My gratitude especially goes to RP and DD for all their help.

A huge debt of thanks to Hon. Robert Mandel, Seventh Circuit Court Judge, for his invaluable tutorial on tribal law and his insight on the grand jury process. Any legal or procedural discrepancies are strictly my own.

Thanks to my husband, Erin, aka Gun Guy, who tackles my firearms questions with humor and patience, and uses my need for "firsthand knowledge" of specific firearms as an excuse to buy more guns.

Thank you to my family for understanding and living through deadline hell with me.

Thanks to the readers who contacted me, asking about the release date of the next Mercy book, since there's been a two-year lag . . . it's good to know Mercy was missed.

Merciless: A Mystery

In *Merciless*, newly minted FBI agent Mercy Gunderson is investigating her first murder case, working in conjunction with the tribal police on the Eagle River Reservation, where the victim is the teenage niece of the recently elected tribal president. When another gruesome killing occurs during the early stages of the investigation, Mercy finds herself torn between her duty to the FBI and her obligations to those she loves, including her fiancé, Eagle River County sheriff Mason Dawson.

When hidden political agendas and old family vendettas turn ugly, masking motives and causing a rift between the tribal police, the tribal council, and the FBI, Mercy discovers that the deranged killer has his sights set on her as his next victim. In order to save herself and protect her family, Mercy must unleash the cold, dark, efficient killer inside her to become the predator rather than the prey.

FOR DISCUSSION

1. Describe Special Agent Mercy Gunderson's relationship with her FBI colleague, Special Agent Shay Turnbull. How does it change throughout the course of the novel?

2. "I was only a quarter Minneconjou Sioux, which was just enough to slightly darken my skin tone and lighten my hair color to light brown." How much does Mercy's Native American heritage help or hinder her in her official and unofficial interactions on the Eagle River Reservation? Consider her interactions with Fergie, Tribal President Latimer Elk Thunder, Rollie Rondeaux, and Saro.

3. "For most traditional Indian families, an autopsy is considered a desecration of the body and the spirit. Especially in children." In what other ways do Special Agents Mercy Gunderson and Shay Turnbull accommodate native traditions and beliefs in their federal investigation into the murders? How does Shay interpret the tribal police's efforts to find the serial killer on the reservation? To what extent do his views differ from Mercy's feelings about the tribal police?

4. How does the nondisclosure rule, which prevents Dawson and Mercy from discussing criminal cases of mutual interest to the agencies where they work, impact their relationship throughout the novel? Do you think it contributes to Mercy's final decision to go after the killer, and do you think this rule has merit for couples? Why or why not?

5. Describe Mercy and Dawson's first hunt together. To what extent is this outing typical of their domestic interactions?

6. How do Mercy's abilities and interests set her apart as a unique sort of heroine in *Merciless*?

7. How does Mason's rodeo accident transform Mercy's relationships with Mason's son, Lex, and with her FBI colleague, Shay Turnbull?

8. Mercy chooses to pursue the killer independently without first disclosing their identity to Shay Turnbull or anyone else at the FBI or tribal police. How does the successful outcome of her pursuit call into question her ethical judgment? Did this decision impact your opinion of her as a character?

9. How did you feel when you discovered the killer's identity? Given the many suspects put forth by Mercy and Shay, which seemed most plausible to you and why?

10. "I'd take this new normalcy in my life for as long as I could get it." Though the book closes on a positive note, Armstrong gives readers the opportunity to use their imaginations in thinking about what might be next for Mercy. Describe Mercy's "new normal" at the end of *Merciless*, and predict how her future relationships might be affected by the events of this book. Consider Dawson, John-John, Lex, and Shay, especially.

A Conversation with Lori Armstrong

Mercy's appreciation for weaponry definitely falls into the category of near obsession. Can you describe your own experience with and knowledge of guns?

My experience with guns is limited to working in the family gun business in the accounting department for a decade. However, my husband still makes his living in the firearms business, so I'm lucky enough to be able to pick his brain when I need to. He handles lots of cool firearms on a daily basis, which I remind myself would be Mercy's dream job.

An unlikely character turns out to be a serial killer and predator in *Merciless*, but the murderer's identity remains a mystery until quite late in the novel. Tell us a bit more about how you plan your books. At what point in your plotting the novel did you know who the killer would be?

That's the one thing I do know when I start a book—who the villain is. The rest of it . . . comes while I'm writing. I usually know the eight to ten black moments, or turning points, in the story before I start it. And I'm constantly surprised by how much ends up in the book that I didn't plan for. Characters show up on the page, or I kill off a character I hadn't intended to. So to some extent it's as much a discovery process for me as a writer as it is for the reader. I figure if I'm surprised then readers will be too.

Mercy Gunderson is an extremely open protagonist—unapologetic about her drinking, honest about her isolationist tendencies, straightforward about her physical needs. What is your favorite part about writing her?

I love when Mercy shows me a glimpse of humor. The darkness and lone-wolf attitude are an innate part of her and are expected, given her background. But it's those moments when we see her sense of humor, or when she tosses off a one-liner that amuse me, because it isn't something I plan. It just happens.

Does Mercy still surprise you as a character? What was the biggest "surprise" she shocked you with in *Merciless*?

Yes, Mercy still makes me scratch my head on occasion. The fact that Mercy showed a domestic side and that she liked it was a surprise to me. She has nurturing tendencies, but she's not had a lot of opportunites to act on them, so her relationship with Lex was a lot easier than I'd thought it would be. Easier, not to write, but easier to believe because we've only seen the barest glimpses of her around children. She's not afraid of kids, but she's afraid of getting too close and losing that connection again like she did with Levi. So I was happy she bucked up to the challenge of Lex living with them, right from the start.

As an author, how difficult was it for you to inhabit some of the "darkness" Mercy has to grapple with in this book? Did it feel like a natural progression from the first two books in this series?

I feel Mercy has adjusted more to civilian life in this book, so she naturally has fewer dark edges—that she lets show—because she isn't dealing with horrific death up close in her face every day like she was during her military service. It's important for me to show that Mercy isn't the clichéd army vet who drinks too much and constantly shoves away everyone who cares about her. The fact that she is in a long-term relationship with Dawson, and she accepts Lex will be in their lives, and she's changed the dynamics of her relationship with both her sister Hope and Jake, proving she wants to be a part of something again.

You've written before about how the racial and cultural diversity of western South Dakota is very much a part of everyday life, both for you as a resident and for your characters. Still, how intensive was your research into Sioux culture and customs?

Not too much for this book, since it deals more heavily with Mercy's new job with the FBI. That entailed much more research, since jurisdictional issues on Indian reservations and the local, state, and federal law enforcement problems arising from those restrictions play such a key role in the book. The one advantage I have in writing Mercy is that she doesn't know how to be Indian any more than I do, so it's an ongoing learning process for both of us.

Much of this book deals with Mercy's struggle to find balance, especially between her work obligations and her family. As a full-time writer who is also a wife and mother, do you identify with this struggle?

I think everyone identifies with the need to find balance. My deadlines have been pretty brutal the last few years and my family has been patient with my lack of balance. Luckily my kids are mostly grown and the one who is still at home is very busy and self-sufficient. But I remember when the kids were Lex's age and how much juggling school and activities and family time were part of our everyday life, as well as trying to find personal adult time, because that's usually one of the first things to go. Both Mercy and Dawson are aware that Lex living with them can change their personal dynamic and they're willing to adjust their lives, but not give up part of who they are to each other.

You also write a bestselling erotic romance series under the pseudonym Lorelei James. What are the major differences for you in writing your cowboy romances versus the Mercy Gunderson mystery series? Do you see a lot of overlap between mystery and romance?

Both mystery and romance have to have a plot, conflict, character growth, and a satisfying ending. So in that respect the story lines are similar. At this point in time, I write mystery in the first person, and it's challenging to write a hundred-thousand-word book from one character's point of view. I write romance in the third person, usually around a hundred thousand words also, but in multiple points of view, so the story gets told from various angles, which isn't necessarily easier, just different. In the mysteries the plot is about the character's relationship to violence. In the romances the plot is about the character's relationship to sex. I find it fascinating that mystery readers don't have a problem with explicit violence, but throw in explicit sex . . . and they run for the hills. I like the challenge of writing both the best aspect of humanity—love, sex and finding happily ever after—and the worst aspect—dealing with violence, hatred, and what makes a person act on those murderous impulses.

We won't ask you to pick favorites, but if you could bring one of your characters from this series to life to spend a day with, who would it be, and what would you do?

I'd pick Mercy and make her take me out shooting. I need help in learning how to ease back slowly on that trigger, every time, with every type of gun. Plus, I think she'd be fun to drink with afterward.

Where do you see Mercy's story going next?

Good question. I leave her a little unsettled at the end of *Merciless*, wondering if she'll continue with the FBI or if she'll find another challenge. I can say I'm kicking ideas around, but the truth is Mercy hasn't told me what she wants to do yet.

ENHANCE YOUR BOOK CLUB

1. As Mercy begins to unravel the secrets of tribal members of the Eagle River Reservation, she uncovers stories from the past that have been concealed to protect reputations and family legacies. Contact family members or friends and compose an oral history of a meaningful, controversial, or confusing event in your past. What surprising explanations are offered by others that shed light on your relationships? Share your findings with your book club.

2. At Mercy and Dawson's party to welcome Dawson's young son, Lex, relations and acquaintances from different parts of their professional and personal lives intersect, some uncomfortably. At what venues and events do the people who comprise your daily life—family, colleagues, childhood friends, neighbors, estranged companions—overlap? You may want to compare experiences with book club members of reunions or gatherings that were notable in terms of bringing out the best and worst in your circle of relationships.

3. Mercy and Dawson seem both competitive and admiring about their respective talents and abilities. When they hunt for antelope, for example, each acknowledges the other's unique strengths. Can you think of a person or people in your life that you admire for his or her special gifts? How do their abilities balance against your own? Explore this dynamic with members of your book group. Whom do they admire and how does this impact the way they interact with one another?

4. Learn about the author, Lori Armstrong, by visiting her online at: http://www.loriarmstrong.com, http://www.facebook.com/pages/Lori-Armstrong/420276695091, or on Twitter at http://twitter.com/Lori GArmstrong.